Title Not Included

The Superstars

To anyone who has ever looked at a book and thought, 'I wonder if I can do that?'

Give it a shot!

ACKNOWLEDGEMENTS

There are many people without whom this book could not have been put together:

Firstly, no anthology could be put together without the authors themselves, all of whom have stepped up to the mark, providing a wonderful variety of stories and poems every month. Thank you all for offering up your scribblings and waiting patiently for this thing to get done.

[Seriously, I genuinely had no idea my mad plan for a writing development group would yield so many pieces of such variety, quality and oddity, and every time something gets posted it always makes me grin. You guys rock, more than Dobby in a sock! - Lauren]

Both Liz and PhoenixShaman have provided some extremely cool art for the chapter headings, which got everyone excited, along with Karelin Victor-Kinzel. Thanks, you guys!

The lovely cover was created through the creative wizardry of James at GoOnWrite.com - thanks James!

Many, many thanks must go to Abigail Ash, who busily edited away, despite having a newborn baby to deal with, and to Lauren, who only had to fit it around her editing work! Also Karelin Victor-Kinzel and Mèlina Lofthouse, who kindly looked over the acknowledgements, and Dominic Hopkins, who read the introduction through.

Several people have contributed to our list of prompts, particularly Gemma, Jess, Dominic Hopkins, Jenni and Lauren. Thanks must also go to Samantha Hopkins, for coming up with a great title!

There are also a bunch of members whose work isn't included in this anthology, but who we love having around. Two of them, whose pieces are always a joy to read, are Kim Hosking and Lina Martindale.

Those members of the club who are always on hand to get discussions going, share creative ideas, read through our work and help us out of plotholes also need a big hand: Helen Bourne, Rebecca Cannell, Holly Crawford, Ben Francis, Clare Keogh, Peter Jeffries, Paul Marr, Carl

Mitchell, Wayne Naylor, Sophie Phillips and Louise Smith. Really, knowing that we have a friendly audience is awesome!

In terms of compiling the anthology, this would not have been possible without the troubleshooting abilities of Niall Fleming, who has a way with computers that seems like an island of calm in a library of chaos.

[It feels bizarre indeed to be writing a thank-you to myself, but I know if I hadn't made myself stick to posting new prompts, bouncing around the club like a crazy person and occasionally hassling people for stuff, I never would have written as much as I have this year. I'm also pretty pleased with how the anthology has turned out, so I'm glad I actually got around to putting it together. Yay! So, um... thanks, me! - Lauren]

Everyone involved in this project would like to thank their family and friends for their encouragement, support and patience, occasional meals and numerous cups of tea.

Picture Credits

Liz Hearson provided the artwork for the following chapters: Dear Kate, Aneurin Strange, The Yellow Room, and Take Flight. PhoenixShaman provided the artwork for the following chapters: Perks & Daily, A Matchbox Full of Memories, The Butterfly and the Lion, Metaphysical Sandwich, Pennies for the Dead, You Are What You Eat, Apricot Heart, and Swimming with Pigs.

Cover art by James at GoOnWrite.com

CONTENTS

INTRODUCTION

Welcome to the first anthology of the Short Story Superstars!

This collection of stories, poems, snippets and experiments is the result of twelve months of prompts, picked at random and posted on the first day of each month. The rules are simple: anyone wishing to participate each month must concoct some form of creative writing of any form or genre, preferably between 100 and 10,000 words, to be presented at the end of each month - in whatever state it's in. Needless to say, these rules are often broken!

The idea was to generate a sort of writing game where people could tell the many tiny stories that we never seem to get around to telling and improve their writing in a friendly and generally rather silly environment. It has to be said that our superstars are all rather odd, which is why we get on so well, and also possibly why all the entries go in totally unexpected directions. This, quite rightly, is all part of the fun - and one of the reasons, when I perused the entries for 'You Are What You Eat', that I was astonished not to find any cannibalism.

Eagle-eyed readers will note that there is one prompt standing forlorn and empty (though arguably J. McGraw's poem covers it in part): Metaphysical Sandwich. This is because everything else written for it was either fanfiction or has been published elsewhere. Given the nature of the prompt, these stories being both there and not there seemed apt.

Our stories range widely, across love and loss, friendship and adventure, murder and magic, fantasy and family.

On behalf of all the Short Story Superstars, we hope you enjoy reading these fragments of our imagination as much as we enjoyed putting them together!

-Lauren K. Nixon

Dear Kate

By Hannah R.H. Allen

"When we get out of this, the first thing I'm gonna do is go see my Kate, and I'm gonna marry her, there and then..."

He had said it a thousand times throughout their time together, from foxhole to blasted foxhole; it had become his mantra, a talisman to be wielded in the face of Death, to cheat him for just one more day.

But the reaper is never to be denied, ever by our side as we marched forth, reaping the souls of enemy and comrade alike as we cut our bloody swath through equals, at the behest of privileged men so much less worthy than those we fought and bled beside. Eventually we all feel his bony hand on our shoulder.

"And what then? After you have been married, what are you gonna do?"

We're hunkered down in what passes for a trench: little more than a ditch, for all that it matters. With the mortar fire falling around our ears it could well be our grave in moments.

"Hey, listen to me. I said what are you gonna do once you have married her? I've seen you writing all those letters – you must have some sort of plan."

He looks up at me, the growing distance in his eyes tells me he doesn't have long; the best I can do is keep him talking, as I try to hold his belly closed.

He rambles about the perfect future he has all set up, the whole white picket fence deal that I have heard a thousand times over, but then each of us in our unit could recite the other's life verbatim by this point. There were no secrets we had not confessed to each other in the dark, as we watched for death from across battlefields, while awaiting death from above.

Suddenly something snaps him out of it, a moment of painful clarity holds him in a fearsome grasp. Grabbing my arm, he forces me to look him in the eye.

"Kate, my Kate – someone has to look out for her... You

have to promise me, she has to know..."

Just as suddenly, it lets him go. He sags back, staring ahead, unseeing.

"Has to know what? Come on, what does she have to know?"

He pulls a battered piece of paper from his pocket, pulls my hand away from the wound and presses it into my palm.

"She was my angel."

His face settles into the most serene smile I have ever seen, and like that he left me: no struggle, no final defiance, just gone.

Finally, I look at the paper in my fist, dog-eared around the edges, now creased and stained with crimson, a faded photo of a smiling girl in the full flush of youth; hair loose, falling over bare shoulders and floral sun dress. On the reverse, in a neat flowing hand it said:

"Keep me near to your heart,

As you are in mine.

Your Kate,

Always."

Beneath that, in a different hand, was a postal address: hers. I recognized it easily from his letters.

*

I took his letters before we bugged out. Read them through God knows how many times, looking for a hint – a way of breaking this that wouldn't seem heartless. After the longest time, I took up my pen and started writing.

"Dear Kate,

The first thing I'm gonna do when I get back is see you, and I'm gonna marry you then and there..."

I don't know why I did it. Maybe I fell a little in love with her as I read the letters; maybe I thought that by pretending it would be all ok, he wasn't really lying cold at the bottom of some crater – he would be coming through the door any second now, talking some poor sod's ear off about how he has the good life all lined up for him when he gets home.

I've lost count of the letters I have sent, and which of her replies came before I began. It's almost like he and I are the same now. I feel like I have always known her. I know when I get out of here I will have to come clean, or perhaps I will die out here and it will solve both our problems.

Till then, I sit with pen in hand and I write:

"Dear Kate..."

Dear Kate

By Hannah Burns

Kate was never a name I liked: I loathed it with a passion, it was as if no one could be bothered to say my full name. My mother sent me letter after letter, always starting the same way.

Dear Kate,

How are you, my dear? Your father and I are on holiday again next week. The South Americas, I believe it is. Somewhere your father has always wanted to go. I think it's going to be too hot for him and he's never going to stop moaning.

Anyway, my love, talk soon!

Mother and Father.

I scan the letter before tossing it aside. You'd think with all these holidays they would at least have the energy to put my full name on a letter, but no. It would obviously take too much paper, or maybe ink was a precious commodity that I didn't know about.

*

I head home from another long day at work; pushing the oak door open I see the familiar brightly colour pink paper. Opening the letter once more, I find that loathsome name.

Dear Kate,

How are you, my dear? America was lovely, though I must preferred the jungles to the cities. So much more danger in the city. I think we're going to Italy next time, not sure about it though, the weather is supposed to be so hot, and well – you know your father.

Speak soon, love.

Mother and Father.

Shaking my head I throw the letter into the drawer beside the phone; after years of use, the drawer is lined with brightly coloured letters, all ripped open and all with those stupid opening lines. Every month I get one of those stupid, idiotic letters. Mother and father off once more on their wonderful adventures, leaving me in the cold and wet of London.

*

Dear Kate,
Met this wonderful man on the beach! Perfect for your age – and he is coming to London. Do you want to meet up, maybe? He's very rich!
Love, Mother.

Once more, the letter is thrown into the pile. It's getting big now and I can't really shut the drawer on it. Maybe I could get Keylee to put a lock on it, or I should just throw them away. No. I'll keep them for now, they might be useful for something.

*

Dear Katrice,
Your father here. We need to talk, please answer your phone. Your mother has passed away. I need you to be there for me, Katrice.
Your father.

My tears drop onto the last words of those pages. The one time they get my name right, the one time they write it fully, and this... this is what is says. The letter falls from my grip as I fall to the ground, slipping slowly down the wall.

Dear Kate

By G. Burton

I'm sorry you couldn't come to see me off. Mum was pretending that she wasn't crying and Dad was being all manly for her: I mean I kind of get it; they don't want too many people finding out about it. I wish you could see the train though! I've not seen anyone else yet, but that's okay because I have an entire compartment to myself. A seat, a bed, desk – even my own bathroom! And there's a fridge with snacks in and a portal thing for cooked meals to come through. There's some serious engineering going into this – you'd be picking it apart like you did with the new car!

I keep looking at the prospectus and the courses – you know me and my thirst for learning! Even when I'm supposed to be on holiday I can't put my studies away. The school just looks so good. You know how much Mrs Dakona struggled trying to keep me busy in class. She wasn't surprised when Dad came in to tell her that I'd been approached for this programme. Though I still haven't worked out why her smile didn't reach her eyes...

Anyway, you know me, I'm going to settle down with a book now and just enjoy the ride to school. I'll write to you once I'm there and let you know all about it!

***

It's so strange being away from home, although I'm sure you're happy that you no longer have to share the bedroom with me. It's really nice here; the buildings are all clean lines and modern architecture – a bit like those government buildings that we saw when Dad took us to the city. The people are all a bit strange still, but I'm sure we'll settle in soon enough. I'm not entirely sure I'll like it. It's just so... different.

The rooms are all fairly plain, save for our timetables and academically associated paraphernalia that the tutors like us to have up. The lessons look like they'll be great; there's the usual fare that we had at school, but there's also classes on astrophysics and string theory if you can believe it!

I found out that we get an older student as our mentor too, which is interesting. I mean, we're hardly scared five year olds; surely we don't need someone to hold our hands and wipe our noses? Anyway, there's an empty bed in my room, I'm guessing for this other student. Goodness knows when I'll meet her.

***

I can't tell how long the post would be from here, so I'm sorry if you get lots of letters at once! Classes started today... though I don't know that they can really call them classes. We had ten minutes of introductions by the 'educational guide' (no teachers here!) before we launched into the first test.

Yep, you read it right, *test*.

They went on, one after the other, for the entire day. We had our last just before I started writing and it's now 8pm. They seem to think we can work without a break too. We had five minutes to eat a sandwich for lunch and then the tests continued. It's also strange that I've not seen any of the extra-curricular stuff that I'm sure they advertised. Perhaps it's just too early in the year for it... Anyway, I'm supposed to be studying now, so I'd better go!

***

There's something a bit odd with my roommate... I mean, she's great and will help me look over my work and study properly (hardly a task as she's always studying too), but she has this weird expression sometimes, kind of like she doesn't know what to do or that something is missing... I don't know.

Classes today were also strange; there were more tests (which isn't that strange – I think that's going to be the expected standard), but what was noticeable was that two of the lads weren't there. Apparently they scored full marks on all of the tests in the last class, so they'd been moved up a group.

So now the pressure is on knowing that we can move up in the school by scoring high on the tests!

***

I did it! The class instructor came to see me whilst I was studying to tell me that I'm moving up to the next class.

But, of course, this means more studying, so I'd better get going. I just thought you'd be pleased to hear!

***

Sometimes, at night, I wonder if you are really there.

Some of the others have suggested that there aren't any holidays. It would fit. We seem to live in this enclosed mess of books and studies.

There's no news from you and we don't have any sense of what's happening outside of the school. Holidays are the least of my worries.

Now that I've spent time here, I can see the horror deep in the eyes of the older 'students'. I fear that this isn't truly the place that we thought it was. That it is, in fact, more government oriented that we first thought.

I don't think I'll be seeing you again, if, indeed, you're still there. Part of me hopes that you are and you just think that I'm busy with school, but I'll never know.

***

Dear Kate,

I don't know why I'm writing. There's nothing to ask and even less to answer. I live for tests. Examinations. Scores.

In fact, I'm convinced you don't exist. That you're a figment of some part of my imagination that has survived the battering of this place. My mentor said I needed to study more. The problem is that I know all of the material. It stays in my mind more easily these days. And that's where the issue starts.

I have ideas. We're not supposed to have ideas. Not in this class. The tests get harder; my ideas grow.

Maybe I do need to study more.

Whoever you are, Kate, I'm sure you won't mind my not writing anymore. You'll understand the need to study. The need to get into the higher classes.

Maybe then my ideas will be able to grow.

Dear Kate

By J. McGraw

When Katy stood upon the cliffs,
The tall ships in the bay;
Her lover proud in red and gold,
Dear Katy waved away.

For war was, in a distant land,
Calling men to fight,
And so the bright and billowing sails
Dear Katy watched from sight.

She sang the songs that all girls sing,
Of sea twix'd her and him,
And for his safe and swift return
Dear Katy sang her hymn.

And when nine moons had been and gone,
A healthy boy she bore.
She named him for that sailor fair,
Dear Katy's paramour.

As the boy from two to three,
Was growing fast and strong,
The sailor sent another boy,
To join dear Katy's son.

'She must not shirk,' the sailor wrote,
'Or treat the boy unkind.
Though he was weak, he trusts his fault
Dear Katy will not mind.'

The younger child was strange of face,
But elsewise kind and good.
To make him brother to her son,
Dear Katy swore she would.

But as regards the sailor fair,

In distant lands transgressing,
A plan to rid him from her thoughts,
Dear Katy set progressing

She took the trinkets left behind,
His tokens of affection,
From which no tender thoughts rose to
Dear Katy's recollection.

She visited the marketplace,
Those tokens for to part with,
And with the coin a mourning dress
Dear Katy fixed her heart with.

Adorned in black from head to toe,
The false news she spread wide,
That in the far ends of the world,
Dear Katy's lover died.

After weeks of funeral black,
Her freedom was regained,
And many young men of the town,
Dear Katy entertained.

She dressed in silks and laces fine,
And out she went a'courting.
'Til with a fine upstanding man,
Dear Katy was consorting.

The lady and the gentleman
They made a happy home,
'Til ships on the horizon guided
Katy's sailor home.

The sailor he searched all the town,
For the lady left behind.
But in another's arms he found
Dear Katy intertwined.

The sailor cried and shouted long
Outside the lovers' door.

He swore his heart would always be
Dear Katy's evermore.

But the sailor's cries were with
Another voice contending.
For in the house a different cause,
Dear Katy was defending.

Her recent husband, proud and shamed,
His anger fierce ignited,
He threw her out into the arms
Of Katy's sailor slighted.

The sailor faced his lady love
His anger unsurpassed,
And with his hands around her neck
Dear Katy breathed her last.

On seeing then what had been done,
The husband howled and cried.
And leapt towards the one who had
Dear Katy's life denied.

The two men fought there in the street,
But sorry was the day,
For war and training turned the fight
Dear Katy's sailor's way.

The husband tried but could not stop,
The knife aimed for his chest.
He staggered, fell, and breathed his last
Across dear Katy's breast.

They hung the sailor in the noose
Until his life did cease.
And now deep down beneath the ground,
Dear Katy rests in peace.

Aneurin Strange

By Hannah R.H. Allen

Aneurin Strange was a strange boy,
A scrap of bone and a hankie for a toy,
And people said, he would be so,
Till he was dead, although...

They did not count on the boy's collusion,
With a strange and squamous God intrusion,
At his behest they came to his home,
Called from long forgotten library tome.

Now Aneurin Strange is strange forever,
And our town sees stranger weather,
Let this be a lesson to those who'd mock,
Beware the boy and his Elder god.

Aneurin Strange

By G. Burton

She grew to the sounds of the underground,
The words that she always said;
'Who would you see about troubled ground?
And why would they even care?'

You think of her as a stranger,
Never seeing her day by day;
She's easy to forget, that Aneurin Strange,
That is, if she says you may.

You know you can't flee,
Or find yourself away;
But you can't find a difference in all you see
Despite what the others say.

The wheezing and rattling you find
To be a kind of song,
You try not to listen but you know
That you can't resist for long.

It's compelling, that wonderful
Underground song, the words so
Frail and clear. You try to forget that
Aneurin Strange, but can't forget that fear.

The mysteries run, the rumours spread,
She's there day by day;
You duck and weave between all the heads
To flee from Aneurin Strange.

You wonder what compels her to stay
In the tunnels and tombs underground.
Part of you wants to ask her to stay,
But you know that she shouldn't be found.

Her history chills you,
Just like the wind. You feel yourself pinned,
Unseen by few and heard by less,
In the wake of Aneurin Strange.

The silence oppressive, the wind cuts through,
The distant cry arrives –
You know you shouldn't, but you can't resist
Hunting for Aneurin Strange.

You find yourself there, on the edge of the cliff,
The darkness looming ahead;
You try to forget that Aneurin Strange,
But you can't until she says.

You remember the news that day in the past,
The harsh, panicked tongues going live,
The haunting chill cut to the heart of the words you speak,
and leaves you breathless at the last.

Others have come and some have gone,
Yet few will understand,
That the day that you see one
Aneurin Strange is the day that you take the stand.

But the days will come when no-one will listen,
When the last one has gone astray.
And the light of the life that was Aneurin Strange
Will soon drift away.

She's used to the sounds of the underground
Of the life that she's come to know.
She's easy to forget, that Aneurin Strange,
That is, if she says you may.

Ysbrydnos Song

By Lauren K. Nixon

He was found on the day the summer died,
On Calan-Gaeaf, when the spirits ride,
Wrapped in a shroud for winter-tide,
So they called him Aneurin Strange.

The brides of Christ who raised the boy,
They never saw in him much joy,
Feared how he'd look upon la croix,
And they shunned poor Aneurin Strange.

They sent him to school so far away,
But he wouldn't talk and wouldn't play,
Just stood and stared out the window all day,
That Anuerin, Aneurin Strange.

His teachers wrote angry letters home,
He seemed 'far too happy on his own'.
Happy, yes, but never alone,
Was Aneurin, Aneurin Strange.

His was a strange and eerie lot,
For he could see what the others could not,
Pale, hollow faces he never forgot,
Not Aneurin, Aneurin Strange.

He saw them in glass in windows of shops –
In the gilded mirror with scratches on top –
In the puddles of mud other children would hop –

He saw them in darkness, all twisted with pain –
He saw them in sunlight, drawn faces quite plain –
And always he saw them in showers of rain –
Did Aneurin, Aneurin Strange.

His mother, she came to his window one night,
And flitted and rippled and shone in the light,

Her eyes a jet black and her skin a bright white,
To comfort her Aneurin Strange.

He slipped from the others on days when he could,
And walked in the rain, peekin' out of his hood,
And watched the silent ones glide as he stood,
Past Aneurin, Aneurin Strange.

He wished that the others he lived with could see
The man at their back or the child at their knee,
But none of them were as brave as he,
Thought Aneurin, Aneurin Strange.

On his fourteenth year, sweet Aneurin knew,
His time on this earth was almost through.
So he sat and he watched the sun as it grew,
Did Aneurin, Aneurin Strange.

To thank the nuns he did not wait,
He packed his things before it was late,
And sat in the sun by the nunnery gate,
Did Aneurin, Aneurin Strange.

There came up a crash and a terrible screech,
They all rushed to help but couldn't quite reach;
The driver was drunk when the wall he did breech,
Over Anuerin, Aneurin Strange.

As they knelt by his form and they wept and they cried,
A toddler who'd run to the place where he'd died,
She looked up waved at the shadow she'd spied,
Of Aneurin, Aneurin Strange.

He waved and he turned and he left them behind,
To some quiet place he'd set out to find,
Far from the life from which he'd resigned,
Did Aneurin, Aneurin Strange.

And to his dark father this boy he did run,
And with open arms, Death welcomed his son,
And told him his work had barely begun,

For Aneurin, Aneurin Strange.

So when daylight is fadin' and you're fearin' the night –
The green hills are slidin' once more from the light –
The heartbeat you're hearin' no longer a-right –

Have peace in your soul and don't take afright –
Look for the boy with the scythe and the sight –
He'll welcome us all with warmth and delight –
Will Aneurin, Aneurin Strange!

Aneurin Strange

By J. McGraw

Don't go down to Aneurin, child. There are dark things that live in the shaded places under those trees, even now. Don't forget the stories of the creatures in those ruined halls, or the insipid, poisonous vines that blanket the ground. Don't forget the tale of the boy who wandered, lost, into those streets and returned without his tongue. Don't forget the girl who was drawn in by visions of her love, who found her way home a half year later, with no memory of being away. Don't forget, child, the tale I tell you of how I ventured into the gloom of Aneurin, and how I became what you see now...

Aneurin may have been a living town once, with people on its streets like blood in stone-clad veins. It may have been filled with laughter, with children running underfoot, with chickens and goats browsing in the yards and crows croaking on the rooftops. When I was younger, though, the life had already fled from the place. Even the trees that had grown up through the shells of houses felt dead, with black, weeping bark and tendrils of pale vines reaching up from the forest floor like a creeping infection. I remember it so clearly, as though the image is burned into my memory.

I was a headstrong youth. The children in my village always laughed about Aneurin, made believe they weren't frightened of it, dared each other to get close, to bring something back. I was the only one foolish enough to follow through. I left early in the morning, so I would have light by the time I reached the ruins. The healthy, living forest between my village and Aneurin began to sicken as I approached, until the towering oaks and sycamores became twisted into unrecognisable shapes.

I think I would have turned back then, expect for a hint of something just ahead. I couldn't say what it was – it kept just out of sight, promising to be visible around the next trunk, but always out of reach. I stopped noticing the increasingly poisoned trees and the cloying smell of decay that filled the air. I stopped paying attention to the path I was taking, or the enveloping darkness. The promise surrounded me with sweetness and security, a warmth to replace the lost light of the sun. I followed it into the heart of the forest, into the streets of Aneurin itself, and there the promise disappeared.

I felt suddenly stripped of all protection. My fear, which had been held back by the promise, returned full force, and my body began to shake uncontrollably. Weak kneed, it was all I could do to lower myself to the ground before I collapsed. But there was no comfort to be found there – the pale vines underfoot were spiky and tough, knife-sharp along the leaf edges. The moment I touched the ground my knees and hands shrieked protests, and I shot once more to my feet. Blood pooled in my palms and stained my breeches. Pain shot down my arms and up my legs. I wanted to go home, but addled as my mind was with the pain and the fear, only one thought shone clearing in my mind.

Find something to take back and make this trip worthwhile.

I pictured the laughter and scorn of returning without proof. My friends would call me a liar. Young as I was, I felt that was a fate worse than the pain that Aneurin had already caused me. Eager, then, to find something that could only have come from this place, I cast my gaze around wildly. A stone from a wall? Too commonplace. A leaf from the vines? No way to collect it without further injury. Bark from the trees?

Bark from the trees. There were no trees like these anywhere else. Black and damp with weeping sap, it would be definitive proof of my coming to Aneurin. With considerable relief I pulled out my pocket knife and made my careful way through the vines to the nearest tree.

The vines were uncomfortable to walk on, promising with every step to cut through the leather of my shoe sole and rip into my feet. I avoided them where possible – once I reached the tumble-down wall of an old house, I climbed up on the stones and made my precarious way along the wall instead. In the centre of the house was the tree I was aiming for. Years past, as it had grown, something had bent it over so that it grew now at an angle, and rested against the south wall of the building. It was also clear the tree was the reason for that wall becoming a ruin – the stones had been pushed out of alignment by the trunk, and teetered unnervingly above a two storey drop to the ground. I tested each step before I took it. It took me a long time, but I eventually reached the tree and the bark I was after.

I was tired after the anxiety of the climb, and my knees still felt weak. After a moment's debate, I steadied myself against the trunk of the tree, trying to keep the cuts on my palms away from the bark. The sap made the bark slippery and soft, though, and my hand sunk into the black mess further than I had expected. It stung where it touched my cuts. Tears sprang to my eyes, but I bit my lip and soldiered on. Once I could cut some bark away, I knew, I could climb down and go home.

My knife felt almost ineffective. In the end I scooped more than cut a section of the bark free, and searched my pockets for something to wrap it in.

Tha-dum, tha-dum, tha-dum. As I pulled out my pocket handkerchief and folded it around the bark, I became aware of my heartbeat. *Tha-dum, tha-dum, tha-dum.* Each beat was a pressure behind my eyes, each stronger than the last, trying to force my head open. It made me dizzy. Precariously perched at the top of the wall, I felt the ground wavering to and fro. Climbing down was impossible – instead, I clung to the trunk in front of me and waited for my head to clear.

Tha-dum.

My hands didn't hurt anymore, I realised groggily. Nor my knees. I looked down and saw the black sap covering me, soaking into my clothes and smothered over my skin. Was something in it numbing my cuts?

Tha-dum.

It was almost suffocating, seeing the sap all over me. It stank terribly, filling my nostrils with death and decay.

Da-dum.

I wondered, if I fell from the wall, whether the sap would be thick enough to cushion my landing. Maybe if I coated the soles of my shoes with it, I wouldn't feel the spikes of the vines as I walked away.

Da-dum.

...

Da-dum.

...

Da-dum.

My heartbeat had changed without me realising. It no longer felt like it was inside me. There was no pressure in my head, no force pushing at me from the inside. Now it sounded like a drum outside my head, not in it. Hanging on to the trunk, I looked around at the empty ruin of a town searching for the drummer. I could see no one, but there were so many trees and walls they could be hiding behind. It was time to go, I knew. Dizzy or not, I couldn't wait here until the creatures of Aneurin found me.

The stones shifted under me as I turned around, but some miracle kept me upright. Tottering back along the precarious path I had climbed before, it felt as though I walked on pegs more than feet. More stones shifted, and I heard them clatter behind and below me, but I hurried on before they could throw me off balance. The world blurred – all that was in focus was the wall at my feet. I only realised I had made it to the ground when I collided with another ruined wall on the other side of the abandoned street.

Da-dum.

The drummer again. He had been silent while I negotiated the wall – now he sounded close by, maybe even just behind the wall into which I had run. I froze. Had he seen me? Did he know I was there? How could he not, given the noise I must have been making.

I felt a tingling on the back of my neck, like someone was watching me. Spinning around, I was just in time to catch a glimpse of movement in a half-standing doorway. There *was* something here. I thought of the stories – no one ever said what sorts of creatures inhabited these forsaken streets. If I could catch sight of one, even for a moment... what a story that would be to take back with me!

Da-dum.

I darted across the street to where I had seen movement, but when I flung myself around the corner there was no one and nothing there. Pausing, I listened for the drumming once more.

Da-dum.

The noise seemed to come from all around me, but as I tried to pinpoint it I saw another hint of movement. Again I ran after it, and again I was too slow, but I was sure I was getting closer. I felt my blood surge with excitement, making my skin tingle. With exaggerated care I looked around again.

There!

I made to run after the shadowy figure, and then I was falling. Why was I falling? It was a slow fall, much slower than it should have been, and as I toppled I had time to wonder, to look around, to spot the vine that had grown up around my right leg. It was almost to my knee, anchoring me to the ground. Why hadn't I felt it growing?

I hit the ground. This time, the vines felt soft underneath me. I lay, surprised, for a moment before struggling to my feet once more. When I looked down, the vine that had been around my leg was gone. Instead, I saw a red liquid mixing with the thick black sap from the trees. I stared at it for a long time wondering what it was. It was all up my arms as well, and along my side where I had fallen. Wiping some of the sap away, I saw the liquid was coming from my skin. It was the strangest thing I had ever seen. Suddenly, I knew what I could tell my friends back home. Aneurin was such a strange place that it made my skin cry red tears. That would be better than any sighting of twisted creatures.

Laughing, I turned and ran for home. I remember the ruins stretching around me as I ran, seeming to go on forever. I remember running on regardless. And that is all I remember.

Whichever way I had run, it was not towards home – a traveller found me staggering along a road heading away from the village, bleeding, laughing, and stopping occasionally to stare at the cuts to my arms and legs. I was told, after they had removed the parts of my body that were too ruined to save, that the black sap was poison. It soaked into my skin, through my cuts, and made me see and feel things that were not real. I was told I had absorbed so much of the poison that it had stained my veins black, and that they would never change back. I was told there were no creatures in Aneurin, and everything I saw there was a hallucination.

Clever men told me these things, after they took my arms and legs from me. They talked in long words I could not understand, and they talked with the confidence of knowledge in the world. But the clever men could not tell me what had lured me into Aneurin when I would have turned back, and they could not explain how, when I had spent so much time in the ruins, I had only been away for a few minutes. Clever men will tell you there is nothing to fear in Aneurin but the poisons from the plants. But we know better.

So look at me, child. See my stumps of arms and legs. See the black veins crawling across my skin and creeping into my eyes. See me, and don't listen to those clever men with all their wisdom. Remember my story, and don't go down to Aneurin. There are dark things in those ruins.

Perks & Daily

By Hannah H.R. Allen

The grey Monday morning drizzle ran streaky down the
windows, collaborating with the condensation to obscure
the view outside; the sound of the urn on a rolling boil
filled the small room almost drowning out the steady
patter of raindrops, its steam forming low lying clouds
within the cafe's delicate ecosystem, drifting lazily past the
wilting pages of the Sunday papers stuffed in the rack on
the wall.

Fresh baked confection nestled under glass bells on the
counter, icing glistening in the yellow florescent lights,
their scent permeating, despite their confines, filling the
air with zesty citrus, and soft brown sugar and cinnamon
notes, mingling with the smell of stewing tea bags, and
bitter coffee grounds.

The morning breakfast rush over, the only signs of
recent occupation; a dusting of crumbs across the counter
and table tops, a scattering of dirty crocks and empty cups,
and a paper; crossword half-finished, abandoned in a
corner booth.

Soon the steady stream of passers-by would resume, a
constant rotation of umbrellas briefly pausing in the stand
below dripping macs, building up to the lunchtime crush,
damp bodies squeezing in to the modestly sized
establishment, more than it had any right to comfortably
accommodate, hunched over steaming mugs, then the last
few stragglers before closing time.

Tables wiped clean, papers returned to the rack
irrespective of date, mugs stacked by the urn, plates
stowed away, everything still and quiet inside, awaiting the
morning rush, while the sounds of revellers passing by, in
search of a take-away, echo down the empty street.

Perks & Daily

By G. Burton

They were simple men whose jobs were fair:
Perks was a man who knew how to be just and care,
His work as a priest some looked on as odd,
But he was happiest when he was doing his job.

Daily was young, and a bit of a gadabout,
People wondered if he'd ever grow out
Of his childish whims and his fairytales,
He wanted to travel and with the sun set sail.

Their paths never crossed, save for one day
When they found each other in the strangest of ways;
The sight of the guns and the mud and the dead,
The pair of them wondered what they'd had in their
head.

For Daily found that his plans were at last
Giving him chance to see sights of the past;
The small country villages and the sounds of the French
Were just what he'd imagined when he had sat on that
bench.

For Perks, however, the place was not
Where he'd imagined himself, laying on a cot;
The dirt didn't bother him, nor did the smell,
Rather, it was the sound of the shells.

He laid there and wondered just why he'd gone,
Out of some foolish notion of what it was to be young?
But it was the day he discovered a man laying there in
the pew
That he knew that he was there for those very few.

The ones who needed him to say they were okay,
To tell them that they were there to keep the homeland
safe,

The ones that they killed were a horrible lot,
But that they were men too, whether they liked it or not.

The men that he fought were just like him,
Wondering what they were doing out in the din.
The families of all whom he saw on the tops,
The sounds of the trumpets now out of their box.

For Perks was a man who saw both of the sides,
He knew that they all fought for someone else's pride.
Yet Daily had come for the show of the brave,
He found it hard to simply stand there and wave.

With guns in the air and the shells on the ground,
Daily found himself not wanting to be found.
He recalled the day that his mother had cried,
Not wanting him to go, but knowing he couldn't hide.

Perks sat down and regaled the man,
As they shared a meal from half of a can,
With the recollections of time when they used to just be,
Not fighting a war to keep them free.

Perks told him of the time that he'd stood in his church
And heard the announcement that war had broken out
He found himself torn between staying and going,
But deep down knew that his calling was flowing

Towards the small dugout that they sat in now,
For support and guidance for those who realised just
how
Their actions were not what they'd thought them to be
And wondered instead what it was to be free.

A friendship was formed, there in that corner
Of a trench dug into the walls of a border.
They were simple men whose jobs were fair,
They certainly never expected things there,

The fight and the furore, the sight of things past;
They wondered whether this meal would be their last.

For years hence the sights of their names
Brought the families tears and those that had doubted
them shame.
The poppies danced and quivered and swayed,
Their merriment harsh in the sounds of the haze.

The wonders of war and the horror of peace
The thoughts of whether it would ever cease;
We stop and we think, of the people so brave,
And wonder just whether we might have been able to
save

The ones that went who wanted to stay,
Of Perks & Daily
Forever remembered for their deaths
In the most horrid of ways.

Perks & Daily

By Jessica Grace Coleman

Samantha Perks and James Daily liked to think of themselves as detectives. They weren't – they were only eighteen years old, for one thing. Also, they knew nothing whatsoever about police procedure. They were, however, from the most boring town in the history of the world (in their humble opinion) and they were currently broke.

No money meant no going out and getting wasted like most of the kids in their year, and as neither of them wanted to stay at home, watching soaps and talk shows with their parents, they would often find themselves at 'The Church', an old abandoned building which James thought was creepy and Samantha thought was beautiful. It had lost most of its roof over the years, which pushed the homeless of Stayford away from the ruins and towards the other abandoned buildings throughout the town, of which there were many. Samantha often thought this place would be a ghost town in just a few short years. Maybe even sooner.

Of course, The Church had a reputation for being haunted, and that kept most of the kids away as well. Teenagers around here weren't too brave.

Samantha lay out on the blanket they'd brought with them and looked up at the sky. From her vantage point, she could see a few stars beyond the jagged edge of the church wall. It was getting chilly now, and she was glad she had taken her mum's advice and put on her giant coat.

"What you thinking, Perks?"

Samantha rolled over, so she was facing James. What she'd been thinking was dark and depressing: how she had to figure out what she was doing with her life, so she wouldn't just end up staying here forever with no plans and no ambitions. She didn't want to simply fade away, or become just another statistic, like so many kids before her. She didn't tell James, this, however. Instead, she just asked, "Will you ever call me Samantha? Sam? S? *Anything* other than my goddamn surname?"

He shrugged, smiling. "Why would I? We're Perks and Daily, the gruesome twosome, the sad loner couple..." he noticed Samantha's scowl and trailed off.

"You don't need to remind me what those morons at school call us, *Daily*. I just can't wait until we finish this year and can leave the whole lot of them behind."

"And what are we going to do then? In case you haven't noticed, we're meant to be deciding our future right about now." He gestured around him, at the dark, dank ruins. "Not hanging out in an old church like some kind of pathetic vampires."

Samantha groaned. James did this every time – moaned about what they were doing and where they were doing it, when she knew that he secretly loved this place. It had such a rich history, and no one cared about it anymore, leaving it to rot and die. It was so sad. "What do you suggest? Because I don't think either of us would fit in very well at Uni, and you know there'd only be a tiny chance we'd both get into the *same* course at the *same* place."

Samantha didn't like to admit it, but the thought of going out into the world on her own – without James by her side – made her feel physically sick. They'd known each other practically since birth, and he was her best friend – her *only* friend – in the whole world. There'd never been anything romantic there, nothing like that, but what they had went deeper than that, somehow. They knew each other inside out, and when they fought, it didn't really matter. They weren't together, so they couldn't break up, and in a way it felt like family. You could argue and fight with your family as much as you wanted, but at the end of the day, they were still family – they always had been, and they always would be, no matter what happened. She and James had a similar thing going on.

"Screw Uni. I'm not going to do another three years of essays and dissertations just to come out with a load of debt."

Samantha rolled her eyes. She knew the *real* reason he didn't want to go; he had no idea what he would study, and neither did she. "So what? We work in a supermarket for the rest of our lives?"

James looked into the distance, as though he were

having some deep, profound thoughts. "Do you think we'd get a discount?"

Samantha laughed. "OK, well what do you propose?"

James – who had previously been pacing around the ruins like some kind of bored, caged animal – went over and sat next to Samantha on the blanket. He pulled her up from her horizontal position and put his hands on her shoulders, firmly but gently. He then looked straight into her eyes. "OK. Hear me out. There's this little office on the other side of town, and there's a 'To Let' sign on the door. It's not huge, but it would do."

Samantha could feel the beginnings of butterflies in her stomach. "It'd do for what?"

"For our very own private detective agency."

Samantha let James's words hang in the air for a few seconds before answering. "You've actually lost your mind, do you know that?"

He moved a couple of inches closer to her, the excited smile still lingering on his face, despite her less than enthusiastic response. "I've crunched the numbers – well, my dad did, anyway – and it's totally doable. I've got my savings and you've got the inheritance from your aunt. We could make that place into a really nice office, and we'd still have plenty of money to kit it out and get loads of advertising sorted to kick it all off."

Samantha frowned at him. She didn't like it when he got this insanely excited about something; it usually ended badly. Either the idea didn't come to fruition, and he was left bitterly disappointed and depressed, or it *did* come to fruition, and Samantha found herself in a ridiculous situation that she couldn't get out of – not easily, anyway. "James... I'm sure you've done the numbers and everything, but these things always cost more than you think."

James shrugged, clearly not perturbed in the slightest. "So we apply for a bank loan. Come on, Samantha, we're both smart; we can come up with a kickass business plan, I know we can. And this is *Stayford*, can you think of a place with more of a need for an independent P.I. company? Think of all the secrets this town holds! Partners cheating on each other, embezzlement, theft... not to mention its 'little problem'. We'd be in business in no time."

OK, on this point, Samantha agreed, but she wasn't about to tell James that. There would definitely be a lot of cheating partners around, and the 'little problem'... well, she didn't like thinking about it, exactly, but it was something that needed to be addressed. After all, no one else was doing it. Sighing, she said, "What about the legal side of things? We have no idea what we're doing, James! We don't know what licences we'd need, or how long it would take to get them, we don't know about insurance, or..."

He cut her off. "So we find out. Minor details, Perks, minor details. We've got the rest of the school year, right? We can plan it all out, get the ball rolling, and then start as soon as we've got everything in place. We can *do* this, I know we can. Come on – how great would it be? Working together, being our own bosses? We've played detectives together since we were four years old. We've watched every single episode of CSI and NCIS and all those shows... and we've got good instincts. We work well together. I think this could be really great."

Samantha was staring at him, and even though she *really* didn't want to, she was starting to feel as excited as James looked. It would be pretty killer. And who wanted to spend their whole lives working for the man, anyway?

James was grinning. "I can tell you're thinking about it." He stood up and held out his hand. "Come on."

Samantha let him pull her up to a standing position. "What?"

"I'm going to prove to you that this is a good idea. Let's start detecting. Right now."

"Er... James? Detect what? We're in The Church."

James looked around him, his smile getting even wider. "Exactly! How many times have we talked about the history of this place? Of how there must be secrets just waiting to be found? I say we look for clues and try and piece them together in some sort of story. We can go and do some research in the library tomorrow and see if we can find anything that matches."

Samantha couldn't help but smile. James was *not* your ordinary eighteen year old... and she loved him for it.

Secretly, she thought the most they'd find around here was some cigarette butts and possibly a couple of gross old condoms, but she'd play along. For now. "OK, I'm in. Where do we start?"

Taking his phone out of his pocket, James turned on the torch function. "Where do you think?"

Samantha groaned, immediately wishing she hadn't agreed to this stupid plan. "I'm not going into the basement, if that's what you're thinking. And anyway, we can't. How many times have we looked for a way in? It's like it's glued shut or something."

James was already making his way over to the other end of The Church, where it sloped down to a little sunken door, barely big enough for a human to pass through without crouching down. They knew it was the door to the basement thanks to some research they'd already done on the place, but they'd tried everything they could think of on the door – including a crowbar that James had 'borrowed' from his dad – and nothing had worked.

While Samantha had been relieved about this, James had been devastated. He'd always wanted to get into the basement because of the rumours. These rumours had been around for hundreds of years, and they suggested that, at one time, there had been secret underground passages running the length of the town. One of them was supposed to end up in the basement of this church, but of course, no one had been able to get down there recently to verify any of it.

Samantha followed James to the door, where they both stared at it. It didn't look like it would be something that would be impossible to budge – it just seemed like a normal old-fashioned wooden door – but their experience with it told them otherwise.

At one point, James had become so desperate to get in there that he decided he wanted to hack it down with an axe, set fire to it, or just blow the door to bits, but Samantha had always stopped him. For one thing, she didn't want to get arrested, just in case she did want to go into higher education (criminal records didn't look great on Uni applications), and anyway, she wouldn't let him touch this church. It had been through enough already, and the last thing it needed was for some idiot to come and accidentally blow the whole thing up. She hoped that one day someone would come and restore this place to its former glory, and secretly, she was kind of hoping it would be her, somehow, someday. Setting fire to it or blowing it up didn't really fit into her plans.

"James, we're not going to be able to get down there. We've tried too many times."

He was shaking his head. "We've tried brute force too many times… maybe there's another way."

Samantha sighed, sitting down on a pile of rubble and watching James as he stared at the door. "Like what?"

James pulled his gaze away from the door long enough to glance at his friend. "I've been researching… not just this place, but churches in general, from around this time period. Some of them… well, some of them were pretty sneaky."

"Sneaky?" What the hell was he going on about now?

James stepped closer to the door, reaching out and stroking the rough wood. After a few moments, he crouched down, blowing at the dust around the frame and running his hands over the surface, slowly and methodically checking every little bit.

Samantha was starting to find this all very funny. "What on earth are you doing? Do you think you're some sort of door whisperer now?"

James ignored her, at least for a few seconds. Then, suddenly, his hand stopped moving. *He* stopped moving. It didn't even look like he was breathing.

"James?"

Nothing.

"Daily!"

That snapped him out of it, and he slowly turned his head towards her. He looked pale. "I've found it."

Samantha jumped off the pile of rubble, the hair on her arms standing up as she took in the change in the atmosphere – a change which had taken place in just the past few minutes. "Found what?"

James turned back to the door, staring intently at his hand. After a couple more seconds, he pushed into the wall with all his strength, and something clicked.

Samantha was frozen to the spot as the door slowly creaked open, letting out a putrid smell of mould, as if no air had gotten past that door in centuries.

James stood up, staring at Samantha as if she were a ghost. "It had it! It actually had a button hidden in the wall! All this time... all the energy we spent on it, and all we had to do was press a frigging button!"

Samantha let out a small, hysterical laugh. It was unbelievable... and even though her heart was now pounding as though it were about to explode, she couldn't wait to get in that door. Taking her own phone out of her pocket, she turned the light on and moved over to James, grabbing his hand. "Let's do this."

James nodded, taking a deep breath before moving towards the door. "Perks and Daily's first case... The Mystery of the Church Basement."

Samantha wanted to tell him to shut up, but the truth was, she was too excited. She knew that realistically there wouldn't be anything down there, apart from maybe a million spiders... but just the thought that they could be the only people to enter that room in over a hundred years... it sent shivers down her spine. Good shivers.

Bending down so they could fit through the small doorway, James guided them both inside.

As soon as they crossed the threshold of the door, it got colder. The change was instant.

Once again, Samantha was grateful for her coat. James, on the other hand, was only wearing a thin hoodie, and he shivered next to her as they looked at what was in front of them.

It was a set of steps – no surprise there – and they led down into what could only be described as a cloud of darkness. No light had hit this place for at least a few hundred years, Samantha was sure of it.

Slowly, James led the way, walking down the steps and shining his phone around in the small space. No spiders. No anything. Just the steps and the darkness.

It felt like an age, but finally they got to the bottom. There was another door here – much like the one they'd just gone through – and James pushed on it, expecting it to be shut fast like the last.

It was. Letting go of Samantha's hand, James felt around the doorframe again, finding another button in a similar position to the one before. Giving a brief glance at Samantha, he pushed on it, watching as the door swung open.

More darkness.

Taking hold of her hand again, James walked into the gloom, with Samantha by his side.

Although the ceiling was very low, this room was clearly a lot bigger, and their phones did nothing more than illuminate a few feet in front of them at a time.

James stopped, hesitating. "Maybe we should go back and get a better torch."

Samantha sighed. "Have you *got* a better torch? Because I haven't. Let's just get this over with." Samantha was excited, sure, but she didn't know if she'd be able to pluck up the courage to come down here a second time, and she definitely didn't feel like hanging around here on her own while James went to source out a better light. Trying to act braver than she felt, she walked further into the room, pulling James along behind her.

There were some old stone slabs dotted around the floor. That was all she could see at this end of the room, and she pressed on, thinking that if there *was* a secret passageway entrance, it would be at the far end, away from the main door.

"What do you think they did down here?" she asked, curious about the slabs.

She felt rather than saw James shrug. "Could be anything as innocent as holding meetings about the church... or it could be where they baptised people. Or... it could be where they prepared bodies for burial."

Samantha stopped suddenly. "Seriously?"

James shrugged again. "I don't know! This place was probably just a front for the secret passageway. If there is one..."

Samantha was beginning to get really creeped out now, and the thought of dead bodies being prepared down here really didn't help. "Let's just find out and then *get* out, shall we?"

James nodded, and the two of them walked into the

gloom, more forcefully this time.

"What's that?"

She looked over to where James was pointing his phone, the pathetic beam of light illuminating something shiny and silver. "I don't know..." Samantha, of course, was imagining horrific ancient equipment, used for cutting into skeletons and God knows what else... but she didn't mention this to James.

They both walked over to the shiny object, stopping a few feet away as they realised what they were actually looking at. It was a knife, and it wasn't alone.

Hanging onto a wooden shelf along the wall was a long line of pointy objects and instruments – actually, it was pretty much what Samantha had been imagining. And worse.

"Do you think this is what they used on the bodies?" Her voice came out quiet and low.

"I... I don't know." James was studying each object closely, and he was frowning.

"What is it?"

James turned to Samantha, his face an illuminated oval in the darkness. "If these are hundreds of years old, why are they so shiny? Wouldn't they be all covered in crap and rust by now?"

Samantha stared at them, trying to think back to her science classes at school. She hadn't taken one in the past two years and she couldn't remember a single thing from them. "Well, they haven't been exposed to any air or anything... maybe they've just been preserved like this?"

James was shaking his head now, an unconscious thing he did when he didn't believe a word that someone was saying to him. "But... don't they look new to you? Like, they look modern."

Samantha stared at the implements again. They didn't exactly look like they'd been bought out of the Argos catalogue, but they didn't particularly look like they were hundreds of years old either. "I guess."

James suddenly stepped back, pulling Samantha with him. "We shouldn't be here."

Samantha groaned. "Oh come on, you're the one who's been trying to get in here for months! Are you telling me that you don't want to explore the rest of the room while we've got the chance?"

James stared down at the floor, and she could tell that he was deliberating what to do. After a few moments, he looked up at her, nodding. "OK, let's do this."

Slowly, they turned away from the wall of instruments and headed towards the back of the room again.

A couple of minutes had gone by, and Samantha was just starting to wonder how long this room was when she trod on something hard, twisting her ankle and making her yell out.

"What is it?" James's voice was full of concern, as well as sounding absolutely petrified.

"I just stepped on something, I..." Samantha pointed her phone down at her feet, getting just a snap shot of the object as the light on her phone went out. Her heart dropped.

"Phone battery gone?" James asked, sounding slightly nervous but not nervous enough – he clearly hadn't seen what she'd just seen. When he got no answer, he held his own phone out at the floor, nearly dropping it as it illuminated a smooth, white bone.

Samantha reached out for James's arm, digging into it with her nails. She couldn't speak.

Neither, apparently, could James. Instead, he just held out his phone with a shaking hand, moving it around the space in front of them.

It wasn't just one bone.

James brought his hand down quickly, shining the phone torch at the ground while Samantha continued to cling onto his arm. "It's fine." His voice was low, almost like a growl.

Samantha couldn't believe what she was hearing. "*How* is this fine? There's got to be at least fifty bodies there! You call that *fine*?"

James turned to her, taking her face in his hands. "OK, Sam, we have to calm down. We're in a church, OK? Outside in the graveyard, there are far more bodies than this."

Samantha took a few deep breaths, trying to get herself under control. "Yes... exactly! In the *graveyard*. Why aren't these buried? Why have they just been dumped down here, on top of each other?"

James shrugged. "Maybe they just didn't get round to burying them. Maybe they were like... homeless people, who had no family or friends to pay for a funeral."

Or maybe it was something much more sinister. Samantha glanced over into the darkness, at where the knives and other implements had been hanging on the wall. "What if they were killed?"

James snorted with laughter, then immediately stopped. In this room, with all these bones, it sounded remarkably creepy. "Why on earth would you think that?"

Samantha took a second to think, while trying *not* to think of all the dead bodies at her feet. "Why would they be dumped down here otherwise? In a secret room full of what is essentially a whole host of weapons... you can't tell me I'm the only one thinking of Stayford's little problem?"

James stared at Samantha, his face – if possible – getting paler and paler. "You're not serious..."

Samantha didn't *want* to be serious, not at all, but it was kind of staring them in the face here. "How many people have vanished from this area over the years? Everyone talks about it like it's some kind of ghost story, but it's real. Come on, James, we both know people who have disappeared. Mark from school? Vince from the library?"

"I know, I know! But... it's just... they could have left. Could have got fed up of Stayford and pissed off to some city somewhere."

Samantha groaned. They'd had this argument a million times. Hell, everyone in town had had this argument a million times. But what if they had proof? Samantha gestured at the bones. "Or maybe they didn't. Maybe they're right here under our feet?"

James slowly turned his phone light onto the sea of bodies again. The sheer amount of grey-white bones was kind of mesmerising, if you ignored the obvious. "Alright, but Mark and Vince... if they were here, they wouldn't be... skeletons, would they? That was recent."

Yes, it was, but reports of missing people had been going on for years and years. That's why no one ever really believed it when someone said the people had just moved away, without thinking to tell any of their friends or families. The number was just too high.

Suddenly, Samantha saw something in the corner of her eye and she grabbed the phone off James, holding it out as far as she could reach, her arm shaking. "Oh God."

James was squinting into the gloom. He'd always had rubbish eyesight, but he absolutely refused to wear glasses. "What?"

Samantha walked forwards a few steps, being careful of where she trod. She didn't want to look, but she had to make sure. Still holding out the phone, the light picked up several strands of long, dark hair. Her voice barely a whisper, Samantha turned to James. "That recent enough for you?"

James was staring at the hair, at the sunken face that could just about be seen underneath it. He was trembling. "But the door... no one's used it for years, how...?"

Even though she felt like she was about to explode and throw up at the same time, Samantha's brain was still working. Just about. "The secret tunnel, remember?"

James laughed, high and hysterical. "We never really believed that, did we? I mean, honestly?"

Samantha gestured at the bodies with her phone. "And this? Would you have believed this? James, listen to me. We have to get out of here and go and tell the police. You wanted to be a detective, and here we are. So suck it up, and let's get moving!"

Without waiting a second longer, Samantha grabbed James by the sleeve, thrusting his phone in his hand and heading back the way they'd come, aiming for the door.

Which was closed. Of course.

Frantic now, both James and Samantha crouched down, feeling around the edge of the doorframe for the magic button.

"Where is it?"

"I don't know! It has to be here somewhere." James sounded adamant, but Samantha wasn't so sure.

After a few minutes of searching, Samantha pulled him away. "James, it's not there. Does your phone have any signal?"

He looked down, his expression turning to one of relief.

Unfortunately, it soon transformed into one of sheer panic. "I've got some signal, but my battery's about to die."

Samantha didn't even miss a beat. "Turn the torch off, then phone the police. Do it!"

James stared at Samantha. "But we'll be in darkness!"

"We'll be in darkness anyway when your battery's gone. At least we'll be in darkness with someone on the way!" Grabbing his phone off him, Samantha quickly turned the torch off, plunging them into a deep gloom. She then dialled 999 and waited for someone to pick up.

"Yes, hello. My name's Samantha Perks and I'm in the basement of The Church – you know, the ruined one on Bailey Street. We've found a *lot* of bodies and we're trapped inside. You can only get in using the small door in the chapel, but there's a secret button to the left of the door that you have to press to open it. Please hurry."

The phone went dead before she could get a response from the lady on the other end, and Samantha could only pray that she heard – and understood – it all.

"Are they coming?"

Samantha smiled at James. "Sure."

James could always tell when Samantha was lying, or at least not telling him the whole truth. "Maybe we should find the secret passageway?"

Samantha looked at him as if he'd gone mad. "When we don't know where it leads to? When it quite likely will lead to the house of some crazed murderer? Really?"

"And what if it just leads into a random field or a sewer or something? At least we'd be getting out somehow!"

Samantha sat down on the ground, pulling James with her. "No. We're staying right here. I'm not going to shove myself into a stupid secret passage that leads to God knows where when there's a chance there's someone on the way. Let's just wait."

James wasn't convinced, but he sat down in the darkness and held onto Samantha's hand. He told himself that he was comforting her, but really, he just wanted to reassure himself that he wasn't alone. Alone in a room full of dead bodies. He shuddered.

A couple of minutes went by, but it may as well have been a couple of hours. There in the darkness – the complete, pitch black – time had no purpose. Their phones had died so they couldn't look at the clocks, and there wasn't even a sliver of light to look at their watches by, so they just sat there in silence, trying not to count the seconds, because every second that went by was another second that no one had come to rescue them.

What if they hadn't got the message? What if they thought it was just kids playing a joke? What if they were here, just feet away upstairs, but unable to get through the door?

Samantha tried not to think these thoughts as she sat next to James, staring straight ahead. At one point, she waved her hand in front of the face – right next to her eyes – to see if she could make out even a vague outline in the gloom. She couldn't.

She vaguely wondered if they'd start hallucinating soon, and she desperately hoped she wouldn't see the bones and the bodies rise up and start walking towards her – or something even worse.

"Did you hear that?"

James's voice pulled Samantha from her morbid thoughts. "What?"

"Someone's coming."

"Oh thank God. Are you sure?"

There was a brief silence before James spoke again. "Yeah, did you hear that? Definitely someone shuffling about!"

Samantha heaved a huge sigh of relief. "I was beginning to think that we might actually –" she stopped suddenly, leaving a huge gaping gap in the air where the rest of her sentence should have been.

"Sam…"

"Shh!"

They both waited in the silence, listening for the tell-tale signs of someone approaching. There was a shuffle, a bang, and a couple of footsteps.

The next time Samantha spoke, it was barely a whisper. "The sounds… they're not coming from the main door. They're coming from the other side of the room."

She let that sink in for a second, but then there was another bang, and she leaped into action.

"What are you doing? If that's the secret passage... let's just stay here at this end and keep still."

Samantha could have slapped James for being so stupid. His brain power must have vanished in his fright. "They'll have a light with them; that would never work."

James's voice was higher now, panicked. "Then what the hell are you suggesting we do? Fight?"

Samantha thought of the knives, glistening on the wall. "Yes. Exactly!" Without wasting another second, she ran over to the wall of weapons, pulling James along with her. She had visions of smacking into the wall and knocking herself out... or of running directly into a huge, sharp knife, but fortunately, neither of those things happened.

Her free hand held out in front of her, Samantha felt the rough wood of the shelf, and then a little lower, the handle of a huge knife. Although by the feel and the weight of it, this wasn't any old knife. It was more like a large dagger.

Fumbling in the dark, she pulled another cold, hard instrument off the wall and handed it carefully to James.

"So our plan is...?"

"Wait for whoever that is to come in here and then charge the shit out of them."

James was silent for a moment before mumbling, "And what if there's more than one of them?"

That thought hadn't even occurred to Samantha, and it stumped her. For about two seconds. "Well, there's more than one of us too."

The noise was getting louder now, and remembering the layout of the room, they could tell it was coming from near the big pile of bodies. They must have been so busy focusing on the horrific mound of bones that they didn't even see that there was a doorway over there – that was, if it would have even shown up in their feeble digital torch light.

Sure enough, a door slowly creaked open, the sound coming from the other end of the room, and Samantha and James both held their breath as a shadowy figure moved into view. It was large and muscly, quite clearly the silhouette of a man. He held a huge torch in his hand, the type that James had been thinking of going and finding just a few minutes before. That felt like forever ago.

Samantha could hear James breathing next to her and hoped it wouldn't carry over to the figure. He hadn't noticed them yet, and they needed to wait until he had turned away from them or was kneeling down before they attacked. They needed as much of an advantage as they could get; if he'd managed to kill this many people, he must have been strong.

Seconds passed, and Samantha honestly thought she was going to faint. The figure still hadn't looked over at them – in fact, he hadn't yet moved away from where the secret passage entrance was. He was shuffling about over there, head down, back bent over.

What the hell was he doing? It was almost as if he...

Samantha gasped.

Two things happened simultaneously. Samantha and James both realised what the figure was doing, and the figure realised that he was being watched.

He dropped the body and glanced around wildly in the gloom, his torch in his lowered hand, forgotten, and his face in shadow.

Time seemed to stop. This was it, this was the time for either fight or flight – apart from there wasn't any flight, was there? Not back the main way, anyway.

This thought hit Samantha at the same time that it hit the figure, and as 'Perks' ran towards the back of the room, the figure tried to back up into the passageway.

"Hey!" Her loud voice rang out in the underground room, sounding unnatural after all of the whispering.

James stood frozen to the spot as he watched his best friend in the whole word hurtle towards what was probably a mass murderer with nothing more to help her than a dagger and a huge dose of absolutely terrified rage.

Then his brain kicked in, and as he saw Samantha disappear into the dark tunnel after the figure, he ran over to the body that had been dumped near the entrance, crouching down over it.

It was a boy, couldn't have been more than fifteen years old. He looked dirty and ragged, like he'd been living on the streets for a while. Sadly, that was pretty common in Stayford. He was either dead or unconscious – James wasn't sure which.

He was torn. Stay and help the boy – who may have been beyond help anyway – or run after Samantha? It was a no brainer.

He stood up and ran the couple of feet to the secret entrance, getting ready to peer into the gloom to try and make out something, *any*thing.

He didn't need to. About ten feet away from him, Samantha and the figure stood, grappling with each other, the large torch swinging around as limbs flailed about, lighting up the rough grey passage around them in large, eerie flashes. The dagger was on the floor.

He could see the man's face now, and it looked vaguely familiar, but then everyone knew everyone around here. He could be any number of the group of generic middle-aged Stayford residents. James shuddered.

"Sam, I'm here!" James was just running towards them when he saw Samantha force the torch out of the figure's hands, raise it above her head, and bring it smashing down on his face.

The figure crumpled to the ground.

"Huh."

Samantha turned to face James, a mix of fear and triumph on her half-lit face. She was just opening her mouth to speak when the sound of a door banging open reached their ears.

Rushing into the basement room, Perks and Daily sighed simultaneously as a couple of police officers stumbled into the semi-darkness.

James just had time to notice that the boy was starting to come round when the officers – one man and one woman – walked over to them, the lights from their own torches dancing around the room as they went.

"Are you the girl who rang the police?"

Samantha nodded, gesturing at the tunnel. "There's an unconscious man in there you might want to get hold of."

They gave the bodies a long glance and then settled their gazes on the two of them and the boy. As the man bent down to look at the casualty and then made his way into the tunnel, the woman spoke. "Everything under control here?"

Samantha smiled as she leaned against James,

completely exhausted.

He smiled back at her, the adrenaline still pumping through his body. He could get used to this.

So could Samantha.

She nodded. "Everything's under control."

Perks & Daily

A poem in three parts

By J. McGraw

Perks and Daily,
(Lizards scaly)
Ukuleles
Used to play.

All the while,
Rank and file,
Judged their style
Too cliché.
~~~~~~**~~~~~~
"Mr Perks, I do declare,"
The lizard Daily said,
"To make our fortunes, different tunes
We'll have to play instead."

"Mr Daily," Perks replied,
"I know we've been a flop,
But think: the music you suggest,
Is little more than pop."

"I understand the urgency
Of our financial state,
But stooping half as low as that
Would all our skills negate."

"Dear Mr Perks," the answer came,
"Our skills aren't so profound.
On ukuleles, lizard hands
Can't even make a sound.
~~~~~~**~~~~~~
The lizards called Daily and Perks
They soon made the most of their quirks.
They traded their ukes

For bow ties and suits
And joined the Department of Works.

Perks & Daily

Purveyors of Unusual Plants and Horticultural Miscellany to the Discerning Gardener

By Lauren K. Nixon

Winter Edition
Special rates available for repeat customers, apply to Ms Perks upon arrival, or if purchasing by post, please address to Ms Mary Perks, Cockleshell Cottage, Little Plimpton.

Creeping Gromwell
Tired of chasing the neighbourhood children away from your house and off your lawn? Plant some *Creeping Gromwell* – with its ATTRACTIVE blue, star-shaped flowers – around your door and you'll never have to worry about knock'n'runs again.

Creeping Gromwell requires two to three days to fully digest an average child, aged between five and twelve. For best results, plant in succession.

Larger specimens recommended for door-to-door salesmen and window cleaners.

Self-mulching. Not recommended for households with young children or animals.

Having trouble with carollers and religious callers? Take advantage of our TWO-FOR-ONE offer. This month only!

Popping Pansies
Want to give a fireworks display with real panache this year? Why not fill your borders with our vibrant range of *Popping Pansies*? Specially bred by Mr. G. Daily for this very occasion, we are proud to offer you an EXCLUSIVE range of jaw-dropping colours that are GUARANTEED to go off with a bang. A hardy variety, this annual is perfect for both Bonfire Night and New Year's Eve.

Displays can be lit an intervals of two weeks throughout the growing season.

Do not expose to a naked flame.
Sold in packs of twelve.

Butterfly Bush
Can't think of the perfect present for your little ones this Christmas? Why not get them a GENUINE *Butterfly Bush* and make them feel like a real fairy prince or princess!

Imported direct from Xanadu and lovingly nurtured by Ms M. Perks, the *Butterfly Bush* is perfect for the younger gardener. Compact and beautiful, this exotic shrub is at home on the patio or in a glasshouse. Unique blooms in a range of different colours will keep all the family happy from April to September.

Got a niece or nephew with a penchant for lepidoptery? Help them dazzle their friends with knowledge, with a GENUINE *Dark Butterfly Bush*!

The *Dark Butterfly Bush,* also known as the *Moth's Mausoleum* flowers from September to March, with sprays of real, live fluttering moths when exposed to moonlight.
Ideal for containers, keep indoors over winter.
Do not over-water.
Do not spray with insect repellent.
Dark Butterfly Bush only blooms at night.

Cockle shells
Line your paths with *Cockle Shells* and you can't go far wrong! This sub-species of land coral forms delicate, shell-like wreaths that glimmer in the sunlight. Perfect for brightening up the garden this winter!

Plant these unusual flowers alongside our GENUINE *Silver Bells* for a stunning effect that will have the neighbours talking for generations!

Requires particular Silicate Potting Compost, available EXCLUSIVELY from Perks & Daily.
Frost resistant.

Snapdragons

Unwanted callers darkening your door? Jehovah's Witnesses witnessing far too much on your street? Plant a posy of *Snapdragons* and they'll soon vacate the area. These classic flowers come with a Perks & Daily EXCLUSIVE TWIST – spliced with dragon's breath by Mr G. Daily himself, these winter blooms will heat up any doorstep discussion.

These traditional cottage flowers grow just as well indoors – why not plant a few in your hearth this year and avoid those tiresome fuel bills?

Do not plant near stores of fuel or near the walls of wooden houses.

Do not plant near Popping Pansies.

Not suitable for young children.

Please wear protective and flame-proof clothing while working with our Snapdragons. Appropriate attire may be purchased from our partners, Messers Tinker, Tailor, Soldier and Spy, who are located on Little Plimpton High Street.

Caterwauling Chrysanthemums

Sick of hearing your neighbours bicker? Tired of listening to Black Sabbath at four in the morning? Plant Caterwauling Chrysanthemums along the edge of your property and you need never be disturbed again. These UNIQUE flowers belt out a succession of increasingly irritating songs, all entirely off-key – and the best part? Due to a fascinating quirk of evolution, all noise is repelled outwards. Do make sure you plant them facing your neighbours – unless you intend to drive your family insane!

Seasonal variations available.

Perks & Daily will not be held responsible should your purchase of Caterwauling Chrysanthemums lead to litigation. Similarly, any accident or injury sustained following the planting of Caterwauling Chrysanthemums is at the owners' risk.

Ladies Fingers

Our ever-popular *Ladies Fingers* are back in stock, perfect for propagating your own potion ingredients. These hardy plants grow best under a *Deadly Nightshade* vine and can be harvested from January to May. HEAVY CROPPER. Plant now for best results. Plant is ripe when fruits most closely resemble human flesh – for best results wait until the blood just starts to ooze from the ends of each finger.

Do not confuse with the mundane Ladies Fingers, which are an African vegetable also known as Okra, and quite useless in anything but a good curry.

Boneless variety available.

Silver Bells

Musically inclined? Can't possibly fit any more wind chimes into your garden? Grow our *Silver Bells* vines across your pergolas and trellises for a MAGICAL effect, every time the wind blows. Our EXQUISITE silver bells can be taught up to five beautiful melodies to delight your family and friends.

Pre-taught varieties available in the following categories: Nursery Rhymes, Seasonal, Heavy Metal, Classical, Lullabies, Classic Rock and 80s Hits.

Prefers shady, damp conditions.

Purple Passionflower

The perfect gift for the one you love this Christmas. Whether you're just starting out or want to spice up a longer-term relationship, the *Purple Passionflower* is the ideal means of creating that little spark of romance. Just plant this EXOTIC vine outside your boudoir and let it work its magic!

Caution, Passiflora Purpurus is a powerful aphrodisiac and should under no circumstances be consumed, planted in the gardens of families with children or on commercial premises, unless those premises are of a very particular nature.

Perks & Daily accept no responsibility for any unforeseen consequences of planting Purple Passionflower. You are all adults and should be using your common sense.

Dandelions

Want a border that really roars? Plant our SPECIALITY *Dandelions* and you'll never be plagued by cats or foxes using your garden as a litter box. Our *Dandelions* have a UNIQUE sense of smell, sniffing out unwanted guests and giving them the fright of their lives. Our *Dandelions* can be taught to recognise several varieties of larger garden pests including cats, dogs, foxes, badgers, sparrowhawks, herons, burglars and religious pamphleteers.

Can be grown all year round, as long as their roots are kept warm through winter with a layer of straw.

Perks & Daily are not responsible for heart attacks experienced by intruders. Plant at your own risk.

Forget-me-Not

An attractive mundane flower, *Forget-me-Nots* also have arcane qualities the discerning gardener may wish to exploit. These pretty blue and pink flowers, when made into a posy or pomander, can help to keep the grower in the mind of the recipient. Perhaps you are in love, or want your CV to stand out – present your potential lover with a posy of *Forget-me-Nots*, or slip a few of the flowers into the envelope with your job application and sit back and wait. It wont be long before you receive that ALL IMPORTANT call!

Do not over-use. Over-use may result in stalking.
Prefers full sun.
Not edible.

Dead Man's Purse

Money doesn't grow on trees – but it does grow on this discrete herbiferous hybrid. Ms. M. Perks has lovingly bred common *Shepherd's Purse* with a few of our more unusual species to create this UNIQUE and SPECTACULAR hybrid.

In financial difficulties? Plant *Dead Man's Purse* and reap the rewards! After a spectacular mid-summer display of red velvet blooms, harvest REAL GOLD COINS every November. This hardy perennial is GUARANTEED to produce a regular harvest of ancient coins for up to five years.

Plant in a secure part of your property.

Owners must be able to produce a bill of sale for the duration of the plant's natural life to prevent prosecution under the Treasure Act.

Rambling Roses

Is trespassing a thorny issue? Tired of chasing princes away from your tower? Sick of fending off well-meaning neighbours? Plant our *Rambling Roses* and your trespassing woes will be forgotten. These hardy perennials produce a dense hedge of vegetation OVERNIGHT, complete with inch-long thorns and semi-sentient branches.

For a more gentile variety, choose a yellow, white or pink hue, which may be trained up trellis and pergolas, but for MAXIMUM GARDEN PROTECTION, select Ruthless Red and intruders will be a thing of the past.

Do not grow indoors.

Requires a mulch of fish, blood and bone every six months. Do not overfeed.

Do not grow Ruthless Red Rambling Roses anywhere near where children are playing, as this is in contravention of national child abuse legislation.

Moonwort

Lycanthropy playing up? Live with someone who's going through a bad run of PMS? *Moonwort* is the answer. Plant this perennial sedge around your doorway and it will soothe the monster within. Moonwort emits a pleasant, minty scent and is delicious in Christmas cocktails.

JUST THE THING for the angry werewolf in your life!

Poisonous to felines.

Prefers a sheltered location. Vulnerable to sharp frosts.

Freezing Freesias
Want to give an unusual floral gift this year? Why not abandon the *Holly* and *Poinsettia* this year and give your loved ones *Freezing Freesias* this festive season!

These EXQUISITE blooms closely resemble their late spring cousins in all but one respect: this rare subspecies produces flowers made entirely of ice.

At their most spectacular at midnight, each transparent and delicate blossom can be kept in a moderately warm room for up to two weeks before melting, with the proper cooling charm in place (enquire at reception). Perfect for that person who has everything!

Can be used in anti-emetic potions.
Frost-resistant.

AND SO MUCH MORE!

Killer Bees
HALF-PRICE SALE on last season's *Killer Bees*.
LICENSE REQUIRED.

*****

KEEP AN EYE OUT FOR OUR NEW YEAR SPECIALS! COMING SOON!

If this is your first time visiting our exclusive nursery, turn right at the Little Nut Tree in the town square and follow the forest road past Peter Piper's Chilli Pepper Emporium and the Solomon Grundy Memorial Cemetery – this should be on your left. Perks and Daily are located on Contrary way, directly behind Polly's Fine Tea Shop. If you are walking from town, the best access is across the fields, by way of the Crooked Style, although do please keep to the edge of the fields.

For a more detailed visit, accommodation can be obtained at the public house, The Shoe (apply to Mrs Hubbard direct). Coaches can be hired from the Cock Horse Station at Banbury Cross.

George Daily would like to make it quite plain that any

indiscretions he is accused of committing in his youth against certain young ladies are entirely unsubstantiated and were fabricated in entirety by the incorrigible blackguard, Wee Willie Winkie. Visits from press and solicitors are not appreciated and litigation can – and will – be taken up at the drop of the old man's hat with Mr Daily's lawyer, Ms L. Locket Esq., care of Jack Horner's Coffee House, Upper Beckfoot. Nor has his nickname ever been – and never will be – 'Porgie'. He doesn't like opera, and it isn't funny.

Ms Mary Perks would like to make it quite plain that the aforementioned Wee Willie Winkie made up all that nonsense about her 'pretty maids', too, and if he comes tapping on her window of a night once more he'll feel the back of her cockle shell.

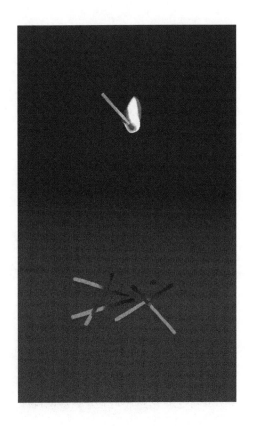

A Matchbox Full of Memories

By Hannah R.H. Allen

The grey October rain streaked the window outside, casting a pall over the house, the lights inside doing little to brighten the rooms inside, it had been a month since the funeral, and she had finally gathered the wherewithal to start sorting through his possessions.

It still didn't seem real, that someone that vibrant could suddenly be gone, every creek as the old house shifted transformed into his footsteps, so much so that she half expected him to walk in and object to her reading through his papers. There were a lot of papers, mostly bills and official papers, but among the disorganised collection there were carefully bundled correspondence, letters from family, friends, and names she didn't recognise, decades of it all stuffed, jammed, and poked into any available space left in the draws of his great sideboard.

It had taken all morning and most of the afternoon to clear out and sort the majority of the draws, neatly packing the papers into boxes to be dealt with later, plucking out the assorted ephemera that habitually collects in such draws; buttons, errant pen lids, pencils, elastic bands, et-cetera, as well as other eclectic artefacts, such as, an impressive collection of lighters, and a selection of penknives with varying degrees of wear.

As she was wresting the wedge of papers from the last draw, the draw that always stuck, she had been leaving it till last for just this reason, all of a sudden the front of the draw gave, and she found herself staggering backwards as papers fluttered to the ground.

"Yes, very funny," she muttered, his laughter echoing in her mind, half-smirking herself. Stooping to gather the papers, she glanced into the draw, and discovered the reason it had been sticking; wedged up against the underside of the desktop, between that and the back wall of the draw, a small matchbox, loosely wrapped in a sheet of paper, yellowing with age. The papers strewn across the floor forgotten, she reached into the back of the draw, and with some considerable wiggling and working she finally pulled it free, turning it over and over in her hands she sat back dislodging a stack of papers that flowed out unheeded across the floor.

The box rattled and shifted as it moved, curiosity piqued, she removed the decaying elastic band picking its dry husk off yellowed track marks, unfurling the paper she saw that it was a series of notes, that at first she took to have been written by different hands. On closer inspection that initial assumption had not been completely wrong, for in a way each note was written by person much different than the last.

The first note in a childish hand, scrawled in the manner of one who does not really expect the note to be read;

"These are the most important artefacts of the grand explorer and adventurer Terry Marr; the all-conquering conker that remains undefeated, the piece of eight discovered in a daring raid of the pirate's hoard, a lucky pebble carried on many adventures.
I hereby bequeath these to the royal museum.
Signed Terry Jacob Marr esquire."

The next note in a neat cursive that spoke of good education, with flourishes that twirled and looped around the text;

"These is T.J's treasures, hands off!
The button from Emily's coat the day we went steady, winner's ribbon inter house football cup, a fossil chipped from the cliff by myself, and the sergeant army man Steve gave me the last day of school.
-T.J "

The next note was still neat cursive, but from a writer that had grown into their own style, and given up the more florid curls to be more expedient and straight forward, as if written hurriedly;

"If you are reading this I am probably dead, know I love you all, I'm sorry I'm gone, I leave these few keepsakes in the hope it helps you remember me.
The photo of the family when we went on that day trip where dad got the car stuck, my favourite piece of whittling & the knife, the geode I found when we went camping.
Love, Terry"

The last note seems decades apart from the others, the writer's hand shakes, the script is neat but matter of fact;

"Whoever you are that finds this, these were the precious memories of a foolish youth, and a silly old man, if I meant something to you then treasure them, if not bury them somewhere my memory can rest peacefully.
My medals & ribbons, my medallion that kept me safe throughout the war, a thimble from our honeymoon, and the most important rings we ever wore.
Signed T.J Marr Esquire."

Hands shaking she slid open the box, sure enough the mementos of a lifetime nestled safely together, desiccated conker rested on plastic army figure, sparkling geode huddled with medal, and fastened together on a white length of ribbon two rings made of twisted grass stalks, the rings they had worn the day they decided to be together forever.

*

The day had been long, he had taken them on a meticulously planned hiking route through the most picturesque views the county had, and as the sun set they arrived at an overlook that took in the sparkling rivers, rolling hills and valleys, and the distant glow of the town, laying a blanket, they huddled together watching the stars come out. They had surmounted the hill as best friends, but alone amongst the beauty of the night, they realised that they were much more to each other, and in absence of traditional means had woven their promises from nature, and in the morning they descended as betrothed.

*

Tears blotched the page in her lap, months of feeling nothing but a hollow pit inside, she began to smile through the outpouring of pent up sorrow, a warmth began to suffuse her soul, like being held close, a final note had been attached to the ribbon;

"Love if you are reading this, I'm so sorry I had to go, but I will always be there when you close your eyes, and I promise when the day comes I will be there waiting to hold you again."

A Matchbox Full of Memories

By Jessica Grace Coleman

This object so small, the possibilities so great.
The fear is increasing; a dull, heavy weight.

This box holds my future, my present and past.
My heart is a drum beat, my blank face a mask.

The memories captured within its four walls
Call out to me, screaming, watching me stall.

The clock here is ticking, the time passing by.
I've longed for this moment, the moment to try.

So with dread and with hope, I pull on the card,
The material creaks, its cover a guard.

Sliding open the box, the stale air leaks.
The inside is dark, desolate, bleak.

This matchbox of memories, supposed to aid,
Instead just mocks me, its edges frayed.

The one clue I hoped would bring it all back
Is gone, taken, faded to black.

The interior is empty, not a speck of dirt.
The hollow void stares, my heart full of hurt.

My memory gone, taken from me.
With nothing to jolt it, I'll never be free.

This tiny matchbox, the one object l had.
The thing I held with me, the only good in the bad.

That moment of terror, that second of fear,
As the headlights approached, too close, too near.

Knocked off the pavement, pushed over the grass,
The frozen onlookers, gaping en-masse.

My arms and legs twisted, my head on the floor,
My mind a blank space, my body in war.

I tried to call out, not making a sound.
My possible saviours gathered around.

My pockets picked clean, my identity gone.
The only thing left: this box, this con.

This box holds my future, my present and past.
My one hope, crumbled, no longer can last.

A Matchbox Full Of Memories

By J. McGraw

Burning.

Memory in flames.

I remember every bonfire night I ever had. The people, the food, the smell in the air and the nip of the cold. I close my eyes and it's all still there, as real as the present. Burnt into my mind.

I remember barbecues as well. Old fashioned holidays in the country, smoking behind the PE shed at school, restaurants with more class than sense, cooking at university. Moments of pinpoint clarity in the haze of my past life. All of them clear in the flames that accompanied them.

I remember, specifically, the moment of realisation. Revising for some exam or other in school. Nothing worked - every fact I learnt turned to haze in a matter of minutes, drifting away with the same lethargy that my memories had always had. No matter how hard or how long I studied, I just couldn't learn.

Exams taken and, unsurprisingly, failed. My teachers couldn't understand, my parents couldn't understand. Everyone was so angry. I picked up my books and ran off. All my effort, and for what?

I sat in the corner of the park that evening, tearing pages out of my books and burning them. Each one slowly shrivelling, charring, fluttering madly in the flames, and then gone, crumbling to ash. I burned every school book I had, page by page, and then I went home again.

Eventually, the re-sits came. My chance to redeem myself for the failures, and to justify the expense of the burned books. I dreaded it. I barely looked in my new books. What was the point, if I couldn't learn? So I put them out of my mind, watched TV, played games. Then the exams were on me, and I entered the hall with as little revision as if they had been sprung on me the day before.

Same situation, but this time something was different. Each question reminded me of a page in my book, a page full of detail. Sentences, diagrams, all lay behind my eyes, exactly as they had been as they went up in flames.

Suddenly, it was easy. Every question as simple as I could dream. I finished in record time, left early. Parents and teachers cross again, thinking I wasn't taking it seriously, but then my results came back...

Cheat.

Top marks, more or less. A few points lost to stupid mistakes – typos, missing information, misreading the question. But only a few. Highest marks of anyone in my year, in all subjects, and all they could say was...

Cheat.

I weathered it. With no proof, there was little they could do. But I had the knowledge now. I've aced every exam since, jumped through every hoop, won every prize. And I told no one, not even my parents. It's been expensive, of course. Extra copies of books, photocopies, printouts. Matches. And of course I couldn't just set fire to things at home. I spent a lot of time in the woods about a mile from the house. Not ideal, but a limited field of view, no passers-by. Slowly, I learnt what I could do, and took advantage.

Skip to now. Good job, good house, good friends. The job was easy – freelance researcher with a reputation for speed and accuracy. The house was essential, full of bookshelves, a photocopier, and a large, functional fireplace. The friends...

I keep them at arm's length. Not that I dislike people, but it's difficult. I had a girlfriend at university, but she hated me disappearing, feared me when she found out. Afraid of fire. I hadn't thought it would be such a problem for us. I miss her now. She was lovely, and I remember her perfectly.

It's not quite the idyll it sounds. Sure, I've been happy, probably more than most people. I enjoy my work, and I'm good at it. I have a comfortable existence. But there's the shadow over me. Flames always create shadows, and the bright points of my life had their dark counterparts.

I found footprints in the flower bed outside my house the other day. Sometimes I look outside and fancy there's someone looking back. I used to think it was paranoia, but there's a face I see in the crowd, and he always seems to be there when I go out. It's been over a month now. I think he might be a private investigator.

It worries me. Someone out there thinks they need to have me followed, have my life reported on like a criminal. I can feel the gnawing in my stomach, the fear that my life isn't private anymore. I can't tell you how many times I have been through the rooms of my house, looking for anything that might look suspicious, that might be used against me somehow. People are so afraid of fire that they judge before they know the facts.

Fire is the only honest thing in this world.

I'll have to confront this snooping PI at some point, before he does any harm. I hope I can make him understand the truth about me, make him see that my fires aren't to be feared or doused before their time. They're part of my life, the best part of my life, truthful and purifying. I hope he can see that. I'm haunted by the memories, crystal clear, of the people who couldn't embrace the flames as I hoped they would. Their cries break into my dreams. But they're free now, and I visit them when I can, in my clearing in the woods.

I'll visit them tonight, let them know about the PI. I'm sure they'd be glad to see another freed as they are, free of fear and hate. I'll prepare his spot under the trees, and then I'll commit him to memory.

The Yellow Room

By Hannah R.H. Allen

She had never liked that room. It was at an odd angle so that the light never seemed to reach it, and due to the building's layout it was an odd shape – a lazy 's', curling round supporting walls and taking in the excess space leftover by other rooms. The wallpaper put her strongly in mind of a book she had once read concerning women running around behind the patterning; that wasn't exactly a reassuring image. There was no real furniture in the room, at least from what she could discern from glances through the door: some plush low seating that put her in mind of opium dens, and yet it was her Grandfather's favourite room. He would spend hours in there, the door locked fast; she would hear him shuffling around, pacing up and down, doing something – Lord only knew what.

It hadn't surprised her that he had left the house to her when he passed; she had been the closest to him over the years, and was also the closet relation still living. What had surprised her was the stipulation in the will; "You may do what you will with the property, once you have seen the yellow room properly," followed by a series of bizarre instructions.

And that was why she now stood on the landing, lingering on the threshold, peering apprehensively into the small room, a set of instructions grasped in her hand.

Breathing deep, like a free diver preparing to launch, she plunged through the doorway, taking a moment to ascertain nothing terrible had happened, and to confirm the absence of demonic looking dolls or arcane paraphernalia. She had flipped the first light switch and left it on for half hour before entering, as instructed. Now she flipped it off, and hurriedly set about the rest of the proscribed preparations.

At the far end was the only window that the room had, recessed into the outward facing curve of the 's'. There was a heavy velvet curtain hung – stage quality from the look of it – from a quite frankly over-engineered curtain rail, as thick as her forearm from wrist to elbow, with decoratively ridged conical end caps. She pulled the curtain across and the room fell into almost complete darkness, only a wedge of light from the hall door slicing through from the inward curling tail of the 's'.

Hurrying back to the island of light, she found a curtain on a much more modest rail, and drew it across, leaving herself now standing in a kind of improvised anteroom beside the door. Breathing hard, she shut the door, the sliver of light round the frame just barely supplying enough light to find the second light switch. She flipped it, closed her eyes and stepped around the curtain, dutifully counting down from ten.

Whatever she had expected upon opening her eyes, this wasn't it: the second light, it transpired, was a black light, and under its glow the walls were ablaze with colour. The sickly yellow paper and it's unaccountably creepy patterning was invisible beneath fantastical landscapes; stretching over the celling, and upper sections of wall was a star-scape full of planets and moons never to be seen from our Earth, picked out in glow-in-the-dark paint. Picking up the first lantern from a collection that was gathered on a low table, the only other piece of furniture in the room, she attached it to a hook hanging just above head height. Turning it on, silhouettes both of light and shadow were projected across the walls, shifting gently as the lantern swayed, sending birds and beasts running across the landscape.

Sinking down into the seating, little more than pile of cushions in the centre of the room, really (although this was suddenly making a whole lot more sense). She stared around in wonder as she pulled out a torch with an improvised slot attached to the front, with a collection of slides to slot in; additional silhouettes of fantastical creatures, knights, maidens, and more. Lastly, she withdrew an mp3 player from her jumper pocket. Pushing the earbuds home, she pushed play, and the voice of her grandfather filled her ears once again.

"These are the stories my father told me as a child, told to him by his mother, told to her by her father, and so on, into the past; these are our family legacy if you will, passed down over the ages."

She glanced over at the low table and for the first time, saw the stacks of hand-bound books on the shelf beneath.

"They have been told, retold, recorded, and rewritten, each generation embellishing on the last and adding their own tales, and this is my addition. The slides should be labelled and numbered for each story." There was a pause, then the next track began to play:

"Are you sitting comfortably? Then I'll begin. Once, a long, long time ago..."

The Last Cookie in the Yellow Room

By Cynthia Holt

I am standing at the counter
in the yellow room that is my kitchen.
I am eating the very last cookie in the last box of the
Peanut Butter Girl Scout Cookies that come
but once a year.
I was not thinking of getting any,
though this is the season for such,
when I happened upon the colorful boxes
and the cheerful girls in their beanies,
outside of the store.
I bought the cookies home, placed them
in a cupboard without saying so.
Curious as to how long it would take for them to be
found.
I came the very next day, today,
to find the boxes opened, ransacked.
One lonely cookie was left
uneaten, last in line,
nestled safely in its plastic tray.
I bit into the cookie
savoring the salty sweet
taste of peanut butter and chocolate.
It tasted even sweeter because it was the last cookie
in the last box, for the year.
It tasted even sweeter to me
because, although for everyone else,
it was the last cookie,
I knew of another box.
Tucked away, unopened.
Where is it?

I'll never tell.

The Yellow Room

By Lauren K. Nixon

Kate stared at the small jar of cinnamon powder.

It was sitting in the middle of the worktop, though she knew she'd tidied it up not two minutes earlier, when she had answered the door to the postman; he'd had more packages for Renee, which she'd put in her housemate's study. They were really beginning to pile up, and Kate had no idea how she could afford it all, given that they were secretaries in the same firm and earned the same basic wage.

Between the packages and the weekends away that she regularly took, Kate was beginning to suspect that she had a wealthy lover. It was either that or embezzlement, and clandestine love affairs were more Renee's style.

The cinnamon had been waiting for her when she came back, right in the middle of the empty worktop. She had the oddest feeling when she looked at it, almost as if it was trying to look innocent.

But that was ridiculous.

Jars of cinnamon couldn't think.

She picked it up, half-surprised that it felt completely normal in her hand, and weighed it, speculatively.

Kate was one hundred percent certain she'd put the jar away – she'd even given herself a nasty papercut on the edge of the recipe book it lived under. Jars couldn't move on their own.

Could they?

It wasn't the first time something had turned up just when she wanted it, or vanished completely when her housemate was looking for it. Just last week, Renee had lost her keys for three whole days, eventually finding them in the hedge at the bottom of the front garden.

She'd decided that she'd been drunk and mislaid them that time, but usually she found a way to blame Kate. Kate, on the other hand, couldn't care less about where Renee put her stuff.

Across the small kitchen, a timer started to beep.

Kate shoved the cinnamon in her pocket, turned the timer off and pulled a tray of perfect oatmeal and maple syrup muffins out of the oven. Their sweet, homely aroma filled the room; Kate breathed it in, happily.

She could honestly say that she was never more content than when she was cooking. It made her feel safe, and warm, and on occasions, a little bit adventurous. There was nothing she loved more than perfecting a recipe, and seeing people appreciate her work.

Not everyone she worked with at the law firm did appreciate it, though, and a few people had dismissed it as 'messing around'. Why should she be cooking when she could be working towards the next pay grade? Renee, who liked to think of herself as Kate's long-suffering housemate, was one of them.

She had stopped taking her cooking to the office after a while, dropping it off at the local homeless shelter on the way in, instead. They were always happy to see her there, though she suspected that this wasn't really a gauge of the food's quality.

She looked over her muffins with a professional air.

They smelled almost perfect, but there was still something missing.

The cinnamon in her apron pocket banged against her jeans; she took it out, thoughtfully.

"Why not?" she said aloud, and reached for the icing sugar.

ooo

"Have you seen my phone?" Renee called up the stairs.

Kate emerged from the bathroom and leaned over the banister. It was late, and Renee's phone had been going none-stop since she'd got back.

"I think it's in the living room," she said.

"It's not there now... I could have sworn I had it a second ago."

Renee's immaculate curls appeared at the bottom of the stairs, like a small, black cloud.

"You were cooking again, weren't you," she said, accusingly. "You know you'll never get anywhere with it."

"Think of it as stress relief," said Kate. "Besides, I don't see why anyone should care."

"Your waist-line cares," Renee called up. "Seriously Kate, you need to take more care of yourself, you're beginning to look like a blimp!"

"Goodnight, Renee."

Kate shut her door quite gently, considering, and let out a long breath.

These days, she didn't let people's comments about her weight get to her. She had in school, until she'd realised that they were attacking her because they were afraid of their own appearances.

Besides, she wasn't actually that fat. She'd never paid that much attention to it, except when she bought new clothes, and knew that she was a perfectly healthy size.

"Really," she said, looking at herself in the mirror, comfortably clad in her pyjamas. "If Renee wants to be a size zero that's up to her. There's nothing wrong with being a size fourteen!"

ooo

The article was stuck to the inside of her door.

It took Kate by surprise, partly because she'd heard Renee talking to her friends on the phone all night, so she knew it couldn't have been her, and partly because it seemed to be sticking to the door through sheer force of will. There was no blu-tac and no pin, but there it was, waiting for her.

She pulled at it and it came away from the door with no resistance at all.

It was black and white – she turned it over in her hands. It looked like it had come from one of those women's magazines in the late 1950s. There was an advert on the back for curlers and scotch tape.

She stared at the headline: *'Marilyn Monroe – Fabulous at Size Fourteen'*.

Kate looked around, perplexed.

There was no way anyone could have got in, and there was no way anyone could have overheard…

Unsettled, she tucked the article in her bag and got

ready for work, taking over the bathroom for the obligatory ten minutes before Renee woke up and made camp.

ooo

"It was pinned to your door?"

"Yes..."

Charlie gave her an odd look.

"Are you sure it's not just Renee, playing funny buggers?"

They were sharing lunch, as usual, in the park across from the law firm. A teacher in his 'real' job, the rest of his time Charlie was a perpetually harassed PCSO who seemed to spend his days off ferrying lawyers to the prison and back again. One of the few people who didn't think Kate should stop cooking; he told her at least twice a month that he'd starve if she did.

"Why would she give me an article about how people my size are vivacious and fabulous?" Kate asked, between mouthfuls of soup. "Just last night she said I was the same shape as a blimp."

Charlie frowned, as if he'd like to have a quiet word with her housemate. "When do you finish today?"

"Five thirty, why?"

Charlie gave her back the article, watching her face carefully.

"Because I want to have a rummage in your attic."

ooo

"Find any stalkers?" Kate asked, waiting at the bottom of the ladder with two cups of tea.

"No..." He backed out of the attic, a small, dusty box tucked under his arm. "But I think I know where the article came from."

They took the box and the tea out to the 'studio' that had come with the house, almost at the other end of the back garden. The landlord had been a little weird about showing it to them, and had given them strange, half-formed warnings about not redecorating.

Kate wouldn't have wanted to anyway. It was painted a

cheery, warm yellow and had just enough furniture for it to be comfortable without you feeling overwhelmed. The furniture and blankets had come with the house, too, and Renee had instantly hated them.

Kate loved it.

It had quickly become the place she retreated to when Renee had her parties. She'd fallen asleep on the small sofa more times than she could count in the last six months, and she always dreamed of sunshine. It was like the walls were infused with it.

Charlie pulled up a chair and together they blew the dust from the lid of the box.

"It was right at the back, tucked under the eaves," he told her, pulling out a glossy magazine dating back to 1957. "Look, here it is – see if your page fits."

It did.

Charlie scratched his head.

"I don't get it," he said. "That attic is inch-thick in dust. I'd be prepared to swear that we're the first people to go near this box in years, but –"

"But this tear looks fresh," Kate finished. "That doesn't make any sense."

"At least we know there's no one living in your attic," said Charlie, after a moment.

"I wasn't ever seriously worried about that," Kate laughed, flicking through the magazine.

"I was," said Charlie, quietly. Kate shot him a curious look and he blushed. "What else is in there?" he asked, changing the subject.

They pulled out another magazine, photographs, seed packets, a couple of sea shells and something that looked like a journal, feeling very much like they were uncovering buried treasure.

Charlie looked through the photographs while Kate opened the journal.

The first page was covered in numbers, neatly penned in faded black ink.

"Conversion tables," said Kate out loud. "Hey, this is a recipe book!"

Charlie leaned over her shoulder as she turned the yellowing pages. Some of them, she noted, with growing excitement, had splotches of flour or sauce around the edges. Others had notes made in the margins, where something hadn't entirely worked. On one page, concerning the proper production of pies, someone had written 'NOT MARGE' in capital letters and underlined it several times.

"This is *fantastic*," Kate exclaimed, reading tips on how to make the perfect peppermint fudge. "I can't believe this was just hiding in the attic, waiting to be found."

"Looks like someone else liked cooking as much as you do," said Charlie, and Kate glanced at him. He was much closer than she'd thought he was, leaning in to peer at the recipe book. His breath tickled her ear.

Charlie met her gaze, went quite pink for a man who spent a good deal of his time shepherding drunks on a night out, and withdrew, coughing.

Kate was surprised how much she missed his warmth.

"These – er – I think these were taken in the garden," he said, not meeting her eyes. He shuffled through the photographs before frowning. "This one's in here!"

"Let's see," Kate said. It was her turn to lean in, feeling strangely awkward. She was sure she was blushing, too, though she had no idea why, since she and Charlie had been friends for months. She immediately stopped worrying, however, when she saw the photograph.

It was black and white, like the images in the magazine, and showed a middle-aged woman sitting neatly on a sofa, wearing one of those cotton dresses that had been popular in post-war Britain, when fabric rationing had finally relaxed. Her hair had been tucked back in a bun at some point, but it seemed to have escaped over the day, leaving wisps of it trailing down to her shoulders. She was giving the photographer a smile of faint amusement, as if she knew something that they didn't; she looked like she was just about to speak

"That's the recipe book," said Charlie, pointing at the slim volume the woman had clasped in her lap. "Look."

Kate looked down at the book: sure enough, they were the same.

"I wonder who she was," she said aloud. "She must have lived here."

Charlie turned the photograph over. Someone had written 'Maggie' on the back of it in a spidery hand.

"Maggie," Kate read aloud. "What a nice name."

"Maybe she was the one who painted the studio yellow," Charlie suggested, looking around.

"Can't be, surely," said Kate. "This paint must be pretty fresh, and the landlord told me he'd been renting it out to people for at least ten years."

"Didn't he tell you not to redecorate when you moved in?" Charlie asked, thoughtfully.

"Yes, he did."

"Did he say why, exactly?"

"No." Kate frowned. "It was all a bit vague, I'm afraid."

"Hmmm," said Charlie.

"There you are!"

Both of them jumped as Renee stuck her head around the door.

"Oh, hi Renee," said Kate. Something – she wasn't sure what – made her stick the journal beneath the table.

"Don't 'oh hi' me," Renee snapped. "I want my bloody GHDs back."

"I haven't seen them," said Kate, frowning.

"You little liar!" Renee snorted – Charlie stood up.

"Now, that's enough Renee –"

"Don't start," she snarled at him. "You're only sticking up for her because you fancy her."

Charlie swallowed. This was news to Kate, who had been about to laugh at the suggestion, but he had the sort of 'deer in headlights' look that she associated with the lawyers she worked for when the boss announced an audit of expenses.

"You fancy me?" she asked, astonished.

"Oh, who *cares*?" Renee asked, exasperated. "I need my bloody straighteners – and don't tell me you haven't taken them. There's only me and you in the house!"

Kate shrugged.

"When was the last time you saw me do anything with my hair other than clip it up?" she asked. "I wouldn't know what to do with them."

"You're taking advantage of my kind and caring nature," Renee complained; Charlie shared an eloquent look with

Kate. "You're hiding my stuff to drive me mad, and I've had enough of it. If they don't turn up by tomorrow morning, you're buying me a new pair!"

She stormed off, slamming the door the kitchen behind her.

"Did you take them?" Charlie asked. He sounded awkward. Kate didn't blame him; she felt pretty awkward herself.

"No," she said. "But she's always losing things."

"Oh," said Charlie, and drank his tea in silence.

Kate began reading the recipe book again. She was dying to ask Charlie about what Renee had said, but she didn't know where to start. Charlie broke the silence after several awkward minutes.

"Does she lose things at work?" he asked, suddenly.

Kate peered at him.

"No," she said, slowly. "Just here."

"But you don't?"

"No – if anything, I find things I don't expect."

She told him about the mobile cinnamon incident.

"And someone overheard you, and pinned an article from this box to your bedroom door..."

Together, they turned to look at the picture of Maggie, lying on the top of the box.

"Kate, there's no such thing as ghosts," said Charlie, frowning.

"I didn't say there was."

"No such thing."

ooo

Charlie had gone, much earlier than he usually did. Renee had caught a taxi to her friend's house, probably to complain about Kate a little more, and to borrow her hair straighteners.

Kate had waited until the sound of her heels clicking on the pavement had faded before venturing out of her room. She went into every room except Renee's, looking at each one more closely than she had in months. The house felt strange tonight: expectant. The feeling that she was being watched settled upon her shoulders, making her uncomfortable.

She left the kitchen until last, dropping the recipe book on the counter. She had been thinking about the peppermint fudge all evening, ignoring the unanswered questions about her best friend and the hot, angry feeling Renee's accusations had given her.

She opened the recipe book to the right page and hurried into the pantry to collect the first few ingredients. It was a fairly straightforward recipe, so it didn't need much.

The book was open at a different page, now. Kate turned it back to the fudge, checking what else she needed. She glanced up at the clock for a moment, hoping she would have time to finish before Renee returned.

A papery crackle made her look down in time to see the pages of the recipe book turning back to the other page, which had a recipe for lavender shortbread. Frowning, Kate checked the spine of the journal, but it hadn't cracked in a place that might make it open. She turned back to the fudge, weighing down the page with the tin she kept the icing sugar in.

She heard it roll off the counter while her head was in the fridge. It was lying on the floor, mercifully un-spilled. Kate peered at the recipe book, which had opened at shortbread again.

The feeling of being watched climbed back up her spine.

"Maggie?" she said, aloud.

The kitchen was quiet except for the ticking of the clock on the wall. Kate shivered and went to turn the light on, though she didn't really need it this far into May.

Turning back, she froze.

The tin of icing sugar was back on the worktop, a little way away from the recipe book.

Forcing her breathing back under control, Kate walked over to it and, hesitantly, picked it up. The tin felt cool in her hands; nothing unusual about it. She looked around the kitchen again, trying to stare into the shadowy pantry without making her eyes hurt.

Could a ghost hurt you? she wondered, weighing the icing sugar in her hand. *With enough provocation and a heavy enough implement...*

"But –"

She whipped around. The fridge, which she had left open, creaked gently closed. She fumbled her phone out of her pocket, breathing hard.

"Charlie?" she said when he answered, in a much higher voice than usual. "How sure are you that ghosts aren't real?"

"One hundred percent." He paused. "Why?"

"Er –"

"Kate?"

A soft thud made her look back at the worktop; there was a sort of 'whum-whum-whum' sound, as a bowl gently rocked itself upright.

The ingredients for the fudge had been joined by a bag of flour and a bowl.

"Are you okay?" he sounded worried now.

"Yeah…" she squeaked, after a moment. She ran her finger down the page of the recipe book.

Take 2oz fresh lavender,' she read.

"Do you want me to come back over?"

"Er – no," said Kate, coming to a decision. "I'm just being silly, it's nothing."

"Are you sure?"

"Really, I'll be fine – sorry for bothering you."

"It's never any bother," said Charlie, and then paused, as if he wished he hadn't. "Look, just give me call if you get scared again, okay?"

"Okay."

"Night, Kate."

"Night…"

She put the phone back in her pocket, thoughtfully.

"Okay," she said. "I don't mind trying the shortbread – it looks lovely – but I've been craving peppermint fudge all evening, and I need to get it started now if I'm going to have it all cleared up by the time Renee gets back."

She swallowed, wondering for a moment whether she'd actually gone mad. She took a few quick steps backward as the pages of the recipe book turned back of their own accord – straight to the recipe for peppermint fudge.

"Er – thank you," she said.

ooo

"This is really good," said Charlie, who was on his third piece of shortbread.

"Yes," said Kate. Absently, she picked at her sandwich, watching the children chasing pigeons across the sunny park.

She heard Charlie sigh.

"Alright, what's going on?" he asked. "First you call me, sounding terrified, because you think your recipe book is haunted, and then you come to lunch with boxes full of goodies and don't eat any of them."

"I'm not that hungry," Kate told him, shrugging.

"That's my point," said Charlie. "It's not like you."

Kate pursed her lips.

"In all fairness, I did gorge myself on fudge last night, so it's not entirely surprising."

Charlie laughed a little, but he still looked worried.

"You're thinking about Maggie, aren't you," he guessed.

Kate nodded.

She'd stayed up all night thinking about Maggie, largely because Maggie kept moving things around her bedroom, apparently delighted that Kate was paying attention. She'd wondered how long this had been going on without anyone noticing.

"I wasn't going to tell you this," Charlie began, "but I went to see your estate agent this morning. To ask about previous tenants."

"Maggie?"

"No," he said, and paused. "She told me they'd had trouble keeping tenants. Some of them complained about strange sounds, things moving around the house."

Kate listened raptly. Maggie must have been in the house for years, trying to get someone's attention.

"The one that tried to repaint the studio in blue packed up the very next morning and left without his deposit and half his furniture."

Kate thought back to her landlord's warnings. "It's got to be her," she said.

Charlie squirmed in his seat.

"I thought you might say that," he said. "So I looked up

the records for the house at the station. I found a Margaret Hanbury, found dead in the studio – strangled when a burglary went wrong – in 1958."

"Oh God, that's horrible," said Kate. She packed her sandwich away, all appetite gone. She took in Charlie's expression: it was somewhere between confusion and annoyance. "What?"

"It's just – there's no such thing as ghosts," he told her, clearly frustrated. "There can't be. It goes against all scientific thought."

Kate nodded, thinking about the way Charlie had frozen when Renee had said that he'd fancied her. Somehow, she needed him to believe her.

"Come over after work," she said. "I'll make something from her recipe book."

ooo

"You're not cooking *again*, are you?" Renee demanded as soon as she got home.

Kate, who was beginning to have had enough of her fellow secretary, shrugged, stirring the stew she had on the stove.

"It's a fairly regular occurrence, having to eat," she observed.

"So go out," said Renee. "Come on, pay up. Those GHDs cost me a hundred pounds, hand it over."

"No," said Kate, abandoning the wooden spoon for a moment to add some chopped potato.

"No?" Renee demanded.

"No," Kate repeated. "I didn't take them, I'm not going to pay for them."

"We'll see about this," said Renee, and stormed out of the kitchen.

Kate stirred her stew, thoughtfully.

"You really should give them back," she said, aloud.

The feeling of not being alone had returned almost as soon as she had got back in the house that afternoon, but it didn't feel oppressive today. If anything it felt comfortable, homely – welcoming.

She put the lid on the saucepan and went to let Charlie

in. He followed her back to the kitchen, glancing around the room as if he expected something to jump out at him.

"That smells good," he remarked, after a moment, and went to investigate the pan, distracted.

Kate smiled. She hadn't realised how much she appreciated his taste in food.

"Okay," she said. "Renee is sulking upstairs. What shall we make?"

"I dunno," he said, taking a seat at the kitchen table. "Anything you make is good."

"I wasn't asking you," said Kate, smiling. She nodded at the recipe book, whose pages were flicking back and forth at speed.

Charlie stood up again very quickly, the chair he had been sitting on falling to the floor with a thump.

"Don't go near it!" he gasped, as she leant over to read the recipe. Kate ignored him.

"'Eton Mess'," she read aloud. "Ooh, I think we have strawberries in. How does that sound?" she asked Charlie, who was staring at her as if she'd grown a second head.

"Er –" he said, looking wildly around the room. "Okay?"

A small sound near the fridge caught his attention; Kate followed his gaze to the box of eggs, which had opened of its own accord. Several eggs were rolling in a purposeful sort of fashion towards the electric whisk.

To her astonishment, Charlie put himself between Kate and the fridge. She could feel how afraid he was.

"I don't think she's going to hurt us," she said, gently. "Charlie?"

"But –"

"She suggested the shortbread, too, and you loved that," Kate told him, and he stared at her. "Besides, she obviously doesn't mind you, or you'd have lost things when you were here, right?"

"I – er –" he paused, staring at her expression. "I think I need a cup of tea," he said, weakly.

Behind her, Kate heard the kettle click on.

"This is *not* normal," Charlie complained, sinking into the chair.

He didn't seem to notice it had righted itself again.

ooo

"I have to admit," he said, licking his plate clean. "Eton Mess was the way to go."

Kate, who had been watching him over the top of her mug, wondering how she'd missed how his smile made her feel, chuckled.

"Er –" said Charlie, glancing at the recipe book. "Thanks, Maggie."

Kate grinned.

"I'm not saying I believe any of this," he assured her, hurriedly.

They both looked up as the doorbell rang.

"Probably one of Renee's friends," said Kate, with a sigh. "We could take the leftovers to the studio, if you want?"

Charlie looked at her for a moment before agreeing, with a slight smile.

They had almost made it to the kitchen door when Renee burst into the room, looking incredibly smug.

"That's her, officer," she said, with an air of triumph. "She's been stealing my things since we moved in, and now she's had my GHDs. Arrest her!"

Kate stared at her housemate, and then at the police constables standing behind her. They seemed to fill the door.

"That's quite a serious allegation," said the larger of the two. "What do you have to say for yourself, Miss?"

"I've never taken anything from her," exclaimed Kate, astonished. She still had a bowl in her hands, which she put on the countertop with dull thud. "This is ridiculous!"

The second constable, who had been looking past her, gave her a bright smile.

"Then you won't mind us searching your room," he suggested.

Kate frowned, feeling rather cross.

"Of course I mind," she snapped. "But feel free!"

"It's this way!" Renee cried, gleefully. She and the larger officer disappeared into the hall and up the stairs.

Kate could hear them moving around upstairs.

"You know," she said, to no one in particular. "I'm really beginning to *hate* her."

She glared at the constable, who to her surprise, laughed.

"Alright, Charlie?" he said.

"I've been better," said Charlie. "This is bollocks, Dan."

"Yeah?"

Kate felt Charlie's hand on her shoulder and glanced up at him, surprised.

"Completely."

The constable nodded.

"I thought it might be, she was far too excited to see us."

"She's like that most of the time, actually," said Kate, slowly. "I'm sorry," she shook her head, remembering her manners. "Can I offer you a cup of tea, or something?"

"That'd be cracking," said Dan. "One sugar for me, none for Geoff. Him-indoors told him he had to cut down."

She listened to Dan and Charlie making terse conversation while she made the tea, the sounds of Geoff and Renee going through her room filtering through the ceiling. It made her feel very vulnerable indeed to think someone was searching through her things.

Charlie must have understood, because he put his arm around her shoulders when Dan went upstairs to help.

"Don't worry," he assured her. "They're good lads – they won't let her get away with this. What?"

"I don't want to have to move," she said, annoyed. "I really like it here."

Somewhere upstairs, someone raised their voice.

"But *I* didn't put them there!"

"I think Maggie may have the problem in hand," said Charlie, faintly.

Geoff came downstairs a few minutes later and gratefully accepted his cup of tea.

"They were in the back of her wardrobe," he told them. "She's got a gob on her, hasn't she?"

Kate nodded, mutely. Renee, by now, slightly hysterical, was still clearly audible through the ceiling.

"I don't want to press charges," she said, after a moment. "She must have just lost them."

Geoff laughed.

"I can see why Charlie likes you," he said, and Charlie's arm – still around her shoulders up to that point –

vanished at speed. "You won't have to. She spent the entire time we were upstairs bad-mouthing you. Even if she did just lose them, calling us out and inflicting us on you is a waste of police time."

"You can't arrest her," said Kate, aghast. "She's a legal secretary – she'll lose her job! I'm sure it was an honest mistake."

Geoff looked like he seriously doubted it, but before he could comment, Dan led a very unhappy Renee back into the kitchen. She was, Kate was astonished to discover, handcuffed.

"There was about ten kilograms of cocaine in her suitcase," he told them, over her protests.

Kate felt her mouth fall open.

"Along with bank statements, receipts and a ledger detailing transactions for the year. There's even a list of wealthy clients. She must have been dealing for a while, out of the major hotels in the region. I wouldn't have looked, only it fell open when I walked past it."

Kate stared at her housemate, who looked angry enough to explode.

"This is your fault!" she shouted. "You sneaky little bitch! You knew they'd find it!"

Maggie...

The constables seemed to be taking the dumbfounded expression on her face into account as they ignored this.

"We'll need you to come to the station with us, Miss, while SOCCO go over the house. Sorry," said Geoff, as Renee was bundled out of the door. "But we need a statement, and until we know you're in the clear you can't be here. You too, Charlie."

"No, I understand," said Kate, whose brain was still having to work quite hard to catch up. "Er – I just need to put the leftovers in the fridge if that's okay? And lock up the studio."

"Studio?"

"In the back garden."

"Fine," said Geoff, affably. "As long as you don't mind me watching."

"Of course not."

"Looks like you might be needing a new housemate,

Miss," he said, while he drank his tea. "Didn't you say you were looking for somewhere, Charlie?"

"I thought you said there were no such things as ghosts," she hissed, as Geoff stuck his head in the hall.

Charlie, still rather red from Geoff's suggestion, shrugged. "Maybe there are such things as Maggies."

The
Butterfly
&
The Lion

Lion and Butterfly vs. Metaphysical Sandwich

By J. McGraw

Metaphysics
Tells me
Butterflies
Exist only when
Observed, and are made of abstract ideas.
Lions, too, are abstract, but I think that
Abstract ideas
Can't eat you.
Screw you,
Metaphysics

Pennies for The Dead

Pennies for the Dead

By G. Burton

It was a job no-one else wanted to do. So, naturally, I ended up doing it.

'Pennies for the dead!'

There were rumours that this was a cursed position. That you spent so much time in their presence that you became one of them.

'Pennies for the dead!'

Ridiculous, I said. You can't become one of them. You either are, or you are not.

'Pennies for the dead!'

It was always cold, the stifling, stale air pressing in on you. Dank and dim; health and safety be damned.

'Pennies for the dead!'

The coin box rattled as I clambered through; there were always people willing to offer their pennies.

'Pennies for the dead!'

Some liked to keep them, hopeful that it didn't mean that they were dead.

'Pennies for the dead!'

At the end of the day, nothing mattered.

'Pennies for the dead!'

They would pay their way eventually.

'Pennies for the dead!'

Pennies for the Dead

By Philip Lickley

"Should I get the blue one or the red one?" Tanya asked, lifting two crop-tops up to her body in turn as she mentioned the colours.

Her boyfriend, Sam, studied the fabrics for a moment against his girlfriend's chest as she pretended to wear them, considering his answer. A couple of beads of sweat gathered on his brow as he realised he was being questioned into a corner, the correct answer having already been determined by his auburn-haired girlfriend. Sam paused for a moment, biting his lip out of habit, and croaked an answer.

"The red one?" he said, the rising inflection in his voice making it sound more like an unsure question rather than a statement of intent. Tanya's face was frozen in the few awkward seconds that followed his three words, before some signs of positive emotion appeared across her face. She nodded in agreement, discarding the blue top back onto the rail it had come from and dropping the red one into the basket.

"I agree," she said.

Sam sighed, but realised that exhalation could sound too obviously like relief, so turned it into a cough at the end, as if he was trying to clear his throat. Having gotten away with it, Sam trailed behind Tanya as they left the clothes aisle and wandered in the vague direction of the supermarket checkouts.

"Is that everything?" Sam asked, once more masking his true thoughts and hopes in an unsure question. He truly hoped that *was* everything as they'd been trawling around Tesco for the best part of an hour and he was hoping to get home for an evening of mindless television and a cold beer from the fridge. Tanya didn't respond but gave a nod as they emerged from the jungle-like clothes department where the shirts were leaves and the rails the jutting out branches, and into the open savannah of the checkout spaces, where a flurry of men, women and children waited to be served. Tanya and Sam joined a nearby queue and waited whilst an old lady with a blue rinse and a kindly face was served by the slowest member of staff in the place.

Sam watched with annoyance as each other queue seemed to quickly diminish around them, but in reality it wasn't long until they were seen, served and dismissed with a swipe of their loyalty card and a handful of change. Emerging out onto the other side of the checkout and now free to make their escape, Tanya and Sam made a beeline towards the exit, Sam a few steps ahead of his girlfriend as he longed to escape the sound of loudspeaker announcements, screeching children wanting presents and couples rowing over items squirreled away secretly into trolleys.

It wasn't long until they had turned the corner from the main shop into the open foyer and that was when they both spotted her: a scruffy looking figure staring out blankly in their direction. Standing about twenty metres ahead, she looked to be a woman in her late thirties but it was difficult to tell from such distance. Her hair was blonde and streaky, but more significantly messy, as if she'd been called away halfway through getting it styled and decided that a windswept look would be all the rage in 2015.

Sam wasn't entirely sure but he thought he could just make out some loose twigs in her hair, as if she'd quite literally been dragged through a hedge backwards, a clichéd analogy that seemed to hold up if the rips in her baggy top and large scratches down her arms were anything to go by, aspects of her look which became much clearer as the woman spotted the pair and began a frantic, hobbling beeline in their direction like a video game zombie triggered to attack on sight. Tanya looked once at Sam, and Sam at Tanya, and they both silently considered their next move as they stood frozen in the foyer area between bags of charcoal and a special offer on outdoor furniture.

To their left was a large glass window that separated them from the car park. If this moment had been slap bang within an action film Tanya would have taken a run to her left and smashed straight through the glass plate, crashing to the tarmac flooring in a shower of shattered glass before running off across the car park to freedom, closely followed by her partner. But Tesco on a Saturday afternoon somewhere outside of Manchester wasn't the place for such cinematic and grand gestures – never mind the fact this this was reality and not the Expendables. They only had one place to go in the lieu of a dramatic escape plan involving duct piping or digging tunnels straight out of a World War Two movie, and that was to face the person head on; a person that was now almost within touching distance.

They could now make out her pained expression, birds-nest hair-cut, raw red arms and damaged clothing much more clearly. Now she was just in front of them, her lips poised to speak, which she did.

"Pennies for the dead," she spluttered, the words tripping off her tongue in a flurry of spittle, her pupils darting between looking at Sam, then Tanya, then back to Sam again. Tanya didn't really catch what she had said through the gruffness of her speech and asked her to repeat herself with a formal, "*Sorry?*"

"Pennies for the dead!" the woman repeated, this time clearer, but with more drama. Both Tanya and Sam, in response, touched their pockets as if they were mimicking an Asda advert in a competitor's foyer, miming the universal gesture for *I've got change in my pocket but I'm not giving it to you, but I'm going to look like I'm checking*. Tanya shook her head, painting a fake show of regret onto her youthful face.

"I'm sorry," she lied, "I don't have any change."

Pennies for the dead Tanya thought. *It's a distasteful name for a charity isn't it? And where is her collection bucket?*

Now Tanya didn't mind giving to charity – she regularly supported many through a series of direct debits – but she found chuggers particularly irritating and would do many things to avoid them, from swift changes of directions on the high street to answering an imaginary phone call.

The unkempt woman now just looked confused as well as crazy, if such distinct emotions could be expressed on her wild looking face. She now attempted to clarify her outburst.

"No," she said, attempting to clarify what she had meant. "Pennies for the dead. For you."

The woman thrust out her hand and revealed two tarnished pennies concealed in the palm of her hand, a hand that had a cut running across it and two red marks onto which the coins were sat, as if they had burnt into her flesh. Tanya looked down at the coins and then into the eyes of the woman, unsure as of what to do next. The woman waited for a moment, not blinking, and thrust her hand further towards Tanya.

"For you," she repeated, jutting her hand out and nodding, encouraging her to take the coins quickly, like a child offering their last two jelly beans to their disinterested parents. Tanya once more looked from her hand to her eyes and then to Sam for help, who just shrugged in response. He was just as unsure as to what this was about as she was. Tanya looked back at the coins and lifted them from the woman's hand, unsure about what to do with them now. Instead of deciding she just stood there awkwardly holding them out whilst the woman sealed her own palm and smiled.

"They're your problem now!" she cackled with more freely flying spittle.

Before Tanya could even react to that statement the woman had turned on her heel and had practically skipped down the foyer away from the pair like a lottery winner would do in a cheesy television drama. Sam half expected her to jump and click her heels together in happiness. Soon she was out of the building and out of sight around the corner. Tanya looked down at the old coins in her hand and then back at Sam, shrugging her shoulders and dropping the coins into the back pocket of her jeans.

"Every little helps, perhaps," she quipped, Sam laughing and wrapping his arm around his girlfriend's waist before they walked off together to their car, depositing the bags of shopping into the boot and preparing to drive off.

Tanya sat in the driving seat, put her keys into the ignition and turned it, slipping the seat belt over her body and preparing to drive, adjusting the rear-view mirror. And that was when she swore she saw it. A figure at the back of the car park staring at them from just beyond the hedgerow, its face masked in shadow. But when she looked back in the mirror, in almost comical double-take fashion, it was gone. She shrugged it off, as if that was the gesture of the moment, and indicated to pull out of the parking space and set off back towards home.

*

Tanya and Sam rented a modest little house on a small street on the edge of town. Nestled between two equally pokey little terraced houses, number five was very much home for them both; they'd picked up the keys from the landlord just six months into their relationship and had just celebrated the third anniversary within its Lancastrian stone walls.

Sam had arrived at the front door first and had let them both in, the bags of shopping placed unceremoniously on the floor as he filled up and switched on the kettle, the rising inflection of its heating mechanism becoming the soundtrack for the next three minutes as coats were removed and shoes placed back on the rack. Tanya made the first attempts at unpacking the shopping, placing an assortment of objects on the side including a bag of loose-leaf tea, some chocolate digestives and a box of cereal that had far too much sugar in it for her tastes, but would keep her boyfriend satisfied for the next week of breakfasts. As she found herself unwrapping the red top from earlier and placing it once more against her skin, Sam returned to the kitchen from a brief toilet break to pour the boiling water from the kettle into two lime green mugs, into which he'd already placed a tea bag each. As he waited for the mixture to work its magic, he leaned against the kitchen wall and smiled at Tanya.

"You'll look great in that top," he commented. She beamed a smile at him as she packed away the last of the shopping, giving him a playful peck on the cheek. "You'd look even better out of it," he added cheekily, and Sam playful tapped him on his leg.

They both continued to unpack the shopping, dancing around each other within the kitchen, the final item unpacked being a tub of butter, which was placed carefully on the top shelf of the fridge. Sam looked at his watch – it was just before seven now – and he began the process of squeezing and removing the tea bags and adding milk to the brews.

"Do you fancy a film?" he asked, passing Tanya her mug, which she grasped with both hands. She nodded and smiled.

"Only if I can pick!"

Sam nodded, though he feared it would be another romantic film, a fear that was confirmed when she skipped through to the living room and removed a DVD from the shelves in the corner, Sam getting a glance at its front cover which clearly showed a young woman staring wistfully into the auburn eyes of a handsome man of a similar age. He sighed to himself but dismissed any disappointment in the cinematic choice as he would be spending some time with the woman he loved, and he joined her on the sofa once she'd deposited the disc in the blu-ray player and settled down. As Sam slurped his tea without any sense of quietness, Tanya laid down and nestled her head on his chest as the familiar sounds of the film began.

After about thirty minutes of the movie – the lead actor and actress had now met up with each other and were clearly disliking each other's company, a sure sign they'd be getting it together by the end – the disc was paused as Sam went to re-charge their glasses. Not with tea this time, but something a little stronger which he'd removed from the fridge and uncorked. As he poured, the satisfying sound of glugging liquid filling up two glasses, Tanya got up and wandered over to the window, staring out to the twilight-coloured street beyond the nets and window as she moved over to draw the curtains. It was as she was contemplating the view as well as wondering whether she should phone the window cleaner that her mind slipped back to their encounter at the supermarket earlier and she recalled the two coins she had been given. Tanya remembered what she'd done with them and plunged her right hand into the back pocket of her jeans and pulled them out, studying them in her hand. They were clearly old and tarnished, but otherwise looked like any other coins she had ever handled. But still, there was something strange about them.

Tanya placed one of them down on the windowsill next to a plotted plant while she lifted the other closer to her face so she could study it more; that's when a strange feeling washed over her and she found herself transported out of the room, her body violently lurching through a daydream that felt more like an out of control rollercoaster. It was a weird feeling; almost like being dropped onto a movie set. She was stood in a field, on a bright summer's day, though the colours were muted and almost sepia in their tones, as if she'd somehow stepped into an old photograph more than a film. Tanya could just about make out two figures over the brow of the hill locked in an embrace and she had to fight the urge to look away, as if staring at their intimacy was somehow inappropriate.

For a few moments she watched as they began to peel each other's clothes off in the heat of the moment and she smiled at the thought of such passion at the start of a relationship, reminding her of the early days of her time with Sam and a particularly quiet car park, but soon joy and happy memories turned to horror as she saw the young man stop moving mid-hug and began clutching his chest, collapsing backwards and writhing in agony and spasms, as his partner tried to help but her actions were rebuffed as his limbs flailed. Tanya found herself moving forward as if to reach them to help, but she found herself only able to walk in an awkward slow motion and she felt like she could see them both clearer but was getting no nearer to them physically.

After a few moments he ceased moving and any attempt at resuscitation by the young woman was unsuccessful. It was instinct that had made Tanya move closer to the scene, but she quickly realised she was an unseen bystander to the unfolding drama and not someone who could help. All she could do was see the still paleness on the man's face and the contorted agony of the girl from closer than she felt comfortable with, tears streaming down her face, before the vision began to fade, but not before she'd spied something from her fresh vantage point: both the girl and her boyfriend shared matching jewellery, as revealed by the bright sunshine reflecting off the pieces as they moved. In attempting to help the young woman had ripped open her boyfriend's chequered shirt to reveal his chest, and a small chain around his neck onto which was affixed a small shiny penny. She too wore a similar coin, but on her on a longer necklace, the coin resting on the top of her breasts.

By this point the vision had faded and Tanya found herself back in the living room, her forehead sweaty and her right palm burning. As her consciousness snapped back into the room she became acutely aware of the heat from the coin and she dropped it in discomfort onto the windowsill so it joined the other one. As Sam returned to the living room with the two glasses of wine she nursed the small circular burn in the middle of her hand, confusion rising up through her chest like heartburn. Tanya turned to Sam, looking afraid, before receiving the glass of wine. Sam looked concerned, his expression of contentment switching almost instantly to one of contemplation.

"Are you okay, T?" he asked, studying her frown and pale skin. Tanya coughed and took a quick swig of wine.

"I think so," she said, unsure of herself. "I just feel a bit weird all of a sudden. I think I must have fallen asleep or something. I just had a really weird dream."

"What about?" Sam asked, still studying the contours of Tanya's face as if trying to work out if she was hiding something.

"I'm not entirely sure," she said quietly. There were then a few moments of quiet as the sentence wasn't followed up by any further words of actions until Sam broke the silence by suggesting they continue the film.

Tanya nodded, swallowed another mouthful of white wine and returned to the sofa, snuggling closer to her boyfriend than she had earlier, as the film resumed. Fifteen minutes later, now wrapped up in the events of the movie, she had all but forgotten about the strange vision, relaxing as Sam ran his fingers through her hair in a pleasingly seductive manner. The mood was only broken a few minutes later by a heavy knock on the front door, which distracted them just as Tanya had rolled over to kiss her boyfriend more passionately, her hand rested somewhere on his upper thigh. Sam rolled his eyes, reached over for the remote and paused the film before getting to his feet, Tanya pivoting herself around on the sofa and taking the opportunity to gulp down a few more mouthfuls of wine.

"No rest for the wicked," Sam muttered under his breath as he passed from the living room and into the hallway and to the front door. From the living room Tanya could hear him turn the key in the lock, remove the safety chain and then pull open the door, and then there was nothing but silence for a minute or so.

After what seemed like a very long sixty seconds, Tanya called out his name but there was no reply. There was then no reply for the second or third calling of it and by this point she was worried. Placing the glass down on the table Tanya got to her feet and walked with purpose towards the front door, spotting it still ajar and Sam's shoes missing from the rack. Tanya called his name once more in the direction of the open door, the darkness of the evening visible through the gap, but there was still no response.

Half-confused, half-startled, with a mixture of concern bubbling under in the pit of her stomach Tanya opened the front door until it was at ninety degrees to the frame and peered out into the blackness, her eyes slowly adjusting to the light levels as the objects in the garden like the trees and the fence appeared first as black outlines then as physical objects. But there was still no sign of Sam.

Flicking on the outside light she stared across the lawn, now illuminated in an eerie orange glow. Tanya could just make out the shape of footprints across the lawn, the blades of grass trampled by Sam as he'd moved across the grass. But there was something wrong about these impressions; they looked to be the wrong way around as if he'd walked out of the house backwards.

Perhaps, she considered, *they're of him coming back.* But if they were, why was he not inside?

Tanya took one step outside and suddenly felt a bump to her side as a figure collided with her body, running across the front of the house. The figure fell to the ground as Tanya jumped back startled. It was Sam, but he didn't look like the man she knew. His face was pale and clammy and he had a large red mark along his right cheek as if someone had taken a sharp object and scraped it down his skin. He got to his feet and walked a few paces towards her, seemingly hobbling as if he'd damaged his left leg. Sam looked panicked and confused and was muttering something, looking around as if expecting something to appear any moment. If ever there was a moment to use the phrase *rabbit in the headlights*, Tanya thought, this was it.

"Run," he croaked, his voice husky and distant. "Lock the door. There's something out here..."

"Sam, get over here," Tanya mumbled, not sure whether to take him seriously or not as if this was some sort of practical joke.

"No," he muttered, "It's too late for me. I can distract it..."

As those words left his mouth he lunged forward, his chin colliding with the hard concrete floor below him, a sickening crack echoing through the cold night air as the bone shattered. Tanya screamed, called his name and then saw something else, a pale bony hand clutched around Sam's ankle, which had forced him to the floor. Horrified, her eyes moved along it to see a skeletal figure grinning manically, scuttling along the path on all fours. She couldn't understand how she had grasped its emotion as all she could see was the bare bone of a skull reflecting in the light of the porch lamp, with no skin or features to truly make such an expression.

As the creature yanked Sam further towards itself, Tanya stepped back and slammed the front door closed, turning the key and replacing the security chain. With her back to the door she slid down its wooden backing and landed with a gentle thump on the floor, lifting up her knees and bowing her head, sobbing into her lap. Why had she left Sam out there? She could have done something. Why had Sam given up like that? Tanya began to sob even harder, her head spinning in confusion with the sudden developments of the last two hours. Her remorse was only broken by three heavy bangs behind her as something was trying to get her to let it in. She refused, sucking up her tears and trying to remain silent, but it was too late and it knew where she was. Three further bangs, this time much more forceful, shook the door frame and she could hear the door cracking under the pressure.

Tanya stirred herself to her feet and returned to the living room, staring out of the window through the net curtains, the main curtains still left undrawn. With her nose almost to the pane of glass she failed to spot the figure at the front door, which now turned slightly. Blinking for a moment, Tanya suddenly found it now almost directly in front of her, its hollow, blackened eyes looking directly into hers, and she stumbled back in fear, backing up and hitting the sofa. She watched as the skeletal figure swung its arms and it appeared to make contact with the porch light; the bulb shattered and plunged the outside into darkness. Tanya, quickly regaining her composure in the situation and manifesting a little energy, pulled the curtains closed, as if not being able to see the creature meant it wasn't truly there.

It was then that she remembered the coins and she scooped them up from the windowsill, her hand groping underneath the fabric, her mind afraid to once more open the curtains and see what was outside.

It must have something to do with those, she figured, looking down at the pennies. As the pair of coins sat in her palm she slipped once more into the dreamlike state. This time with not quite the same bump – any reluctance she had to lose contact with reality and protect herself from the monster failed in the presence of the all-encompassing vision, which took her mind over like sea-sickness. Her heart filled with pretty much the same feeling of unease and dread.

Tanya was now the witness to an emotional goodbye in a back room of what she figured was a mortuary, the cold soulless, clinical steel furniture at odds with the heartfelt farewell happening in the room before her. The young girl from the earlier vision stood over the cold body of her boyfriend, her eyes welling with tears, her throat dry and bitter. In her hand she held her necklace, a small coin dangling from the end, and she studied the matching one around her boyfriend's neck, which she gently lifted from his person, both coins together at last.

At least they can be reunited.

The girl studied them for a moment before slipping them into her pocket and leaving the room, nodding to a middle-aged man in a pale coat, who was stood in the corner, almost camouflaged against the walls and unnoticed due to his silence. He followed the young girl out of the room and flipped the light switch, the room now plunged into darkness leaving Tanya in the dark, in the cold, and alone.

She decided to clamber out the room, guiding herself along the wall by only her sense of touch. Eventually she felt the door and turned the handle, but as she did a series of flashes and images startled her with their vividness and speed, as if opening the door had simultaneously opened Pandora's Box.

The visions came thick and fast:

One was of the young girl and a car, the screeching of tires making Tanya's heart race. There was the sound of sirens, a beeping machine, and then the steady flat lining of the same sound as the occupant of the car died from her injuries after she'd manipulated the car to avoid a skeletal figure that had suddenly risen from the back seat of her car, its bony hand grasping onto her shoulder, the tips of its fingers burying into her flesh.

Next there was a vision of a jeweller's shop and a young loved-up couple buying some second hand jewellery of a style Tanya recognised from those of the previous pair, juxtaposed with flashes of the same two figures cowering in a cellar, him with a large blunt object readied in his hands, his legs splayed, as some dark figure approached them from the gloom. This vision ended in darkness aside from the sounds of screams and of the blunt object being waved in defence but offering little in the way of protection.

Then there was a vision of a computer with a teenager sat lazily in front of it, buying something from an auction site, with a heavy package soon landing through his post-box. It was as if time was being condensed, further days disappearing in an instant before a knock at the door delivered a terrifying vision of death, pain and darkness.

These quick series of images continued until the final one burst into Tanya's consciousness and left her reeling on the floor, her heart racing and her skin sweating. She had seen the woman they'd met in the supermarket, but she was practically unrecognisable.

She was firstly sat at home with a cup of tea and a magazine, laughing and smiling, her hair neater and no bruises or cuts present, before the scene switched to her being presented with a lucky coin by her partner as a birthday gift. This in turn shifted painfully to a darker, more foreboding scene of the woman being chased across a field by a dark, lumbering figure, before she found herself seeking sanctuary in a dark alley way. A sharp voice echoed out around as if bursting from radio interference. It was distinctly female, but with a deeper, depressed tone to it.

My love was taken from me it called. *Why should others not have to suffer what I have suffered?*

Eventually this woman would find herself back in town, finding salvation in the foyer of a supermarket, escaping the curse by passing on the coins, the cursed coins that had made their way from the doomed couple, through the hands of the soon-to-be-dead, and now to her. Tanya now knew what she had to do – rid herself of the coins – but she feared it was already too late. Upon coming around from the vision she found herself now collapsed on the floor, a position which gave her a unique vantage point of the front door, which she saw had been broken open. A bony foot was at her eye level, suggesting the figure was literally standing over her. As she tried to lift herself up from her prostrated position the creature reached out bony fingers, ready to take her.

Shuffling backwards to try and get a better view of the figure and to escape its clutches, Tanya found herself now with her back against the skirting board, but these few moments allowed her to get some purchase on the wall and an understanding of her situation, lifting herself to her feet and trying to make some form of logical decision against her racing heartbeat. She was now stood face to face with the figure, her eye level matching its.

It was like something out of a horror movie. There stood a skeletal figure, its bones hanging from small remnants of cartilage, bones missing from all over its body where parts of it had rotted away, peeling and hanging lank, as if it were a snake shedding unneeded skin. At its uppermost part it stared at Tanya through the two empty sockets in its skull, as if the power of reanimation after death had given it the ability to see without needing something biological to see *with*. A bony hand with just two fingers left was outstretched, trying to grasp hold of Tanya, who was backed against the wall. Coming to her senses, all it took was a swift kick to its chest to make two ribs fall out.

The arm collapsed in on itself; the whole length of arm from finger to shoulder blade clattering to the floor in a shower of bone dust. Tanya seized this moment and shuffled around the figure, striding across the living room floor and out of the hole in the broken front door, into the darkness of the garden.

She had just a few moments to stare down at Sam, his body lying motionless and broken on the path. Tears began streaming down her face, but she knew she had to make her escape, and she began the difficult journey of navigating the garden in the pitch black, cursing as she collided with several pots as she progressed, scraping her side on the brick wall that ran around the perimeter of the property. Groping and flailing in the dark, with only a smidgen of moonlight to guide her now the clouds had separated slightly, Tanya finally reached the end gate. Out of breath, from her quick escape and her racing heartbeat, she rested on the end of the wall, gathering what little air she could get into her lungs. From her pocket she took the two coins again and studied them. They looked just like ordinary, but old, coins. No one would think from looking at them that they were anything other than normal units of money, and no one would bat an eyelid if they were given them in their change. From here she could properly end the curse though, and not be palming them off to an unsuspecting person who would then become the creature's next victim. Tanya hoped this would work and that the creature would stop pursuing her. She just hoped that it wasn't the case that she would have to literally pass on the problem.

Tanya studied the first coin momentarily in her hand, then with a flick of her wrist unceremoniously skimmed it downwards to the nearby drain, watching it clatter and spin on the metallic grill before seeing it fall through a gap and disappear down into the drains, a faint splosh just about audible as it began its journey through the unseen underground waterways that powered the city. Tanya figured that it was either that or discarding it in the waste as the best way of making sure the coin would never get into the hands of anyone again, and with no rubbish bins to hand the drain was the next best thing. Already the coin would be somewhere a fair distance away and hopefully would get stuck underground somewhere to remain undiscovered by human hands again.

Now it was time for the second coin, and then she would be free. She wasn't entirely sure why she'd not thrown them both at the same time; maybe this was her last connection left with Sam and she wanted to savour that moment? But it was now the time: Tanya held the second coin in between her fingers, looking at it shining in what little light there was. But in pausing for these few moments to take stock of the last hour, she had given the skeleton time to reach her – a creature which didn't have the capacity or the fear to worry about injury in the darkened garden and so was not slowed down by fear of injury.

It was now, unknown to Tanya, bearing in on her on the opposite side of the hedge and as she passed by the tall bush that ran from where the wall ended she was grabbed by its one remaining arm, its muscle-less pull still incredibly strong, yanking her off her feet and into the hedge where she gave one final scream before her voice got muffled by the overgrown shrubbery.

The coin slipped from her hand and rattled on the floor. In one swift movement Tanya was gone, the creature clawing at her face and anywhere her flesh was exposed, ripping her clothes and slicing across her neck. The last thing Tanya saw before the creature overpowered her was the coin almost completing its journey to the drain – but not quite. Her failure the last thing she would ever experience. At least there was little time for her to curse the bad luck of gravity.

Now everything was quiet and for a couple of hours the coin just sat there on the edge of the pavement, concealed to the few people who walked along the path in those one-hundred-and-twenty minutes. It was almost as if Tanya's plan had worked.

But sometimes things don't always go the right way.

*

It was just after eleven when two figures made their less than quiet way down the street, one drinking from a can of lager, the other with his hands thrust into his trouser pockets, both dressed smartly. They were both chatting away loudly on a range of subjects from how much they were going to drink that night; to the women they were hoping to meet; to how smart their clothes were. As the lager was finished and the can thrown into a nearby hedge, scaring a cat that had been sleeping there – it hissed in retribution – the pair continued to make their way noisily along, waking up at least a couple of the local residents. They appeared to slow down as they approached the scene from earlier, but more to do with the fact they were engaged in conversation rather than any knowing change of pace.

"Once I get to the bombs tonight Rob, I am going to be well and truly fucked."

"I think you are already Josh," his friend commented with a smirk, noticing his wobbly walking. The pair were heading out to a friend's party at a nearby pub and many shots had been promised. Rob was also hoping to meet up with Jennie, a young girl with a bright face and compelling personality, whom he had a crush on; he was hoping to make his move that very evening.

But this was for later on that night. By this point Josh, in his merry state, had spotted something on the pavement and had already bent down to pick it up. It was a small, scuffed penny that had shone mysteriously in the street lamp and had somehow attracted him, as if he'd developed magpie tendencies. Rob looked at him with a raised eyebrow.

"What are you doing? It's filthy. It's hardly going to help with another bomb."

Josh inspected the coin in his fingers. "It's that old

saying Robbie. Find a penny, pick it up, and all the day you'll have good luck!"

Josh flicked it over to Rob who caught in his palm, a slight burning sensation as it made contact with his skin confusing him. He looked at it: it was just an ordinary coin.

"You'll need the luck more than I will, Rob, if you're wanting to get anywhere with Jennie..."

Josh laughed as Rob pocketed the coin and continued to walk onwards towards their drinking destination.

"All the day you'll have good luck?" repeated Josh.

"Who gave you that phrase?" Josh asked, walking after him. "Your gran?"

"I think so," laughed Rob, entirely unaware that, as they both turned the corner onto the next street, already a figure was stepping out of the shadows and heading towards them, a glint of menace in its empty sockets...

Pennies for the Dead

By J. McGraw

Darkness filled the cave, complete and unbroken. Anyone standing there would have felt the pressure in their ears of solid rock around them, but there was no one. Or rather, there was no one who could feel.

Shouts sounded in the distance, growing closer. Several voices, all questioning. More, growing louder behind the leaders. But when light entered the cave, it didn't belong to the shouting crowd outside.

A glow flared up against part of the cave wall, flicking in the way only fire can. It grew more intense, and then the torch slipped into the room ahead of a nervous, shaking young man. He held the flame at arm's length, and above his head, and moved as though against his will.

In the dancing light, the cave glowed. It wasn't a large space – the light bounced from wall to wall, highlighting the crystals in the stone, making everything sparkle. The light bounced, too, from a line of coins on the floor, stretching from one wall to the other. Gold and silver sparkled as gaily as the crystals in the walls, and the movement of the light almost made them come alive, a line of smartly dressed soldiers standing guard. In the centre of the cave lay the body of a man, and around him the coins lay scattered.

"He's still here!" the young man called as quietly as possible. As two more men entered the cave, the first shrank back against the wall, staring at the back of the cave with wide eyes.

The eldest of the three took the scene in quietly, taking care over his examination of the body and the coins around it. The silence was almost torturous, but the man broke it after long moments.

"Go outside and talk to the people. See if they have any gold, any silver."

"Precious metal in the village...?" The third member of the group, quiet until now, sounded doubtful.

"Some have heirlooms, jewellery and the like. Some may

be silver. If we have to melt it down, so be it."

"There's no time!" the young man whispered. "It's almost dark, and the line's broken..."

"Go!" the elder snapped. Like the young man, he kept his voice low, but it acted like a whip. The young man started, then lent the torch against the rock and hurried away.

"He's right. There is no time," the second man said.

"There is little time. It is not the same." The elder turned and put a hand on the other's shoulder. "You know the words? You know how to reassemble the line?"

"As well as you do." The man looked worried.

"But I cannot do it. It is almost night and the line must not remain unbroken. Help me move the body."

Between them, they managed to lift the body high enough to move it away from the line without disturbing more coins. With the line cleared, the hole in the line looked like a wound.

"What killed him?" the man asked.

"Crossing the line. There is too much building up behind it every day, every night... just a toe on the wrong side will cause it to burst out. He must be watched tonight. A group of men, all with blades, all alert."

"You think he's still a danger?"

"I think it is impossible to know what flowed through him when he broke the line. He may wake again, he may not. We must be sure."

With slow, creaking movements, the elder lowered himself to the floor directly in front of the break in the line. He was a frail man, and the corpse belonged to a healthy farm hand, but by crossing his legs, kneecap to kneecap, he just filled the gap.

"You can't sit there!" the younger man exclaimed, finally realising what his elder was doing. "We'll find the silver, we'll fill the gap. You don't have to..."

"Can you not feel it?" the elder interrupted quietly. "The darkness is falling outside, even as you protest. The spirits can feel it. They're becoming restless. They know there's a hole, a weakness, and they're desperate to break through. I can hold them at bay tonight. You have until sunset tomorrow to beg, borrow, or steal whatever you need to repair the line."

"You'll die."

"I will die one day anyway. If the spirits break through, I will die in the night, alongside my family, and alongside yours." The elder looked up suddenly, searching for the man's gaze in the flickering light. "This is my duty. Come tomorrow, it will be yours. We keep the line whole. We keep the dead at bay." He fixed his eyes on the man until he received a defeated nod, then turned back to stare at the back wall of the cave. The light didn't reach far enough back to light the walls back there, but it did briefly reflect something moving in the dark.

"Take the body out. Let no one in until morning, and then only to mend the line." he took a slow breath, in, out. "Do not let my wife see me."

The man stared, helpless, then placed a hand on the elder's shoulder.

"Peace," he muttered. Then he stooped to collect the body, and left.

Pennies for the Dead

By Lauren K. Nixon

Cat curled in the corner; sunflowers in a jar.
Coffee and a newspaper. Two cups.
Oranges in a bowl.
The smell of toast.
Flowers for the living, pennies for the dead

Sunlight on the bright white sheets, leaching colour.
Hands folded, tucked in pages of a fallen book.
A chest, rising and falling.
The sanctity of sleep.
Apples for the doctors, pennies for the dead

A helping hand.
Fingers pressed tight; comfort taken and comfort given.
The scent of bleach and lilies.
Counting backwards from ten.
Ether for the surgeon, pennies for the dead

Time stretched out like elastic, ready to snap.
Rumbling on in fits and bursts.
Cold hands and cold hearts. Squeezing breaths.
Each second a lifetime, the minutes an age.
A breathless flicker of sunlight on car windows. And
then you know.
Whetstones for the reapers, pennies for the dead

Long hair brushed, laid on that final pillow.
Hands clasped again. Gentle.
Flowers in her hair.
All our little rituals.
Hearts made of glass, filling up with silence.
Ribbons for the undertakers, pennies for the dead

"I'm sorry for –" Tea now, not coffee, and something
stronger.
Eulogies and elegies. Prayers in the dark.

Words that grasp like pleading.
Please don't leave – "– for your loss."
Whiskey for the preachers, pennies for the dead

No cold like church cold, seeping into bones.
Filling up the marrow like snow in March.
A strike and a burst of sulphur.
The candle catches, sputters and goes out.
You think of her hands.
Candles for the angels, pennies for the dead

Cat curled in the corner, looking up at floorboard creaks.
Coffee and a newspaper. One cup.
Oranges in a bowl.
The smell of toast. The memory of sunflowers.
A dream of life.
Whispers for the spirits, pennies for the dead

Take Flight

by Philip Lickley

As the door slides open with a metallic groan, the thumping in my head suddenly and without warning becomes much more apparent to me, the throbbing, pulsating ache washing over my scalp like a tide of jellyfish, with the same amount of venom and fear. I can feel a mixture of emotions: the pain of the headache; a dryness in my mouth; the absence of memories. I look around to try and establish where I am. I appear to have stumbled, almost as if intoxicated, out of an aircraft toilet, my eyelids heavy and my eyes blinking as the light from the main cabin perforates my retinas. There is the line of windows; there are the chairs filled with passengers drinking, eating or listening to music; there are the overhead lockers containing hand luggage of various shapes and sizes. But everything else is like a void. Who am I? What am I doing on a plane? Why is my head throbbing so badly?

Stumbling over to the edge of the aeroplane I find myself supporting my weight on the edge of the aircraft, only a thin sliver of metal keeping me from the outside air, the pressurised cabin only adding to the thump-thumping of my head. I look back to the toilet cubicle and see that I'd closed the door behind me. Already I am arousing suspicion on the craft, with several passengers looking over towards me, their eyebrows raised in bemusement. One particularly nervous looking passenger – they're sat in their seat nervously sucking on a sweet, a stiff glass of whiskey in one hand and a sick bag poised in the other – is giving me the evils. I realise I must look suspicious, hanging around the toilets with a pained expression on my face. He probably thinks I'm a terrorist about to hijack the plane or something. I need to go incognito, but first I have to find my seat, and with my memory an empty register that is not an easy undertaking.

With my eyesight a painful blur, my surroundings

moving in and out of focus like someone trying to badly operate a camera, I cough and try to stand up straight, suppressing the screams of pain from my head just enough to walk casually down the aisle, past several rows until I spot one empty seat in a sea of filled chairs. I hazard a guess that that is my seat and slowly move towards it, passing two young men and placing myself in it. Neither of the individuals to my left and right – one a young man in his mid-twenties in a blue t-shirt and intentionally ripped jeans listening to music on his mobile phone, the other a lady in her mid-fifties with a bouffant hairstyle and clothes that were much younger than she is – bat an eyelid as I sit down there, suggesting my appearance in the seat wasn't entirely unexpected. I look casually across at the older lady to my left who doesn't even look up from the book to acknowledge me. I must be in the right seat, and now I am just another passenger on a crowded flight, of whom no one is taking a particular interest.

It is now time to try and work out who I am and why I am here. I pat myself down, from the jacket I am wearing down to the pockets of my trousers. In my left trouser pocket is a travel wallet but all that is in it is cash – dollars, fifty – and there is no phone in there. In my right pocket is a solitary key with a bland, unassuming key fob attached to it, engraved with the letters K.L. In my right jacket pocket there is nothing but in my left there is what feels like my passport, but on pulling it out and examining it, it turns out to be a form of identification, but not just any form of ID. It is an FBI badge. I blink a couple of times to try and place it. Am I a member of the FBI? I certainly don't remember anything about that but then much of my memory is hazy and incomplete. I can't even remember my name never mind whether my initials are or are not K.L. One thing I do know, though: they certainly don't match the name on the FBI identification, which from studying the clear formal type is David Richmond. David Richmond? I mull the name over in my head and feel a slight trigger of recognition. Yes. I have seen that name before. Some memories start coming back to me. I'd earlier got up from my chair, walked swiftly down the aeroplane aisle and into the toilet. Then all is blank. I return the badge into my pocket and recline slightly in the seat, wondering whether there would be any hand luggage above me that would give me any further clues.

"Well I'm not reading anything by *her* again…" spluttered the lady to my left. I look over to her as she closes her thick paperback with as much force as she could muster, the intentional force of the closure not exactly threatening in sound as much as tone. I speak to her, my words difficult and stuttering, as if the syllables were sticking, no clinging, to the back of my throat.

"Not a good book?"

"Not at all," she replies quickly, her gaze meeting mine. "I've read better stories from my grandson, and he's five."

More words struggle to come to me. I instead just nod. By this point the lady next to me has placed the book into a small satchel and is instead looking out of the window. There isn't much to see other than an immense blueness. After a few moments she turns back to me.

"Are you feeling okay?" she asks me. "You look a little pale."

I tell her that I'm not feeling at my best.

"Your visit to the toilet didn't help then?"

I fill her in on my sudden bout of amnesia. "I can't remember anything," I confess. She looks concerned.

"What happened in there? Did you slip and bang your head or something? It's pretty serious not to even remember your name."

"Did I introduce myself earlier?" I ask. She shakes her head. "Not even as David?"

She stares at me blankly before shaking her head once more, her hairstyle not flinching as she moved. To my side the young man shuffles in his seat. A hostess ambles down the corridor in the middle of the plane with a trolley; the passenger requests a coffee and once it is poured he sits there nursing it.

"You didn't really say a word to me at all."

"How long have we been up in the air?"

"About thirty minutes."

"And I got up to the toilet?"

"Yes. You looked agitated, fiddling nervously in your pocket. I think it was a phone."

"A phone?"

"You know, one of those iPhone things. My grandson has one."

For a couple of minutes our conversation diverts onto a tangent. I ask her about her grandson. He is eight, doing well at school, popular with the teachers. She tells me how he often comes around after school – at least twice a week – and speaks animatedly about what he'd learnt that day. Science is his favourite subject. She smiles as she thinks about these memories. After a few moments we get back to the subject of my earlier movement.

I ask if she is sure it was a phone as I don't have it on me anymore. She nods, but looks unsure. It was something concealed in a pocket. But what has happened to it?

"Perhaps you left it in the toilet when you went?"

I nod and look over to the toilet. I consider going in but there is a young woman in her mid-twenties already heading for the door, her blonde ponytail swaying in the stale recycled air of the budget airline. My stomach growls. I realise I am hungry, that familiar emotion and desire breaking through my still throbbing head and frustrated confusion that the memory loss had brought on. My eyes follow the woman as she enters the cubicle. It's not long before she lets out a scream, stepping backwards out of the smallest room and looking much paler on her exit. A couple of flight attendants are with her in seconds and they too study the room, looking shocked. I look back at the lady next me.

"What do you think they've found?" she asks me. I realise it must be more than my discarded tablet. Unless I'd been watching something particularly dodgy on it – which didn't feel like me deep down, even with my memories vacant – it would hardly make someone recoil in horror. I decide to act, getting up from the chair and scurrying over to the toilet. The taller attendant stops me with a firm hand.

"Sorry sir you can't come any further. We have an," he says before stopping and studying me, noticing my pained expression and a speck of blood on my collar. "Incident."

I try to look around him into the toilet but my view is blocked. I explain that I'd just been in there but something had happened and I am struggling to remember. He looks at me suspiciously.

"If it helps," I say, retrieving the badge from my pocket and deciding to dismiss any confusion over my true vocation and saying it firmly as I truly became the owner of the pass, "I'm from the FBI. David Richmond."

The attendant, with a thin pencil-moustache and the most piercing grey eyes I'd ever seen, examines the badge closely and then my own eyes before passing it back to me.

"You had better see this then."

He lets me past.

*

What I see in the toilet cubicle takes me by surprise. There, sprawled on the floor of the small room is a man, about six foot, his eyes open and fixed in panic, his mouth drooped open. There is a huge gash across his forehead and blood has seeped from the wound onto the floor, pooling at the base of his skull. His left arm is twisted and in his right hand sits a small tablet computer, but it is bulkier than I would expect thanks to something connected to it. Scanning around the room I spot a phone in the corner. It has been thrown, and clearly has smashed against the wall. A large crack is visible across the screen and already the familiar rainbow colourings of a damaged screen are appearing. *That must be my phone*, I realise.

There is something about this scene that triggers something and a powerful vision hits me, as if the scene laid out in front opens a tap in my brain, and memories start to flood through. A voice booms out. *FBI. Freeze.* There is a struggle. I fall down, my head hitting the sink. And then the other man hits the side of the toilet and slumps to the floor. The phone goes spinning. The tablet lays there on the floor. I bend down to pick it up. The screen is displaying something. A countdown. I remember studying it and looking to press a button but then the other individual in the room moves, grabbing me by the ankle. I come crashing to the ground and hit my head hard against the wall. I am out cold. My next memory is of waking up and stumbling blindly out into the main part of the aeroplane.

I shake myself from this vision and lean down, picking up the tablet. I study its case for a moment: it looks to be a standard Android-based device but with an extra component thrust awkwardly into the USB socket. This extra section has a distinctly homemade feeling to it, albeit of a pretty good construction. I press the button to switch on the screen and I'm presented with a piece of software, again looking distinctly homemade. It doesn't look particularly intuitive but it does display some sort of countdown. My first thought is that it's some sort of game, but something doesn't feel quite right. There is one button on the bottom. It reads 'Abort'. I press it and it asks for a pin. I look back at the attendants.

"What do you think?" he asks. I swallow hard.

"If I was to make an educated guess, providing this isn't some elaborate game, I'd say that our friend here is looking to blow up the plane and from the look of this device I'd say that plan is still in action. And if this countdown is true we have twenty minutes."

"Twenty..." the attendant begins, unable to contemplate the situation or complete the sentence. "Are you sure? I mean look at that, it looks like a game. Bombs don't really have countdowns on them. That's just Hollywood..."

His chatter tailed off as if his vocal chords had run out of steam. I can't disagree with him.

"Is the guy...?" he asks. I lean down and feel for a pulse. There is nothing. I nod.

"If he knew the pin then that knowledge has gone with him."

The attendant studies the tablet. "That's not big enough to be a bomb."

"This must be just the trigger. I'd hazard the real bomb is somewhere in the luggage. The countdown ends, bang."

"But if that's the case, why put an abort on it? Surely if you wanted to blow a plane up," he says, hushing his voice so as not yet attract the attention – and concerns – of the passengers – "you wouldn't give the guy a way of getting out of it, if they got cold feet."

"Maybe the abort is for another reason. Is there anything special on this plane, in the cargo?"

The attendant thinks for a moment. "Not that has been told to me."

"What about a person on board? Any celebrities or scientists? Anybody that would be a bartering tool for a terrorist?"

The attendant shakes his head. "We usually get briefed on that. Not that many celebrities travel budget."

I look confused but at least the drama unfolding has pumped adrenaline around my system which masks my throbbing cranium. But that is currently the least of my worries. The second attendant, who had been there outside the toilet at the start had earlier quietly left but now returns with a message.

"I just got called by the pilot," she reveals, standing in the doorway, her face pale yet clammy. "Air traffic control have received a message from an organisation calling themselves *Take Flight*. They have said that if they don't receive $1billion wired to them within twenty minutes the plane goes up."

So that is why they had the abort button. They get the money, they cancel the explosion, though that still didn't entirely make sense. Surely a ruthless terrorist organisation would get the money and still blow up the plane? Or perhaps there was something we don't yet know.

"Are they going to give them the money?" I ask the others within ear shot. The male attendant shakes his shoulders.

"It's unlikely. The American Government doesn't make deals with terrorist organisations – well, not officially anyway – and the owner of this airline is tighter than this cubicle. He'd charge his own grandmother for using the toilet onboard if he could. He won't pay, and that means. Well. I won't spell it out."

I grimace, my stomach continuing to do cartwheels. I look down at the man, dead on the floor. In tackling this man earlier I'd managed to suppress the human threat but clearly had made things worse. Dead men don't tell tales or reveal de-activation codes. There are eighteen minutes left. I have to face facts. The chance of me guessing the code in that time correctly is very unlikely, and even if I try it wouldn't be unfeasible for the software to activate anyway with a few incorrect entries suggesting a sabotage attempt by a third party.

"You'll have to tell the passengers," I say. The attendants nod, head out of the toilet and go for a protocol-breaking swift glass of whiskey each ("If I have fifteen minutes left to live bugger the disciplinary!") before delivering the sombre message over the intercom. Naturally this isn't best received, with many starting to scream, sob or break down, aside from one or two that have seemingly resigned themselves to the fate. Meanwhile I am there, staring down at the dead man in front of me, silently cursing him for getting us into this situation. I don't want to die. Granted, I can't remember who I am or my past, the throbbing of my head still consuming most of my senses, but I must have some friends and family I'd want to see again and, besides, the haze is starting to lift and hopefully soon my thoughts would return to me.

I continue to study the device and think. What would they have used as a pin number? A particular pattern? A birthday? A significant date? If I had been told by my bosses, or had an idea of what it could have been, my lack of memory is masking those facts. The abort code is now my only hope to save everyone on the plane and I either don't know the number or it has been forgotten. I check my pockets again. Perhaps I'd brought some case files with me onto the plane in which there might be that information. There is nothing on me, of course, but perhaps there would be in the overhead compartment above my chair.

Perspiration is now gathering on my forehead and a sick feeling continues to ebb and flow from my stomach. I look around the room and study the blandness of the aeroplane toilet cubicle, its white walls and cream-coloured minimal furnishings creating a bland offset for the drama unfolding. I slowly realise there is little I can do in this space and that there's very little point me spending my last fifteen minutes like this. I return casually to by my chair, walking zombie-like through a fuselage of chaos and emotion. I quickly open the compartment above my chair but it's empty. I sit back down next to the lady from earlier who seems remarkably calm.

"I can't believe that's the last book I'll ever read," she moans as I came within ear shot. I look at her and ask her how she can remain so calm.

"Whatever will be, will be. That's what they used to sing many years ago and it still applies now. There's no point worrying over things you can't change. I've had a good life, it's just a shame I won't be able to see my grandson again. But I've just tried to leave a message for him on Facebook. Here's hoping he'll get it."

I feel sick. What sort of monster would do this? And how can she be so calm and accepting of our fate?

"Don't beat yourself up," she tells me after I confess my anxieties to her. "You did the best you could, going in there and trying to stop the terrorist. You weren't to know their plan was already in motion. You weren't to know."

"But I should have done better than this. I should have been able to save everyone."

My head suddenly pulses with a flash of pain unlike anything I'd yet felt. Clutching my head I wait a few moments and it fades, giving away to a more clear tranquillity against the backdrop of an aeroplane in uproar. Some memories flood back and they make me feel ill.

I am now watching myself from across the plane as if a neutral observer; it's my movements from earlier. My other self gets up from my seat, my exterior calm but a few beads of sweet on my forehead giving away that I'm not as calm under the surface. I spot another man behaving suspiciously across the aeroplane, looking at me. I have to act. I get up, subconsciously feeling for something in my pocket before heading across to the toilet, sliding the door closed and pulling from my pocket a tablet device. But before I can lock the door I see a foot jammed between the sliding part and the wall and a figure bursts in. 'FBI,' he calls and I panic, quickly going for him and we scuffle, battering each other against the walls but somehow quietly enough to not attract attention, the door having conveniently slid closed. I start winning the fight and overpowering him, and I push the man over, and his head makes contact with the sink unit. He falls. I lean down and remove a badge from his jacket pocket, examine it in my fingers and study his name vividly, and then place it in my own jacket. I retrieve my tablet from the floor onto which it dropped during the scuffle. Thirty minutes to go. But then I am tricked and realise the man was just playing possum. He grabs my ankle and I fall, whacking my head on the sink and my vision blurring. I begin to lose consciousness, but as I do I realise that was the last attempt of a dying man as the agent begins bleeding. By this point we are now both unconscious. But the clock is still ticking.

The vision fades. I feel sick. I turn to the lady to my side.

"I'm sorry," is all I can utter, my throat dry.

"What do you mean?"

"My memories are back. I'm not who I think I am. I think I am the terrorist. I brought the bomb on board..."

She just sat there, looking speechless. A tear forms in her left eye. I swallow hard, but there's hardly any spittle to lubricate my throat. I blurt something out to her:

"I don't want this. I don't want to die. I don't want any of you to die. What have I done?"

A thought comes to my head. I wouldn't have the case files; they'd be with the actual agent. I try and locate the other empty seat belonging to the FBI agent but in the chaos of the aeroplane with everyone now either standing or having moved about it, it is impossible. Concealing my true identity for a little longer from the attendants I ask them if they knew. They check the records and find him – David Richmond. Seat C15. I find the seat and the compartment and there is a briefcase in there, but it's locked. I take it out, and bash it a couple of times on the floor, but unsurprisingly it doesn't budge. The attendant comes to help and delivers me a Swiss-army knife. I look at him.

"You allow knives on planes?"

"Not really. It's mine. I keep it hidden in case we ever, you know, got hijacked. It's my insurance. My girlfriend suggested it. My bosses don't know."

"It's ironic then you're giving it to me,"

"What do you mean?"

"Nothing," I mutter, my gaze switching back to the briefcase. I use the knife to cut open the latch and it flips open, but inside there is very little aside from a few identification papers and a map. No intelligence; no numbers; no nothing. I slam the briefcase closed and return to my seat.

Remember! Remember! I demand of myself, trying to recall the abort code. After a couple of moments of self-investigation the male attendant is back at my side. He is smiling.

"It's unbelievable. They're actually going to wire over the money."

"That's all fine," I say, "But we still can't stop the bomb." I then reveal my secret to the attendant and he recoils in horror. I bow my head.

"I'm sorry. I never meant any of this. Well, I must have, but I don't now. But I cannot remember the number."

Five minutes.

"So we're doomed then. Resigned to our fates. The pilot has tried to aim for a nearby airport, one off the flight path but that's still twenty minutes away."

"We could try and ditch in the ocean?"

"Too risky."

"What have we got to lose? Potential death vs actual death?"

The attendant nodded and left, and after about thirty seconds I feel the plane jerk downwards. The pilot is attempting it. We could actually be saved, though a water landing is not particularly an easy thing and it is probably equal to suicide. I turn to the lady next to me who is still in a form of zen-like calm that belies the situation we face.

"If I could only remember the fucking number..." I curse in frustration. I am frustrated with the situation, with my inability to stop it, with my reasoning for joining *a group so desperate to cause destruction.* Why would I do such a thing to myself and to all the people onboard? Desperation perhaps? Money? What good would money be to me?

A voice begins to fill my head. It is distant, like a past memory. I'm in a briefing room with two other men in suits. It doesn't feel like a terrorist training camp. I imagine these to be in a ramshackle hut in a desert somewhere but this feels like a more professional outlet. The men are in suits. There is an electronic smart-board on the wall.

"We demand the money," the voice rasped. "Then when we get it you can abort the bomb. The plane then lands. You'll be arrested of course but you'll be alive. Your family gets the money. We, *Take Flight*, pay off your debts. All will be well."

I am a desperate man. Drowning in debt. *Take Flight* is just that. I take the flight, my family takes flight with the money to live a better life than the one I was providing them.

I then hear my voice. "But what if they don't pay and the plane goes up? What about my family then?"

"That's why we recommend this," the shadowy figure said, sliding a thick document across the table in front of me. "Life insurance. Set it up then in six months, result. Extra cash anyway."

I nod.

"And the code?"

My heart beats faster. Is my memory finally delivering the answer?"

"It's 7-2-3-9. Memorise that. It's the only way you'll stop it on the day."

"You'll tell me that again though..."

"Oh yes. In the pre-event briefing."

That phrase made what is happening sound like preparation for a business lunch not mass murder.

*

I had the number; relief swept over me like a refreshing tide on a warm summer's day, or something like that. But I can't think too clearly about such metaphors. I have to act. I turn to the lady next to me.

"I've remember the number. I can stop this!" I declare perkily. "You will see your grandson". She smiles.

"Then it's a good day."

"I'm sorry for all of this. I must have been desperate," I say. I nod and get up from the chair, walking with purpose over to the attendants who have the tablet. Two minutes. I take the tablet from them and click the 'abort' button, the number pad appearing on screen. I tap in the first three numbers. Seven. Two. Three. One more figure and it's all over. But for a moment I lose myself, thinking about the scenarios. In one-hundred seconds the bomb is likely to go off. In fifty seconds we're likely to hit the water; will that be enough time for us to escape; but I also have the ability to stop the bomb with the code, but have I got enough time left to disarm it and then get the pilot to pull out of the dive? These questions float around my head and I feel like I'm wasting time. But there's another conversation coming into focus in my head as if someone is tuning a radio next to me, one that is much more muffled than the previous ones, as if overheard from a corridor or something, as if the message was said about me but not to me and only my subconscious heard it when it actually happened, but was now teasing me by introducing it freshly to me in my last few moments. I feel slightly guilty for letting it play in my head as my finger hovers over the 'nine' graphics.

"That's the benefit of over-rides," the voice said without hint of emotion in its flat, monotone voice. "It's the safety net for anyone recruited. They think they can stop it from happening if they have a change of heart or chicken out. It helps recruitment if they know there's a way out. But, of course, the abort button does nothing but set the bomb off earlier even when the correct PIN is entered. It makes it easier that way. *Take Flight* can't have our members ruining our well set up plans."

I swallow hard and close my eyes. This isn't me. I don't want any of this. I just wanted to secure my family's future. That's the only reason I got involved with *Take Flight*. I didn't want to take the flight. One minute. Either way it's over. I feel the plane falling towards the sea. In a few seconds we will land on, or in, the water. Will we survive or will the water consume us? Will the time limit seal our fate or will I? A piece of modern classical-style music comes out of nowhere in my mind, its notes washing through my head and subduing the still throbbing pain. For a moment I feel at peace, a calming sensation spreading throughout my body, but a tear still forms in my eye as thoughts of my family start to come back to me, as well as thoughts about everyone else sharing the space with me. I take a deep breath. I look out of the window and the blue sky is being replaced by the blue of water. Still the music echoes through my head.

I press the number nine key and wait. A message appears on screen.

I'm sorry for everything.

Take Flight, or Daedalus

By Lauren K. Nixon

Louis slowly teased out the feathers, taking great care not to damage any of the barbs.

The bird, a fieldfare, looked strangely false in death, as though someone had made an intricate model of a living thing. It was still faintly warm. He had seen its moment of mortal struggle, that awful moment when it had rebounded off the great glass expanse of the windows in the library. His mother hadn't been inside, which was lucky, and he had scooped the airy little thing into his pocket.

He had carried it with him all afternoon, through a particularly arduous three hours in the schoolroom. Although, as a rule, he enjoyed geography, today he had been unable to take his mind off the tiny corpse in his pocket. Over the afternoon he had lent it a kind of false existence, so now when he came to examine it the warmth under his fingertips was partially his own.

He applied himself to the grim task. If his family or tutors were to find him, they might have assumed that he enjoyed it, but he took no pleasure in the manipulation of a dead creature – particularly birds. To him, they were creatures of exquisite spirit and he often felt more connected to them than to his own family.

He took out a charcoal pencil and opened his notebook. Beginning at the tip of wings and moving down along the beautiful creature's body, he listed the measurement of each feather, each bone. He examined the angles of each part, both at rest and how he imagined them in flight.

His family had little enough idea about him as it was; distant, elegant creatures, too caught up in their own social bubbles to bother with a small boy who seemed more at home with his books than anywhere else.

He preferred to be forgotten. The worst days were the days he was noticed. His sisters seemed to revel in their cruelty. His brother, when he was home, simply didn't seem to realise he was there. Once, at a party he had been forced to attend, escorted by his tutor, the distant, older boy had patted him absently on the head and given him a strange, squashy kind of sweet that tasted of rosewater. He was grateful for that. Perhaps, he had imagined, being away in the army so much had made him value the things at home a little more.

His parents, when they spoke to him at all, used that time to admonish him for his many and varied failings. Low school marks; imagined transgressions; the annoyances of his sisters; being too loud; being too quiet.

He was not, he had been assured, worthy of the family name. Louis didn't have a problem with that at all. He didn't pay much attention to last names, only to the names of species. A Swedish man, Carl Linnaeus, had classified every plant and creature he had known into different categories. One day, Louis decided, he should like to meet him. He felt his grandfather would have liked to as well.

He finished his measurements and began to sketch the fieldfare, from every conceivable angle. His strokes weren't particularly skilled, but he was improving. That and his enthusiasm for the sciences were the only things his tutor could praise him for. He spent a considerable amount of time drawing birds. It was all part of his plan.

Once he had spent an entire, gloriously peaceful day watching the flight of the birds above the cornfield their coach had broken down in. It had been a stolen season, those neglected hours, as his sisters flirted with the grooms and his parents went out to shoot the wildlife. They disgusted him. To Louis, the creatures of the forest and field were infinitely more valuable than his boorish relatives, who never seemed to enter a room without destroying something.

He moved to the basin in the corner and carefully washed his hands so that no trace of the charcoal remained. He tucked the sketchbook behind the loose wall panel under his desk, along with the increasing collection of string, feathers, wood and glue, filched from the house and grounds at every opportunity. The prize of his collection were the remains of his grandfather's tent – the only thing he had been able to salvage before his effects were disposed of – and a book of botany that had been left to him in his grandfather's will. His family had laughed at that, but no one could find a reason he shouldn't have it, so he had been allowed – to his concealed delight – to keep it. He wrapped the corpse of the bird in a white handkerchief that he knew from past experience would be replaced without complaint and tucked it back into his pocket.

Not that nature wasn't also destructive. No student of the natural sciences could live under the illusion that there was a surfeit of kindness in the world. Almost everything ate almost everything else, and even the flowers in the most serene of summer meadows fought a vicious battle for survival. He had learned that the day his kindly, quiet grandfather had died. He was the only member of his family who seemed to feel that Louis's existence was worthwhile.

He had spent many happy hours sitting on his grandfather's knee, flicking through the books on botany that filled his much disapproved of study; examining the pictures of butterflies on the wall; caring for the precious and exotic orchids he had brought back from his youthful travels; listening to his stories of freedom and adventure. The day he had succumbed to the lung sickness that had confined him to his study, Louis had been beaten for weeping.

It had made him, unconsciously, as a little boy of five, a confirmed atheist. No longer could he conceive of a god so cruel as to let his elderly friend – his only protector – die in such pain, while his loud, vulturous family cavorted so carelessly.

Nature wasn't cruel, like the god who had taken his grandfather; nor was it kind, like the god the preacher lectured them about on Sundays. Nature was indifferent. Louis had respect for indifference. But for all that, he had witnessed a stark kind of humanity amongst his fellow creatures.

Louis listened carefully at the door for a few moments, glad, as he always was, that the corridor outside was lined with creaky floorboards. He slipped out of his door and moved silently across them, knowing exactly where he had to step. He made it to the kitchens without any trouble and slithered unnoticed between the forest of legs.

The fieldfare was despatched into the furnace at the back of the room with ease and little ceremony. Ideally, he would have liked to bury it, to afford it the respect he felt it deserved, but there was no way for him to reach the gardens without being observed. Consigning him to the flames was the best he could do. He watched the fire flare for a moment, as the bird's perfect feathers disappeared, thinking of the way it must have felt to stretch wings against the warm summer breeze.

When he was eight, walking back one day from the chapel on the estate, he had seen fox cubs playing together on the edge of the woods and one of them had become entangled in the fencing by the edge of the road. He had snuck away from the group to free it, and its siblings had scattered. The cub, freed, had peered at him for a few moments, no longer afraid, before briefly nuzzling against his itchy woollen sock. He had made it back to the others before his absence was noticed, and carried home within his heart the first moment of gratitude he could remember since his grandfather's death.

That was the day he had made his decision.

He had been on time to dinner and no one had spoken to him. Forgotten, he had walked quietly back to his room and waited, patiently, until everyone in his part of the house had gone to sleep. Most of the staff and all of the family and their guests were engaged at a party, as they were most evenings. This one was a birthday celebration for his eldest sister and he had been expressly forbidden to attend.

It was a perfect opportunity.

Working quickly, his heart hammering against the inside of his chest, he pulled out the sketchbook and began to construct the thing he had designed over years of observing the birds. It needed a frame, strong enough to bear his slight weight and to draw the light, tight-woven canvas tight across itself. It was a painstaking job and he took his time. It had to be perfect, he knew, or he wouldn't stand a chance. He had made smaller models to test them and the results had always been the same: perfection was the key. Nature was indifferent, after all.

He would be Daedalus, soaring off into the still night

and to his freedom.

He had been storing food that wouldn't perish for weeks and had snuck into his father's study a month before, as soon as he had known that his plan would work, and stolen the exact amount of money that his tutor had told him was intended to be his inheritance. His grandfather had left him a small amount of money, but his sisters wanted it for themselves – they, to no one's surprise but their own, had been overlooked by the aged naturalist.

No one had noticed. Money was such a fluid medium in the house that it was possible that no one ever would.

He knew carrying money was a risk, but it was one he would have to take. He knew from his studies that it would take him five days to make it to the coast, where he would find a boat that needed a boy. Any boat would do, as long as it took him towards Uppsala, where Linnaeus was based. There, he would find a way to speak to the man, or at least find a way to study the garden.

And from there? Louis didn't know. He rather liked the idea of having no set direction. He could flit wherever he wanted, like a bird.

He would change his name – he had already chosen it: Merlin. His grandfather had told him of the bird, one happy, sunlit day, and then the story of the ancient magician. Although Louis couldn't imagine having such power over the world, his grandfather had told him that Merlin had also been a student of nature. Louis was his grandfather's name, so he had decided to keep it.

His family might look for him, he supposed, but not as far away as Sweden. They assumed he was an imbecile because he seldom spoke. His tutors might have better luck. They knew he had a mind, though they often disapproved of what he used it for. They would have preferred him to pay more attention to poetry and history, but he thirsted for science. That was the real magic now. If Merlin had been alive, science would have been his discipline – Louis was sure of it.

By the time he was finished, the sounds of the party were winding down, just a couple of hours before dawn. He packed a change of clothes, and a few warmer garments, his sketchbook, his book of botany and his charcoal pencils. His money he concealed in different parts of his bag – a trick his elder brother had taught him when they were younger and he had remembered that one of his sisters was, in fact, a boy. The food, the feathers and the rest of the string, along with the knife he had stolen from one of the gardeners, were distributed amongst the pack.

He crept out of his room and moved through the house as easily and as noiselessly as a shadow, pausing only by the door to the room that his grandfather had occupied during the last years of his life. He would have wanted Louis to go, he thought. It had occurred to him that if he stayed here, he might simply disappear.

Although there was always someone roaming the grounds and the vulnerable ground floor regions of the house, Louis knew there would be no one on the roof. He had the only key, liberated from the butler earlier in the day. He climbed the staircase, a sense of great anticipation building in him.

Peering over the edge, the wind ruffling his hair, he felt oddly calm. He had imagined that this moment would fill him with fear. After all, he knew exactly what a fall from four storeys would do to the body of a twelve-year-old boy. He looked down over the estate, across the woods and formal gardens. Beyond it, the deeper shadows of the village that served the estate hunkered down in the valley. From here, it looked like it was trying to be unobtrusive, camouflaging itself against the hills.

He fastened the glider to the belts he had clamped around himself and strapped his pack to his front. Louis hesitated at the edge of the roof. He had no illusions about what failure would mean.

For a moment he looked back at the door leading into the house, weighing the key in his hands. He could go back. He could hide his glider and pack and try again on another day. His family might remember him, or perhaps he could find a less dramatic means of escape.

Out in the stilly night, an owl called. Louis, whose eyes weren't as good as the owl's, followed the sound, searching for the silent wings. Owls could glide through the air, so why couldn't he?

He dropped the key over the edge, listening with

satisfaction as it fell on the gravel path below. Someone would come across it and the butler would not be inconvenienced. He took a breath, eyes on the stars, and began to run.

He was not Icarus. He would be Daedalus. He would soar. He would –

It occurred to him that his feet were no longer in contact with the roof. The wind rushed around him, buffeting him higher, wrapping him up in a cocoon of noise and movement. He felt dizzy; simultaneously weightless and intensely heavy. The glider creaked under his weight, but the knots and folds he had taken such time on held.

The park rushed past below him and, for a moment, it seemed like *he* was still and the *world* was moving. It was getting steadily closer, too. His shoes brushed the tips of the leaves above the trees and then there was only open space.

Louis began to run again, in mid-air, suspended above the river that marked the boundary to his family's land. His feet crunched against the ground and suddenly he was flat against the ground, curled between his pack and the glider, utterly winded.

He lay there for minutes, simply breathing. It was a privilege to be alive. He listened to the rushing water of the river, ambling past on its own journey to the coast.

By stages he managed to move, first his hands, then his arms, then his legs, and finally his whole body. His fingers were numb and he had bruises all over his body, but he had made it. With shaking hands, he disassembled the glider, still too numb with shock to fully process his achievement. The tent would come in handy in the days it would take him to reach the coast; perhaps on the boat, too.

He would tell them that his middle name was Daedalus. He had earned it.

He closed his eyes for a moment, consulting the map he had memorised of the route he needed to take to the nearest port. When he opened them, he saw another pair of eyes across the river: the yellow, patient eyes of a vixen. He smiled, for the first time in years, and nodded. The fox flicked her tail and disappeared back into the wood – the only farewell he wanted or needed.

Calmly, and with the conviction that he was understood, at least by one living creature, he set off across the fields towards the road. He would be alright.

He was Daedalus; he had wings.

You are what
you eat

The Great Brutal Bake Off

By Philip Lickley

Gerald Woodstock was a burly old man in his mid-fifties whose costume of choice was a pair of grey slacks, an ill-fitting t-shirt and a gravy-stained apron. He had owned and run *The Full Monty Café* for almost thirty-five years, a small but well-patronised greasy spoon on the edge of Oxford Road and Carlton Green. His speciality was the fried breakfast of "olde England" and men, women and children would come from miles around to sample his fry-up, or at least, so he would boast occasionally. One night, a cold February night, Gerald wondered to himself, as he lay in his bed at night, how many full Englishes he must have served up in his career, and he came up with the number 1,102,503. He admired such an impressive figure before turning over onto his side, farting and falling asleep, the smell of half-eaten breakfasts and subsequent served-up dinners still wafting from his skin. This had successful put off anyone sharing the bed with him for a third of a century.

The Full Monty itself, though, wasn't in the greatest of shape, much like Gerald himself. The paint of the door was peeling, the glass in the windows cloudy and shattered in places, and the brickwork in desperate need of re-pointing. But inside it actually wasn't too bad: the metallic tables were well-kept, the cutlery shiny and the kitchen tiles spotless. Gerald prided himself upon keeping his business premises at a high rate of cleanliness.

Each morning Gerald Woodstock went through the same daily routine, pretty much unchanged over the years. Though his moustachioed upper lip had become bushier and his belly overhung his trousers by a greater degree, he was still doing exactly the same thing he'd always done. At five-thirty sharp his alarm clock went off, which he subsequently silenced with his palm before he rolled over in bed, scratched himself and lumbered through to the bathroom where he emptied his bladder, shook a few times and washed his hands roughly with a nail brush and carbolic soap. He would then have a quick shave, brush his teeth and scratch some more, before a return to the bedroom heralded a stripping off of his vest and boxers and into that day's clothes. Now ten minutes after the alarm brought him back to consciousness he would half-heartedly lumber downstairs, switch on the café lights and begin preparations for that morning's service: namely, switching on the fryers so they began to heat up, receiving a delivery of fresh eggs, meat and milk from his regular supplier – Billy "The Butcher" Bradshaw, who had been in his job almost as long as Gerald himself had been in his – and giving the tables a once over with the back of a cloth.

For many years this repetitive series of drab, daily events included a wave through the window across the street to Clive Waddington who owned the bookshop across the road, who didn't really have a particular reason to be up and alert in his shop at such a time in the morning other than he would have often consumed a whole bottle of whiskey on the previous evening and thus woken up with a start, and a hangover, amongst some chosen classics that had been knocked from a shelf onto his intoxicated body. Waddington, by this point in his early seventies, had run *The Bookworm* bookshop for over forty years and would have considered doing so well into his late seventies and early eighties if it hadn't been for a freak turn of events, now a couple of years ago, when his order of sixty-seven copies of bestseller *'Fifty Shades of Grey'* had turned up a day earlier than every other bookseller in the area and he'd found himself crushed to death by the early morning stampede that was a knot of thirty-three horny housewives, desperate to get their fingers on the story of Christian Grey. Gerald had naturally attended Clive's funeral and had been heard to curse the circumstances of his friend's passing as the coffin had rolled into the furnace, but many couldn't help seeing the funny side in his premature passing away.

Since Clive's early demise under the feet of the local women, the premises that had once housed *The Bookworm* had remained vacant, the books packed up, shipped out and sold off by his surviving relatives shortly after the accident, but no buyer could be found to step into

Waddington's shoes. Rumours of a curse on the building, which included evidence such as a plumber scalded by a rather enthusiastic tap as the water was switched off, and the supposed sight of Clive occasionally through a window some mornings, remained unconfirmed, but this didn't stop further rumours circulating that Clive was still haunting the building.

So days, weeks, months and years passed. Gerald would continue to do the same thing: switching on the fryers, listening to the heat bubbling; receiving string-tied parcels of bacon from Billy; and wiping down the surfaces. He would often pause at the window, remembering Clive, before switching on the television in the corner and turning on the radio. In a weird combination of dis-co-ordinated audio and visuals, many customers would consume their eggs and bacon under the watchful gaze of Jeremy Kyle, whilst Ken Bruce would rattle on over the radio. Occasionally it worked much to Gerald's amusement when the subject matter synched, such as 'Burn Baby Burn' playing when the televised caption read 'My ex-girlfriend gave me gonorrhoea'.

And so the rhythm of daily life continued. At six thirty a.m. Gerald would slap on his apron, walk over to the front door and grope sleepily for the key, turning it and hearing the door unlock with a satisfying clunk. He would then turn the sign round from 'Closed' to 'Open' and retire briefly to behind the counter, preparing for the first customer of the day. As he waited, he would clean his spectacles on his apron, adding to the grime already on the apron and probably not actually making the lenses of his glasses any more suitable for seeing through. Without fail, within a couple of minutes, the customers would begin to trickle and then pour through: older couples wanting company; builders and other workmen looking for some satisfying sustenance before a hard day of manual labour; and school children cheekily grabbing a bacon sandwich before assembly. Some would come in, take a seat at a table and await a fry-up delivered to their table, complete with runny fried eggs, crisp rashers of bacon and chunky slices of black pudding, alongside beans, fried mushrooms and half-a-tomato, joined alongside by a cup of strong, sweet tea and three whole slices of freshly buttered toast. Others just settled on the edge of chairs, downing a quick cup of tea and perhaps a bacon sandwich whilst flicking through a copy of the Sun. A further group would just scurry in, make their requests, pay up and scurry back out again with a take-away sandwich in a white paper bag, either eating from it as they walked down the street or devouring it in a van parked up on the side of the road.

After a couple of hours of breakfasts the room would empty before the lunch run began, businessmen and women, and many others in the community, arriving to take away sandwiches of all shapes, sizes, colours, textures and combinations, whilst others took seats at the freshly cleared away tables to consume a warm cottage pie or a hearty soup and bread roll. Then, once this selection of customers had come and gone, the sign would be switched back to 'Closed', the door locked, the place cleaned and the fryers switched off. Gerald would then head out the back door for a quick cigarette, to undertake a walk to the local newsagent for a copy of the evening newspaper, a scratch card and a half-pint of milk, and then to slowly waddle home to read the paper in front of his television, an object he would remain glued to for the rest of the day, accompanied at different periods by a pint, a hot meal or a coffee, before heading up to the bathroom for a short, sharp, cold shower and then a quick read of some sports biography or other before bedtime.

This unchanging chain of events continued day-in and day-out, with only the variance of the weekend crowd and the occasional public holiday offering anything fresh. Months would go by with little fluctuation, until one day when everything suddenly shifted. As Gerald looked out of his window one Wednesday morning in memory of Clive, he spotted activity in the premises formerly known as *The Bookworm*. At first he didn't pay it much attention, shifting his gaze from the shop and pushing back the net curtains, his familiarity with these same actions from every other morning kicking in without him contemplating what he'd just seen. It was only when he did a comedic, almost cartoon-like, double take that he began to take in the situation. The front door of the ex-shop was open and a couple of men in paint-splattered overalls were walking in and out at regular intervals. A young man in a casual suit (without a tie, Gerald noted to himself) was stood outside, his hands in his trouser pockets looking up at the building. Gerald assumed this must be the new owner. It would be good to see the shop re-opening and he wondered if it would be a bookshop once more.

There was no indication of what business would be replacing *The Bookworm* over the next few days, only the continued to-ing and fro-ing of the decorators in and out. It was only on the Thursday, eight days after the first sign of activity, that Gerald realised what the new shop would be as a new, pristine plastic sign was hoisted up onto the front of the building. He looked aghast at just after eleven as he looked through the window, prompted by a customer who had just come in muttering something about competition.

'Caf-ay Up' said the sign in huge red letters. Gerald scratched his head, confused by the lettering. He returned to his familiar, almost comfortable, place behind the counter and then to the kitchen to finish splashing oil over the top of a fried egg. He then used a fish-slice to drop it onto a pre-buttered slice of bread, onto which a second slice was layered on top before it all went into a small grease-proof bag. With a spin of his wrist, Gerald sealed the package and passed it to the customer who had alerted him to the new addition to the shop across the road.

"Well, it's good ol' Yorkshire slang," Albert Peters said, gesturing in the rough direction of the sign. "You know. 'Ay up'. Like 'hello'. It's quite witty."

"But this is Norfolk," Gerald spluttered. "It doesn't make sense. We don't speak like that here."

"Well I think it's clever anyway," Albert remarked before slipping two pounds into Gerald's hand and leaving the shop with his breakfast wrapped up tightly. Gerald's lip curled as his gaze moved from the customers in his café to the sign outside, still visible between the slats of the blind.

The breakfast crowd and the lunch crowd soon passed in a flurry of buttered bread, boiled water and cleaned cutlery and soon the tables had been washed down and the kitchen closed. But today, instead of heading outside to the back for a cigarette Gerald slipped out of the front of the building and into the street to get a proper and lengthy looking at what was now seeming to be a competitor to his own business. There was no one around now, even though it was early afternoon. It looked like the contractors, having spent considerable time and energy – not to mention cups of tea – had called it a day. And Gerald, realising there was little he could do about it at the moment, did the same, bypassing his usual cigarette but continuing through the rest of his usual activities.

The next day soon came and by just after nine the main breakfast rush was out of the way and only Sue remained in the café. Sue was one of Gerald's more eccentric patrons. Dressed in a flowery top, un-matching striped skirt and a permed haircut rinsed in considerable purple dye, she never failed to stand out when she was there to eat. Each day she came in at twenty-to-nine, ordered the same thing (eggs, bacon, black pudding, two slices of toast – no butter, and a sausage – well done) and demolished the breakfast over a period of twenty minutes or so, all whilst seemingly enamoured by whatever images were flashing over the television like a toddler seeing a magic show for the first time. But she was usually no bother, keeping herself to herself and only occasional tutting at what she saw on the TV, so Gerald felt it perfectly acceptable to leave her in the main body of the building whilst he slipped out into the back room to make a phone call. Lifting up the landline handset he read a number of a scrap of paper that he had held tightly in his fist and waited for an answer. When an answer came it was naturally a recorded voice dictating a series of options to him which Gerald reluctantly followed, finding himself wading through the automated telephone service equivalent of a garden maze, each left or right turn pushing him deeper into the construction but with no sign of the centre in sight. Eventually, after around seven to eight minutes, a human voice finally appeared on the other end, a Welsh woman with a guttural voice and the sound of a cold in its early stages. She introduced her safe as Megan and concealed a slight cough off-mic.

"Good morning, finally," Gerald spluttered in rage. "My

name is Gerald Woodstock of the Full Monty. I discovered yesterday that a new café is opening up quite literally across the road from me and I want to know who in the council has given permission for it to happen."

"Thank you for your query," Megan muttered, as if reading from a script. "All enquiries about new businesses need to be sent in writing by post or e-mail..."

But Gerald wasn't listening and he just continued speaking, words springing from his mouth like jets of water. In the background there was the sound of a chair scraping backwards as Sue finished her meal and got up to leave, looking around confused at the absence of Gerald who was usually so attentive in clearing away her cutlery and crockery and wishing her a good day. For a man who was so used to things happening in a way that could be described as just-so, today was turning into a day of shifting schedules.

"I find it frankly absurd," Gerald continued, sending out his wall of words, "that anyone in planning could even consider locating another café only metres from my front door. I have run this business for probably more years than half of your staff have been on this earth and for that I demand some respect, not to have some cocky upstart fresh from cookery college coming here and challenging my livelihood. I will not stand for it, you hear?"

And Megan did hear, but didn't really respond in anything other than how you'd expect a low-paid member of staff reluctant and unwilling to deviate from the script printed out in front her by her manager, would respond, the script currently pinned up on a noticeboard next to a photo of her and her boyfriend (Kevin) on their last holiday (Kent) and an old bus ticket she couldn't remember why she'd kept. Megan continued, in her spittle-filled Welsh-heavy accent, to confirm the need for written confirmation. After playing verbal tennis between his anger and her refusal to budge from protocol, alongside the appearance of Sue peering around the doorway from behind the counter wondering where Gerald had gone, he realised his attempts at reason were futile and ended the call in an abrupt manner. He replaced the handset in a half-slam and stormed back through, pushing Sue back into the room like you would move a stubborn dog towards the vet and toward the door, wishing her a good day in a tone of voice entirely contradictory to that statement before shutting and locking the door, confusing two men in high-vis jackets who had just been moments away from popping in for their late-breakfast meals of bacon sandwiches. Gerald gave them a hint at how he felt by returning to the door and turning the 'Open' sign back to 'Closed'. He needed ten minutes break to compose himself after the call. And, of course, a stiff coffee which he began brewing from himself.

It was only as he was pouring some coffee granules into a cup he noticed that there was a man sat at one of the tables, a figure he sort of recognised but he couldn't put his finger on where from. As they made eye contact the man got up from the seat – on which he had only been temporarily sat, sat at right-angles to how you'd normally sit on one – and approached the counter.

"A bacon sandwich with a fried egg please," he requested. Gerald's gaze moved from staring into the man's eyes like the star of a perverted rom-com where the romantic lead was an overweight older man in a grease-stained apron and the object of his affections was a thinner muscular builder, to the rest of his body. Then it clicked.

"You're one of the men working across the road aren't you?" Gerald asked with venom laced around each word. The man nodded.

"On the new café? Yes," he confirmed verbally. There was a momentary pause between them, the sort of pause you'd get from a lion studying its prey before deciding to pounce and devour the unexpected victim. But this time it was Gerald, an angry human being, ready to pounce, and pounce he did with a loud growl from deep within his chest.

"How dare you!?" he exclaimed, grabbing the man by his collar and almost choking him, surprise etched on the builder's face as he was pulled forward from the unexpected grab. "Get out of my café!"

The man didn't need telling twice, yanking himself out of the grip and stumbling backwards, his eyes bulging with shock. Regaining his composure and use of his tongue the man issued a few choice insults in Gerald's direction before turning to leave, his departure not quite as smooth as he would have liked, due to the locked door. Only a fumble with the key, a turn of the handle and an awkward bump into the two men still stood outside waiting in the hope of *The Full Monty* opening up again, meant the builder had made his escape. Gerald by now had followed him to the door, thrown a few choice words of his own in the direction of the fleeing builder and dismissed the two men waiting with a narrowing of his eyes. One man raised a finger in query about whether *The Full Monty* was open for business but Gerald silently confirmed otherwise by slamming the door closed again and locking it. For the first time ever on a day that wasn't a public holiday, Gerald's business was closed early. And he was fuming.

*

A cigarette, an afternoon in front of the television and a reflection on the day's events had turned Gerald into a calmer figure overnight and it was business as usual the next day, and the day after and the day after that. In fact things continued in a familiar rhythm for much of the next ten days. It was only when a cold and rainy Monday morning heralded the appearance of a bread van and a butcher's van in quick succession to the new café opposite – the vehicle's arrivals seen through narrowed eyes through even narrow blinds – that Gerald realised battle was now commencing. *Caf-ay Up* was open for business.

Not much happened at first other than a few whispers and the occasional irregular customer swayed to give the new kid on the block a try. But then it started to build momentum: firstly the occasional customers jumped ship to the new venture then some of the more regular customers, and then even some of the hard-core customers who had been coming for years started disappearing. The final straw for Gerald was when even Sue, who had always, always come to the Full Monty for her morning sustenance stopped coming and became a regular of *Caf-ay Up*. Soon numbers were low and there were times when *The Full Monty* was entirely devoid of any customers, something that had never, ever happened. It was after one particularly slow day that Gerald grabbed Sue on the street as he walked to the newsagent and her to bingo.

"What is it about this new place that is so good?" he asked her. "Is it because it's new?"

Sue paused for a moment and thought. "Well it's cleaner than your place. The food is nicer. But ultimately it's because he's cheaper. Your full English is £5.80. Theirs is £4.99. It's simple market economics."

Gerald would normally have been taken aback by a) Sue's bluntness and b) her use of the term *simple market economics,* but was instead distracted by the poster in the window of his competitor that he'd never noticed before. It was simple. It was bright yellow. It had big capital letters emblazoned in red. And it said. 'Our full English is much nicer. All that you want for under a fiver'. Part of Gerald admired the inventiveness of the slogan, but the vast majority of him despised it. He was being undercut and with margins like that there was nothing he could do about it. Now was the time to act.

Gerald wished Sue a reluctant 'Good day' and dismissed her company, walking with determination over to the front door of his rival café, banging on the entrance with the back of his fist. It was quickly answered by the young man he'd seen weeks earlier. He smiled. Gerald didn't like him already.

"What the fuckin' hell are you playing at?" he asked, the swear-word sitting so prominently within the question it felt considerably at odds with Gerald's usually pleasant demeanour. The young man in front of him blinked once, but otherwise didn't waver at, or react to, the question. Instead he peeled off a blue hygiene-boosting glove and thrust out his arm as if to receive a handshake. It wasn't reciprocated.

"I take it you are Gerald? Of *The Full Monty*?" the man asked. The older, taller, gruffer man staring at him made a gesture with his head that could have been interpreted as a nod. "I'm Ollie. Nice to make your acquaintance at last. Now I know what you're thinking; that I've come here and upset the applecart or whatever. But it's only business. Competition is good right? It helps give customers choice..."

But Gerald wasn't listening. He just choked some insults

back and instead waggled a finger in Ollie's direction, his face unnervingly close to the other man's face it was worrying. Ollie could smell the stale tobacco and coffee on Gerald' breath.

"You listen here Oliver. Either you play ball around here, or face the consequences. I will not go down without a fight."

There was a pause as Gerald waited for Ollie to make his move but he remained resolutely unfazed. "In that case," he said crisply. "May the best man win."

And it was those five words that started it all off.

The rivalry between the two businesses started off small with a succession of price drops that saw customers ping-ponging between the two cafés as the price of a full English switched venues for being the cheapest each day. But when that became unsustainable the battleground went online, with the Facebook pages of each café the new home for the trading of insults. Gerald didn't even know how to use Facebook – the page had been set up by his nephew – but he had help in posting comments and more across the network. And soon it began to ramp up with hate-tweets, hate-mail and hateful words being spat across the street by the two patrons. At what point Gerald was even sent a poison pen letter where Heinz ketchup had been used as the ink.

Soon the rivalry between the two businessmen became newsworthy after Ollie hung a banner outside his café promoting 'Count on us for the best breakfast' which some wag had edited over night with a pair of scissors and a black marker to remove much of the sentence and change the first word to something less savoury. Soon journalists were interviewing the pair and the die-hard customers of the respective cafes in a headline that read *'Breakfast Club becomes Fight Club'* though there was much disdain in the office that they could find no pun-filled headline to rival the battle between two rivals fish and chip takeaways from a few years ago that went documented under the strapline *'A Tale of Two Chippies'*.

It wasn't long before the battle between the two

businesses was the talk of the town and Gerald and Ollie's on-going attacks were the subject of every piece of gossip shared on street corners and of idle chats in the post office, as everyone had their own thoughts of who was in the right, with many heated discussions coming out of divided loyalties. Pints were even thrown in anger in one particularly loud and violent discussion in the local pub one Thursday evening, which saw the quiz cancelled after the host was knocked to the ground by a surprisingly hefty punch from one Ollie-supporter.

Soon the battle came to a head one Friday lunchtime when Gerald responded angrily to what he deemed to be the final straw: opening up a fresh delivery of eggs to find a swear word appearing letter-by-letter over each egg in red felt tip. He stormed out of *The Full Monty*, charged across the road and demanded Ollie join him outside, which he soon did, finding Gerald standing in the middle of the street in a pose that resembled Clint Eastwood if he had been a middle-aged man with a beer-gut and a stubbly chin at the height of his fame. He stood with a sauce bottle in one hand and a spatula in the other, grasping them like guns in a holster – what *High Noon* would have looked like if its conclusion had been plagued by product placement and directed by Henry John Heinz instead of Fred Zinnemann.

Ollie, in response, grabbed a pair of tongs from the side shelf of his kitchen and a bottle of vinegar and mimicked his pose further down the road. A knot of intrigued locals gathered on either side of the street. What little traffic there was about came to a standstill. The postman stopped what he was doing and waited the next move from either of them with baited breath. Gerald was the first to speak.

"You came here Ollie and have tried to ruin me. I will now and ruin you."

Ollie smirked and tried his best to construct a witty reply. "The only thing you could ruin," he said with a theatrical bent to his voice as if trying to appeal to the crowd, "is a fried breakfast, which you do each morning!"

Gerald's lip curled. "As the famous saying goes, you are what you eat. In that case you are a soggy mess served up on a cheap platter."

Ollie struggled to follow up that insult – he had hoped Gerald was serving Spotted Dick so he could work that into an insult, but the dessert board instead promoted a chocolate flan – and so instead settled for something unashamedly crass. "Then you too are what you eat. And what all your customers eat. A little shit."

Gerald's face reddened. "I'll give you shit," he called before charging forward. If the movie analogy was continuing the movement of the two men running toward each other to engage in battle was like the final fight in a *Matrix* movie, only the two protagonists were running in an awkward uncomfortable stance and instead of trading blows like trained ninjas it was more like handbags at dawn, a messy fist-fight ensuing that saw Ollie receiving a spatula to the face and Gerald tongs to the crotch, whilst sauces were deployed all over their opposite numbers like a culinary Jackson Pollock gone wrong. Pedestrians either side of the road began cheering and booing in turn, egging them both on, as metallic utensil clashed against metallic utensil, in a battle of wits and cutlery, both fighters panting with exertion and struggling to maintain focus.

Soon supporters of either establishment were joining in to stop the two men accidentally killing the other as they realised things were getting serious, but they too soon found themselves covered in sprays of ketchup or vinegar, yelps coming from those receiving red sauce or sharp, acidic liquid to their eyes. Soon small throngs of supporters had broken off into their own little fights, scuffles over the qualities of both establishments and tiffs over their respective pricing structures. The battle only finished as both of the central two men dispensed of their utensils and condiments and grabbed each other by the shoulders, forcing each other to the ground and engaging in a bare knuckle battle on the zebra crossing, like two apron-wearing pugilists, failing to correctly scan a bar code with their bodies. It only ended when both retired hurt, out of breath, bruised and black and blue, laying on their backs still clutched to one another like a romantic liaison gone wrong. Not that many romantic liaisons where both parties were out of breath and tired also included the location of the middle of a street, in broad daylight, surrounded by retired men and women.

Gerald and Ollie soon found themselves both removed from the scene by ambulance, such was the drama of the occasion, with the threat of police action not too far away as two tall policemen cautioned them about causing a disturbance with their food-based fracas. As the emergency vehicles darted away the street soon returned to normal, the traffic flowing once more and the postal deliveries concluding.

The ambulances soon arrived at the hospital whilst the police went to deal with an escaped sheep from a nearby farm, but with the promise they would return to question the two individuals later. After being patched up by doctors over the next few hours, both men were ready for recuperation, but in an exercise of NHS bed-blocking, Gerald and Ollie somehow ended up in beds next to each other in the local hospital, but as both were tightly bandaged up – Gerald's leg up in plaster, Ollie's arm held tightly in place by his side – neither could continue the fight and instead could only exchange words of venom across the small gap between them both.

But soon something miraculous happened and they began to form a sort of truce, both men seemingly swallowing humble pie – something not really ever imagined on either of their menus – and working out their differences over a couple of hours. Gerald began by apologising for his behaviour and soon Ollie was saying sorry for his choice of business, and admitting he'd always wanted to be a greengrocer ("I love the smell of a ripening marrow. I'm actually a vegetarian. I've not eaten bacon in twelve years") but his father – who was funding the business – had said there was no money in such a venture and demanded he opened a café instead.

"On reflection," Ollie admitted, "I should have followed my heart all along. I'll speak to my father when we're out of here and set things right."

The pair would have shaken hands on this decision but the state of their limbs prevented them from sealing the deal. After just a handful of hours in hospital they were now firm friends and could laugh about the events of the last few weeks ("I don't know what I was thinking writing a letter using ketchup – it was bloody difficult!"), and they had something finally to enjoy that afternoon as Joseph Carpenter arrived with a large wicker basket that he placed down in the middle of them both on a small table. He lifted up the lid to reveal that it was stuffed to the brim with delicious looking fruit and vegetables, all shiny and fresh.

"For you both," he said with a smile, "To aid recuperation."

Joseph beamed at them both before adding "I hope you've both worked a way forward together."

"We have," confessed Gerald. "Ollie here will be changing his business back to where his heart really lies. *Caf-ay-Up* will be no more. He will instead be bringing fruit and vegetables to the people!"

It was only as the words left Gerald's mouth that he realised what he had said, and his smile faded. Joseph looked back at them both, his eyes narrowing. It was then that he was joined by his daughter, Amy (a petite girl with a pleasant grin and even more pleasing eyes), who placed a final piece of fruit – a pineapple – on top of the basket, her beaming smile infectious. But it was soon wiped from her face as Joseph turned to her and spoke.

"Looks like Oliver here is setting up competition against us," he said, thinking of his very own *Carpenter's Fruit and Veg* on the high-street just down from *The Full Monty*, who had provided fruit and vegetables for over two decades. "I think, Amy, you should return to the van and fetch up those coconuts."

"But they're not ripe yet and really hard."

"I know," Joseph said with relish, licking his lips and staring hard at Ollie laying there in the hospital bed. "The harder the better for our friend here. It's time for me to practice my old cricket throw I think."

Ollie swallowed hard and looking over to Gerald. It seemed that battle was about to commence once more.

You Are What You Eat

By J. McGraw

Patient records for Mr Julius Maldavern, Esq., day patient at the Pluisant Hospital and Home for the Imbalanced on 2nd Augur 921. Patient No.:MAL2564. Attending physician: Dr. G.Q. Teneslaw.

2nd August:

Mr Maldavern was admitted by his wife, who described a series of extraordinarily peculiar symptoms which were, initially, dismissed as imaginings brought on through stress. Having conducted a thorough examination, I found no physical ailments, while the only mental trouble appeared to be an unwillingness to speak. None of the symptoms which his wife had reported were visible at that time.

Being unwilling to admit the man solely for substandard communication skills, I returned with him to his wife and explained the situation. It was then that Mrs Maldavern produced a lunch box and requested a moment more of my time.

I will admit to being ill-prepared for what she then showed me. Within the lunch box were a series of carefully prepared morsels of food, ranging from bite-sized pieces of meat to slices of vegetables, and even half a boiled egg. Explaining what each morsel was, she proceeded to feed it to her husband.

Upon eating a cube of beef, Mr Maldavern pushed his chair backwards and fell to all fours, producing a lowing sound and attempting to graze on the carpet. Feeding him a piece of chicken resulted in him crouching, with his arms held close to his sides, and making a soft clucking noise. The half-egg made him roll into a ball and lie very still. Mrs Maldavern found it difficult to make him eat in this position, but eventually managed to feed him a stick of carrot, which had him back on his feet, standing very straight. Mrs Maldavern explained that her husband now had a very restricted diet where vegetables were concerned, as she found it difficult to watch him attempting to force himself into small spaces as a result of eating peas, or trying to curl himself up to form a bell pepper.

Further conversation revealed that Mr Maldavern was capable of mimicking the food he ate even when he was unaware of what that food was. To demonstrate, she produced a final piece of meat which I could not immediately identify, and fed it to her husband. From his reaction, I guessed the meat to be pork, which she confirmed. With her permission, I attempted this experiment myself, using a slice of lamb from the remains of my lunchtime sandwich. I refrained from explaining what the meat was, and as it was sliced so thinly I do not believe Mr Maldavern could have recognised it. No sooner had he tasted it than he was on all fours again, but this time he began barking angrily and jumping up at me. I attempted to restrain him while Mrs Maldavern produced another stick of carrot, but despite all my care Mr Maldavern managed to bite me sharply on the hand, drawing blood.

Immediately, he stopped barking and stood upright again. With immense embarrassment, and in a tone exceedingly similar to my own, he apologised for his behaviour and for causing me harm. We shook hands, and he suggested to his wife that they return home. Her amazement left her speechless for some minutes after this remarkable transformation, allowing me to interrogate Mr Maldavern properly.

Mr Maldavern was, he says, aware of his actions since the moment the illness took hold of him, approximately one week prior to our meeting, although he was not in control of it. He praised his wife for a diet predominantly composed of long, straight vegetables, as he believed that had saved both of them a great deal of trouble, and had hidden the extent of his illness from their neighbours. He also believed that he was feeling quite himself again, and once his wife had recovered her senses, thanked me profusely for my help and took his leave.

This episode occurred two days prior to this report being written. Currently, I await further news of Mr Maldavern's condition, although if he had suffered a relapse I suspect I would have heard of it before now.

Addendum: Although not relating directly to the case, I feel I should add that I have reported my ostensible lamb sandwich to the canteen management, and will no longer be eating food provided by them.

You Are What You Eat

By Lauren K. Nixon

Maisie hugged her mother's case tight to her front.

Of all the tasks her mother set her, this was her least favourite. Even scrubbing the floor of the laboratory, with all the viscous and unpleasant liquids that somehow accumulated there, was better than this.

She stood warily in the small patch of dry pavement beneath the porch. Maisie had been coming to this particular shop at this particular hour, every other Thursday since she was four years old. Back then, of course, her older brother had been with her; it seemed like a long time since he had left for school and far away shores.

In a few years she, too, would depart and one of her mother's assistants would have to come here in her stead.

She bit her lip, staring up at the gold lettering on the glass, bubbled and flaking with decades of rain and sunlight. Gathering all the courage she possessed, she squared her shoulders as only a nine-year-old could and reached for the bright, brass handle. It was warm under her hand, and clammy – like some living thing. She let go of it as quickly as she could and wiped her hand distractedly on the skirt of her pinafore.

Every time Maisie walked through this door, she imagined (with unsettling clarity) that she would never again be able to leave.

The shelves towered above her, dusty and distant. It was always dark inside the shop and it always took a few moments for her eyes to adjust. Maisie held her breath, trying not to pay too much attention to the hammering of her small heart; she was sure it was loud enough that anyone might hear it.

Or any*thing*.

Something, deep in the gloom, went 'gloop'.

Slowly, the familiar jars and boxes emerged from the shadow. Maisie tried not to look at anything too closely. Sometimes she was sure she saw things looking back.

With great trepidation, she approached the counter. In her many visits to the shop she had learned to anticipate it; for a few seconds before it happened, the dimly burning lamps that smelled faintly of hot tin would flare, responding to the crackle of energy in the air. It had taken years, but she had begun to be able to sense it, that sudden lens flare before the fact, and now it seemed strange to her that there had been a time before she had known how to see it.

With the sense that the air around her was being squeezed somehow, Maisie peered into the gloom above the counter. It was empty and then, quite suddenly, it wasn't.

Maisie bit her lip hard enough to draw blood. She hadn't screamed. She hadn't even flinched this time.

"Very good, Miss Hawthorn," came the voice, coarse and gravelly as the grave.

It always reminded her of the cemetery she walked through on her route home. The cemetery didn't frighten her nearly as much as the shopkeeper did. The people there were sleeping: this one really wasn't.

A hand extended, pale and withered; expectant.

"List."

Maisie hurried to comply, pulling the carefully folded scroll of parchment out of the pocket of her dress. It was snatched from her fingers with the usual temerity. She suppressed a shudder as the thin, cold fingers brushed her own.

"I see the doctor's research has moved on a pace," he observed, scanning the list.

Maisie tried not to look at the pale, stretched skin around his lips, or his dreadfully yellow eyes.

"Yes, Mr January," she said, though her voice came out as nothing more than a whisper.

"You're a good child, coming in each fortnight to help your mother."

"Yes, Mr January. Thank you, Mr January."

The skeletal creature nodded, once, their bi-monthly pantomime complete: Maisie Hawthorn would pretend that she wasn't afraid and Mr January would pretend to have any feeling for a being under the age of twenty.

He began mumbling to himself, selecting items from the shelves and marking them off against the list.

Wordlessly, Maisie handed over her mother's case. Mr January took it from her without a second glance, which was somehow better than conversation. A small concession for her, perhaps, or a rare example of fellow feeling.

When he talked she could no longer pretend that all this was simply a bad dream.

The jars were lined up on the counter as if they were queueing up to get in the bag. It was the only place in the whole shop where Maisie couldn't avert her gaze. Instead she stood, rooted to the spot, staring at their grisly contents: a liver; a heart; two ears; a whole jarful of eyes.

It was different each time, though some things remained the same. Her mother always bought tea, for example, and more ink for her assistants, who seemed always to be running out. Sloppy record keeping was one of Doctor Hawthorn's pet peeves. There were always matches and candles, and old, worn pennies for the gate.

There were always dark, slippery things that defied description and still beating hearts, pulsing away in their glass cages, uselessly pumping fluid. The subjects had to eat, her mother told her, and Mr January sold the finest specimens.

Maisie tried not to think about where he got them from.

Maisie eyed the jelly-like eyeballs warily, watching them eyeing her back. She hated carrying eyes – it always felt like they were peering at her, even from inside her mother's case.

Mr January packed them carefully into the case. When he was done, Maisie expected him to ask for money; she was used to settling the account for her mother. Both she and Mr January knew that Maisie could be trusted with money. The terror of being locked inside Mr January's shop or, worse, in the cages with her mother's subjects, was just too horrible for her to contemplate changing the amount on the receipt and spending a penny on sweets. Besides, her mother didn't approve of sweets.

This time, however, Mr January put the list down on top of the case and moved towards the partition in the counter. He lifted it carefully and beckoned to Maisie.

She stared at him, stunned. Not once, in five years, had Mr January asked her to go behind the counter. Nor had he asked her brother, who had found the task just as unpleasant as she. Years ago, before he had become little more than a series of letters and a doll on Christmas morning, he had joked that anyone who went behind that counter was never seen again.

Staring, horrified, at the ancient shopkeeper, Maisie couldn't shake the conviction that *exactly that* was about to happen.

"Come," said Mr January in a commanding tone. When it became clear that Maisie wasn't going to move, he took her arm, his sharp, bony fingers closing around her flesh.

She didn't cry out; she couldn't. Her mouth didn't seem to be obeying her brain.

Inexorably, Mr January led her towards the back door of the shop, the dark wood looming large and impossibly terrifying before her.

A horrible sawing noise came from above her and she couldn't help it, she looked up. Maisie stopped dead, unable to decide whether this was actually more frightening: Mr January was laughing.

"I'm not going to eat you, child," he said, though Maisie wasn't entirely sure she believed him.

He met her eyes.

"You may believe me."

Maisie chewed her lip. He did seem to be fairly earnest – and of all the times she had visited the shop he had never shown any interest in eating her... Though of course, he could simply have been biding his time. She glanced over her shoulder and thought about her brother's stories, and her mother and the assistants back at the laboratory. They would notice if the supplies didn't arrive on time – they would know exactly where she was.

The pressure on her arm wasn't painful, either, simply an act of guiding her.

Finally, realising that Mr January was actually waiting for her permission to continue, she nodded, still frightened, but taking comfort in the gentleness of a walking corpse.

"Thank you," he said, and released her arm. "The doctor

requires a special order this week," he explained, walking towards the door.

Maisie followed him tremulously, her entire body shaking with fear.

"I keep my special collections in the back."

The door ahead of them creaked open without any obvious instruction and Mr January strode through it.

There were more shelves back here, but fewer body parts, which was something of a relief. Despite her fear, Maisie began to peep at every shelf, every packing box. Each item was carefully labelled in faded, spidery handwriting. She caught snatches of text: 'Butterflies, Blue', 'Egyptian Amulet – Definitely Cursed', 'Curried Eels', 'Soot – Fire of London', 'Shrouds, Assorted'.

She caught up with Mr January, who appeared to be waiting for her, a cryptic expression on his face. Three feet from the end of the row, Maisie stopped dead in her tracks. Something – some deep, primal instinct – had stopped her in her tracks. She felt it in every fibre of her being; it was as if her skin was vibrating from the sheer, raw power ahead of her.

"You can feel it?"

She looked up at Mr January, surprised. Of course she could feel it. This was a magic so loud that everyone in the street should be able to feel it, except... She frowned. Clearly, they couldn't feel it, if none of them had complained or moved away.

"Yes," she whispered.

"Curious." Mr January beckoned her again. "They cannot harm you."

Swallowing hard, Maisie turned the corner, forcing herself to put one foot in front of the other. She stopped again. She had been prepared for dark artefacts, for more body parts, for people, even, trapped like the butterflies in the packing cases. She hadn't been prepared for them to be beautiful.

This entire room – which must have been an annexe to the original building – was full of glass jars of every shape and size. They covered the walls, the ceiling – there were even jars in compartments in the floor. Each one of them glowed, soft and bright at the same time, seductive. Maisie wanted to reach out and caress the brilliant balls of light and, after a moment, she realised she was walking forwards, arm outstretched.

Unnerved, she forced herself to stop and turn back to Mr January. He was watching her closely.

"Curious," he said again.

Maisie frowned, unsure. She took a breath.

"What – what are they?" she asked, her voice seeming quiet and small in the room of brightly coloured orbs.

In all the years she had been coming here, she had never asked him a question before, and Mr January regarded her for a moment before speaking.

"Curious."

Maisie wasn't sure if this was an answer, or a comment on her behaviour. Mr January reached for a tall jar, containing a deep green orb, and held it out. Trembling slightly, Maisie took it.

Immediately she was struck by the overwhelming sensation of motion; she swayed, clutching the jar, feeling an overwhelming sense of melancholy. She felt deep and boundless and empty, ancient: like there was no end to her at all. She tasted salt and seaweed, heard gulls crying.

The jar was gently removed from her fingers. Maisie reached up and was surprised to find tears on her cheeks.

"The sound of the sea," Mr January explained, putting the jar back on its shelf.

Maisie shivered. She had never felt anything like it. She had never even seen the sea, or heard a seagull. She didn't understand. Mr January pointed to another jar, this one red and rosy, like an apple. She reached out for it, hungry for more.

This time the sensation was softer, sweeter. In her mind's eye she could see a river in summer, hear the laughter of children. Something sweet and warm in her mouth.

She managed to put the jar back herself this time.

"The taste of cherries," said Mr January. He pointed at another jar, and another. "The smell you get after it rains; light on the water; tears at a funeral; a baby's sighs..."

Maisie looked around, her eyes following his pointing finger, pleased that she had been brave enough to follow him into this extraordinary room full of extraordinary things. She realised that she was no longer afraid – only curious.

"How?" she asked, hoping that this strange impromptu lesson would continue.

"They are the fragments of souls," said Mr January, and Maisie's eyes went wide. "Captured moments of life. Your mother intends to feed them to your subjects – to give them a kind of consciousness."

"But that's – that's *awful*," she exclaimed, forgetting herself. "You can't steal people's souls!"

She slapped a hand over her mouth, horrified. Strangely, though, Mr January didn't seem angry at her. He seemed pleased.

"You are quite right, Miss Hawthorn," he said, and she thought she heard a note of approval, though she wasn't sure why. "To steal another's soul is a crime without equal. But to take a moment – an echo of that person's true being – that is perfectly acceptable. Nothing is stolen from the person."

Maisie thought about this.

"Like – like a gramophone?"

"Yes," Mr January nodded, slowly. "A little like that." He peered at her. "Can you hear them?"

Maisie frowned, confused.

"No, I –" she paused and put her head to one side. Before he had spoken she had thought the room was silent, but now, just on the edge of hearing... "I think so."

Mr January nodded again.

"Curious."

Maisie pursed her lips.

"I'm sorry, Mr January, but what is curious?"

"You are."

Carefully, he selected six jars from the shelves and began to make his way back to the shop proper. For a moment, Maisie was torn – she badly wanted to stay in this little room with all these singing, shining souls, but she was a well brought up young lady, and there was something about how badly she wanted to touch the jars that made her wary. She hurried after the shopkeeper, feeling an unaccustomed pang of regret.

Back in the shop, Mr January tucked the jars of souls into her mother's case and Maisie payed the balance of the account.

He paused before lifting the case off the counter. It would be heavy and Maisie was not looking forward to carrying it home through the rain.

"Are you afraid of me, Miss Hawthorn?" he asked, softly.

"No," said Maisie, and realised that actually, this was quite true.

"Good. Wait here a moment."

He lifted a quill and slip of parchment from the desk at the back of the shop and began to write. Maisie peered over the counter, trying (and failing) not to look too nosy. Mr January folded the parchment with a flourish and turned back to her.

"You will forgive my manner, Miss Hawthorn, but I wish to make you a proposition," he said, peering down at her. "Very few have the talent to detect the Moments and fewer still have the strength of will to resist them. You are a child of nine years old and you managed it in two attempts. I have seen you pause a moment before I appear and I suspect you can sense that, too."

Maisie gawped at him, then nodded.

"I thought as much. You have magic, Miss Hawthorn, a rare and dangerous talent. A talent that can destroy you and everyone around you if left untutored and unchecked." He lifted the parchment, sealed with black, shining wax. "I have here a letter for your mother – an offer of apprenticeship. The terms are thus: you reside here, above the shop and act as my assistant, carrying deliveries and learning the proper upkeep of my collections. You will receive room and board, and tuition in the art of magic – and, if you are careful and diligent, the art of taking Moments. You will become the next Soul Eater."

Maisie's heart began to beat faster and faster. To learn magic? That was a rare chance indeed.

She opened her mouth to speak, but the slightest movement of January's hand stilled her.

"This decision is not to be taken lightly, Miss Hawthorn," he told her, sternly, his voice soft and silky. "There is a cost. This aged body you see before you, this soul is over five hundred years old."

Maisie had absolutely no trouble believing that.

"The Moments take their toll. If you take this path you will age slowly – ever so much more slowly than everyone else. You will watch the ones you love wither and die."

Maisie swallowed.

"Your mother, your brother, your friends... should you fall in love, have children, you will lose them all in time." There was a pain in his voice now, a pain that Maisie couldn't quite quantify. "After all pass, you will remain. Do you understand me?"

"Yes," Maisie whispered. "I would become what you are..." She frowned. "Can you die?"

"Very easily," he responded, "but not of illness or old age."

That sounded like a bit of an advantage to Maisie, but she didn't say anything. It was comforting to know that the shopkeeper had a pulse.

"You will consider carefully," he told her, and Maisie realised that this wasn't an instruction, but an order. "And bring me your answer when you visit next."

"Yes, Mr January."

"Then perhaps we will speak further," he said, and handed her the letter.

Hands trembling – through excitement now, rather than fear – Maisie tucked it into the pocket of her dress.

She looked up to bid Mr January goodbye, something she had never considered before, but he was gone.

Maisie looked around; suddenly the jars of eyes and hearts were a lot less scary. It struck her that a man – even one that so closely resembled a zombie – who was so adamant about the proper treatment of souls wouldn't take body parts from anyone who was still using them.

She hefted her mother's case and struggled towards the door. Before she could reach for the handle, it swung open, an air of politeness about it. Maisie gaped at it for a moment, uncertain whether it had been her, Mr January, or the door itself.

"Thank you," she said, just in case, and started home.

Home. In two weeks, she would have to make a choice that could cast her onto a dark, uncertain path. In two weeks it might not be home at all.

She trudged through the rainy street, wondering if her mother might see her after dinner, when she enjoyed her nightly cigar. There was no question in her mind.

She would be back, and next time it would be her own case she was carrying.

Apricot

Heart

Apricot Heart

By Hannah Burns

She always used to buy them. Every Sunday she would walk down to the local market, where a little old man would sit every day from eight to three, churning out these decorative fruit pieces, but she always only every got the one type. I never remember why she started to do it. I just remember one day, an overcast Sunday, she went out to meet some friends, she came back with whole box of them, transfixed with how they had made, leaving it to the last possible moment to buy them.

The shop owner always has a box ready now, though now it's the shop keepers' son these days – the old man passed many years ago. It wasn't long before she became unable to walk down herself, so our Justine would go and always bring back that box for her; she always had the biggest smile on her face when she opened them, always saying that that boy had pick up his father's talent and love.

"I'm not sure now, what he will do with all his boxes, Mom, now you're gone, but I have one last box for you now. Your favourite: Apricot Hearts. Rest in peace Mom, and I'll remember to bring some up with me when I next see you."

The Chance Encounter of Apricot Heart

By Philip Lickley

If I were ever to interview my father, for whatever reason, there would only be three questions I would ever ask him. The first would be rather straight forward: why a goatee beard? My personal preference, of course, is for a well-groomed, clean-shaven man, but I can see the positives of a man with a well maintained beard, and the rugged look that entails. (Please don't judge me, we all have our personal tastes, okay? My friend likes men with nose piercings. That sort of thing turns my stomach!) But why a goatee beard? It's either the sign of someone who is too lazy to fully shave, or had found their shaver battery dying before the job could be finished. Or a way of hiding a double chin.

My second question would be about his childhood. I very rarely shared any stories with him other than my day-to-day goings-on and his work and I feel like I'm missing things about him as a young man. What did he do? Who did he hang around with? What were his hobbies? These questions and more still remain a mystery to me.

But my third question would be the most important. Why, father, did you pick the name *Apricot Heart* for your one and only daughter? April is a nice name. Then there's Natalie. Mary. Charlotte. All great names and normal. But *Apricot Heart?* Sometimes I would daydream about how the conversation would go, walking up on my father sitting in his chair reading some newspaper and asking him that key question.

> *A day dream:*
> *"Dad?"*
> *"Yes sweetie?"*
> *"Why did you name me Apricot Heart?"*
> *"That's easy. After my favourite fruit and body part."*

I hoped that if I ever did ask him the question that would not be the answer, but whatever his reasoning

Apricot Heart I was named and Apricot Heart I am. You can probably find me quite easily on Facebook. I am the only girl on their called Apricot, hidden somewhere amongst the fan pages for jam. Seriously, look them up. Some people have too much time on their hands – and jam seeds, I would assume. Twitter is more of a challenge. I'm nested between a collection of robotic accounts who re-tweet any mentions of apricot jam in recipes. Those people also have clearly have too much time on their hands, and some admirable programming skills too.

Sometimes I would console myself with other thoughts after I was old enough to realise the unusualness – some would say absurdity – of my moniker. I wasn't the only person I knew with a daft name. I went to nursery with a Holly Bush, who I'd often spend afternoons finger-painting away with. At school I heard rumours of a Roger Butts, but that could well have been an elaborate prank. Richard Head, a flat mate at University, was real though. He didn't take kindly about his first name being shortened to Dick, for obvious reasons. It didn't make his time in the rugby team a particularly great one. Many drinking circles were dedicated to a Carry-On level of euphemism when he was involved.

But, you know, having an unusual name sometimes helps. If you want to get recognised for something or have an application stand out it helps to have something unusual that will jump off the page for people, more so than a John Smith or Anthony Jones would. Plus it's a talking point if you would ever need some facts about yourself, like an ice-breaker at work or a television quiz. I'd often thought what I would put down as my five interesting facts if I ever got onto a show like Pointless or whatever – a friend once got through to the audition stage of The Chase and told me such personality pointers were actively sourced – and outside of my unusual name and the fact that as a party trick I can dislocate my left arm there's not much else worth mentioning that makes me standing out. I suppose I'm good with computers but isn't everyone these days? Most kids are born with a tablet in one hand and a mobile phone in the other.

Which must make giving birth painful.

The machine beeps.
"I'm sorry Mrs Smith but the baby's coming iPad first.
And it's a first generation fully sized one. Nurse! Pass the
sedatives!"

Yesterday, though, my unusual name certainly came in
useful. To fully round out the story there are a few things
you need to know about me other than my name, my lack
of sharing stories with my father, my dodgy left arm and
my occasional drifts into fantasy. I live in London and
work as a receptionist for a taxi firm. I travel daily on the
Tube to work from home and back again several hours
later. And I'm also single. Not necessarily by choice, but
more habit. I wouldn't class myself as a confident person.
I've never really plucked up the courage to ever ask anyone
I've fancied out on a date. Well, that's not entirely true. A
couple of months ago I did ask an acquaintance if they
wanted to go to see a film and get something to eat at the
tail end of a conversation and though my suggestion was
accepted it was sort of accepted in the way you'd say yes to
grabbing a pasty from Greggs on the way to the bus
station. It's not often that you can ask someone out on
what is essentially a date and them not even realise that
was what it was. That, in a nutshell, is my life.

"So, maybe a film and dinner? Oh and here's a box of
chocolates and fancy a coffee, maybe back at my flat?"
"Oh – I didn't get the subtext..."

So yesterday I'd gone to work as usual, packing my
belongings into a small shoulder bag, heading out of the
door and onto a bus, which took me within a few metres of
the nearest Tube station. I was particularly tired, so much
so I didn't even bother playing bus driver roulette ("Will
they smile and return my 'Good Morning' or just stare at
my ticket like a vulture with piles, eyeing up a kill?" – it
was the latter, miserable sod) or even read a copy of the
Metro which sat alongside its other tabloid friends in the
plastic box on the bus, proclaiming on one page how a
female singer had told them she was tired of only being

known for her relationships and not her music and on the next page, without any hint of irony, talking about this same singer's new pop-star boyfriend. Instead I just sat in the one free seat, next to a balding man who had failed to use enough deodorant that morning, and fiddled on my phone, flicking absent-mindedly between Facebook, Twitter, 9gag and Candy Crush, before settling on a forum I enjoyed reading, not because it was something I was interested in, but because the comments were usually so absurd it was funny. You've heard of Godwin's Law? Basically that says that if any conversation online goes on long enough someone will be compared to Hitler or the Nazis. In the case of this site it's more about how quickly the conversation mentions something that even UKIP would find distasteful.

Classic example:
Bill posts: "I went to the chip shop yesterday and the fish was awful."
Michael: "It's under new owners. The last ones were much better. These new ones cook in vegetable oil and not beef fat. It's not the chip shop way!"
Simon: "I saw the new owners are Asian. Probably Muslim. It'll be halal. No wonder it's awful."

Having rolled my eyes and chuckled to myself about the weirdness of people, I was off the bus and into the underground, battling through crowds of people ebbing and flowing through the interchange like mindless zombies, cocooned in their worlds of newspapers, music and smartphone games. I grabbed my ticket, passed through the barrier and ambled along the concourse, down and over to my required platform, staring up and down the space at the smattering of people there. Many, it seems, were also lost in their phones or their music but there was one there that seemed different. He was tall – I'd say about 6-foot-2, with a mop of brown hair and a slightly rough unshaven face from two days growth. Sorry, I'm mentioning beards again. I think it's an obsession of mine. Maybe I should start a Tumblr account about it? I shall make a note of that and come back to that thought later...

He was dressed in a white shirt and dark-brown jeans, with a pair of converse shoes completing the look. There was no phone in sight, instead he appeared to be reading a book, though I couldn't make out the title from the creased spine. Intrigued I slowly and self-consciously made my way towards his general direction without trying to look as if I was actually heading over to him. Within a minute or so, though, I was within about a metre of my target. My handsome, rugged, tall target. Sorry, I'm drifting off again. I coughed as if to attract his attention but he didn't flinch. I coughed again but still nothing. I found myself, I think, biting my lip as if to think what to do next, which was, I discovered, to speak up. With all this coughing I'm surprised I wasn't attracting attention.

"Excuse me," one commuter would say. "Are you trying to attract the attention of that man you fancy or do you have Bird Flu?"

"I'm not sure," I would confess and the commuter would go back to fiddling on his mobile phone. Probably playing Angry Birds 2 new out this week. Ironically.

(I did mention that I enjoyed technology? I'd not played the new Angry Birds game yet. Don't judge me.)

"What's your book?" I asked in a croaky hoarse voice that couldn't really be heard over the generally noise of a large and rapidly filling Tube station that was punctuated with the background noise of shuffling feet, tinny bass and occasional tannoy announcements. Clearing my voice I repeated the three words again and this time he looked up from his book.

"It's called *Cloud Atlas*" he said in a friendly and warm voice, which made my heart flutter – a feeling I'd not felt for a long time. Come on Apricot, it was only four words. "It's about..."

"I know, I've seen the film!" I interrupted beaming. He smiled.

"Well it's better than the film. You can only really judge it once you've read the book."

My smile faded even though I think my face remained held in a static grin. He was a book snob, I was an ignorant kid who had paid twice as much to see the book on the screen rather than tackling it the proper way. My heart sank. I'd been here before.

"I'm a huge fan of the new Godzilla film. Very true to the originals," I said to a friend.

"I'm not so sure," they replied without a crack of a smile. "If you're familiar with the Ishirô Honda you'll find some serious flaws in the TransAtlantic adaptation..."

But, it wasn't all lost, it seemed, and with some careful manoeuvring – or in truth some ham-fisted attempts at starting a new conversation – we got into a lengthy and friendly chat about all sorts of subjects and all thoughts of my first question were forgotten. The five minutes that were there between my arrival at the station and the departure of my train disappeared quickly and after an announcement – which barely registered with me – my train was here, the doors sliding open. I made a gesture to walk onto the train with my newly found conversational partner, but in the moment I spent sort of gazing into his hazelnut-tinged eyes (sorry), three businessmen in suits yabbering into their phones, a young man with a skateboard and a woman in a tight dress and too much make-up had separated us and followed the man onto the train. I found myself being pushed back away from the carriage and I had to enter the train through the next door along. As the doors closed as the Tube prepared to depart I let me eyes jump from face-to-face in the carriage to try and find him, eventually my pupils settling on his face and I smiled. He might be twenty-thirty people away from me, but he wasn't out of reach. It's hardly *Total Wipeout...*

The announcer blares: "And now contestant Apricot Heart will attempt to walk swiftly across the train carriage of danger, past the commuters of doom and attempt to wrestle herself onto the moving cliff-face of the mysterious stranger. Oh wait, she's failed miserably, and fallen into the water."

All I can hear is Richard Hammond laughing at my failure. Presumably before going to collect a large cheque

from Amazon and making sure his colleague's dinner is
warm enough. Sorry. I'm digressing...

All I had to do now was get back to him, swap phone
numbers and bingo!
(That's my description of how it would feel like, not a
plan for a first date. Who would go to bingo on a first
date?)

Me: Hey, I thought it'd be cool to hang out with loads of
old women and students on our first date.
Him: Er... great. Then maybe after this we can go
crown green bowling or perhaps knitting?
Me: I suppose? Have you got a dabber?

For a moment I thought about how such a situation
could be turned around and most of my thoughts rested on
using the word dabber as a euphemism, but I shook such
thoughts from my head. I would not be taking him to
bingo. There is only one location for a first date and that's
for a meal. I clearly have set thoughts about what
constitutes a date. Maybe I should find a book to expand
my horizons? Pippa Middleton has probably written one.
With the carriage emptying slightly at the next station I
could finally make my move, squeezing through some gaps
to get a couple of metres closer. He'd now made eye
contact with me and smiled. I raised my eyebrows back in
a motion that I thought would say *I see you* but possibly
could be interpreted as wind or an unfortunate facial tic.
But he didn't seem to be put off by it and over the next few
minutes and two stations I got closer and closer until I
finally reached him, avoiding total wipeout. Sorry Richard
Hammond. Maybe next time.
"My station is next," I said, a little flustered. "Would it
be possible to like, swap numbers?"
"Sure," he said. "But I've left my phone at home in my
other jacket. Realised as I got to the station. That's gonna
make today difficult..."
"Don't worry!" I exclaimed perhaps a little too excitedly.
"I've got my phone, I can take your number, if you know
yours off by heart..."

What a stupid question. Who our age doesn't actually know their number off by heart?

I quickly opened up my shoulder bag and took out my phone and pressed the on button, and then my heart sank. It wasn't switching on. I'd not charged it last night. I pressed the button. Held it in. Tapped the gorilla glass like a monkey in a cage. None of these futile tactics made any sort of difference. Then what happened twelve hours ago came flooding back to me like a day-nightmare. I'd put my phone on the side and not on charge as I'd left the charger downstairs, and with the night being cold I hadn't been inclined to get out of the warmth of my bed and go to the chilly sitting room to pick it up. I cursed my laziness and I cursed my lack of heating. And my filmsy Winnie the Pooh pyjamas that looked great in the shop but offered very little warmth. I had to confess to my acquaintance.

(About my uncharged phone. Not my Winnie the Pooh pyjamas. I'd never confess those to anyone.)

"I seem to have forgotten to charge my phone. Perhaps I've got something to write with..." I said, thinking out loud.

Which is weird, as I usually think more internally in a sentence or paragraph tabbed right once to distinguish itself from the main crux of the story. But now my mind is truly wandering...

I began to scrabble around my shoulder bag for a piece of paper and pen but neither was forthcoming. The closest I got was a small pack of tissues and a lipstick but that would not do. "I don't suppose..." I half asked him and he shook his head.

"I'm travelling light. I can't even be trusted to remember my phone never mind pen and paper..."

I began to curse modern life under my breath and in my head. Damn phones and their poor battery life. Damn humankind for constantly striving for the latest technology at the expense of everything else. Damn my computer for being old and tired and not being able to play Netflix films at anything other than a snail's pace. I want my *Game of Thrones*. You know nothing Jon Snow!

That last observation might not have been that relevant to the current predicament I found myself in, really.

My predicament summed up life in 2015 though. Our phones do everything. They're our phone book, messaging service, social life planner, calendar, note taker, music player, camera and God knows what else. And when the battery dies through too much use we're then back to a temporary dark age. Want to phone a friend to meet up? Sorry, our brains have given up remembering people's numbers. Want to take a photo of a cute dog you see on the street? No phone, no camera. Want to remember what shopping you needed to get to restock the fridge? It's not accessible until you get home and charge it, and by then it's too late. Curse you, modern technology and the fact I no longer carry around a notebook and pen. I made a vow now to rectify this for the future, knowing full well I'd end up ignoring myself just like the time I thought about dragging around a digital camera 'just in case'. Or I'd end up like some sort of hipster carrying around old technology to make a point.

"Sorry I can't travel without a back-pack. I've got to have somewhere to carry my jotter, Polaroid, Sony Walkman, typewriter, notepad and wallplanner. Now excuse me, I have to head off to Paperchase to buy a pencil case in the shape of Harry Potter's wand… it's, like, limited edition!"

I smiled nervously at the man I had suddenly become so enamoured with. "Maybe I can remember your number?"

"079," he began. I nodded, committing those numbers to memory. I repeated them back. This wouldn't be difficult. It's hardly Mastermind.

"And today's contestant is Apricot Heart. And your chosen specialist subject is, the mobile numbers of everyone you know and care about. Question one. What is

the mobile number of your best friend Susie..."

"Pass."

John Humphreys sighs and wishes he was playing golf or something.

"536", he continued. I remember them. I recalled all six. He then gave me the remaining five. I read them back wrongly. This wasn't going to work.

"Your name!" I blurted out after thinking about some other ideas.

Your address? Too much like a stalker. E-mail? What if it's something even longer? Twitter handler? Come on. Who asks for a Twitter address off someone you fancy?

Me: Well I thought maybe I could express my feelings for you in 140 characters #unlikely

Him: Lol. #awkward

Me: Here is an emoticon of how I feel about you. No – not that button – that's the little poo with eyes. Oh God!

Part of me wondered why I'd not asked him his name earlier. Surely that's like first up on dating 101. Hell, it must be first on general introduction 101.

"It's Chris Evans," he told me. I stared at him blankly. Chris Evans. Now unless he's the radio DJ – which from the colour of his hair he wasn't – or the actor famous for being Captain America – which he wasn't, even if his chest did seem teasingly buff (sorry) – finding him out of many Chris Evans' again would be difficult. Imagine trying to find someone with a common name on Facebook, squinting at profile pictures and hoping that drunken shot of a night out in Ibiza is actually the man you met and not some weirdo who'll try and befriend you when you send a friend request. That wouldn't work.

"Yes, this is me, the Chris Evans you met on the train."

"Are you sure?" I'd say. "You look a balding forty-year-old man who still lives with his mother."

"My name!" I said a little too loudly. "You can find me. My name is Apricot Heart Williams. There's only one of me!"

I could see Chris mouthing my name subtly as if his

brain was trying to work out whether someone with such an eccentric name was eccentric themselves. If he did find my name funny, he didn't laugh. Which makes a change.

"Cool," he said smiling. "I can find you then."

And with that the train pulled into the station and I had to say goodbye to him, piling out of the carriage and onto the new platform, watching as the train shortly pulled away and disappearing into the dark tunnel with a hum of electricity and clatter of metal-on-metal. I raised my hand as if to wave him goodbye and to my surprise he returned the gesture. I smiled and that warm feeling barrelled through my chest again.

*

Work was, that said, expectedly tedious with little to report other than that it for once didn't rain on my lunchbreak when I ventured across the road to Starbucks for a café latte and a chocolate muffin, and it meant I could enjoy the lukewarm coffee and treat on a bench under a tree rather than back at work. That was another benefit of an unusual name in that they mostly spelt it right on the cup though I didn't often get into some endless conversations.

"Name?" asked some spotty youth who wished they were back at home playing Halo 5.

"Apricot."

"No, you didn't order a Vanilla Apricot White."

"No, that's my name."

"Apricot."

"What sort of name is that?"

"My name."

"Really."

"Yes. Now give me my fucking coffee or one of these over-priced date and walnut cookies are going up your nose."

I watched as the world went by, as the saying would go, all the time thinking about my encounter that morning. With my coffee and muffin polished off I took out my phone and checked. Nothing on Facebook. Not even an invite to *Mafia Wars*, that's how unpopular I was. Depressing status, self-publicity status, a quote attached to a picture of a stupid bloody Minion. It was all there just nothing from Chris.

I assumed that would be the way he'd find me right? He wouldn't just randomly Google my name would he? I hoped not as that would not be a great start. After finding a website about a construction company and a perfume that shared my name, he would get results back I wouldn't be particularly enamoured by.

3. Student Apricot Heart wins award for highest attendance at school [Too geeky]
4. Apricot Heart's Blog about boy band the Vamps [Speaks for itself]
5. "Why the shopping centre needs a Lego shop" [An article I wrote ten years ago that still haunts me.]
And the less said about the image results the better. That fifth image of me from a school production. Embarrassing, to say the least. I never made a good living tree.

It's now two days after my chance encounter with Chris and I wished now that my life was like a movie. No, not full of explosions like my whole being was directed by Michael Bay, or with Russell Brand making an unwanted cameo. In the respect that I could have merged the forty-eight hours of getting up, having breakfast, trudging to work, enduring work, getting the Tube home, making dinner and going to sleep, all whilst nervously checking my phone for any signs of a message into one short-running montage that I didn't have to live every minute of. Sadly life doesn't work like a movie – unless you mean it's expensive, often a little boring half-way through and ends too quickly – so it was two days of hell.

Maybe he's playing hard to get? Maybe he has developed sudden amnesia and forgotten my name? Maybe he has suddenly joined the Amish movement and can no longer use technology? It was painful waiting. Perhaps it was just not my week. Everything else seemed to be stuck in a loop of waiting. I was still waiting for an Amazon parcel in the post. I was still waiting for a plumber to come round to fix my drip-drip-dripping tap. And I was still waiting for my computer to update to Windows 10 when it had for everyone else. God, even Bill Gates hates me, and he even helps strangers in Africa.

But then, finally, after three days it happened, a Facebook notification. He had requested to add me as a friend. Naturally I didn't want to appear too eager in accepting so let it wait thirty minutes but it was with a nervous hand that I clicked accept and saw the confirmation of our new found digital friendship. A few moments later I then got a message.

"So, what are you doing Friday evening?"

I replied promptly.

"Nothing much. You?"

"Well I was thinking of going out for a meal. Fancy joining me?"

"Sure."

Not too eager. Not too forward. A good reply.

"Great. Then I'll see you 8 p.m. at Charing Cross."

"It's a date."

I immediately regretted posting it but my fingers were too hefty on the screen to reach the delete key quickly enough. I meant, it's a date in the calendar term of course. Idiot.

"I suppose it is. Looking forward to it!"

I smiled.

*

Without the aid of a montage still absent from the film that is my life...

"Coming soon to cinemas," blared the film-guy narrator, *"The Chance Encounter of Apricot Heart. See one young woman battle social anxiety, poor life choices and a diet with far too poor chocolate-to-vegetable ratio in a thrilling battle of surviving. Total Film called it "surprisingly bland", Empire gave it two stars..."*

Friday took an age to come naturally, especially as when you're waiting for something, time drags. But it wasn't a huge wait before I found myself at three minutes to eight – according to the large digital clock – standing on a busy and bustling Charing Cross station, the familiar buzz of smartphone-handling commuters ambling about with something you'd hope was purpose. The digits of the clock switched over to the hour and as if on cue Chris appeared dressed in a short-sleeved chequered shirt, black jeans, well-polished shoes and a hat. Yes, a hat. That was unexpected. I felt a little over-dressed though, wearing as I was a blue dress that rested neatly on my hips. My look seemed to please Chris who beamed and complimented me on my look, which was directly from the House of Primark. It's popular, I'd heard, on the catwalks of Milan, New York and Morecambe.

"You look beautiful," he said. I could feel myself blush.

"You scrub up well yourself. So, where are we going?"

"To a little bar I know, a couple of stops down. After you," he said gesturing at the half-empty Tube train that had pulled into the station. We both got on and sat together.

"At least this time we don't have to shout across a carriage," I noted in a sort-of embarrassing attempt at making conversation, to which I added, "and I charged my phone up."

Chris nodded as if actually managing to plug a power cable into a phone was some sort of major achievement. He added: "And I remembered mine, which is always a good start. Perhaps we could finally exchange numbers."

I nodded and we did.

The second stop shortly appeared alongside the dusty carriage windows, the doors sliding open, and we left the underground, moving up into the twilight of a shopping street still surprisingly busy with people milling around with shopping bags, the crisp night air hitting my face as we stepped up from the last step. Chris gestured with his muscular arms – sorry, too much detail again – and I followed in the general direction he pointed.

"Where are we going?" I asked him after a couple of

minutes, my dress not really providing the necessary warmth on the evening. I might as well have turned up in my Winnie the Pooh pyjamas for all the good this dress was doing.

He responded with one word – *here* – and I looked up at the building. It was a fancy-looking cocktail bar called *Juliet's* with the bar's name emblazoned in hefty florescent pink neon above an equally flamboyant awning. Chris gestured for me to go in and I took a couple of steps up and into the building.

Inside, Juliet's was surprisingly small but well fitted out, with an expensive-looking wooden bar, retro neon lighting and an attractive man behind the counter shaking cocktails. At least my dress fitted the room. As we took a secluded seat in the corner, some Spanish-language-version of *Don't Let Me Be Understood* began playing, its smooth South American vibe really suiting the mood. I smiled as I looked around the dimly-lit room and reached for a menu, running my finger down the cocktails. It must be classy; none of the cocktails have rude names. Chris smiled.

"You don't need a menu, I've ordered us something special."

"Already?"

"I'm a regular." He made a friendly hand gesture to one of the waiters who nodded and five minutes later – after we enjoyed a flowing and really bouncy conversation about the perils of catching trains – two reddish cocktails were placed onto the table. I lifted up the glass and twisted it around in my hand.

"What is it?" I asked.

"Try it," he said. I nodded and lifted the glass to my lips, taking a small sip of the drink. Here's hoping it wasn't spiked. The cocktail, instead, tasted delicious, the flavour familiar but I was unsure how.

"What's it called?" I asked looking at the menu, trying to place the taste with the ingredients listed. Chris laughed.

"It's not on the menu. I got them to make it especially for you. It's syrup, mint leaves, chilled orange pekoe, rum, lemon juice and Bailoni Gold. I call it the *Apricot Heart*."

His description and final reveal took me by surprise

mid-gulp. I looked at him in shock, apricot liquor sliding down my throat. I found it hard to get the next few words out. "The cocktail is named after me?"

"Absolutely," Chris said. "Thought it would be a nice treat for you. After all I could only get in touch with you because of your name."

"Well, yes, three days after we met."

"A man cannot appear to be too eager."

I smiled and took another mouthful of the drink. It was sweet and refreshing. And tasty. At this point I could compare the drink to my table partner but that would be a little crass and cheesy. But in truth I was thinking it.

"So the Apricot Heart..."

"Tastes great, with a sweet centre."

I smiled. That was perhaps a little cheesy to be honest but I let it slide. For the next hour we laughed, joked and enjoyed each other's company and tucked into a variety of cocktails on the menu, along with those knocked up out of our own imaginations. I don't think I'd felt like this in a long time. It was great. It was only on leaving the table to let nature take its course due to the five – or six – cocktails I'd consumed that things shifted. On leaving the toilet I glanced at my phone to see six missed calls, all from my mother. I cursed myself that I must have somehow switched my phone to silent.

Coming out of the toilet my gaze met Chris' and I nodded, gesturing that I was popping outside. He nodded, spotting me with my phone. I left the noise of the bar – the music continuing to sound like a higher class Nandos, that simile not quite capturing the classiness of the venue in truth – and headed outside to return the call. It was rare for my mother to call once never mind six times. My call was accepted and my mother spoke on the phone and told me what she needed to.

Oh shit, I thought.

*

I'm not a great fan of hospitals. The white corridors, blue scrubs, metallic surfaces. It's all very cold, as if all emotion of human life has been sucked out of everything. But here I was anyway, sat on a chair in a lifeless corridor nursing a rapidly cooling cup of coffee. After a few moments my mother emerged from side room and walked over to me, her face pale and make-up-less, bags hanging under her eyes like suitcases of sadness. Or something like that.

I placed my cup down on the floor and embraced her tightly, only pulling away when I sensed she was calmed.

"How is he?" he asked.

"Okay," she croaked. "He's speaking if you want to go in."

I nodded and left her in the corridor as I headed over to the room she had just come out of it, though she did stop me shortly before entering.

"Apricot," she called, a slightly mischievous grin drifting over her face, "who's the guy you came in with?"

"Just a friend," I beamed, the sadness of the moment sort of temporarily clearing as we shared a moment of mother-daughter bonding where she knew I was lying without me saying a word. She smiled and nodded as if she understood, knowing full well those three words didn't paint the entire picture.

Leaving my love life behind for a moment I entered the side room to find my father laid there in bed, his face pale and unshaven, a machine beep-beep-beeping in the corner and a drip snaking around his arm and into the fold in the limb. He smiled weakly as I entered.

"Hey Dad," I called, taking a seat next to him and nervously fidgeting with my hands.

My father had had what they figured was a heart attack earlier and was lucky to be alive. I asked him how he was, knowing that there was no easy or reassuring answer to that most vanilla of questions. He replied pretty nonchalantly, something about having luck on his side. If I'm being honest I wasn't truly listening, my mind flicking back to Chris waiting in the corridor. I quickly felt guilty and subdued the pangs by turning back to my father and chatting about everything yet nothing in particular for the next thirty minutes.

Eventually my father made his excuses as exhaustion took over him and he said he would have to sleep. I nodded, got up, kissed him on the cheek and made for the door. But something made me stop and turn, looking back at his weary persona lying in the bed. I hated seeing him like that.

"Before I go could I ask you something? Well, three things."

"Sure," he said wearily.

"Why do you always have a goatee and not, like, a full beard?"

My father chuckled, which metamorphosed into a chuckle. "What a question. I just like a goatee."

"OK. Secondly, when you're out, could we like have some father-daughter time. I feel like it's been ages since we'd talked. There's so much I'd like to know about your time growing up."

"Sure. But you're buying the coffee."

"And thirdly. Why Apricot Heart? Why that name?"

My father looked up and at me and smiled. "We were in a room not unlike this and I looked at you in the arms of your mother and I was overcome with how you looked, so sweet lying there. But I knew you'd also be like your mother and very determined and made of steel. And that's what makes a good person growing up. Sweet on the outside but determined and strong on the inside like an apricot heart."

I smiled and watched as my father turned over in the bar and drifted off to sleep. My question had been answered.

I didn't have the heart to tell him that apricots had stones, not hearts, but even if he hadn't been asleep and such a comment redundant I wouldn't have said it. That would have surely ruined the moment.

*

The next time I was in hospital was a much happier time. My father, you'll be glad to hear recovered. I went on another date with Chris, and another, and then several more; soon we moved in together and, well, the rest followed on: nights in, nights out, engagement, marriage. The next time I was in hospital I was about to give birth, Chris stood by my bed holding my hand and reassuring me in his cool, collected manner.

Woah, woah, woah. Thirteen pages about train travel and random asides and several key life choices are brushed off in one paragraph? If my life was a film then it's rubbish. It's like two movies in a trilogy setting up a huge battle then the final fight is a post-credits sequence of the third. Who is scripting my life – Peter Jackson?

Anyway. After much panting, screaming and pain I was able to hold in my arms a healthy baby girl. I smiled at the little bundle in my arms and Chris leant over and kissed me.

"I suppose we should name her," he said. I smiled.

"I have the perfect name," I told him, thinking back to what my father said. I chose my words carefully. "This young girl will be as sweet as Blossom but as solid as a rock."

Chris's smile faded. "Sweet as Blossom, solid as a rock..." he muttered, the cogs in his head whirring. "You mean... No. You can't."

I laughed. "I'm only kidding. I quite like Charlotte."

Chris nodded. "Yes Charlotte. I can live with that."

Good. Welcome to the world Charlotte Evans. Now, as I was saying...

Apricot Heart

By J. McGraw

Bite! The fruit is soft and sweet,
The stone is small and hard.
Such a lovely thing to eat,
But please be on your guard.

Don't throw that stone into the bin,
Don't be so cruel, my dear.
For this is where new lives begin...
The faeries come from here.

Inside the stone, inside it's heart,
Inside a seedling grows.
Until the stone is popped apart,
And out the faerie goes.

The seedling breaks through earth to air,
It grows from seed to tree.
The faerie tends it, full of care,
They're close as two can be.

Sometimes 'neath the flesh you'll find
The stone's already broken.
The faerie's fled, to fate resigned,
The seedling can't be woken.

But if it's whole, please let it grow,
Be kind to those that hide there,
For you've been told, and now you know,
That lives begin inside there.

Apricot Heart

By Lauren K. Nixon

The child turned it over and over in his hand. Of all the things on his grandfather's desk, this puzzled him the most.

The desk was old and well used, but also well kept. It had a curious sheen to it, as though the wood was still somehow alive. Sometimes he would come into the room and mistake the creaking of the floorboards for the movement of the desk. Desks couldn't move, of course, or grow extra decorative details. He supposed it must be his imagination – that perhaps he didn't remember it properly – but there were still moments of doubt.

Most of the time, he ignored it. His grandfather had travelled the world, and the relics of those adventures – many of which the man had enjoyed with his wife, who had died before he was born – were collected on the desk. It was like peering into a whole lifetime of stories.

There was a little globe that showed the whole world; an astrolabe that had once been used to determine the progression of the stars; a green flint arrowhead from a path in Kent that his father said had been walked for thousands of years; there were fossils from even further back, ammonites and trilobites and shadows in the rock that might once have been fish; there were stones that shone like jewels or glowed when struck; there were masks and weapons from distant tribes; there was a dagger that his aunt had told him had belonged to the real Conte de Monte Cristo; a pen that had belonged to Jane Austen; a locket that his great grandmother had worn...

It was a treasure trove, and he loved the stories, like little pieces of his grandfather's heart, absorbed into his own through the telling.

The one thing that puzzled him, though, was the little apricot stone. Of all the things on the desk it was by far the simplest. It almost looked out of place, like his grandfather had been eating his lunch one day and simply forgotten to throw it away. It barely drew the eye; in fact, it was years before the boy had even noticed it. There were so many other treasures to marvel at.

The older he grew, the more his eye was drawn to it, as though it was the keeper of a great secret. He had intended to ask about it today, at that time after dinner when the old man would tell him or his sister to choose a treasure and hear the story of it. His grandfather had beaten him to it, though, as if he had known. As if this was a date that had always been set in his mind: the day he told them about the apricot heart.

It wasn't a sweeping adventure, like some of the others, or full of exciting twists and turns. It was simple and quiet and a little bit ugly, like the stone itself.

It was the story of how he had met and fallen in love with their grandmother. He had seen her through the glass of an exhibition at the British Museum, gazing peacefully at an obsidian blade, dreaming the story of its manufacture. They had taken tea together and seen each other twice a week through spring and into summer. He'd bought her a ring and offered her his heart.

"What a strange thing to offer," she had said, her toes trailing in the cool clear waters of the river they were picnicking beside. "It's not like you can take it out of your chest, is it?"

"Well no, but —"

She had laid on him a gaze that had stolen his breath.

"I will marry you, and I will love you my whole life," she said, with a smile brighter than July, "but you cannot have my heart. I need it. I cannot give it to you, nor can you give yours to me..."

She cast around and seized upon the remains of their lunch, the fruit they had picked from the orchard that morning.

"But I can give you this, if you want it. A poor analogue for my heart, I know, but if you truly want it, this is all I have to give."

He had taken the apricot stone in his hand, turning it over and over between his fingers.

"Then," he had said, when he could trust his voice, "I will take it, if you will have me."

"I will," she had laughed, and let him put the ring on

her finger. "Your heart is in the right place!"

It appeared to the boy that she had always seemed more than halfway made of magic to his grandfather.

"I wish I could have met her, Papa," said his sister, reverently placing her grandmother's heart back on the desk.

"You would have loved her," he said, gently. "As she loves you. Look for her in the spring, when the apricots are in bloom." He patted his granddaughter's bright golden hair. "She is always watching over you."

"I wish..." the boy began, when his sister had run out of the room and into the summer sun. "I wish I could meet someone like her, Papa."

"Maybe you will," his grandfather laughed. "I think you might, one day, but not just yet."

They shared a smile, the old man and the boy, and followed the little girl's laughter out into the garden. Separately, side by side, they watched her run and dreamed of a grassy bank, of sharing fruit while the sun shone on the river, of bare feet touching only just, of a smile like sunlight, and the way the perfect, wrinkled oval of her heart fit in the palm of their hands.

SWIMMING
WITH
PIGS

Swimming with pigs

By G. Burton

It all started with that travel advert on the telly.
Swimming pigs. Who knew they could swim?
I've always wanted to do that, she said.
What, swim with pigs, says I.
No, you daft berk – swim with dolphins. She hit me on the arm.
Oh, dolphins. They're not pigs.
Very much not pigs, she agreed.
But why dolphins?
Well they're supposed to be right intelligent –
Oh, like us?
She laughed.
Me, perhaps, but you? Nah.
Thanks. I love you too.
So, dolphins?
Why stop at dolphins? Maybe we should try swimming with pigs...

The Rise and Fall of Rick Rotten

(Singer, aged forty-two-and-three-quarters)

By Philip Lickley

Sometimes truth is stranger than fiction. But sometimes certain prompts in life mean that fiction has to get pretty strange.

The translation of Rick Rotten's Latin tattoo found across his shoulder-blades, which he got done in 2017 at a cheap tattooists, somewhere in Brixton.

*

We all love reality television, comedy shows and other such programmes. But how does one get a career in such a thing? Do you come up with a great concept and get lucky? Do you have to be born into a family already in the business? Do you have to find yourself sleeping around with senior management in the hope that you, well, perform well enough to get a commission? Maybe there's some dark secret to how shows come about that isn't common knowledge.

Well, few people in the world know how such things come about: a shady group of individuals more mysterious than the Masons, more secretive than the Illuminati, and more unbelievable that the Scientologists. Many of the few were television executives; some were heads of production companies; a few computer programmers at the top of their game. We will probably never know exactly who is part of the selected group of people, but what I, personally, know to be true is that one of the select few was a below-par singer from London, and a Cockney wide-boy who just happened to know the right people. And this is their story. A crazy, wild story about music, casual sexism, pigs and the far future. But that's me getting ahead of myself. Let's firstly get some background.

Richard Rotten was born in June 1980, just after having

the surname Rotten would have been cool. But sadly for little baby Rotten – who would later adopt the shortened first name Rick to appear a little more punk – there wasn't much scope for a punk rocker in nappies in the early part of the nineteen-eighties. Growing up in Brixton, Rick had an unconventional childhood before getting in with the wrong crowd, as many looking down on him would have said, and experimenting with a range of drugs, alcohol and women, each one of those three temptations experienced with a certain amount of excess.

It wasn't until he was in his late thirties, at an age quite late to be any sort of pop-star, that he had a one-off number one hit with the delightfully un-PC title of '(I Love You) Now Get Into Bed', which came about as part of a drunken bet with his friend and part-time agent Craig Waddington and the availability of a local run-down recording studio that happened to have a spare two-hours between a rapper laying down the final few verses of his latest mixtape and the arrival of a local pub singer with delusions of grandeur.

This surprise chart topper set Rotten on a surprisingly speedy journey into minor celebrity and soon offers were piling up in his inbox to open various shops, pose open-shirted in some lads' mags and appear on television, alongside many more weird, wonderful and eclectic offers, all of which he agreed to without any thought of quality control.

Soon he was to be seen everywhere, in print, on screen and on-line, including in a series of ill-advised low-budget television dramas on some obscure digital channel where his surname soon became synonymous on the wooden-acting-scale that stretches from Danny Dyer to Larry Fine and onto Eve Best. Anyone who had had the displeasure of watching '*The Attack of the Killer Kangaroo-Monster*' late on a Saturday night when there was little else on would be able to attest to Rotten's lack of acting ability, even in the face of a cheaply made robotic kangaroo model that occasional broke down and collapsed on some underpaid runners from the local college.

There had been some luck – divine or otherwise – in Rotten's rise to fame. He had managed to secure a number one record more by luck than good management, and certainly with Craig as the closest thing he had to an agent he didn't have anything close to good management. Released in January, the numbers required to reach the top spot were lesser and coming a week before the release of One Direction's comeback (they were, by this point, down to just three members), many of the music-buying younger generation were saving their pennies to buy that track. Throw in a tongue-in-cheek Buzzfeed article that made fun of the cheesy single of Rotten's creation, which actually fulfilled the famous saying of 'All publicity is good publicity', and a programming glitch on iTunes that actually placed the record as 'Single of the Week' for a short, but crucial, four-hour period, and you had the making of a snowball effect that catapulted Rick Rotten to the peak of the charts, and it was hard to know who was more surprised: Rotten (who received a phone call from BBC Radio 1 announcing his success and inviting him on air to talk), the music-buying public (who had spent a week re-tweeting jokes at Rotten's expense), or the gobsmacked radio presenter who had to interview an intoxicated Rotten over the phone with nothing but a collection of hastily written questions on a scrap of notepaper and a quick prayer that the famously foul-mouthed Rotten wouldn't give Ofcom a reason to come knocking on the BBC's door the next day.

Overall 'I Love You (Now Get Into Bed)' sold just under 1000 copies, the lowest number ever for a record reaching number one, fuelling more ammunition for the tabloid press in decrying the relevance of the chart. Unconfirmed rumours on Twitter suggested Rotten had got some of his less desirable contacts to somehow hack into many computers in the week of the singles release and making them secretly and repeatedly stream copies of the record over and over again, boosting the song's chart position. Rotten – and Craig – naturally denied this but by the time TMZ published grainy long-lens photos of an infamous black-hat computer manipulator coming out of Rotten's London house there was little that could be done to stop the runaway success of a song whose opening lyrics were 'I really like your brain, I love the way we chat, but babe that don't mean nothing, unless you're your back'. A delightful number, anyone would admit.

But, although such a song was successful for the week of the chart, it was soon knocked off the top spot by Pharrell Williams' latest comeback, who celebrated his own achievement by buying a bottle of champagne and a new hat, and this triggered off a series of ill-advised follow-ups by Rotten, from a second single that sold, quite literally, only a dozen copies and an album that was so badly laid down in the studio it should have been told to move on by the police.

This string of failures didn't deter Rotten. In fact, it had quite the opposite effect, and mobilised him into sparking some sort of come back, albeit one through the medium of reality television. There wasn't one show that Rotten would not sign up to, and his name soon began to replace that of Christopher Biggins as the name people immediately thought on when they conjured up an image of an over-exposed celebrity. Biggins himself was furious and the mild-mannered celebrity even found himself coming to verbal blows with Rotten in the corridor of Channel 4's Countdown, when their paths crossed between two shows they were working on independently.

But none of this really impacted on Rotten who continued on regardless seemingly trying to win an award for getting on as many television shows as possible in as short a time as possible, hoovering up cheques and appearance fees like they were lines of cocaine ready to be consumed, which he did, of course, with some of the money he raised.

He did pretty well on his debut appearance on *'Celebrity Come Dine With Me'*, coming second to Noel Edmonds even though he'd managed to set both a trifle, and Dane Bowers, on fire during his main course. Rotten wasn't quite at home on *'Strictly Come Dancing'*; when he was out in the first week for a sub-par American Smooth. He did manage to become the first celebrity removed without going to a telephone vote after swearing on air, calling Bruno Toniolo an insult not suitable to repeat here, and making an off-colour joke about Bruce Forsyth, much to Tess Daly's visible distress. Weirdly this bad behaviour only made his star shine brighter and he was courted onto *'I'm A Celebrity, Get Me Out Of Here'* (stretching the requirements outlined in the programme's title to their extreme) possibly because of the hope he'd doing something to generate more publicity for the flagging programme, but, alas, such publicity wasn't forthcoming as he found himself being stretchered off within five minutes after getting hit in the face by a bird as he crossed the bridge onto the site.

And so it continued. Out in the first round on *'Celebrity Fifteen to One'* (Even Adam Hills struggled to converse with him on anything suitable for the family show); scoring the maximum 200 points on *'Pointless'* with his partner Keith Allen; and finally, *'The Great Celebrity Bake-Off'*, a new spin-off of the popular show, where he took the show's instructions too much to the letter. When Sue said they should "just follow the directions" Rick did, namely to Tesco on his sat-nav before the show to pick up a fancy cake which he attempted to smuggle onto the show (without much luck, I might add): an attempt that saw him be disqualified. And this is now where we find Rick, post *Bake-Off*, with Mary Berry's fury still ringing in his ears.

*

The Dog and Duck was an old-fashioned spit-and-sawdust pub of the kind that no one really wants to find themselves in, but are often the last refuge to escape from the rain or the family. The wooden bar had seen better days, the panels having had names, rude words and dates etched into it over the year. The barman was gruff, impolite and corresponded in a series of grunts, and the customers weren't much better. It was in such a rough part of the capital that individuals still smoked indoors and flouted the law, with most police officers reluctant to come anywhere near the pub never mind inside it. Rick was sat in the corner of the dark pub sandwiched between the family area – empty – and a *Deal or No Deal* gambling machine that somebody had got annoyed with several Fridays before and had ripped out the speaker. Rick took a long drag of his cigarette, stubbing it out not in the overflowing ash tray, but on the Carling beer mat, cinematically exhaling the smoke so it spiralled around his head. He stubbed out the rest of the fag in the tray and took a long gulp of his lager which tasted as foul as the room smelt. He barely glanced up as Craig walked over to his table with a matching, but fuller, pint of lager and a packet of pork scratchings, which he opened after sitting down and offered with a rough hand gesture to Rick, who declined.

"I know it's not a bleedin' fairy cake," Craig said, in a Cockney accent that was so clichéd, he would fit in well on some sort of gangster movie.

"I went out in the first week remember."

"You were disqualified. That hardly counts as going out when you weren't really in anyway."

Rick nodded. "I don't even know how I got onto the bloody show in the first place. Perhaps Dean Gaffney wasn't answering their calls."

Craig smirked and took a long refreshing drink off his pint. He wiped his mouth clear of foam before continuing the bland conversation with Rick.

"How many shows have you been on now?" he asked rhetorically, which was good as Rick wasn't planning to answer. Rick had lost count anyway, somewhere around *'Celebrity Crocodile Wrestling'* (which had aired for one rather lacklustre series on Sky Living). "You must have tidied away a good number of cheques from all of them!"

Rick nodded, but without commitment and this led to a few moments of silence between them both as conversation dried up and the only thing flowing was lukewarm lager from glasses into mouths. It was Rick that eventually broke the silence.

"I mean. *'Celebrity Crocodile Wrestling'*. Who comes up with that as a format? Who was sitting in a boardroom going, you know what would get bums on seats and keep the advertisers happy? And everyone asks what, and he – as it could only be some idiotic teenage scrote fresh out of college - answers *Celebrity Crocodile Wrestling*. And then they all pat each other one the back and go off for shots of Sambuca and lines of coke at their local trendy wine bar. It wouldn't surprise me if there's some hidden room deep in the bowels of Television Centre or wherever where there's some massive fuck-off computer the size of a room into which they plug audience figures and celebrity names and it vomits out show titles which then get commissioned. It's the only explanation for two series of something like 'Famous Philately'."

"Famous Philately?" Craig questioned, pausing with his glass half way between grotty table and stubbly chin. "As in stamp collecting?"

"Yeah," Rick grumbled as he finished off his pint. "It was on Channel 4 for a couple of years before *Countdown*. Part of those years where programmes were popping up everywhere to try and make up for dropping advertising figures. Do you remember *'The Great UK Mowing Challenge'*?"

"No..."

"I'm not making it up," Rick said, gesturing to the man behind the bar for another pint. "It genuinely happened. Fifteen celebrities and fifteen gardens each week with points given for the best trimmed lawns. The third week saw them spice up the formula with them using scissors to neaten up their borders."

"You're taking the piss..."

"I only wish I was. You've seen some of the crazier ones. *'So You Think You Can Whittle'; 'Keeping Up With the Krays', 'America's Next Top Cosplayer', 'The Only Way is Egg and Cress'*. That last one saw celebrities working in a sandwich shop, and its name comes from another bloody reality show. The television industry is consuming itself."

Craig forced a laugh as the barman delivered Rick his new pint. "So which show is next?"

Rick thought for a moment. "I've either been on them all or been declined for them. It only leaves one remaining that's open according to the website I use."

"Which is?"

"Quite possibly the weirdest idea for a celebrity themed show you could imagine."

At this point Craig tried to imagine such a thing, his eyes narrowing as he considered some outlandish suggestions.

"Celebrity hairdressing?" he proposed. Rick shook his head.

"They've already done it, and besides that's pretty run of

the mill."

Craig thought again. "Famous people working at an undertakers."

"Too obvious."

"Celebrity Topiary."

"Channel 5, last year."

"Then I don't know…"

*

If Craig and Rick had been living in a sitcom at this point he would have spat his lager across the table in a comedic fashion. But as it wasn't a sitcom and instead two grown men sitting in a dingy bar in a dodgy part of town for no other reason than needing something to do he instead just sat open mouthed.

"You'll have to run that past me again," he admitted, scratching his head.

"Swimming with Pigs."

"No," Craig said after a moment or two of reflection. "Still nothing. That title is just too absurd to even contemplate. If I was – say a commissioner or a writer or something and was given that brief – *Swimming with Pigs* – I would just sit there, open-mouthed unsure what to do. I mean, it's just nonsensical. If it was a story, never mind a television show, what would you write about? A young child on the verge of dying of some incurable disease but the dolphins are ill, so they go to a budget bucket list centre where people swim with pigs? Is it slang for the police? I just can't get my head around it."

Rick nodded. "I tell you: automated computer, basement of Television Centre. Previous successes are fed in and something comes out. In goes *Total Wipeout, Countryfile, Splash*, out comes *Swimming with Pigs.*"

Craig shook his head. "Nope, I still can't imagine the chain of events that could lead to somebody coming up with something like *Swimming with Pigs*. I mean, what does it even mean? You might as well have a show like *Juggling with Chameleons* or *Boxing with Springboks*, or *Dancing with Dingoes*. It's ridiculous."

"You're telling me but it's out there. They're casting it

now to be shown on some obscure digital channel next autumn."

"An obscure digital channel? Surely you want more exposure than that?"

"Absolutely," Rick noted, supping once more from his pint, "But ten grand is ten grand. I'm not in a position to turn my nose up at that."

"OK, you've got me hooked, explain to me the concept."

*

The journey from concept to screen for *'Swimming For Pigs'* was a relatively speedy one. Rumour had it on the televisual grapevine that an eccentric commissioner called Clive "Sandy" Sanderson had gone on holiday to the Bahamas and found himself at a beach side bar late one evening, having had four-too-many Pina Coladas and a few drugs that he shouldn't really have consumed, with names that sounded like children's comic books from the 1950s. Attempting a drunken walk home after a couple of Mississippi Mudslides and a few lines of *bang* and *whizzee*, he had come across an advert for an unusual tourist attraction where people could actually swim with pigs. There was even some folklore built up around the animals to entice in tourists. Though Sanderson had scoffed at the idea, just before tripping over a sand dune and nursing his hangover over an uncomfortable night collapsed on a beach, he woke in the morning with a renewed sense of vigour, a clearer head and the flyer wedged into his shorts. That's when the cogs started turning, and over a few more cocktails and through a conversation with a naïve young runner from a local college who didn't have the heart or the confidence to say no, or question the clearly absurd idea, a gentle tourist attraction had formed into the craziest game show ever.

The basic premise of the show would be an animal-themed *Total Wipeout*, with a smattering of round each based on a task and an animal which would vary each week. One round would see a celebrity pair trying to play a game of underwater chess whilst sharks bashed into the cage they were in; another would see a game of orienteering in some woods, in which bears were known to live; another, a high-wire rope challenge surrounded by beehives. Naturally the runner had questioned the safety of all these suggestions but this had been dismissed by a now clearly sozzled Sanderson, who muttered something about filming it in Latvia or something, and then proceeded to come up with more outlandish ideas, within the restrictions of a) a random game, b) a dangerous animal.

Naturally the title of the series had to come in somewhere and thus the final was set in a large swimming pool containing twelve pigs, each with cards attached to their bellies, which contained prizes or amounts of money. The lucky contestants would just have to swim after the pigs, collect the envelopes, and hopefully get some great prizes by the end of the sixty seconds. At this point the runner nodded as they sat under the shade of the beach hut, discarded cocktail glasses littering the table, each one testament to a crazier idea than the last. He could understand the relevance of the final round but not the title of the show.

"If you have rounds featuring bears and sharks and crocodiles ("Hop-scotch, with alligators!" Clive had exclaimed at some point between two White Russians) then why not call the show something more exciting like *'Swimming with Sharks'*?"

Clive considered such a suggestion and noted that that would be a more sellable title, but seemingly his drunken brain had already settled on the title, perhaps because he'd already generated a series of pun-based catchphrases the host could use.

He could hear it now...

"Let's see which celebrity will win the £10,000, who will win the roast beef, and who will be going wee-wee-wee all the way home with no money. Let's play *Swimming with Pigs!*"

*

By now the wheels were in motion for Rick Rotten's final attempt at fame. If fame, of course, could be obtained by appearing on a crazy show on a minor channel. But it seemed that things were playing into his hands. Firstly, his audition went really well and secondly the producer took a shine to him. Apparently he had been a big fan of his earlier single and, coincidentally, one of the twelve people who had got a copy of his album, though he had to admit it had been given to him as a joke present for his birthday. But, the fact still stood, that prank from years earlier got Rick Rotten onto his latest reality show, and he soon found himself onboard an EasyJet flight to Latvia with a clutch of other minor celebrities – and much to his own annoyance, Christopher Biggins, who wasn't pleased to see Rotten again – heading to the filming area which was a hastily repurposed former military base with fifteen-foot high walls, barbed wire and the unmistakable feeling of despair. The grey concrete and security towers were certainly at odds with the brightly coloured sets erected in the main concourse, housing the assault courses. The cheap plastic and unconvincing décor certainly wasn't deterring the celebrities from taking part, neither was the large forest just outside the walls of the base, from which animal calls could occasionally be heard, not to mention the ones coming from the rusty cages positioned in certain dark corners of the centre.

Even Rick felt apprehensive about certain elements of this experience; this coming from a man who once faced down a man with a gun in a dark alley whilst both he and them were drunk. The combination of wobbly sets, animal calls, a host who was seemingly a little tipsy with his breath smelling of cheap Russian vodka, and a disclaimer with conditions on it that would unsettle Chuck Norris, wasn't adding to a great welcome for the celebrities. Rick began to fear that elimination wouldn't be by telephone or text but by a swipe from a bear's paw in a momentary lapse in health and safety. Rotten feared that there was certainly a lack of risk assessment around here or anything involving a duty of care towards the men and women at their respective points of career desperation. (Rick was sure at least two of his fellow contestants had won the *X-Factor* at some point but he wasn't entirely sure).

But actually, for all the fears of the group on that first initial visit, the filming went remarkable smoothly, with the worst injury being a broken finger when the post-wrap party got a bit out of hand and a stray glass hit some *Hollyoaks* actor on the hand. Over the course of the week the group of celebrities who wished they were as high as Z-list ran through woods to the sounds of wolves howling, collected goodies from snake pits, and headed to the nearby coast to swim with stingrays. It all felt a little dangerous at times but they'd all come out of it unscathed, and the actual swimming with pigs – or boars as they were here – was probably the most fun part of it. Rick Rotten, for his efforts, came second to a weatherman from ITV, but he was happy with that and he returned to England tired but happy that good things could come from his new television appearance.

But sadly, like everything in Rick Rotten's world, from the time he developed chlamydia after his first sexual encounter to the time he got locked in the bathroom of a friend's house who was away for the weekend with no access to a phone and a window that also jammed, good luck wasn't always shining on him. And, like always, his way of recovering from such things involved a pint or several at the *Dog and Duck* with Craig.

*

Several months on and the bar was still as dingy, poorly lit and unwelcoming as ever. Rick wouldn't really have it any other way. The barman was scowling at a young couple getting a little intimate in the family area (not necessarily a euphemism, but it could well have been) and someone had put a considerable amount of loose change in the jukebox and selected the entire back catalogue of REM to play on random. Rick would have wanted something uplifting to help him like *'Shiny Happy People'*. What he was instead getting was *'Bad Day'*, which was at least fitting.

"So are the dark glasses a fashion choice?" Craig asked, having just arrived in response to Rick's garbled and drunken request to meet up. Craig had appeared at the table with a pint but even though it was only just past one in the afternoon was already four pints and three whiskeys behind his friend. Rick drank for his glass and shook his head, his speech slurred.

"Not really," he confessed, looking around nervously. "More out of necessity."

"Why the secrecy? Is it because your star is ascending and you don't want to be recognised? I don't think I saw any one from TMZ hiding in the bushes."

"Sort of..."

"Cheer up, for fuck's sake," Craig said, his mood quickly changing from jovial to annoyed. "*Swimming with Pigs* was a huge success. You banked ten grand, a holiday to Barbados and a flat screen television – and the show was a ratings success, the best performing show in that timeslot. It even beat *The Apprentice: North Korea* and you know how popular that show is with the Instagram crowd.

"I mean," he continued in a monologue fashion. "It's pretty depressing that the best two shows on a Tuesday evening at 8 p.m. involve picking prizes off pigs or Alan Sugar's bald Korean counterpart, but that's what we get I suppose since they abolished the licence fee..."

Rick still didn't respond.

"Come on Rick, what's up? Is it the music single? You must have been able to find one you like to fulfil that contract? It's what you always wanted, a new song on the back of your new-found fame. Again."

Rick cursed under his breath. His appearance on what was now the most popular reality show format had been everything he'd wanted and more: money, fame, a new recording contract. But it had with some caveats that even he found uncomfortable. And he blamed Tumblr.

*

Before Rick had flown to Latvia he had never heard of Tumblr. He'd barely heard of Twitter until he had trended following a particularly disastrous live performance on some internet music show. Apparently his appearances on 'Swimming With Pigs' had set the social network alight, animated GIFs of the challenges spreading like wildfire, especially the ones where he had accidentally grabbed one of the pigs in the final round in a rather personal location. Now, according to the internet, he was in some sort of fictional relationship with said pig. Said male pig. Said male pig called Mick. At his last count there were 14,592 posts about their relationship, six fan-fictions and over a dozen slash stories that made even the world-wise Rick Rotten blush. He didn't like it but, he supposed, it was getting him fame.

"You're not still embarrassed about those online stories are you?" Craig asked. Rick shook his head. "All publicity is good publicity..."

This stock phrase was apparently the straw that broke the singer's back and Rick started to bubble like a volcano slowly on the way to erupting. He spoke through gritted teeth like a poor Alan Rickman impersonator.

"Do you know what's worse than getting fame online for your unintentional intimate involvements with a pig?" he asked rhetorically. Craig didn't answer anyway as it's not a sentence you can really truly follow up without sounding flippant. Rick told him anyway.

"I'll tell you anyway," he confirmed. "It's being plastered all over the front page of the fucking Metro."

Rick pulled a tabloid freesheet from under the table and placed it down in front of Craig. On the front cover was a publicity shot of Rick holding a pig from the show, next to a grainy image of Rick, taken on the street, of him eating what looked to be a bacon sandwich. Both images were under the headline *"Failed Singer in Pig Trouble"*. Craig scanned the headline and the opening paragraph to ascertain its meaning.

"Not since Labour leader Ed Milliband was photographed making a meal – quite literally – out of a bacon sandwich has a lunchtime snack brought someone down. Former singer and Z-list celebrity Rick Rotten, 43, has put his latest comeback in jeopardy as Metro photographer catches him enjoying a bacon sandwich a day before his new music single is due to be released."

Craig chose not to read any more and folded up the paper, drinking from his pint. It was a shame as the free tabloid also promised the latest on Ellie Goulding's love life and Katie Hopkins' thoughts on the unemployed. Rick responded first.

"I mean, this is celebrity culture all over. They big you up and they bring you down. Just because I eat a bacon sandwich doesn't mean I don't like pigs," Rick said, a sentence he couldn't believe he would have ever found himself saying. Craig laughed at the absurdity of the situation.

"You know what your next step should be? Get someone to write your biography. This would make a great story!"

Rick scoffed. "This would make a ridiculous story. Do you really think someone would read this and believe it? A man from my background releases a music single which leads to going on the *Bake-Off* and then a show involving swimming with pigs and my downfall is eating a bacon sandwich? I don't know which would be worse. Someone having to read such a bat-shit crazy idea or someone actually writing it."

Craig laughed. "I don't see what other avenue you've got now. The public will turn against you. There's nothing more that the British public like than animals, unless it's queuing, casual racism and Jeremy Clarkson."

Rick's lip curled and he smiled. "Let's be honest, I'm now a toxic brand. No one is going to touch anything I do. I'll never be on television again, my music career is dead and I'm hardly going to be the face of the Pig Trust now..."

Craig muttered something about *There's always Danepak*. Rick chose to ignore him.

"There is one thing we could do, and it involves something even crazier than this wild ride so far."

"Okay," Craig said, downing his pint in anticipation that they were about to go on a trip. "Enlighten me."

The jukebox switched to '*Man-Sized Wreath*' by REM. It seemed appropriate.

*

"You weren't joking were you?" Craig asked, the light from his torch bouncing off the walls. Both he and Rick were dressed head to toe in black with only their eyes showing through balaclavas. Craig was holding a torch in his gloved right hand and Rick a badly scrawled map. It turns out that if you have the right contacts, Television Centre is not a difficult building to break into, especially when the security company was on strike and operating a skeleton staff – and an old school friend of Rick's had kindly left a window ajar. Both men were now skulking down the corridor, moving from door to door and flashing the torch light on individual signs. One was labelled 'Dressing Room', another 'Server Cupboard'.

"It's definitely down this corridor," Rick muttered in a volume slightly louder than a whisper. Craig didn't sound convinced.

"This thing does not exist. It just cannot exist. It's like the Holy Grail. Lots of people think it is real but it's just a myth conjured up by nutters and fantasists."

"Oh ye of little faith," Rick said, studying the scratty piece of paper he clutched onto. "Next left."

Craig stopped at the next door and tried the handle but it was firmly locked. He rattled the handle again but it didn't budge. Rick wasn't quite so restrained and with two swift lunges, kicked the door off its hinges. Craig narrowed his eyes and stared at his friend, shaking his head in frustration and following Rick into the room. There they stood, looking around the space; it was mostly empty, apart from one computer terminal. Rick approached it and sat down on the chair and began tapping away on the keyboard.

"It's a little smaller than I imagined," Craig said. Rick nodded.

"But it exists and that is all that matters."

Craig laughed. "I cannot believe that there is a computer hidden in a room that commissions all the shows on television. Like that's even possible." He thought for a moment. "Though I suppose that does go some way to explain the career of Ricky Gervais."

As those words left Craig's lips Rick got up to his feet. "It is done," he said as the cursor on the terminal blinked on and off. "That's now one sure way of me finding favour once more."

"But firstly," Craig said as he thought he heard footsteps, "We have to get out of here. If you're found to have broken into the BBC then the only career you'll have is on prison radio. Come on, let's get out of here."

*

Twenty years later

When people think of the future people think of it as a really hyper-futuristic time of flying cars, robotic servants and slightly dystopian, where whole countries and civilisations have been wiped out by trigger-happy senators. But in fact the 2040s aren't much different from what you'd know now, except the mobile phones are more powerful, the televisions bigger and the cars more automated than you'd expect. Otherwise, very little has actually changed. Trains still run badly; cities are still a hodgepodge of listed buildings and futuristic looking modern skyscrapers; and humankind still oscillates between war and peace in a regular fashion, in different parts of the world. Advancements in healthcare are commonplace, but much of the change comes in personal technology. Celebrities have continued to emerge, bands have got older and been replaced, rampant piracy continues to make music, film, books and now other products with the rampant rise of commercial 3D printing cheaper and cheaper. Social networking is still as all-pervasive as ever. People still moan about having little time even though gadgets help them do much more much quickly. Politicians are still economical with the truth, Saturday night television is still tedious, and the weather is still as poor as ever. Simon Cowell still has a career.

At this point it's a warm and sunny July day and we find Craig sat on his balcony overlooking London, sat next to his wife Maria and their young soon Billy. All was at peace until an alarm went off on Craig's mobile phone. He lazily glanced at his smart-watch and realised it was almost eight o'clock according to the flashing digital screen which was attempting to manage his social life, insofar as listing all his Facebook interactions, tweets and Instagram shots of friend's dinners. He turned to his wife.

"Hey Maria. It's time. He'll be on in a second."

She nodded and turned over to tan the other side of her body as if his words were important to her but not so important she'd abandon her tan. Craig smiled, leant over to kiss her on the forehead and left the balcony to go to their living room. He ambled over to a nearby huge curved-screen television on the wall and switched it on by speaking a series of commands that it understood with surprising clarity. The credits of the previous show were playing with a continuity announcer babbling on over them, mentioning something about hashtags and an application on tablets.

"And that was the last in the series of John Bishop's *Chess Champions*, but there will be a new series starting next year. Next up is Harper Beckham, with her live chat show and the interview we've all been waiting for, as Rick Rotten reveals all about the secrets of television."

Craig smiled as he watched a series of trailers played out on screen, which appeared to be interacting noisily with his smart-watch and waited for the next show to start. Just as the titles came on Maria lazily sloped in and smiled kissing him on the cheek.

"Fancy a cuppa?" he asked. She nodded and he pressed a few buttons on his smart-phone that appeared to trigger the kettle to start boiling in the kitchen. There was a low hum from along a corridor as their robotic vacuum cleaner decided to do a quick clean of their bedroom floor. Craig turned up the volume on the television just in time to hear the introduction for the show from an attractive young lady in her late twenties.

"Over the last few years we've uncovered such incredible secrets on this show. Who could forget two years ago when we revealed the truth about Area 51? Or last year when we discovered for a fact who Jack the Ripper really was? Or only last month when the first pictures came back of a new galaxy? And this year we have got another incredible revelation as A-List celebrity and movie star Rick Rotten reveals the secrets behind some of the biggest television shows and television stars of the last fifty years. Ladies and gentlemen – Rick Rotten!"

As the audience burst into spontaneous applause a figure emerged at the top of the steps in the studio whilst some on-screen graphics popped out of the screen in three-dimensions, announcing the guest's name and some appropriate contact details. Though the figure descending the steps was much older it was clearly Rick, still with the cheeky smile hidden among a few layers of mid-21st-century face lifts. He continued to descend the staircase towards Harper and the sofa. Meanwhile Craig was receiving a phone call.

"Simon!" he said with enthusiasm answering the call through a concealed receiver behind his ear. "Are you watching this? It's Rick's big moment." But there was something about Simon's voice that unsettled him. Simon was Rick's agent of ten years and was always never less than chirpy. Here he just sounded haunted.

"Craig. You have to get out of there now."

"Where? My flat? Why?"

"Go. Now. Do you really think that the executives of this show would let Rick reveal everything?"

"But they wanted the ratings. You were in those meetings with us, how keen they were! Do you know how many people are watching the show?"

"Oh they'll get their ratings alright," Simon said. "Just not for that revelation. They're coming for you, too, Craig. Go. Now."

Craig heard a noise from behind him and everything seemed to switch into slow motion. He saw Rick, who had just shaken hands with the presenter, and sat down on the sofa, now slumped over said piece of furniture, lifeless, whilst camera crew and runners dashed up to him. Someone had shot him live on television just as he'd uttered the words 'Here is television's biggest secret....'

Both Craig and Maria stared at the screen open-mouthed. Rick had been about to confirm the existence of the machine that commissioned shows, an incredible piece of technology that had been at the heart of television for so long. The machine that had, twenty years ago, given him his own television show which had set him finally on a path towards fame and fortune, alongside many other contemporary stars, and his best friend and co-conspirator Craig. His own chat show had led to a series of lucrative reboots (*Rick Rotten's Generation Game; Big Break with Rick Rotten*; and even *The Great British Bake-Off with Rick and Craig*); and then into some mid-budget Hollywood films. But this was a secret that they wouldn't let out. But at least the show would get some incredible ratings where the golden boy of television was killed live on air. Craig swallowed hard.

"We have to go," he muttered to himself and his wife, his eyes glancing around with panic. He turned off the television with a few stuttered commands and called for this son, but before they could move there was a knock on the door and then three quick rings on the doorbell.

"Craig Waddington, please open the door," came a voice, with menace.

He was frozen to the spot. He couldn't answer. They repeated the request twice more. All Craig could think about was how everything they'd been through would make such a fantastical story, but one that would never be fully heard. The people at the door called out once more. And then they could wait no longer. They held a master fob against the electronic door receiver and the front door slid open. Craig saw a flash of metal, and heard a scream, and as some shots rang out, everything seemed to move in surprising slow motion.

'Shit', he thought, one word that didn't quite sum up the end of his life in its entirety but felt, as he hit the floor, surprisingly apt, considering the quality of television that had got him to this point.

Swimming with pigs he thought as his vision failed. *Fucking ridiculous*. And he couldn't help but chuckle to himself.

Swimming with Pigs

By Shaun Martindale

Hmm. Well, this was a change.

A bit wetter than I am used to, I have to admit. But, well, I kinda like it.

I bobbed up and down a little bit and spun about, flapping my stumpy legs gleefully through the murky water.

A broken bit of fence drifted past. Funny that.

My tall-not-pig was standing not too far away, the water up to his knees. He was shouting his loud noises into a brick in his hand. Silly tall-not-pigs.

A feathered-not-pig drifted past. I said hi and she looked quite surprised to see a snout greeting her from the waters. She quacked a bit and sailed on. Fine.

The tall-not-pig had finished making his noises and was splashing noisily towards me. He picked me up in his arms and splashed a bit more through the waters.

He made a noise that I hadn't heard before – sort of like how a feathered-not-pig would sound if it flew into a cloud-not-pig – and fell into the water with more splashing and waving of not-pig-trotters.

With some low grumbling the tall-not-pig picked me up again. I smiled at his face and wrinkled my nose. I hope it cheered him up. He seemed a bit mad.

We got to the big wooden box and pushed open the moving bit. The water was much less here, but still wet. He reached up and set me on a shelf covered with lovely straw and patted me on the head. He lowered a wooden frame in front of me so I wouldn't fall off and left to do some more shouting.

Sighing about the short end to my adventure, I turned around and saw my brothers and sisters lying down in the straw, slowly drying off. Now THAT looked like a good idea.

I shuffled over and snuggled into the warm mass and was asleep before I could even wonder where the water had come from.

Swimming with pigs

By J. McGraw

The bus pulled up to a stop, letting on dripping, shivering passengers. Among them was a middle-aged man, travelling alone, with his trench coat pulled tight against the weather and a fedora jammed securely on his head. He slid into an empty seat behind two young women, wiped a hand over the fogged window, and stared blandly out into the grey New York streets as the bus pulled away again.

The women in front were talking about the rain, and how beastly winter in the city was, and how weather like this would be so much more bearable if they were somewhere nice, like Paris or Rome or London. The conversation fell into a lull, and the man leant forwards.

"Excuse my interruption, ladies. I couldn't help hearing your conversation, and I have a very interesting fact that I thought might cheer you up, if you'd like to hear it?"

"We could do with some cheering up, couldn't we?" One of the women nudged her friend, who grudgingly nodded.

"Well, I was reading the other day about an island in the tropics where, if you go down to the beach, you can see groups of pigs swimming in the sea."

The first woman looked oddly startled, and her friend scoffed.

"Swimming pigs? That sounds like utter baloney."

"I've heard about them," the first woman said quickly. "It's in the Bahamas, isn't it?"

"That's what I read, yes." The man gave a quick nod and a smile to the first woman.

"That sounds marvellous."

"You can't be serious?" the friend exclaimed. "It sounds perfectly hideous, Moll."

"I think it would be quite a sight, to walk down to a beach and see pigs swimming around."

"Pigs are filthy things."

"But not if they're in the sea," the first woman, Moll, reminded her friend. "They'd be perfectly clean."

"Hmmph." The friend turned back in her seat, ignoring a disapproving look from Moll.

"Well, I think it's fascinating," Moll said to the gentleman. "And it certainly has cheered me up."

"If I were in the Bahamas, I could think of much better things to do than watch pigs." The friend sighed, then shot upright. "Oh lord, this is my stop! Out of my way, Moll. Driver, wait a moment, please!"

Chaos reigned for a moment or two, as the friend clambered ungracefully out of her seat, blew a kiss to Moll, and ran down the aisle of the bus to the street, clutching her hat to her head. Moll laughed as she watched, and waved energetically as the bus pulled away.

"Sorry about her, sir," she apologised once they were underway once more. "She's a bit outspoken, but she means well."

"No problem." The man tipped his hat, and turned back in his seat. For a moment there was no sound but the traffic outside and the roar of the engine, and then the other passengers, realising there would be no more hi-jinks, turned back to their own affairs.

Once the general background chatter had built up again, the man pulled a magazine from the inside pocket of his coat and leant forward once more.

"I wonder if you'd be interested in hearing more?" he asked quietly, unfurling the magazine and opening it to a random page.

"Are you Eddie's friend?" she asked quietly, barely moving her lips. The man nodded ever so slightly. Moll sighed in relief.

"You know, you gave me a proper shock. Eddie gave me that code phrase ages ago. I was beginning to think no one would ever use it."

"It's taken us a little while to get things sorted, Miss Winston, I know. Thank you for being so patient."

"Is Eddie going to meet me?"

"He is. He wants you to go home now, then at eight o'clock tonight head down to the grocers on your corner and wait. He'll arrive in a Model T with a red handkerchief trapped in the front passenger door. When he pulls up, climb in the back, not the front. Don't take anything with you but your handbag – he says you can buy whatever else you need when you get where you're going."

"Eight o'clock tonight?" Moll's face fell. "Jack wants to take me to dinner tonight. He's picking me up at seven."

"Can you get out of it?"

"Did you ever find out what happened to his last girl?" Moll asked acidly. The man gave a conceding grunt.

"Still, it has to be eight o'clock. You'll have to leave earlier and wait somewhere."

"Jack has men everywhere!" Moll tried her best to keep her voice low. "If I'm not there, he'll come looking for me, he'll know I've..."

"Miss Winston, calm down," the man said in a deep, easy voice. "Do you have a friend you can visit? It'll only be for an hour or so, until Eddie can get to you."

"No, there's... there's no one. Until I met Eddie, Jack was the only one I had. All my friends are his friends."

The man was silent for a while as the bus pulled in at the next stop. Two gentlemen boarded, and sat near the front, talking quietly. Neither looked their way, and as the bus pulled away once more, the man turned back to Moll.

"Go see a movie. The theatres are always dark, and if anyone comes in to look for you it's easy enough to hide. But take a watch and keep an eye on the time. Eddie can collect you from outside the movie theatre at eight o'clock, instead of the grocers."

"He'll definitely be there?" Moll sounded uneasy. "I can't cross Jack if I'm not leaving town."

"Miss Winston, getting you out of the city is a priority for us, don't worry. Your testimony could help us put Jack away for the rest of his life, and we're not going to jeopardise that."

"Okay," Moll replied, feeling relieved.

"You remember what I told you about the car?"

"Um... a Model T with a red handkerchief in the door."

"And get in the back, not the front."

"Why the back?"

"It'll be safer for you."

"And we'll leave town?"

"Eddie is going to get you as far away from here as he possibly can, Miss Winston, don't you worry."

"Somewhere even Jack can't find me?"

"Somewhere Jack definitely can't find you." The man grinned suddenly. "Maybe even as far as those swimming pigs, if you like."

Swimming with Pigs

By Lauren K. Nixon

If I had one wish
My wish would be
To swim with pigs
In a sapphire sea.

AUTHORS

Hannah R.H. Allen

Han, also known as PhoenixShaman, is a gender fluid humanoid being, who loves to create and tell stories through many different mediums, is an avid LARPer, and revels in being the weird one in any social group. They currently reside in York, where there is plenty to inspire them, along with a mischievous black cat called Imp.

You can find more of their work here:
http://phoenixshaman.deviantart.com/

Hannah Burns

My name is Hannah Burns. I am a sporadic writer who gets random ideas at random times. Don't usually get them into an order, but sometimes when I can, they can be enjoyable. Read and enjoy all that you can.

G. Burton

G. Burton is a working professional from Yorkshire who writes. Her writing has bubbled from a love of literature and a lifelong desire to put words to paper. She is currently working on her first novel-length piece of work, and on developing her book review blog, The Forensic Bibliophile (**www.theforensicbibliophile.wordpress.com**).

Jessica Grace Coleman

Jessica Grace Coleman lives in Stafford, England, where she writes by day and writes more by night. She runs an editing/ghost writing business and self-publishes her own novels – when she can find the time.

You can find out more about her writing services at **www.colemanediting.co.uk** and about her own books at **www.jessicagracecoleman.com**.

Cynthia Holt

Cynthia Holt is a Chionophile, Bibliophile, and Insectophile.

Her favourite words are hiraeth, petrichor, susurrus and apothecary. She collects words, stories, secrets and the occasional bit of paper.

Cynthia lives in New England with her bees, a husband, three children, the standard dog cat combo and a grouchy hedgehog.

Read more about her silly adventures over at No One Sleeps Naked In This House:**nicrophorus.blogspot.com**

Philip Lickley

By day Phil works at a University, attempting to let people know what's going on whilst also supporting the media areas and entertainments. By evening he prefers to either put on a pair of headphones and grab a microphone to broadcast radio, slap on a pair of shorts and an ill-fitting top and go running, or grab the nearest keyboard and do some writing. Having already published an e-book under a pseudonym that has had at least seven reads (!) he likes to write short stories and sketches in the hope that he can get readers into double figures and maybe make more of his thirties than he has his twenties!

Shaun Martindale

Shaun is a working professional who also writes, living in the spiritual home of mint cake with his partner in crime, Lina.

In his spare time he practices martial arts and makes chainmail.

J. McGraw

J. McGraw is museum professional and osteoarchaeologist, but manages to raise herself out of the monotony of the coolest job in the world through science fiction/fantasy writing. In her spare time, she works in The Wooden Tooth Factory, a place where stray thoughts, characters, and plot lines gather for company. Some say this is the place where the rest of her first name went to live a full and happy life, but she doesn't like to talk about it.

Pay a visit to the Factory at **woodentoothfactory.blogspot.co.uk**

Lauren K. Nixon

An ex-archaeologist enjoying life in the slow-lane, Lauren K. Nixon is an indie author fascinated by everyday magic. She is the author of numerous short stories and the Chambers Magic series. Happily, there are many things to keep her occupied, and when she's not writing or curating the Short Story Superstars club she can be found gardening, singing, crafting, reading, playing the fool and playing board games.

You can find out more about her writing, and the weird stuff she finds herself researching, over at her website: **http://www.laurenknixon.com/**

ARTISTS

PhoenixShaman

PhoenixShaman, also known as Han, is a gender fluid humanoid being, who loves to create and tell stories through many different mediums, is an avid LARPer, and revels in being the weird one in any social group. They currently reside in York, where there is plenty to inspire them, along with a mischievous black cat called Imp.

You can find more of their work here:
http://phoenixshaman.deviantart.com/

Liz Hearson

This is me, dressed as a dragon.

18963193R00151

Printed in Poland
by Amazon Fulfillment
Poland Sp. z o.o., Wrocław

Introduction

You may find yourself living in a shotgun shack
You may find yourself in another part of the world
You may find yourself behind the wheel of a large automobile
You may find yourself in a beautiful house with a beautiful wife
You may ask yourself, well, how did I get here?
You may ask yourself, how do I work this?
You may ask yourself, where is that large automobile?
You may tell yourself, this is not my beautiful house
You may tell yourself, this is not my beautiful wife
Same as it ever was, same as it ever was, same as it ever was, same as it ever was
Same as it ever was, same as it ever was, same as it ever was, same as it ever was...

(lyrics ©David Byrne, Brian Eno, Chris Frantz, Jerry Harrison, and Tina Weymouth, 1981)

...well no, not the same as it ever was. How did I get here? Now that's a long, long story.

I could probably fill a dozen pages with dedications and thanks, but that might minimise the contribution of each, so some of you may have to wait for the next book. In this one I'm going to keep it short and sweet. Special thanks have to go to David Bradley, perhaps the most annoying friend, muse and supporter in the world, but without whom this may not have been finished. Further special thanks go to Lee Ballantyne, who was my unofficial editor and proof reader, and who pointed out all the silly little mistakes that come with writing some 87,000 words. And none of this would have been possible without everyone who bought and read my novella and gave me the encouragement to move onto bigger things. To you, and to anyone else who contributed, my thanks a thousand times over. And special thanks to Jason McCreadie (Syntax/Vectraits Illustrations) for the marvellous front cover.

S.W.P September 2014

FOR JOHN AND SARAH DONNELLY

THE LIGHTS MAY HAVE GONE OUT BUT THE CANDLES ALWAYS BURN

Prologue

This is not a true story, though some of it is based on actual events and people. Nor does it seek to condone drug use of any type. I believe that such activities, just the same as the use of alcohol or tobacco, should be a matter of personal choice. As long as what you choose to do with your life does not cause any form of harm to others, then what right do governments have to prohibit such activities? Why have we seemingly evolved as a species, yet seem to have moved backwards as far as allowing others to dictate the manner in which we live our lives?

Graham is a fictional construct. But parts of his life mirrors my own, both in the good and bad choices he makes, and indeed in the path he follows. There are many real life figures appearing in this story, some of them from the world of music, and some of them from everyday life. Nothing portrayed in this book is intended to indicate fault, guilt or wrongdoing on the part of those characters, or to insinuate criminal behaviour of any type as the situations in which they are placed are purely fictional. But on my own pathway through life, fate has brought me into situations where I have mixed and socialised with many of these people and similar and those interactions have helped shape me as a person as well as being signposts on this marvellous journey we call life.

But I truly believe that my mistakes and bad choices have led me to the place I am now, just as they do for Graham in this first novel following his own, often stumbling steps. So, this is not meant to be a guide to how to live your own life, or a ringing endorsement of drug use or any of the other 'lessons' one could take from Graham's adventures and misadventures; it's just a story about one ordinary little boy growing up, or sometimes trying to grow up too hard. I don't want you to judge Graham harshly, or me, or in fact yourselves or those around you. We all make mistakes, we all take wrong turns now and again, but it is those errors and wrong turns than make us who we are, which is not always who we want to be or who others want us to be.

Steven W. Palmer, April 2014

"Though the road's been rocky it sure feels good to me."

— Bob Marley

"The path to our destination is not always a straight one. We go down the wrong road, we get lost, we turn back. Maybe it doesn't matter which road we embark on. Maybe what matters is that we embark."

— Barbara Hall

You could say with some certainty that until the night my cousin John gave me a new look at life that I'd led a fairly average childhood. I was an only child, though unfortunately (or is that fortunately?) not with the stereotypical spoiling you'd expect.

Mum and dad were ordinary, hardworking good folk. They came from very working class Paisley roots and had been born in the 1930's, so had seen what it was to be poor and to really go hungry, especially during the war years. I think, though I never asked, that one of the things that drew them together was recognition in the other of that persevering spirit, and one that was determined not to go hungry or without again. Mum got shafted pretty badly by her family; she was desperate to train to be a nurse but in those male dominated days of the 1940's, she was forbidden to, and was sent out to work to enable her older brothers to attend college. The irony is, she probably achieved more in her working life, and earned more respect, than either of them ever managed.

Dad started off working in the J&P Coats thread mills (In those halcyon days, Paisley was still the thread capital of the world) and also worked weekends and the odd evening in a butcher's shop, while attending evening school a couple of other nights in order to increase his chances of promotion. Mum, before she met dad, worked in a variety of jobs, from the Co-Op to a car showroom and then the thread mills, where, of course, she met my dad. I don't know if it was ever a mad passionate relationship; it's not the sort of question you ask your parents, but I do know that they loved each other and remained together and loyal for some 40 years.

Time passed…they married in 1954. Dad had worked his way up the ladder and was now an assistant mill manager. The company sent my dad to Turkey for 2 years at the end of the 1950's; an exotic location for 2 working class Buddies (for the non Scots among you, Buddies is the term given to Paisley folk). Perhaps this was a prophetic trip in terms of what would happen to Britain's industries over coming decades, as my dad's job was to get a new factory up and running in Istanbul (where labour costs were, even then, a fraction of Britain's)

I remember one funny story my dad told from their stay there. In those days there was not the same level of foreign travel we have now, so expat numbers were small and they tended to group together. The preferred location was the bar of the Istanbul Hilton. Expats and the occasional tourist would gather here, make new friends and sip tea in the afternoons and martinis in the evenings. One evening my mum and dad met this American who had just been posted to the US Embassy there. They got on really well and my dad gave him an open invitation to visit them in their apartment. Unfortunately, the day their new American friend chose to visit was the 25th April 1959. To most people outside Paisley, this date will mean nothing. And indeed, to many Paisley folk, the date will also mean nothing unless you actually follow the local football team; St Mirren. For that was the date that St Mirren won the Scottish Cup for only the second time (and it had been 33 years since they first lifted the trophy and would be another 28 till they did it again). Now my dad was a fanatical St Mirren fan and had attended matches since he was a boy. He was therefore understandably gutted that he was in another country the day his team were in a major final.

My mum told me how he spent the first half of the day trying out their radio in a variety of positions within the apartment in an attempt to find the best position for a half decent signal from the BBC World Service. There was nowhere that produced a clear signal at all, just varying degrees of 'not as crackly as over there'.

Having finally established the 'least bad' location, dad settled down with the (hastily moved) armchair and a cold Turkish beer to cheer his team on. 108,000 were at Hampden that day, an amazing figure considering neither of the Old Firm were in the final (St Mirren having dismissed Celtic 4-0 in the semi). St Mirren had taken the lead but the match was getting a little rough when Asuman, the Turkish maid/housekeeper provided by the company, ushered in the American, who, in the traditional way of Americans through time, entered with a loud and hearty 'Why hello there John, how are things?' to which my dad (having consumed several beers by this point) turned and shouted at him 'Fuck off you arsehole'. Now it has to be noted at this point that: a) my dad was never a drinker – the odd lager, a few whiskies at Christmas and that was that; and b) nor did he swear with any regularity at all. In fact I can only recall him swearing on some half dozen occasions throughout my childhood (and around half of them were when my mum was driving)

Of course the American was in total shock and turned and walked out the apartment. Mum sent dad off to see him the following week with a bottle of whisky and an apology. But as St Mirren had won 3-1, dad was more than happy to eat humble pie.

And so, after 2 years in Turkey, they returned to Paisley and decided it was time to start a family. I cannot imagine what they went through in the years that followed, but 4 times mum fell pregnant, and 4 times she miscarried. And when

I think about how there was no counselling or support groups or online forums in those days, it breaks my heart to think what she, what they went through.

They decided, despite advice from doctors not to, to give it one more try and this time there was no miscarriage, no heartbreak, just a gorgeous, smiling, beautiful (am I going overboard here?) baby boy born on the 17th July 1966, who they decided to call Graham William Robertson (the William after my Uncle Bill who was killed in North Africa during World War II). The downside was mum was told she would not be able to conceive again, but after all the heartbreak they were both just happy that mother and son were healthy.

As I said earlier, the first 12 years of childhood were fairly nondescript; though of course at the time every day seemed like a new adventure. When I arrived, mum and dad had moved from a tenement flat on Paisley's Glasgow Road to a new build in the village of Elderslie, just a few miles outside Paisley. Our house was in the second last row, and beyond that were open fields and, within walking distance, the Glennifer Braes. It was a good place to grow up; open spaces for football, woods for hide and seek and massive games of Japs and Commandos. No worries about child predators; we used to (in the summer holidays) leave the house at breakfast with a bag packed with lunch and juice, and not reappear till early evening for dinner.

I suppose it was an idyllic enough childhood and, without sounding like some whingeing old arsehole, the kids of today don't know what they missed.

Yes, there may be internet and games consoles and smart phones. And yes, foreign holidays may be more common and there are more food choices in supermarkets and restaurants. But do they have the imaginations we did when we were their age? When a patch of waste ground and adjoining woods could become South East Asian jungle? Or when a bit of wood could become a sub machine gun? Or unseen shadows in the trees monsters and demons?

So yes, it was fairly blissful. I was lucky enough to never have a major illness, never to go hungry, and to have parents who loved and nurtured me, even as the dreaded teenage years approached. But those years dreaded by parents would prove to be my awakening and set the foundations for the life ahead.

Chapter 2

I suppose at this point I should introduce John. He was my Aunt Mary's son in law; Mary was 18 years older than my mum, and that, combined with the fact that I was quite a late baby, meant that John was 35 when I was 12. For many years he had been the black sheep of his family because of his involvement in the music business, mainly working as a roadie (though he preferred the term 'guitar technician'). He'd worked with nearly all of the big names of the 70's rock scene; from T-Rex to Average White Band to The Who. He counted folk like Rory Gallagher and Alex Harvey among his close friends, though it wasn't till I was much older that I appreciated just how cool all of that was.

But no-one in the family, other than an impressionable kid, thought that this was an actual career. His job had taken him all over the UK and Europe, and even further afield on a few occasions, so he was certainly the well-travelled of our family.

Two years previously, he'd finally met my cousin Marion, someone who he felt gave him a reason to calm down a little. They had got married within 6 months and within another ten months, Linda had given him a baby girl who they had named Amy. This had given John even more reason to stay at home, and, for the first time ever, he got what my mum called a 'real job', working as the assistant manager of a music shop in Glasgow. He also gave guitar lessons in the evenings (he was later to say that his attempts at teaching me guitar had been among the most frustrating times of his life) and would still do some 'guitar technician' work for folk like Alex and Rory when they were in Scotland.

I'll also take this opportunity to go over my family dynamics as briefly as possible. We were not an overly close family, and in fact the two branches of my mum and dad's side hardly met due to various reasons peculiar to our geographic area in Northern Europe, but seen worldwide in differing forms. Despite my dad's strong Scottish surname, he came from a long line of Southern Irish Catholics dating back to the foggy and often overly romantic mists of time. Apparently we had a strong link to the historical O'Donnghaile clan and could claim royal blood going back almost twenty centuries. But given the historic prolificness of the Irish at producing large families, coupled with the interminably large number of small fiefdoms that the island had produced, it had been calculated by a team of crack scientists at Munster University that 96.7% of all people with Irish roots could lay a similar claim so I wasn't rushing to be fitted for a new crown just yet.

The flip side of this genetic coin was that my mum's side of the family were Ulster Protestants, staunchly pro-Union and more orange than a huge vat of

Kia Ora. John was the black sheep in this respect also, even though an in law, (nearly all the Orangeheads married other Orangeheads) and had long forsaken the singing of the Sash for the singing of rock classics. My Aunt Mary wasn't too rabid either, and I always felt close to her as we shared a birthday which meant she spoilt me rotten. But my other cousins could be seen marching the streets of the West of Scotland on a regular basis throughout the 'season', proudly celebrating their Protestant heritage and ignoring completely the way this was designed to divide the lower classes. This did produce a rather amusing (to me) incident later in my life when I was going through a radical phase and met some of aforementioned cousins on a counter march to the 'Troops Out of Ireland' demonstration I was at the front of. None of them talked to me after that till a family funeral some years later. I only had one grandparent alive: my dad's mum, who eventually passed on when I was eleven. I'd love to say we had a warm and loving relationship, but truth be told, she was a crabbit old bitch who was constantly causing problems for my dad and who never accepted my mum (filthy Protestant). My dad had two siblings; a sister called Moira who had a faux poshness that irritated me even at an early age, and a brother called Daniel who had downs syndrome and stayed with my Gran until her death, at which point he was decamped to an awful care facility that constantly smelt of urine and a lack of understanding. When I see the progress made today and how integrated downs syndrome children and adults can be, it makes me immensely sad to think of the utter lack of quality Daniel had in his life. Moira's marriage, to a poor downtrodden little man called Duncan, had produced one child, the cousin I was closest to afterJohn,Elizabeth, and we had even practised snogging on each other in our formative teenage years (in my defence, she was two years older than me and seduced me!)

My mum had at that time two brothers and one sister. Her brother John had never married (although he finally did when aged 53), while her brother James had two sons, Jim and John (there seemed a little lack of imagination name wise on that side of the family), and Mary had two daughters; Catherine and Marion (who was married to my mentor John). To underline that lack of imagination, Catherine had married a guy called Ian; they had two children, and named them...Catherine and Ian. Methinks that if they had put half the energy they put into sectarianism into the thinking of children's names, then my family may have had more variety in the nomenclature department.

So that was my family in a nutshell. There were a couple of honorary aunts and uncles but they play little part in the gist of the story so we will pass them by for now. You can probably understand why we never had any major family gatherings. It would have been akin to staging a re-enactment of the Battle of the Boyne with potentially similar levels of bloodshed.

It was now 1978. Punk was in full swing, and I was on the teetering cusp of awkward teenager status. My music taste was developing slowly; for some reason I never took to The Pistols, but from the first moment I heard 'White Riot', I was a Clash fan for life. There was such a gritty rawness that was tempered with true musical talent, and Strummer has to be the most influential and talented songwriter of his (and any other) generation.

Much to my horror, parts of my body had also started sprouting hair. At this point we had not studied the infamous 'Science, Section 6' that constituted the ineffectual sex education in the Scottish school system at the time.

My knowledge of the female body was limited to pictures from 70's porn mags like Club International, purloined from friends' fathers (despite Indian Jones levels of searching, I never found any of my dad's, and can only presume it was not his cup of tea). But these sudden sproutings had me terrified. And the first time I had an erection nearly made me run screaming downstairs. (Luckily I thought better of it). My mum and dad were pretty old fashioned and I had no conversations with them regarding sex until I was around 16. So, I sort of stumbled into puberty; a maelstrom of confusing psychological and physiological changes that had me all over the place emotionally. The anger of punk suited that moment to a tee, and mum and dad hated every chord, every lyric with a vengeance. Or maybe it was my accompanying mood swings, sulks and sudden ability to answer back that rubbed them up the wrong way. John was my escape, and added a new facet to my musical education. He had a vinyl collection that was of ludicrous proportions, though after the arrival of Amy, the records had all been relegated to the loft where John had installed his (damned good) stereo, a few cushions and posters in order to make a bolt hole from the realities of family life. John and Linda lived around a half mile from my school, so it was a convenient escape plan one or 2 evenings a week to escape to, help Linda with the baby, and await John coming in to take me further into his record collection.

Ah yes; school. I suppose I should really give some background on my 'wonderful' schools. As I mentioned, we were living in Elderslie; a small village between Paisley and Johnstone. I attended Wallace Primary (so named as Elderslie was the birthplace of Scottish hero, Sir William Wallace). Primary was fairly non eventful; usual boyish hi jinks, couple of completely dramatic and non-violent fights, and the statutory fear of impending secondary school. Where we lived fell within the catchment area of Paisley's John Neilson High School; an institution that had existed in one form or another since 1852. The current grey concrete monstrosity bore little resemblance to the grand old Victorian version, affectionately known in the town as 'the porridge bowl'. The school's catchment area covered three main areas of Paisley and surrounds;

Elderslie as mentioned, Millarston, and Ferguslie Park; at that time known as one of the three worst housing estates in Scotland. My mum was panicking more about this than anything else and had urged my dad to send me to Paisley Grammar. But my dad pointed out that the Grammar was at the other end of Paisley, and that they would not shield me from the realities of life, especially given their own working class roots.

And so it was that in August 1978, I started secondary school with punk as my soundtrack and the onrush of puberty as my emotional commentary. There was the expected jostling for position; who's the hardest first year? These spots, in fact most of the top ten, were quickly filled by Ferguslie Park boys, though there was one of our crowd, Willie, who was in the top 3 from day 1; mainly because he had this couldn't give a fuck attitude of someone much older and more jaded. But once those initial few weeks of sussing everyone else out were over, things settled down to fairly banal normality. The back of the gym was quickly identified as the clichéd and ironic spot for the secret smokers, and it was here I was first introduced to the wonders of Regal cigarettes. They say you always chase that first high, and I can still remember that first heady rush of nicotine mixed with the sulphurous aftertaste of the match, the almost euphoric dizziness that followed, and the inevitable coughing up of the guts as the poison hit your lungs. But I was hooked.

First year at secondary seemed to fly by. Other than one altercation with a particularly nasty prick called John McLeod, I managed to avoid any violence. I did however seem to develop a habit of getting the teachers' attention, usually for all the wrong reasons (and usually for saying things I shouldn't at the most inopportune times). In those days, Scottish schools still employed the tawse as a form of corporal punishment. The tawse was a strip of leather with the end divided into several 'tails'.

It was administered to the palm of the hand, and the usual level of punishment varied according to the misdemeanour, but could vary between 2 and 6 strokes. Some teachers had developed the use of the tawse as an art form, and I often trudged home at the end of the school day with stinging hands. There was even one teacher, close to retirement, who had been a Japanese POW, and was banned from using the tawse after breaking one pupil's wrist.

So, school life meandered on in that way it does when you are 12 going on 13. I saw and touched my first naked breast around 6 months into the school year thanks to the lovely Elaine McCardle. This first, tentative grope soon developed into a passionate (for that age) affair of touching and feeling and, after 2 months of furtive, uneducated heavy petting, I eventually got her fully naked. The not so romantic setting was the fields behind Stoddart's Carpet

Factory in Elderslie. Neither of us really knew what we were doing; no condoms, no education, and luckily I came as soon as the tip of my penis touched her pussy. Otherwise, I may have been a very young dad, with a backside severely tanned by both sets of parents. Probably just as lucky is that the relationship went sour soon after, and it would be many a moon till I came that close to sexual adventures again.

Chapter 3

First year ended, and the summer holidays, which always seemed so much longer in those days, began. When with my mates, the soundtrack of 1979 had The Clash, The Ruts, Dead Kennedys, The Buzzcocks, Joy Division, Tubeway Army, Kraftwerk and many others on it. When with John, it could be anything from T-Rex to Deep Purple, ELO to Steely Dan and Rush to Van Morrison. So it's fair to say that my musical education and tastes of the time were pretty damn eclectic. On the radio, it was nearly always the amazing John Peel, but on a Wednesday, it was our local radio station, Radio Clyde, that we always tuned into. Street Sounds with Brian Ford; the only alternative music you would find on an otherwise abysmal station more known for the likes of Tiger Tim than a Peel fan playing punk and new wave. It was also the first summer I got drunk. It soon became apparent that 9 out of 10 adults, when asked if they would go into the off licence to buy you booze, would readily agree. (Just try doing that now). So my first real drinking session consisted of 4 cans of Sweetheart Stout and ¾ of a bottle of El Dorado (a truly awful fortified wine around the 17.5% abv mark if I remember rightly, that was mostly known by its nickname 'Electric Soup'; a name used years later by an underground Scottish comic in the style of Viz). I was truly and utterly pissed, and as the group split up at the end of the night, the paranoia set in as to how to enter the house in my inebriated state without mum and dad noticing. I decided stealth was the order of the day, so let myself in, mumbled an 'I'm home' in the general direction of the living room, and headed up to my bedroom. Two minutes later, my mum's voice called me from the bottom of the stairs. I made it out my room and stood there swaying, like a wonky tree in a gale force wind. 'Have you been drinking?' asked my mum.

Rather than replying, I chose this moment to perform a triple twisting backflip somersault, all the way down the stairs, landing at my mother's feet, and finished my display of acrobatic prowess with some major vomiting all over her slippers. Needless to say, I was grounded for a month. I also swore never to drink again (though this pledge lasted perhaps 8 weeks).

The end of the summer holidays approached, but with a month to go came that huge milestone; becoming a teenager. And so it was; on 17th July 1979, I passed from childhood to the era of hell (my parents' description, not mine.)

Now, there seem to be lots of different suggestions as to why the number 13 is unlucky, but my personal view is that it was because it marks the beginning of the symbolic years of hellish behaviour, fumbling promiscuity and making your parents' lives unbearable.

More importantly, for me, it marked an extension of freedom. I was now allowed to get the bus from Elderslie to the big, evil city of Glasgow. That first Saturday journey, with a pocket full of birthday money, was like entering a whole new world. Paisley was a large town, but this was a city! A big city teeming with people, some of them very strange looking, traffic everywhere, and a complete smorgasbord of places to spend my money. The original plan was to buy some clothes, some shoes and some records, but the fondly remembered Listen records ended up with the whole £30 of my birthday cash. I can still remember every LP bought that day; Tubeway Army – Replicas;

Simple Minds – Life in a Day; The Clash – Give Em Enough Rope; Ian Hunter - You're Never Alone with a Schizophrenic (a definite John influence); The Rezillos - Mission Accomplished But the Beat Goes On; Ian Dury – Do It Yourself; Joy Division – Unknown Pleasures; David Bowie – Lodger, and The B52's eponymous album. Not a bad haul for thirty quid and had money left over to visit the chippy before the long bus journey home.

To make the month even better, John got permission from my mum and dad to take me to my first gig as he had a couple of freebies. So, on Tuesday 31st July 1979, John and I set off in his rather chic beige Morris Marina for The Glasgow Apollo to see Ian Dury and the Blockheads. There were two support bands who were so forgettable that I forget their names. But Dury…sweet fucking Jesus. I was hooked on live music from this point. I was already addicted to some of the grittiness I listened to on vinyl, but to see that in a live setting, with Dury's showmanship and the Blockheads' musical ability had me buzzing more than any substance I have ever found in my life (like that first cigarette, I was always chasing that first high). John, of course, was a veteran of live music, and though he found my exhilaration amusing, he also conceded that it had been a gig of the highest quality. He'd even used his influence to get me to the backstage area so I could collect autographs of the band. At the time it seemed amazing to someone of my age, and it meant even more later in life when I still revisited Dury's music.

From that point on, every penny I could save, scrimp or earn (I had the obligatory paper round as well as the more unusual egg round) went towards records or concert tickets.

Next up was Gary Numan in September (who had shortly before changed his name from Tubeway Army), supported by OMD the The Buzzcocks supported by Joy Division in October (this has always been a weird one to recount; while The Buzzcocks were amazing, most people later in life were more impressed that I saw Joy Division, who were, frankly, pretty bloody awful!). Next up were the Boomtown Rats (when they were still good) a week later, AC/DC at the end of that month (another John freebie), Hawkwind in November (again with John), The Jam in December, and rounded off the year with my Xmas present from John; tickets for Blondie on Hogmanay (from the opening chords of the first song, 'Denis', I was in love with Debbie for life.)

So, for me, that year, and becoming a teenager, marked the true beginning of my life. I was 13 but felt like I was 19. I smoked, I drank, I went to gigs, and I had already seen a pussy close up. But it was February 1980 when my real epiphany happened.

John and Linda rarely went out together, but as I had spent so much time with Amy, and was now a (hah!) responsible teenager, they decided to trust me with my first night of babysitting. It was only going to be for 3 hours as they were just going for a meal and a drink. Amy was already sleeping when I arrived at 6.30, and John took me out into the kitchen.

'Listen. I know you're a smoker these days. Have driven past the bus stop at the school a few times and seen you puffing away. Plus can smell it on you every time you visit. Just as long as you are eating mints before going home – your mum would tan your arse. Anyway, here, in case you don't have any, I've left you 3 roll ups (John only ever smoked rolling tobacco). My only rule is that you smoke them outside the back door. If I smell one bit of baccy in the house, I'll give you a good slap'

With these words of warning ringing in my ears, John and Linda headed off to their meal and left me to settle in front of the box. (I remember vaguely Jim'll Fix It being on; now not as much of a retro flavour as it once was!). After half an hour of watching inane dreams come true, I headed up to look in on Amy. As always, she was fast asleep (she was one of those rare babies who usually slept right through). On returning downstairs, I decided to try one of John's roll ups, so headed out the back garden, leaving the door slightly open so I could hear Amy if she did wake up. As I took my first few draws, I noticed a slightly strange flavour, but put it down to the difference between rolling and cigarette tobacco. Once finished, I settled back down in front of the TV. It so sticks in my mind that the musical Seven Brides for Seven Brothers was on, because for some strange reason, every song was making my heart beat faster, every colour on the screen suddenly seemed a thousand times more vivid than before. I wondered if I was coming down with something, and hoped I wouldn't have to settle Amy just in case it was a bug and I passed it on. Another half hour passed, so I again went outside for another smoke. This time, on returning to the sofa, the whole room seemed to be spinning and things appeared to be moving. I began to panic, rushed to the kitchen and gulped several glasses of water before opening the door and taking deep breaths of fresh air. What the hell was going on? I'd never felt like this before, not even during my alcohol experiments. The panic began to recede slightly and I went back to the sofa and lay down. Next thing I knew John was shaking me awake with a smile on his face.

'So, you smoked the roll ups then?'

Yeah, I had two cuz, but been feeling really weird. Sorry I fell asleep.'

John grinned; 'There's a good reason you were feeling weird. I'd put some afghan hash in each of the roll ups. I know all those daft wee pricks you hang about with are sniffing glue and gas. If I ever find out you have indulged, I'll give you the kicking of your life. You ever want a wee high, you come to me and I'll share a joint or two with you. And it goes without saying; not a word to your mum.'

I looked at him in horror. 'You gave me drugs? Why the hell did you do that?'

He laughed. 'Graham, a bit of dope now and again is pretty harmless, especially compared to that shit all your mates are sniffing. One question; how do you feel'

'Well, now the panic is gone, I'm actually feeling quite good. Sort of all happy on the inside.'

'Exactly. Much better than that evo stik shit. But I have some rules; you only have a smoke at weekends, you never tell your mum, and you don't go bragging to your mates'

I nodded. 'Promise cuz. I'm not that stupid. This will be our wee secret'.

And thus was born my lifelong love affair with cannabis. I'm not going to get involved in long moral debates here. Experiences in later life, and the recent changes in the law, have convinced me that my early fears that I would become a drug addict were nothing more than childhood naiveté. And I don't want you to think I suddenly turned into some sort of 'Reefer Madness' type dope fiend. I only smoked at weekends, and not every weekend either. And it would be 9 months before John even let me take some dope away with me, ready rolled, as I had a party to go to, and again with a promise of discretion and secrecy.

So otherwise life rolled on as normal (no pun intended). School meandered along in its own bland way. I continued to be a regular visitor to the rector's office on disciplinary matters. I had a couple of girlfriends, though none would allow me further than those wonderful early fumblings with Elaine. The biggest regret of 1980 was missing The Clash in Glasgow at the end of January. I had tickets, but was laid low by a nasty, nasty bout of gastroenteritis and had to pass them on to a friend. I never did make it to see them as a band, though in later life got to see both Joe and Mick perform in their respective new bands. What I did get was my first ever proper 'meeting a star' moment, when John took me to see Alex Harvey at the start of the month. I was ushered backstage by John, into a small crowded room, wreathed in smoke and smelling of whisky.

John introduced us, and I stood there star struck, amazed that at 13 I was shaking hands with one of the greatest rock musicians of his era. I ended up sat in a corner watching and listening to strings of profanities, groupies being groped in corners (I have always wondered if 'grope' should be the collective noun for groupies), and an endless stream of alcohol and drugs being passed round. John kept a close eye on me and only allowed me a lager and some of a joint as he knew he had to drop me off at home later that night. But it was another moment of epiphany; I knew this was the world I belonged in. I wanted it all; the glamour, the women, the drugs and the alcohol, and that I'd do anything to be part of that world. I blurted this all out to John on the way home and he laughed.

'It's not all glamour mate. There's long nights and days stuck in a van or a bus stinking of sweat and with no sleep. There are endless hours in practice and recording studios trying to get the sound right. And most bands struggle to make enough for petrol for the van. Alex is lucky; he is a star, but even with that there can be a price to pay.'

Despite his cynicism, I elicited a promise from him to teach me guitar, and as we headed back down the road, my mind was full of dreams of stardom, beautiful women and a life on the road.

Even though there had been the huge disappointment of missing The Clash, 1980 was a great year for me musically, both live and on vinyl. Over the course of the year I went to see Madness, The Stranglers (another band who were making a big impression on me, though John called them a poor Doors copy), The Ramones, The Tourists, Stiff Little Fingers, Thin Lizzy, Black Sabbath, Mike Oldfield (John's choice – I found him boring but he was supported by Gong who became another of my lifelong loves), The Undertones, Rush, Roxy Music supported by Martha and the Muffins, The Specials, Gary Numan (again), The Skids, Captain Beefheart, Hawkwind, The Jam, AC/DC and Motorhead. There was also the weirdness of seeing Ian Gillan open the Glasgow Virgin Megastore, with The Skids playing from an open top bus in the city centre for the same event. All in all not a bad haul of gigs for a 13/14 year old with pretty strait laced parents.

I experienced my first sense of loss with music on 18th May that year when it was announced that Ian Curtis had hung himself. I'd really identified with his lyrics, even though I thought they had been shit live the year before. I spent the entire evening replaying 'Unknown Pleasures' till my mum told me to switch off that 'bloody miserable dirge.' Their second album was released posthumously and, in my very humble opinion, still stands as a masterpiece of that era.

My vinyl collection was also growing steadily. Nearly all my pocket, paper round, egg round and chore money went towards music related products. Unfortunately, my other music related plans were not going as well. I have always had quite big fingers and any ability to play even the most basic guitar seemed beyond me. To give John his due, he persevered for several months before finally giving up in frustration. He even borrowed a bass guitar to see if that would suit me better, but all in all, it seemed that if I wanted to work in the music business, it would not be as a musician.

Chapter 4

And so 1980 segued into 1981. Much to my disappointment, and despite every effort, I was still a virgin, which made my next bout of trouble at school all the more ironic. Just before Christmas, I'd started seeing a girl in the year below me called Sandra Wilson. Cute little thing, and when I got more than a quick feel on only our 3rd date, I began to think that another teenage hurdle would soon be crossed.

Nearly every lunchtime we would head off to the park adjacent to the school for long sessions of amateur snogging and various gropes and feels. I was in paradise, but little did I know there were dark clouds gathering on the horizon.

We were in the middle of a class, I can't remember which subject, when there was a knock on the door and another pupil came in and spoke to the teacher in hushed tones. Everybody sat with bated breath; these sorts of incursions only meant one thing. Someone was in the shit and their presence was required by one of the senior staff. The teacher listened to the message, nodded, then looked up.

'Robertson! Report to Miss Cooper's office immediately.'

I looked up in shock, oblivious to the sniggers and mutters around me. I had not been up to any of my usual tricks the last week or two, perhaps the positive effects of young love, well young lust anyway. I hadn't even answered back to any of the teachers, even the stupid ones, for at least a week. Bewildered, and to a chorus of catcalls and jeers, I left the class and headed off on the long walk down to the administration block where Miss Cooper had her office.

When I arrived, I reported to the admin office and was told to take a seat. Five minutes turned into ten, which then turned to fifteen. Finally the door to Miss Cooper's office opened, and an older pupil came out, his hands tucked in his armpits to try and dull the sting of the freshly received punishment. I waited...

'Graham Robertson? Come in!' came the rector's stern voice.

I walked into the office I knew so well, shutting the door behind me, and standing sheepishly and confused in front of Miss Cooper's desk.

'Sit down Graham. Would I be correct in stating that you are currently seeing Sandra Wilson of S2?'

'Em, yes Miss.' I replied, wondering what the hell Sandra had to do with this.

'This is a very worrying situation Graham. You do realise that Sandra is only 13 and well under the age of consent?'

'Sorry Miss, I don't understand what you mean.'

Miss Cooper sighed impatiently. 'What I mean is that Sandra is 13 years old and it is a criminal offence to have sex with a 13 year old.'

I stared at her dumbly, my mouth hanging open. 'I know that Miss, but I still don't know why I am here.'

Her face darkened. 'Robertson, your 13 year old girlfriend is pregnant. To get someone pregnant you need to have sex with them. Now do you understand why you are here? Sandra's parents are on their way here now, as is someone from social services, and it may very well be the case that the police are involved by the end of the school day.'

I gasped in shock. Sandra pregnant? It must be a mistake! Our fumbles had not progressed as far as any inter genital contact at this point, and even a naïve 14 year old knew that a finger could not get a girl pregnant.

I stammered. 'B,b,b,but Miss. I've not had sex with Sandra! We have been going out for 2 months but nothing like that has happened.'

She stared at me with clear disbelief on her face. 'It would go better for you if you were completely honest about this Graham; this is a very serious matter.'

I stared back defiantly. 'Miss, I am being honest. We have not had sex at all.'

'Do you deny that you both spend nearly every lunchtime in the park or that you have spent time together there after school?'

'No Miss, not at all, but just because we spend time together there does not mean we are having sex!'

She sighed again. 'Very well. There seems no point in continuing this discussion if you refuse to be honest. I have no choice but to suspend you from school while we and social services look into the matter. I have phoned your mother and told her of the situation and she will be arriving to collect you shortly. It may also be the case that social services, and the police if they become involved, will want to come and speak to you. You could be in a lot of trouble. Now go and sit outside the secretary's office till your mum arrives.'

I stormed out the office, half of me angry as hell at being accused of something so serious, half of me confused and scared at what my parents' reaction would be. I sat down, eyes glued to the floor and refusing to look up at anyone who passed, even though I heard the odd giggle from passing students.

Finally a shadow entered my field of vision and remained there. I looked up. My mum stood there, face like a Scottish winter sky.

'In the car, now! We will talk when we get home.'

That fifteen minute drive was one of the worst of my life. I wanted to blurt out protestations to her, to shout my innocence out loud, but I knew better than to start an argument with my mum when she was driving; she was always very low on patience when she was behind the wheel. We arrived home and I went to head to my room to drop my bag and get changed.

'Don't bother going to your room to hide. In the living room now.'

I went into the lounge and sat down, my mum taking a seat on the sofa opposite.

'Mum, I really don't know what is going on. This is all rubbish. I've not had sex with Sandra, honest!'

'Then why are social services involved? How is she pregnant? It all makes sense. Since you started seeing this girl, you've been coming home later and later from school. You explained away most of your lateness as basketball practice and games because there was a competition coming up, but Miss Cooper says you dropped out of the basketball team just after Christmas. You do realise police could charge you for this? Never mind the fact of that young girl having a baby at that age and you having to be a father.'

I had indeed dropped out of basketball at the start of the new term. The prospect of running about putting balls into a hoop was far less exciting than the idea of my balls getting emptied by something other than manual means.

'Look mum, I have no idea how she got pregnant. I didn't know she was pregnant till today! But I do know this is nothing to do with me!'

'Right, go to your room till your dad gets home. You obviously do not want to talk to me about this so maybe you will be more honest with your father.'

For the second time that day, I stormed off. I stomped upstairs, slammed my bedroom door shut and threw myself on the bed, hurt, angry and confused. Why did no-one believe me?

The next couple of days were hell. My dad's arrival home that first night had commenced with mum and him talking downstairs, then me shouted down to the living room, and then a major argument for the next hour or so, still with no-one willing to believe that, perhaps for once, I was totally innocent of what I'd been accused of. Day 2 saw a visit by two social workers to interview me, though when I looked back when I was older, the term 'interrogation' would probably have been more appropriate. Sandra was apparently refusing to say anything; a fact that angered me more than anything as with one sentence she could absolve me of any and all responsibility. Why was she not clearing my name? Of course, I couldn't phone her. In fact, dad had gone so far as to put a lock on the phone in case I tried to contact her while mum was busy and he was at work.

Dinners were eaten in silence, and I spent all of the day in my room, reading and listening to music. Even that caused more conflict as my anger and frustration made me pick not only my loudest, angriest records, but to constantly turn the volume up till mum or dad came and shouted at me to turn it back down.

Day 4 finally came, and with it a phone call from the school asking if my mum and I would attend the school for a meeting with Miss Cooper that afternoon at 4pm. We drove there in silence; everything that could have been said had already been said (or shouted) over the previous three days. When we arrived and announced our presence to the admin office, we were told to go straight through. My mum knocked and Miss Cooper's voice told us to come in. We both sat down in front of the desk and Miss Cooper began.

'Mrs Robertson, Graham. Thank you for coming in today. Graham? I'm afraid I have to apologise to you. Sandra finally told the whole story to her social worker this morning, and the test results from her doctor back up that she is telling the truth. She is pregnant by her last boyfriend, who is apparently 17, which is why she was so reluctant to tell the truth and to let you off the hook. She told social services that she thought that because you were only a year older, you would not get into trouble with the police. But when it was explained to her that you might still face charges, she admitted that it was nothing to do with you. I can only apologise again for what your family has gone through these last few days but I hope you understand that we have to take situations like this very seriously.'

I'm sure there must have literally been steam coming out of my ears at this point. Although there was a huge amount of relief, I was angry beyond description. No-one had believed me, and Sandra had held back the truth to protect some 17 year old prick of an ex-boyfriend. There was probably a bit of me that was equally angry that I had still not managed to lose my virginity but that she had been shagging her last boyfriend. I was so lost in my thoughts that I missed most of what Miss Cooper had been saying.

'…and of course that is the matter finished as far as Graham is concerned and we look forward to seeing him back on school on Monday.'

'Miss, there is one thing I don't understand; did everyone just assume it was me because we recently started seeing each other? And how did you know we spent all that time in the park'

For once the roles in this office were reversed, and it was my school rector who looked sheepish and embarrassed.

'The matter was brought to our attention by one of Sandra's friends, well probably former friend by now, who apparently had a thing for you Graham, and was aggrieved when you chose her friend over her. So, when Sandra confided in her that she was pregnant, she saw a chance to cause some trouble. She has been dealt with and is suspended from school for a fortnight.'

The fucking bitch! I knew exactly who she meant. Sandra's friend Lyndsay, who had sent me a note about two months before Christmas asking me out, but I'd had no interest. She was a chubby wee ginger thing with bad spots, and at that time, I was far too young to manage the ten pints necessary to face something like that. I would be having some stern words with that wee cow when I saw her next, never mind that slag of a girlfriend, no slag of an EX-girlfriend after these last few days.

The journey home was nearly as uncomfortable as the one a few days previously had been. I knew mum wanted to apologise, but stubbornness has always been a family trait. Finally she broke the silence.

'Graham son, I'm sorry we didn't believe you. But you can see how it looked to use. Everything added up, and with you lying about playing basketball, how could we believe you about this lassie?'

I was still seething at the betrayals and the lack of trust. 'There's a damned big difference between a wee fib about playing basketball and lying about getting that silly besom pregnant!'

My mum went quiet again, not even pulling me up on the use of the word 'damned'. (I think, over my mum's lifetime, I swore in front of her on maybe 4 or 5 occasions, and each incident other than this was met by a stern rebuke, no matter what age I was)

'Aye son, I'm sorry. Maybe we should have realised you wouldn't lie about something so serious. And I can normally tell when you're trying to get one over on me. You seemed genuinely upset about these accusations.'

'And I still am!' I shouted. 'Just wait till I see that besom in school next week.'

'Graham, there's no point in going in and kicking off. That daft lassie has made some big mistakes and I think having a baby at 13 is punishment enough for her. Just go back to school on Monday and act like nothing has happened.'

I didn't reply. Mum just didn't understand; I'd been suspended from school, so there would be multiple interrogations as to what had happened when I returned. Then inwardly I smiled. I'd seen a way to turn this to my advantage. There was a good chance that the news of Sandra's pregnancy had leaked, and that this was why I had been suspended. But it was also likely that people would know that it was her ex who had got her pregnant. Where it could go well for me was kudos value; although I had escaped blame for her pregnancy, there was no reason for people to know that I hadn't been shagging her. This would raise me up amongst my peers, as there were only 2 folk in my year that I knew of who had admitted to popping their cherry (and one of those claims was suspect.) It still meant I had the real line still to cross, but I could walk into school with my head held high and a knowing smile on my face.

And so it was that as far as my peers were concerned, I lost my virginity in a public park to the school bike. Maybe not the most impressive thing to put on your resume, but when you're that age, it impressed your mates. The downside, however, was that it became more difficult to pull a girl. They all thought now that as a non-virgin, I would expect sex in any relationship (and I suppose they were right. Love does not really come into the equation when you are that age, and respect for the opposite gender was an island I still had to visit.)

Chapter 5

The rest of 1981 was fairly uneventful. I managed to avoid any more major trouble at school. I continued to visit John and have the odd smoke with him, and I continued to rack up gigs. I'd gone to my first non-Apollo gig at the start of the year. New Order at the Eglinton Toll Plaza. The band that had risen from the ashes of Joy Division had moved to a different sound, influenced hugely by the New York club scene, and Bernard Sumner had taken over vocal duties. I think I actually cried a little when they dedicated 'Ceremony', the closing song, to the memory of Ian. Tiffany's (now the student meat market that is The Garage in Glasgow) was next on my list of new venues for U2. Much as I hate what they have become, especially the swelling of Bono's ego to a size that threatens to swallow all the air on the planet, I have to say that they were brilliant live in the early days when they had not reached the levels of stadium arrogance. I even went back to see them at the same venue in December, though by that stage, the success of 'War' was beginning to manifest itself in the growing egotistical swagger of their singer. Tiffany's sort of became my venue of choice for gigs with friends as John was not really into the new wave/new romantic scene at all. (It elicited several old fogey comments about boys in make up till I pointed at Bowie, Bolan and The Sweet). My 'fashion' sense then was as eclectic as my music taste. (If you can credit a 14 year old with fashion sense). My mum and dad had never approved of the more outlandish styles, but my best friend David's parents were a little more liberal. So I had managed to accumulate a few pieces of clothing specifically for gigs that were stashed at his house. Included in this wardrobe were a couple of red satin shirts (and yes, with ruffles), one black with red detail and the other vice versa. I had a couple of pairs of black drainpipe trousers, and one obligatory pair of high waisted (though not to Cowellesque extremes) baggy trousers in black with white piping.

My 2 items that were my pride and joy, however, were a buccaneer jacket (sort of like the Adam Ant one, but with horizontal gold braiding across the front), and the most ludicrous pair of winklepickers I'd been able to find in Glasgow. Let's just put it this way; if at any point I'd been confronted by a wild animal or a pack of rabid dogs, I could have removed these shoes and used them as spears. The early part of the year saw me hit Tiffany's for Gang of 4 and Simple Minds in March. Gang of 4 were simply amazing live but had attracted more of a punk crowd that night so there were a few glasses (full and non-full) thrown about during the gig which really pissed me off. Simple Minds were another band who were amazing in their early days, but, for me, became rather bland when they reached stadium status later that decade. Though at least Jim Kerr's ego remained a milli-fraction of his contemporary in U2. In May, I'd finally met a girl who did not know of my alleged misadventures from the start of the year (mainly because she was at a school on the outskirts of Glasgow). The scare of the Sandra incident seemed to have calmed my hormones a bit, and though I was all up for a bit of heavy petting, I was reluctant to even think of taking it any further. I'd met Mary at The Cure gig at Tiffany's. She was a vision of gothic beauty; white make up and dressed all in black with hair that she must have backcombed for hours. She was also a year older than me, twice as confident (even though I was a cocky so and so at that age) and had initiated conversation by offering to buy me a snakebite and black (the de rigeur drink of the era). I wouldn't say it was love; can a 14 year old have the maturity to be in love? But she was funny, clever and absolutely gorgeous. She also introduced me to make-up (now you need to remember that the whole new romantic and new wave scene had some very androgynous styles and style icons, mostly deriving their influence from Bowie who was seen as the Godfather of the new romantic movement). Nothing overboard; a bit of eyeliner usually.

First time I wore any out (applied expertly by Mary) I was nervous as hell, but then realised that 80% of the guys around me were also wearing some; from the subtle to the ridiculous. But I soon lost that self-conscious feeling and was happy with a bit of slap on! That gig was one of the best of the year; Teardrop Explodes and The Delmontes. Cope was on top form and was another act I stuck with throughout my life. Trips to Tiffany's that year (usually either with Mary or David) included Duran Duran, The Beat, Bauhaus (Mary in full Goth mode) and Killing Joke.

The other side of my fashion 'sense' was bog standard teenager. Jeans and t-shirts and trainers, and this tended to be both the outfit I always left the house wearing, and what I would have on if attending gigs with John. He regularly got free passes for The Apollo, and most of the bands playing there tended towards the 'rockier' side of the music scene. I did dress up for the Adam and the Ants gig there in March, and John nearly had a coronary when he saw me. Again I had to remind him of the flamboyance of Bowie and some of the 70's acts he had followed and worked with. But over the course of the year, we managed to get to see The Who (superb), Elvis Costello, The Undertones, The Kinks, Stiff Little Fingers, Toyah, Kraftwerk (this time with Mary; John kindly gave us both the passes for it), Siouxsie and the Banshees (with John and Mary. He was quite impressed that I had a seemingly decent and steady girlfriend), Ultravox, Madness, Tangerine Dream, Thin Lizzy, OMD, Human League, The Stranglers and a second Toyah gig (this one notable as the wonderful Fad Gadget were the support act). I was gutted (and feeling jinxed) to miss The Clash again, as my bloody mum and dad decided to choose that week to have our first ever October holiday away from home. But overall, I felt that by the end of the year I had racked up another list of great and amazingly eclectic gigs.

My musical experiences were head and shoulders ahead of my peers, though this was mainly down to John as I had not paid a single penny for one of the Apollo gigs, and he'd even managed to wangle us guest passes for a couple of the Tiffany's shows.

As the end of summer approached, I was a happy lad. I was going to gigs regularly; I had a beautiful older girlfriend, good friends all around and was enjoying the odd smoke at John's. From the dark clouds that had started the year, blue skies seemed to be all around as the year ended.

Chapter 6

Although 1981 had brought with it panic and trouble at school, it had also brought an incident that would be another major part of my life's jigsaw. A couple of times at gigs, I'd bumped into an older guy from school called Eric. Eric was in 5th year and had the honour of being the 'school DJ'. Although in retrospect a Citronic Hawaii in a custom case is not that glamorous, at 15 years of age, he was like a pop star up on that stage at the school discos. (albeit a slightly pimply pop star with red hair). He had started chatting to me more and more at school as he realised I was serious about my music, and when he found out I spent a lot of money on vinyl, he asked if I'd thought about being a DJ. This was a 'Eureka' moment of the highest magnitude. I had realised that I had little or no musical talent at all when it came to instruments, but was still determined that I wanted to work in the music business. Suddenly visions of being the new John Peel surfaced in my mind.

What made the offer even more inviting was when Eric showed me he had built in hidden compartments to the DJ console and that therein, he regularly kept a half bottle of vodka and a couple of ready rolled joints (obviously not for smoking in the middle of the stage). He said he would train me up on how to use the equipment, and that initially I would cover breaks for him; maybe 20-30 minutes at a time so he could nip outside for a smoke away from the prying eyes of the teachers. The 'training' was pretty simplistic. This was well before the days of beat mixing, and a DJ still had the 'pleasure' of using a microphone between the odd track or to make dedications. I actually cringe when I look back at it in some ways but it was all part of both the learning curve and the building blocks for the rest of my life. Although Eric had similar tastes, we mainly overlapped in the rock or guitar based side of music. He was not really into the electronic or new romantic scenes, so it was agreed that this would be my niche. So, my first ever DJ gig was in February 1981. I can't remember the exact set lists I played that night (so wish I had noted each and every record) but I do remember playing Human League, Siouxsie, Teardrop Explodes, Tears for Fears and Bowie. It went down pretty well, with the hall floor never less than half full. But once again I had found a new buzz; the feeling of dropping a tune and looking up to see the crowd react was one that I would never grow tired of (though I was glad when the DJ microphone became a thing of the past). Surprisingly (to me) my mum and dad were quite approving of this new hobby, though a hobby was what they saw it as rather than my vision of a potential career. Mum did a lot of stuff through the church (a hobby I had abandoned at 13) and one of the things she was involved in was hospital visits, so she suggested she put me in touch with Hospital Radio Paisley, who 'broadcasted' to most of the hospitals in the area. She thought she was just encouraging a hobby, but this, for me, offered yet another career chance, as I knew quite a few of the Radio Clyde DJ's had cut their teeth on hospital radio stations.

So, one Saturday morning, I traipsed along to their dingy offices in Paisley's High Street for an interview and to see around the studio. I had expected glitz and glamour; what I found was dark, gloomy rooms, coffee mugs everywhere and a cloud of smoke permeating every corner. Colin, the studio manager took me into an office and chatted to me about the various tasks volunteers undertook. My dreams of being on air within a week or two soon evaporated as I realised I would have to start at the bottom with hospital visits to collect requests for the shows before moving on to the production side of things (basically collating the records from the library for any particular show) before finally getting to go live. The hospital visits were tedious and boring. You would go from bed to bed with your little clipboard and ask the patients if they listened to Hospital Radio Paisley. If they did, you would ask them if they wanted a request played, and on what show. If they didn't, you would extol the virtues of the station and suggest they give it a try. I did this dutifully for a month before someone leaving the station gave me a chance at learning production. This was much more fun. Though to be honest, the playlists were not exactly at the cutting edge of the music scene. Not such a surprise given the average age of many of the patients. But at least it was more interesting than walking round disinfectant soaked wards. Most shows were 2 hours long (we 'closed' at 11pm and took a feed from Radio Clyde from then on. There was a station playlist that certain songs had to be played from, there were the records the presenter him/herself wanted to play, there were the requests to sift through and identify what was suitable (and what we actually had), there were news and weather slots, and some shows had features (current affairs etc). It was my job to put all these things together into a 2 hour show, to make sure all the records were stacked in order, and that all required jingles or pre-recorded features were ready on cartridge or tape. Despite the lack of musical quality to the station, I enjoyed the organisational side.

Although it was the presenter whose voice was heard by the listeners, it was the producer who constructed the show and made it what it was. Colin was impressed that I was throwing myself into the work with such enthusiasm, and also allowed me to start studio training to learn how the various bits of equipment worked and how to present a decent show. Eventually, on Sunday 25th April 1981, and thanks to the regular presenter being ill with flu, I got my first chance to go live on radio all by myself. It was not the show I would have chosen. The 12 to 2pm Sunday show was an all request show, I had little to do in it other than introduce records or link to the news and weather, but it was still, for me, a momentous day. Now I could embellish things here, talk about how the young soul rebel dropped Dexy's Midnight Runners or Bowie into the mix, but this tale is about being honest about my experiences, so I need to tell the truth that my wonderful debut on the airwaves opened with that underground cult classic, 'One day at a time' by Lena Martell. Not that I was going to disclose this to any of my mates at school. Oh God no. They were regaled with tales of spinning The Clash and Depeche Mode and long segments of talking about the new wave scene.

But anyway; it seemed to go well, there was only one major mistake (putting a 45rpm 7" single on at 33rpm) and Colin said I could soon have a regular spot. This took another two months to come to fruition, but till then I continued with production and covering for absent presenters. But at the end of July, I finally got a Thursday night show from 5 till 7pm and even managed to slip in the odd record of my own for the rest of my time at Hospital Radio Paisley.

Chapter 7

I realise I have not really said much about friends over these first teenage years. There was one constant in my life, and indeed we are still in touch electronically though it has been many years since we actually saw each other. David Collins lived one row behind me in Elderslie. I could see his bedroom window from mine which made communication easy (though our parents put a stop to the string/tin can system we wanted to install). I can't remember how, or why, we became friends, but from the age of 7 we were a dynamic duo of mischief, plots and pushing our respective parents to the limit. The friendship never faltered, though there was one rocky period I shall come to shortly. We never had a physical fight (Well, not a full on one), though there were verbal altercations as every friendship must have. We would stick up for each other, lie for each other and always one of us would call in for the other on the way to school. There was an 18 month period when David was gone. His dad worked for IBM and was sent to America on secondment for a while when the first ATM machines were being rolled out. David came back with a healthy tan (they had lived in San Diego) and with American wonders that were not freely available at home. His was the first skateboard seen in Elderslie (or indeed Paisley) and very probably the first American football too. We had Frisbees, but they were cheap plastic things from Woolworths, while David brought back some semi-professional model used in the US, as well as a whole range of tricks he had learned. There were other friends in the group too; David's wee brother Stuart was only a year younger so would often tag along. There was Graham 2 (to avoid confusion), Steven and Martin, all living within 5 minutes walking distance. Other friends we only tended to see at school, at weekends, or if we went into Paisley, but those first names were the core of our group through the main part of my childhood. I'd mentioned one fall out with David, and it came in September of 1981.

I'd split up with Mary the month before. Well, I say split up with but the truth was she had dumped me for an 18 year old she'd met at a gig in Edinburgh. I was heartbroken for all of 3 or 4 days. It's strange how that childhood innocence helps you deal with these situations easier than when you are supposedly older and wiser. There was a girl David and I both knew called Fiona. She lived a couple of doors from our friend Tam down by the (infamous) carpet factory and, for a girl, she was a good laugh and not as self-obsessed as most of the girls we knew seemed to be. We both fancied her like mad but neither of us had the balls to do anything about it. Then one day, she phoned me at the house and, much to my despair, told me that she really liked David and asked if I could set them up on a date for that coming weekend. Looking back from later in life, I realise that this was the first ethical dilemma I ever faced, and, much to my shame, I failed it miserably. I sat in my room for around an hour, The Buzzcocks on my record player, and tried to decide what to do. David was my best mate and I knew he liked Fi, but I was really into her too and did not want to lose her to anyone. My mind made up, I went back downstairs and phoned her.

'Hi Fiona, it's Steven.'

'Oh hi. Did you speak to David?'

I took a deep breath.

'Yes, just off the phone to him there. Listen Fi, I'm sorry, but he says he is only interested in you as a friend.'

I could already feel the gates of hell beckoning for my lies.

'Oh. But I was sure he liked me. Ach never mind, but that's my plan for the weekend gone then.'

I took another deep breath.

'Fiona? I know it's not what you wanted, but we get on really well. Why don't we go to the pictures this weekend instead?'

The die was cast. I was damned for eternity.

'Well…why not! Yes, that sounds a great idea Steven. You sure you don't mind keeping me company?'

Company? I had far more devious plans than just keeping her company.

We arranged to meet at Elderslie Baths on the Saturday afternoon and get a bus out to the Kelburne Cinema on Glasgow Road. I was ecstatic! I had a date with a girl I had lusted after for ages. So why did I feel so goddamned guilty?

We met as arranged, and duly headed off for the Kelburne on the bus. I was desperate to see Conan The Barbarian, but realised it might not be the ideal 'date film' so took the easy way out and said that Fiona could choose. Luckily she chose my second choice; Dead Men Don't Wear Plaid, so I was happy that we had not been stuck with something like the Julie Andrews musical comedy, 'Victor, Victoria.' (Weirdly I watched and loved this film years later but it wasn't really one that would fall within the then taste parameters of a teenage boy).

We collected the tickets and the obligatory supplies and made our way into the cinema. Fi was dressed casually in jeans and a Fruit of the Loom sweatshirt, but boy did she fill them out for a 15 year old girl. I could feel the testosterone levels rising as we took our seats and I hoped and prayed that my friend betraying machinations would at least have some sort of payoff). The cinema was fairly quiet with it being the afternoon showing and I had tried to not be overly obvious in picking a row two or three down from the back one. I felt like I was in one of those old cartoons where there's a devil on one shoulder and an angel on the other (a theme that would recur throughout my life), one urging a path of good, the other a path of sin (and fun). Eventually the winged cherub lost the argument and I subtly, or as subtly as a teenage boy with raging hormones and a tent in his pants could manage, let my hand slip down to cover Fiona's hand. To my surprise and joy, she reciprocated and shifted in her seat so she could rest her head on my shoulder. I made sure my left arm was casually draped across my lap so she wouldn't notice my unequivocal state of excitement, and moved my right hand and arm around her shoulder, my fingertips only brief frustrating centimetres from her right breast. I'd completely lost interest in the film, and was now only concerned in the next move. To my shock, and utter delight, it was Fiona who initiated the next step some ten minutes later (well she was the older woman, albeit only by a few months).

Her head seemed to nuzzle deeper into my shoulder then I felt her head turn upwards toward mine. Thinking she was going to say something, I mirrored her movement and declined my head towards her. But instead of words, I found soft teenage lips seeking out mine, with of course the obligatory amateur bumping of noses first.

She was an expert kisser, far more adept than my supposed level of expertise, and her probing tongue was firmly in control. We kissed for what seemed like ages, then she whispered to me;

'We don't seem to be watching much of the film. What say we get out of here and buy some cider.'

I suddenly became aware of the very obvious erection straining at my jeans.

'Em, sounds like a plan Fi. But let's wait five or ten minutes first.'

Her left hand lightly brushed across my lap and my hard on. I jumped. Fiona giggled.

'Oh dear, I seem to have got you a little hot and bothered. I suppose we better wait till you can actually stand up.'

After what seemed like an eternity, I felt able to get up without thinking everyone would be staring. We walked hand in hand along the road, the cool early summer evening a counterpoint to the heat I was feeling inside. There was an off licence on the corner of Lacy Street, and Fiona headed over to see if she would get served with her false ID. Within five minutes she was back, proudly clutching a plastic bag with two bottles of Olde English cider in it.

'So, where will we go to drink this?' I asked. 'Barshaw Park?'

'Best place really. And should be fairly quiet at this time.'

Barshaw Park was a medium sized park to the east of Paisley, shortly before an unseen border marked entry to Glasgow. It had the usual shit; crappy little pond, pitch and putt, and a golf course to the back.

We headed up the hill to the side of the 'lake' and Fiona opened the first bottle of cider while I lit us both a Regal Small. There were a few other folk on the hill, mostly illicit drinkers like us. Fi took the proffered cigarette and let out a contended sigh.

'Well, the weekend's worked out okay then. Maybe just as well David didn't like me enough.'

Oh fuck. The attack of the rampaging guilt morality pixies had returned. And the sweet little devil perched on my shoulder suffered a sudden sucker punch as the bastard angel sneaked up on him.

'Em, listen Fi, about that. I've been a bit of a prick. I never told David that you liked him. I fancied you too much myself.'

Fiona sat straight up and stared at me. Damn; that was the hormones back in the cage again. Then she laughed out loud.

'What a sneaky bastard! But I suppose I should be flattered. I actually sort of liked both of you, but I still thought you were getting over Mary and I was getting bored with no boyfriend.'

Result! Half of my ethical burden had been removed in one fell swoop, and she hadn't slapped me and stormed off. I could handle the David half of the problem at a later date.

She put the cider down and moved in for a kiss, her hand pulling me closer. God, this girl knew how to take control, and my hard-on was back in full effect. Fiona noticed this quickly (note to self; must get jeans that hide erections better.)

'Why Graham, I do believe you are all excited again. Why don't we head over to the golf course and find somewhere a little more private?'

I gulped. Then I gulped again. And for good measure I gulped a third time. I had no idea what she had in mind, but whatever it was, I was fully supportive of it. We headed down the other side of the hill and made for Barshaw golf course. There was a thick row of bushes bordering the course, and Fi pulled me towards them. We managed to find a small clearing in the midst of them and made ourselves comfortable on the grass. Fiona took another long drink of cider and smiled at me, a twinkle in her eyes that spoke of far more experience than her 15 years suggested.

'There are some rules Graham. Don't think you are getting to shag me on the first date, but I'm feeling pretty randy so we can have some fun. If you're good, I may even give you a blow job.'

I returned to my previous habit of repetitive gulps. Could the betrayal of a friend really lead to my first ever experience of oral sex? And what did she mean; if I was good? She passed me the cider and in keeping with my state of mind, I took several gulps. I handed the bottle back and she placed it on the grass and moved closer to me. I leaned towards her and kissed her greedily.

'Hey, slow down Graham. We're not in a rush are we?'

Well I was actually. Even though Mary had been older, she had allowed me no further than clumsy groping of her boobs. Any attempt to head further south had been met with a slap to the hand and a serious look. Now all of a sudden I had a girl beside me who had virtually offered to give me a blow job. (Though the 'if you're good' was still confusing me)

I kissed her again, this time more slowly. Her body pressed against mine and my hand moved to her pert teenage breasts. She moaned gently and pushed herself harder against me.

'Hold on a minute.' She whispered. 'Let's make this easier.'

With simply amazing dexterity, she reached up her sweatshirt, unhooked her bra and with some twists and turns somehow managed to take it off without removing her top.

'There. That makes it a lot simpler.'

Gulp. Gulp again. Well, you get the gist by now. My hand eagerly sought her now naked breasts beneath her sweatshirt. God, they were wonderful.

'Graham, play with my nipples.'

Em, okay. This was a new one. My prior breast exploration experience had mainly consisted of, well, holding them, and sort of rubbing them. So girls liked their actual nipples played with? No-one had told me that! I hesitantly put a finger on her nipple, not entirely sure what to do next. She sighed.

'You've not done this bit before have you? I can see I have a lot to teach you.'

Can you guess what comes next? That's right; gulp to the power of 10.

She pulled up my t shirt and took my right nipple between thumb and forefinger and gently at first began to squeeze and tease it. I gasped and gulped. I'd never thought my own nipples could be a source of pleasure. Have to add that to the wanking sessions.

'See? Like that. Start gently then squeeze a little more firmly. You'll know if I like it.'

I tried again, mimicking what she had just done to my own nipple. She let out a little moan as I began to roll her nipple between that magic thumb and forefinger.

'Oh yes. That's it. Much better. And don't just play with one. Play with both.'

I twisted round so I could get both hands up her top. As my learning fingers played with her responsive nipples, her moans and gasps became more frequent.

'God yes, those fingers are amazing. Let me take this off.'

She pulled back from me and removed her sweatshirt. I gulped (yes, again) and gazed at sheer perfection with an open mouth. She laid her top out on the ground and lay back on it, shocking me still further by undoing the button on her jeans.

'So...we've taught you how to play with nipples properly. But do you know how to suck them?'

Gulp.

'Yes, well I think so. I mean, I have kissed them before. Maybe you should show me again.' (Hey, quick thinking Batman)

Fi sighed again then hooked her fingers in the bottom of my t-shirt and pulled it over my head.

'Like this...'

Her head bent forward and I felt her soft tongue find the tip of my nipple. I shuddered. God, this was amazing. Her tongue began to circle my nipple then her lips enveloped it and she began to gently suck. I gasped and gulped. My erection was in full effect now. I couldn't remember my body feeling like this ever before. Then she began to lightly bite my nipple, alternating between that and soft licking. This was amazing.

'Now it's my turn.' She purred, and lay back down on the ground.

I lay beside her and followed the game plan she had just shown. Her moaning became louder now and I worried for a moment that a passing golfer may hear us, before realising that the vegetation would muffle any sound. Her body gave little shudders as I changed techniques. All my previous clumsy petting seemed so amateurish now compared to what Fiona was teaching me. As I continued with my attention to her nipples, her hand grasped mine and pushed it downwards, further south, toward the holy grail of boyhood fantasies. She kept her hand on top of my own and guided me.

'There, feel that little bit sticking up? Like a button? Rub that gently, not hard. I'll tell you when to do more.'

Her guidance had left my fingers on top of said 'button' and I gently began to massage it, noticing with delight that her body responded to each little movement and that she was moaning more and more.

'Yes Graham. Oh yes. Now, feel how wet I am down there? That means I'm excited. Slowly slip one finger inside me, but keep playing with my clitoris with your thumb.'

Clitoris?? Was that what her 'button' was called? I realised that what I had thought was 'man of the world' knowledge had been nothing more than 'boy of the village'. I followed her instructions and tenderly slipped my forefinger insider her while still massaging her apparently named clitoris.

'Oh god, yes, yes. Those fingers are amazing. I can see I will have a lot of fun with you. Now move your finger in and out of me.'

I complied, a mere student to this font of sexual learning. Her body began to shake more and more and her gasping became more frequently. Suddenly her whole body convulsed and she let out a long moan before falling limply backwards. I sat up in shock. Had I hurt her?

'Oh my God, are you ok Fi? Was that sore?'

She breathed heavily for a few minutes then laughed quietly.

'Oh no Graham, you didn't hurt me at all. That was me coming, and God it was good.'

The penny dropped. She'd had an orgasm! I felt an amazing sense of pride. This was the first time I had given someone an orgasm! (Well apart from self-inflicted ones, but that goes without saying for a developing teenage boy). It was also a moment of epiphany. For the first time I realised that sex was not a selfish act.

It wasn't about seeking the maximum amount of pleasure for yourself, but for both of you. I curled up beside her, my head on her chest, listening to her racing heart and tracing light patterns across her belly.

'You know Graham, that was a nasty trick you pulled on David, but I'm sort of glad you did. That was amazing.'

I smiled. My ego was well and truly massaged and praised, though I had to be honest; Mr Tenty was actually beginning to hurt now. I wondered if I had been good enough to cross that magic threshold of sexual progress.

'Well, you've made me smile and come, so I suppose it's only polite to return the favour.'

Gulp, gulp, gulp, gulp, gulp.

She rolled over and pushed me onto my back then kissed me long and deeply before moving her mouth back down to my chest and repeating her earlier play with my nipples. I could hear my own breaths become faster and my heart pound against my chest wall as her fingers traced their way down my body and lightly rubbed me through my jeans.

'My my, someone is happy to see me. Let's see how happy...'

She expertly unzipped my jeans and pulled them partly down before freeing my hardness from my boxer shorts. I gasped aloud as her fingers encircled it. I didn't think I could last very long with this level of total excitement and I think Fiona sensed this too as she moved her head down and kissed the tip gently before taking it in her mouth. I cried out loud. This was wonderful. This was more than wonderful. This was sheer heaven on earth. She slowly began to move up and down my shaft, surrounding it in wet wonderful warmth. My breathing had reached almost critical level now and I knew the end was near. What did I do? I had no clue as to the etiquette here at all. This was new territory for me. I made a snap decision. Fi had been in charge throughout and knew far more than me, so it was best to hand control to her. (Who was I kidding; she had been in control from the first minute)

'Fi, oh Fi. That's so good, but I can't last much longer.'

She paused momentarily.

'Don't worry babes. Just let yourself go when ready.'

Gulp.

She returned to her expert ministering and I could feel me reaching critical point. Then she did something with her tongue and I exploded, a wave of pleasure racking my body. She stayed where she was, still gently sucking at my now softening penis before finally finishing and sitting up with a smile.

'I'd kiss you just now but I'm afraid my mouth is a little sticky you bad boy. Was that nice?'

I was lost for words for a moment and just nodded, a probably idiotic smile plastered to my face.

'God yes. Amazing. Need to be honest; no-one has done that to me before.'

Fi laughed. 'What? Seriously? I thought you were a man of the world Graham.'

'Yes, so did I, but I was obviously wrong. Thank you. Maybe the best Saturday I have ever had.'

'Only maybe? I'm disappointed!' She threw back, a mock look of hurt on her face, and we both collapsed in fits of giggles.

We lay there for a while, curled up in each other's arms and sharing what was left of the cider and my dwindling supply of Regals. Eventually, as it became darker, she looked at her watch.

'We should make a move soon. I'm starving. Let's grab some chips from that place by the Grammar then get a bus home. And let's do this again soon.'

Do it again? Damn right!! Now I'd crossed that real threshold of female induced orgasm, there would be no going back!

We sorted our clothes out and headed back down to Glasgow Road via Arkleston Road, hand in hand and giggling like the young lovers we were. Telling David seemed a far and distant country at that moment and I would make that journey when I felt ready.

We reached the chip shop and I bought a bag of chips for both of us as well as the obligatory polo mints so we could both remove the aroma of cigarettes and cider from our breaths. We only had to wait about five minutes outside before a Johnstone bus came along and we both headed for the top deck. Far too soon the bus was heading up Glenpatrick Road and we were getting off as it turned into Abbey Road. Fiona lived on Burnside Road and it was a 10 minute walk across the fields to my house, so it made sense to get off at the same stop. As the bus pulled away, we spent a final ten minutes snogging in the bus shelter before saying reluctant goodbyes and made promises to phone each other after school on Monday. (Fiona went to a different school so we would not see each other during the day). The walk home across the fields was an easy one, there was lightness in my heart and it felt like I almost floated that last mile or so.

The next two weeks were awkward. Fiona wanted us to be a public couple, but I was still scared of telling David. Finally Fi put her foot down and said she wouldn't see me until I came clean with him. With heavy heart I realised I had no choice but to tell him everything. I decided to do it after school the next day as we had about a fifteen minute walk from the school bus to where we both lived. The skies were grey and heavy and suited my mood as I was terrified at how he would react. I made my move as we turned into Douglas Avenue.

'David mate, I need to tell you something. I've been a bit of a prick and it's really bugging me.'

David grinned in unknowing innocence.

'What have you done now then?'

'Em…well…you know Fiona that lives down from Tam?'

'Of course I do you fud. And I plan on knowing her a lot better soon.'

Gulp, but a gulp of an entirely different nature to the ones that Fiona induced.

'Well, that might be a problem. I sort of did a sneaky on you. I know you fancied her, and she phoned me a few weeks back and asked me to set you two up. But I liked her too, so I lied to her and said you weren't interested and I took her out instead and we've sort of been seeing each other since.'

I could see the dark skies reflected in David's face as he stopped and glowered at me.

'You're fucking kidding, right? This is a wind up. You knew I was really into her!'

'I'm really sorry pal. I feel guilty as hell about it.'

I didn't even see the punch coming. One minute I was apologising, the next I was lying on the pavement with blood streaming from a burst lip while David disappeared up the road. I picked myself up and cleaned the blood as best I could. Oh great. Falling out with my best mate, punched in the face, and facing explaining to my mum why there was blood on my school shirt.

It was three weeks before David even spoke to me again, and several more before friendship had overcome the resentment and things were back to normal.

As we moved deeper into the school year, things became easier, and, when he pulled one of Fiona's friends one evening, things began to go much better.

Fiona and I continued our steamy affair till distance separated us with her taking the teaching role for much of it, and me happy to be the student. I never got to cross that final hurdle with her though. While she was happy for lots of heavy petting, it seemed she wasn't ready to go all the way yet, and I resigned myself to waiting.

Chapter 8

I had turned fifteen on the 17th July that year and felt I was another step closer to adulthood but knew I had much still to learn. I was still spending a fair amount of time at John's and my smoking career went from one high to another, but I felt there was more to come, and I was right.

Given our problems of that summer, it was both surprising and fantastic that it was David who initiated the next stage of my substance using evolution. The summer holidays were over and we'd started back at school, regaling long unseen friends with tales of adventures both real and imagined. (Though strangely for a teenager, but perhaps mindful of David, I disclosed nothing of mine and Fiona's sexual frolics in various countryside locations). As September drew to a close, David told me one day that his mum and dad were going away for a few days at the Glasgow holiday weekend and leaving him and his siblings home alone, though his Gran would be there part of the Saturday to check on them and cook dinner.

He then suggested a little adventure on the Saturday night that I had read about in various books but had not yet seen myself embarking on:

Magic mushrooms.

Since I had started my 'education' with John, he had really expanded my reading list as well as my listening list, providing me with books or names of books that he thought I would like. And so I had plunged into the wondrous pages of everyone from Lewis Carroll to George Orwell, Ken Kesey to Hunter S Thompson, Aldous Huxley to Tim Leary. I'd realised that within these pages was a world I wanted to inhabit but had always been hesitant to ask John for anything other than a bit of dope. I also felt (perhaps a little arrogantly at such a young age) that I identified with many of the characters within the pages I read. I wanted to be Kerouac in 'On the Road', taking road trips to a background of jazz, poetry and heroic doses of amphetamine. I wanted to be Kesey in 'Electric Kool Aid Acid Test', riding a bus 'furthur' than anyone else to a background of The Grateful Dead, nonsense rapping and even more heroic doses of LSD. I felt that I had been born out of time; I wanted to be in San Francisco in the 60's (albeit minus all that hippy gear) and listening to the wisdom of Ginsberg and Leary. But I was 15, in a post new wave Glasgow of the early 1980's; a million miles in time and culture away from the world that was fascinating me. My world was dope, furtive fumbles and three minute singles. But all that was about to change...

David had bumped into this guy he knew from Johnstone Castle called Billy. Billy had picked a bumper harvest of mushrooms from some sacred (to the mushroom pickers) fields on top of Glennifer Braes and David had bought 80 off him for £2. He'd used the odd bit of dope with me when John had let me take some away with me, and thought this would be a bit of a giggle (understatement of the decade as it turned out). The fateful weekend arrived. David's younger sister was going to be staying with his Gran but David and Stuart would have the house to themselves on Saturday and Sunday, with his parents due back on the Monday evening. After tea (dinner) on Sunday I headed round to David's house. My mum and dad were going to a dinner dance and I had said that David's gran was staying the night so I would sleep over. To be honest, other than what I had gleaned from books, we had little idea what to expect. David had asked Billy the best way to take them and had been told to make 'tea' with them; simply boil the mushrooms in water, strain through a cloth, and add tea or coffee and lots of sugar to mask the awful taste. His gran had already left, and Stuart was away out to play football with his mates, so we headed off to the kitchen to prepare what would be, for me, a true moment of epiphany. We measure out about 3 mugs of water into a pan and added the mushrooms, then stood back and waited for the pan to boil. The concoction did not look particularly appetising; the water turning a sort of earthy brown as the water heated. After about fifteen minutes, we decided it was ready. David got a fresh cloth from the cleaning cupboard and we carefully strained the mixture into each prepared mug. Once milk was added, the drink took on a strange, almost oily look, which did nothing to detract from a sense of almost impending doom. We headed back to the living room and sat and waited for our brew to cool. Nervous glances were exchanged across the room, and it felt like each of us was waiting for the other to take that first tentative sip. Finally I decided to take the plunge and raised the mug to my lips. That first taste (the first of many to come) nearly made me gag.

Even with four sugars in it, there was an underlying taste of soil, earth, leaves; natural yet weirdly and attractively repugnant at the same time. David had followed my lead, and by the look on his face was experiencing the same contradictory sensations. I made a snap decision; no way could I drink this one sip at a time, so, like some medicines, I decided it was better to get it over with quickly. Steeling myself against the inevitable gag reflex, I drained the drink in one go, and am sure my face exhibited all the pain and suffering of a torture victim given the laugh that came from David. But he realised that my chosen option was the best idea and followed suit, allowing me to reciprocate the laughter when I saw his face twist and contort. Now the deed was done, and all we had to do was wait…

Billy had said to David that for a first trip, it was always good to watch something funny on TV. Given the dire nature of British television programming in the '80s, we had gone down to the video shop earlier that day and got some videos out. We'd gone for three comedies; Time Bandits (which weirdly, has a place much much later in this tale), Stripes, and Mel Brooks' 'History of the World: Part 1'. If Billy was right, then these seemed like perfect choices for the evening ahead. We put on the Mel Brooks film first. I'd seen 'Blazing Saddles' up at John's the previous year (was NOT the type of film my mum or dad would ever watch) and had spent the entire duration almost doubled up in paroxysms of near hysterical giggles. If this was even half as good, then it should catalyse the mushrooms very quickly indeed.

As it turned out, we did not have long to wait anyway. Even as the main titles were coming on, I could feel the beginnings of a new and strange sensation start to course through my body. There was also an underlying feeling of nausea (which did not worry me too much as had read in some of my books that feeling sick often accompanied the early stages of a hallucinogen trip) but it was being drowned out by a rising tide of almost euphoric awareness. My vision was also affected; the edges of the picture on my retinae were going slightly blurry, and the sound from the television assumed an echo that should not have existed in an anchored reality. I tried to communicate this feeling of new perceptions to David, but to my mutating ears, the words came out in a foreign language I could not speak. I was now struggling to focus on the television, and even with the foreknowledge of what I was watching, I found myself confused that there was a hotel/casino complex called 'Caesar's Palace' in Ancient Rome. The dialogue was shifting in and out of aural focus now, but when the words did manage to be deciphered by my increasingly addled mind; even the weakest jokes were inducing convulsions of laughter. I felt as if the world around me was moving away, leaving me drifting in an isolated vortex of madness. Trying to cling to a swiftly escaping reality, I made an attempt to get up from the sofa but found that my centre of balance had shifted to somewhere in Asia and instead found myself crawling across the floor, desperately seeking the main window which seemed to offer a path back to the world of normality. Reaching this doorway to sanity, I peered outside in the hope of bringing myself back to some sort of level of sense, but instead I was horrified to see that David's mum's collection of garden gnomes had come to life and were moving towards the house in a maelstrom of vertically challenged horror. Previously harmless fishing rods and garden tools had become implements of impending death and I could see the crazed and malevolent looks of violence in their glowing eyes. I screamed, or I think I did, and shrank back to the sanctuary of the bean bag in the corner.

Yet this was only temporary solace as the satanic gnomes began to materialise from the carpet, pulling themselves up from some gnomic underworld and, with steely resolve, gathering their tools and focussing on their immediate target, which unfortunately seemed to be me. Yet something seemed to be protecting me for as the nearest gnome came within striking distance and maliciously raised its fishing rod to strike, it disappeared in a puff of smoke. Then the same happened to the next one to attack, and the next, and I became convinced that some hidden telepathic power I possessed was shielding me from these tiny attackers. Finally the last one vaporised in front of me and all that was left was a forlornly abandoned wheelbarrow on its side, one wheel still spinning. I took deep breaths as I realised how close I had come to being destroyed by these seemingly harmless garden ornaments. Leaving the safety of the beanbag I crawled back towards the sofa, pausing to focus on the clock above the fireplace and realising with shock that the entire attack had taken almost two hours though in my addled mind it seemed that only thirty minutes had elapsed since we had taken the mushrooms. I looked round the room as things slowly swam back into a sort of focus and realised that there was no David in sight. I panicked. Maybe some of the gnomes had got to him while I was still battling their army and had dragged him back down to their Stygian lair. I desperately began to hammer on the living room floor and call out David's name. Suddenly I heard a weak and echoic reply and realised he was still alive. There was still hope of saving him, though I had no idea of how to break through their nefarious magic barriers.

'David! Can you hear me?'

'Yes I can hear you...'

'Look around you. Tell me what you can see. I'll get you out of there somehow.'

'Well, there are cupboards on the walls, and a fridge in the corner. The sink is underneath the window and the cooker is next to it.'

I was confused. I had expected some sort of sombre and murky cavern lit only by flickering torches.

'David, can you see any sort of way out?'

'Em...yes. There is the door out to the back garden and the door through to the living room.'

I thought for a minute. Though it may have been five as my mental processes still seemed to be on go slow mode. Cupboards, cooker, fridge, door to back garden. Finally the low wattage light bulb flickered to life above my head. He'd not been abducted to some demonic cave below the house! He was in the kitchen! I finally managed to regain enough balance to stand up and headed through to the kitchen. Sure enough, there was David, hunched up in the corner behind the fridge.

'You okay?' I asked.

'Yeah. Well at least I think I am. That was a bit mental for a while. What was all that banging about?'

'Don't laugh, but I was convinced your mum's garden gnomes had come to life and had abducted you to some underground lair.'

'Oh I won't laugh. All I can remember is every bloody piece of furniture shrinking to dolls house size any time I went near it. Finally I think I gave up and hid in here till the madness calmed down.'

I smiled. 'Seems like we've both visited the land of insanity in the last couple of hours. I still feel weird as hell but at least know what's going on now. That was strange, but damn good now I'm looking at it from this side.'

I retrieved one of my ready rolled joints from my jacket and we stood at the back door, letting the smoke calm our muddled minds. It was getting cold, so we quickly finished and went back into the living room, David relieved that the furniture had returned to normal size, and me ecstatic that the killer gnomes had not reappeared. We stuck on 'Time Bandits' for the next couple of hours, still enveloped in a warm fuzziness of psilocybin wool. There were still moments when the world took on Daliesque qualities, but they were far less intense than the dimensional sojourns we had both made earlier. Stuart came in around 10pm and looked bemused when his questions as to how our night went were met with furtive exchanged looks and an outbreak of giggles.

When the film finished, I realised I was feeling totally drained, both physically and emotionally, and decided on a last smoke before crashing. David and I stood at the back door, the cold chill of a September night offset by the warmth of the Afghan black John had provided. We agreed that our first experiment in the world of hallucinogens had been fun, if at times a little unnerving and definitely something we wanted to repeat. Though maybe not for a little while.

And so I entered a new era of my life, albeit one that would develop slowly at first.As I lay awake for a while in the spare room that night, I realised that the mushrooms had touched something deep inside of me. I'd given up on religion a few years back, but for some weird reason I felt tonight I'd discovered my soul. Or something. My yet maturing teenage brain did not really understand all the feelings and experiences I had undergone that night. But I knew there was some…I don't know, 'presence' out there, or maybe in there. But, whatever it was, it excited me in the way the first view of a new country must have enthralled early explorers, and I realised that part of my life would be devoted to the searching of these new undiscovered territories of inner space. It sounds almost trite writing it down in retrospect, but to a semi naïve teenager, it did seem like a religious experience, and I wasn't even close to understanding the processes or feelings that I had gone through.

Chapter 9

Still basking in the warm reflective afterglow of my first psilocybin experience, I had little idea that there were storm clouds gathering on the periphery of my life and that I would soon undergo the first major upheaval of my life. I'd noticed mum and dad having 'serious' talks, and the conversation always seemed to cease abruptly when I entered the room. Not that this fazed me at all. To a self-absorbed teenage boy, there is little that matters outside the immediate sphere of his own day to day life. But that world was about to collapse around me one October evening. I came home from school, wet and bedraggled from a typical Scottish autumn day. As soon as I got in the house, I knew that all was not as it should be. Mum and dad were sitting in the living room with sombre looks on their faces and no television or radio on. I took off my coat and mumbled a greeting as I went to head up to my room. Instead dad called me into the living room and told me to take a seat.

'Graham, we need to talk to you son. We've not wanted to worry you until we saw how things worked out, but it's time you knew what's going on. My manager called me in six weeks ago for a chat. Coats are shutting down huge parts of the mills. Unfortunately, my job is one of the ones that are going.'

'God dad, that's awful. What are you going to do?'

'Well that's what your mum and I have been talking about. As soon as I knew, I started looking for another job. I had an interview for one last week and they called back today and offered me the position.'

'Oh that's great dad. What's the job?'

'It's another production post. But in a slightly different field. It's with Burton's the biscuit manufacturers.'

Initial fantasies of bags full of free wagon wheels and other biscuity goodness flashed through my mind. Then I paused for thought. I hadn't seen any biscuit factories around the Paisley area.

'Where's their factory then? Is it up in Glasgow? '

'Well, no. That's the thing. The job is in Edinburgh.'

Naiveté and stupidity mixed again for a minute.

'Edinburgh? Does that mean you'll have to drive through and back every day?'

'No son. Though I will have to do that for a few weeks anyway. But it just wouldn't make sense to do that journey 5 days a week. We're going to have to move through to the east.'

Life as I knew it was ending. Friends. School. John. David. Fiona. My musical adventures in Glasgow. Everything I knew, loved and enjoyed was going to disappear. Although Edinburgh was a mere hour along the M8, it may as well have been in a different galaxy.

Plus they all talked a little funny through there. I didn't want to move and of course, being a recalcitrant teenager, I made my feelings very clear and finished making my point with a flourish of an exit, storming upstairs to my room and slamming the door so hard that the shock wave caused a small tsunami to hit Rothesay. I lay on my bed staring at the ceiling, Strummer's defiant vocals reverberating round the room and the entire house due to the volume I'd cranked Sandinista up to. Inevitably my mum soon arrived and reduced the volume. She sat on the edge of the bed.

'Son, I'm not happy either. I've lived in Paisley and Elderslie my entire life. I've got the kirk and the guild and I'll miss those things. And I'm going to have to leave my job at the Southern General.'

I should add as an aside here that my mum had been working as an auxiliary in the neurosurgery department of the Southern General Hospital in Glasgow for the last seven years, the closest she'd come to her childhood dream of becoming a nurse. In the way typical of my mum however, she wasn't an 'ordinary' auxiliary, but worked in the operating theatre, and in further inimitable mum style, ruled the place like she was the matron. She'd even wangled getting me into watch from the observation room, giving me an all-powerful anecdote for school of having seen a skull drilled into and cut open and the human brain being operated on. The down side of her job was the she often worked nights, which meant dad and I were regaled with gory tales of horror from the night before while tucking into breakfast. Really added something to that runny egg. Her best tale from work concerned a night when a young guy had been admitted with his skull impaled by a screwdriver; ah the joys of Glasgow pub fights at the weekend. The two surgeons, being in possession of equal amounts of brilliance and arrogance, were arguing in the scrub up area as to the best way to perform the operation to remove said screwdriver, all while the patient lay prepped and ready on the operating table and the rest of the theatre staff twiddled their thumbs. Finally my mum, being my mum, went into the tool box kept in the prep room and removed a screwdriver, marched into the scrub room, brandished it in their faces and declared; 'We were fed up waiting for you two to settle your argument so we just removed it ourselves!'.

This of course resulted in two eminent neurosurgeons left speechless and with mouths agape.

'But there are no jobs for your dad in the west at all. He's been trying hard and phoning any company he thought might have him. We haven't told you till now as we didn't want to worry you and dad still hoped something would come up through here.'

I took my sullen mood and placed it back in the emotion cupboard till it was needed next. Maybe it was time to stop being selfish and putting my own wants and needs before mum and dad's.

After all, they were both giving up so much too and if we were going to do this as a family, it had to be as a united family.

'Sorry mum, it just came as a bit of a shock. And I suppose it's not really another planet, even if the folk sound a little weird.'

Mum laughed. 'That's better. We all need to pull together. It's not going to happen overnight. Your dad starts the job in two weeks and will have to commute for a while, but we're going to have to put the house up for sale here and house hunt through there too. We may not move till close to Christmas, or even afterwards.'

Most of the run up to Christmas seemed to pass in a strange daze. David, Stuart and the gang couldn't believe I was moving, though David promised he'd be through for any good gigs and that I could do vice versa. We also pledged that the last few weeks would be as much of a full time party zone as two fifteen year olds could fit in between school and homework. A huge part of the October holiday and nearly every weekend was taken up with driving through to Edinburgh and its environs looking at house after house. If mum liked it, dad didn't. If dad liked it, mum didn't. If I liked it, neither of them liked it. And so on we went on our little merry go round of house hunting frustration. Balerno, Currie, Linlithgow, Livingston, Haddington, Dalkeith, Cramond, Corstorphine, Murrayfield, Bruntsfield, Craiglockhart…the list seemed to go on and on, and I began to realise that after these trips I knew Edinburgh better than Glasgow. My former reluctance to the move had slowly begun to defrost as new possibilities opened themselves up to my hungry and imaginative mind. A whole selection of new girls at school and wherever we eventually bought this elusive house. And, having now heard the Edinburgh accent on a regular basis, which of these East Coast hotties could resist a sexy West Coast accent coming direct from a sexy West Coaster? And I already knew there was hospital radio (several) through in the East, so surely my undoubted rise to being the new John Peel would not be hindered? And surely John would keep me supplied, even if I would see him far less often? Everything that had appeared as a barrier and problem to this move was slowly melting away and a soupçon of...dare I say excitement...had crept into my attitude. There was however one 'nasty' surprise about my impending new home. One Saturday, after a second viewing of a rather, in my opinion, dismal house in Musselburgh, it had got quite late so mum announced we would find a chippy and park up by the front to eat before heading home. It was a pleasant October evening; crisp and cold but with clear skies and only a hint of sea fog. We found a decent looking fish and chip shop on the road by the car park and headed in to make our choices. The problem arose once my fish and chips was on the paper and the server looked at me and asked;

'Salt and sauce?'

What the hell? Salt and sauce? Had he made a mistake and said sauce instead of vinegar?

'Em, salt and vinegar please.'

There followed what seemed like an eternity of confused silence coupled with that blank look of the terminally stupid.

'No, salt and sauce. We don't do vinegar.'

It turned out, that because of some weird evolutionary quirk, or perhaps even recessive genes, the fish and chip sector of Edinburgh and large parts of the East coast offered 'sauce' instead of the usual, normal, societally acceptable vinegar. And it wasn't even real sauce, but rather a watery concoction of vinegar and cheap brown sauce that on its own looked almost faecally unappetising.

I accepted the second rate condiments, collected my fish supper and followed a bemused set of parents to the car. I realised in that moment of culinary disappointment that despite my new found enthusiasm, the move ahead still held certain challenges.

Finally, on a cold morning in November, we hit the jackpot. We viewed a house that all three of us liked (well I say a house, but we actually viewed a show home followed by a muddy plot with random piles of bricks that would allegedly soon resemble the sparkling showpiece we had just toured). And it was in a place that all three of us liked. (At this current rate of miracles I was expecting the second coming of Jesus and me losing my virginity by 6pm). The place was a semi sprawling new private estate called Echline; surgically inserted between the beautiful and historic village of South Queensferry and the main road to Boness. To the rear of the plot was a small embankment, then the aforementioned Boness road, then sprawling countryside. The agent stated we were in the last part of the development and that no more houses would be built around us. (She forgot to insert the words 'for now' at the end of that statement.) From what would be the front, you could just see the Forth Road Bridge and, with a little bit if squinting, a small rectangle of the silvery Forth itself. Once we'd viewed the house/plot itself, we drove down into the village itself, an almost palpable excitement building in the cars as we drove down the narrow cobbled centre street, past old stone cottages and terraced houses, and then finally round a corner towards the Hawes and the majestic sight of the Forth Bridge itself (the rail one). Majestic but red and rusty in the afternoon light, testament to the engineering of a bygone age, the bridge towered over the river and the small cluster of buildings at the Hawes Pier. We parked by the Hawes Inn, itself a historic icon and mentioned in Stevenson's 'Kidnapped' (as this was one of the few historic Scottish novels I had read by this point, this fact made far more impression than the magnificence of the bridge). We walked along the front for a half hour or so, then retired to the Inn itself for a welcome warming cup of hot chocolate (my request for a shandy was greeted with a scowl from mum and feigned ignorance from dad). As discussions progressed (mainly excluding me) it became apparent that South Queensferry had rapidly become a very hot favourite. Location was good, transport links to dad's work were good, the local school was good (hold on, just how long have you two been considering this place? I thought it was a last minute viewing), plenty of local shops and surrounded by gorgeous countryside and a river on (well 5 minutes' drive from) our (potential) new doorstep. It seemed we had gone from countless weeks of frustration and disappointment to finding what could be a dream house in the space of one single, but very important day. The way mum and dad were talking; it appeared that the only barrier to this house was the sale of our old one in Elderslie. They talked about something called a bridging loan (this confused me for a minute as I thought we were buying a house) and dad eventually said to mum he would go into the bank on the Monday.

And so we headed home. As we would our way up the narrow and leafy streets of South Queensferry, I wondered if this was the place I would call home for the next 2 or 3 years. I already knew it would never be another Elderslie.

That had been the cradle of my life for some 15 years. It had seen adventures and misadventures, excitement and disappointment, and would always be the home that had a place in my heart. But I was also very aware that though still naïve in many ways and stupid in many others, that I stood on the brink of adulthood and that an entire world lay before me as a plaything. My heart and mind were telling me that these next two to three years would be like a training course for what would follow after. And I was right…

In the end the moving date was set for after Christmas due to the lengthy process of paperwork and contracts and all this other kerfuffle I didn't quite understand yet. Our old house hadn't sold yet, so the fabled bridging loan (nothing to do with bridges) had made its appearance and we were good to go. The date was set for 16th January 1982.

David had promised we'd make the last of my time in the West as mental as possible and we did pretty bloody well. There was a raft of gigs to attend in those last couple of months. November and December at the Apollo saw us heading to see Adam Ant, ABC, Siouxsie and The Jam, and John took me to the same venue for Whitesnake in December. There was also a new venue for us in Night Moves, and we managed to catch the breath-taking Birthday Party and the sublime Southern Death Cult there before Christmas. Then of course there was my venue of choice; dear old Tiffanys. How I'd miss her musty darkness filled with the aroma of stale lager and furtive joints. Managed three final visits while still living in the West (though I would return for nostalgia boosts) and saw Danse Society (brilliant), Blancmange (quirky) and finally China Crisis (bland and insipid).

Despite the let-down of China Crisis, my time living in Elderslie had ended on a high. There was a couple of great drinking and smoking sessions with David over the Christmas holidays. There were also a few heavy snogging and petting sessions with Fiona who seemed genuinely sad to see me leave. Alas, not sad enough to offer me up the Holy Grail of losing my virginity, but some damned good fun nonetheless. But through the excitement of the impending move, came a continuing wave of melancholy. Everything I knew, everything I was, every mistake I'd made, every experience I'd had, from birth to where I found myself now, had been part of a world of growing concentric circles with their origin and root at that little semi-detached house in Dunrobin Avenue. I was leaving the only world I'd known behind me in the West and entering what was a virtual unknown. What had previously been a cauldron of teenage hormones was slowly changing into a vessel of almost adult emotions. I was sad, scared and excited all at the same time. I didn't know what this next chapter of life may hold for me, but in my heart and head, I felt that there were some momentous times ahead.

PART 2

Chapter 10

From a meteorological perspective, 16th January 1982 was what the professionals would call an absolute stinker. Since very early morning there had been a constant downfall of that horrible wet snow that never lies but still manages to stick to you if you venture out in it. But, strangely, despite the slightly higher temperatures, there was still a biting cold wind swirling down from the braes. It was definitely a day for snuggling up in front of a fire with a good book or film, and definitely not a day for emptying an entire house, driving some 54 miles along the M8, then moving contents of old house into a new house which, dad had just informed us, would be a little cold as he'd forgotten to set the heating there the day before. Of course, there was very little real work for us to do. Those wonderful Pickfords elves had been hired for the day, and, other than a few of my mum's prized possessions, they would be doing all the packing. I'd been commanded (literally) to have all my things in neat piles in my bedroom so they could be packed and labelled, transported, then decamped in my new (much larger) bedroom in South Queensferry.

I'd taken a leaf from my mum's book and had written large scrawling 'Handle with Care' signs on the piles of my beloved vinyl. Once the removal men had arrived and started for the day, we headed off to my Gran's house for breakfast and temporary goodbyes. The removal men had estimated that it would take around three to four hours to pack up the house, and a further ninety minutes to drive the van to our new house. Mum, being her usual highly organised self, had packed a couple of boxes in the boot of the car with all the makings for coffee or tea, as well as a cool bag filled with sandwiches and cold drinks. We eventually left Gran's at 1pm and, with a brief stop for fresh milk, headed off to our new beginning.

It was even more miserable in South Queensferry. Although there was no wet snow, there was a constant rain coupled with that grey depressing haar so peculiar to the east coast. You could see the curtain twitchers around us busy observing who their new neighbours would be, but my attention was more caught by the girl coming out the house diagonally opposite from us with a dog. She looked about fifteen, long blonde brown hair and what, even under the several layers of clothing she wore, looked like a curvy little body. Hmmm, yes, I could enjoy living here if this was my first view of our neighbours! The house seemed forlorn when we entered, probably not helped by the cold inflicted by my dad's forgetfulness. Mum immediately headed for the kitchen to unpack the food and drinks. A new fridge freezer had been delivered a few days before as the one in Elderslie was probably about as old as I was so all the drinks and sandwiches were transferred to it before unpacking, filling and switching on the kettle.

As it was, the Pickfords crew didn't arrive for another two hours due to the weather and traffic. I was dispatched out the house with the dog for a walk.

Ooops, sort of missed out the other family member (perhaps due to another nomenclature embarrassment moment). My mum had, for some bizarre reason, taken to naming any pets after a geographical feature near to the kennels. So their first dog (already a few years old when I arrived) had been a nasty yapping little Pekingese called Feuch (after a river in Aberdeenshire) and our current dog was a Shetland Sheepdog we had got in the borders of Scotland near to a very famous river, which resulted in my mum calling her Tweed. (See what I mean?). Her last dog, later in life, was the same breed, this time named after the island of Islay. Tweed was a great little dog; I just hated having to shout that stupid name if I had her off the lead. I realised that this walk would give me a chance to do a reconnaissance of the area and also to have a couple of fly cigarettes. Making sure I had the necessary equipment (cigarettes, matches, pack of extra strong mints), I wrapped up against the horrible weather, put Tweed on a lead (Ah, was trying to avoid rhyming couplets anywhere in this) and headed off into the relative unknown.

There wasn't really much to see. Anyone with a modicum of common sense was indoors with fires or heating on and not outside in a miserable Scottish January. So, other than my (hopefully) new little blonde friend across from us, the only people I met were fellow dog walkers, mainly middle aged, who all seemed to exchange reluctant and cursory nods of greeting to my hearty West coast hellos! It did give me a chance to gauge the geography and lay out of the area most proximate to the new house. Our house lay on the last road of a medium sized estate, with the Bo'ness road behind us, a chunk of the estate to our west, and to the east a large empty field then the approach to the Forth Road Bridge which was mostly hidden by the haar today. I walked to the southern boundary of the estate where the main village road swept under the grey lofty spires of the road cathedral and down into the village proper.

I followed the path up to the bridge approach road, and then walked back along the Bo'ness road till I found the house. I had been gone for well over an hour and was almost soaked through. Mum sent me upstairs to change which confused me for a minute till I realised that through sheer chance my boxes had been last in the van which meant that they had been first out. I headed straight for my number one clothes box and retrieved some jogging bottoms

and a t-shirt and got out of my sodden things. Task number t
to my carefully labelled system (with cap doffed to my mum f
to retrieve my deck and some vinyl, and soon the slowly fillir
the sounds of Devo's 'New Traditionalists'. All my furniture
so I started unpacking things and sorting places for them. !
and so had that partial view of the road bridge, though for now it was s....
obscured by haar. As I organised my room, I kept glancing out the window in
the hope that my potentially cute neighbour from earlier would reappear. To my
joy, she made an appearance with her family, and my joy was increased
further by the realisation that not only was she as cute as I had suspected, but
that she had two equally cute looking sisters. I had been in our new house less
than 4 hours and already the tottie forecast was looking extremely favourable. I
switched the music to The Associates' 'Fourth Drawer Down', Mackenzie's
charged octave vaulting falsetto voice a seemingly perfect counterpoint to the
drab weather outside. Next stage in the room organisation was, for me, the
most important after speaker/stereo placement. Where was I going to put my
burgeoning collection of posters? There had been some argument with my
mum over the use of blue tac on the walls, but my dad had helpfully ridden to
my rescue and pointed out to my mum that a teenage boy could not be
expected to live in a room with only some tasteful prints of classic cars.

I'd been lucky in that I had, through John's contacts and my own audacity,
managed to amass a serious collection of posters, postcards and signed
photographs, and my biggest problem was deciding what would go on the
walls and what would remain in my cupboard. One easy decision was to place
my pride and joy above my record player; a signed copy of the promo poster
for Magazine's 'Shot by Both Sides' that had been given to John when he
worked with them in 1978. They weren't his cup of tea at all, but being a
compulsive hoarder of music paraphernalia (and probably the cause of my own
lifelong hoarding of trivia) he had kept it for years then given it to me when he
found out they were one of my favourite bands. Next up, placed above my bed,
was my large poster of the London Calling cover by The Clash, featuring the
iconic photo by Pennie Smith of Simonon smashing his bass up. Another
promo poster, this time for Tubeway Army's 'Replicas', filled the space beside
the Magazine poster. The last space, poster wise, went to an oversize poster
of Joy Division's 'Unknown Pleasures'. Various other spaces on the wall and
cupboard door were filled with promotional postcards, gig tickets (of which the
collection was also growing rapidly) and assorted signed pictures and flyers
including Gary Numan, Dury and the Blockheads, Rory Gallagher, The
Teardrop Explodes and of course John's old friend, Rory Gallagher. I was
pleased with the way the room was taking shape. It was quite a bit bigger than
my old room in Elderslie and as I sat on the bed with The Associates'

age Oblique Speech' as my soundtrack, I realised I could be quite happy
e, even if it was to be for a shorter duration than my old home.

Sunday was a brighter day, a cold crisp frost greeting me in the morning as I
let the dog out the spacious back garden (as a corner plot, our garden here
was around 4 times the size of the one in the west). Mum was already hard at
work cooking breakfast and simultaneously organising the kitchen beyond the
level she had organised it to the day before. I decided to skip any possible post
breakfast chores and offered to take the dog (I shall try and refrain from using
that cursed name too often) for a long walk. This plan served the added
purpose of exploring further than the boundaries I had reached the previous
day. After breakfast, as I headed down the driveway, my cute neighbour from
the previous day emerged from her house – result! I hurried to make sure that
our paths would cross sooner rather than later. As I got to the main path that
led down through the estate to the village, she was around 5 yards ahead of
me and looked back. Yes! My original estimate of high levels of cuteness had
been bang on the mark if not a little below how pretty she was. She smiled. My
heart began to melt, even in the sub-zero temperatures of a January morning.

'You've just moved into the corner house, haven't you?'

Wow! She'd noticed me too. Things were looking promising here.

'Yes, we moved in yesterday. Have you been here long?'

'We moved in about 3 months ago. Seems a pretty decent place. I'm Gillian by
the way.'

'Graham. Nice to meet at least a half expert on the town then. What school do
you go to?'

'St Oggy's, sorry, St Augustine's in Edinburgh. You for the local high school
then?'

'Yes, but not looking forward to it. Hell of a time to change schools. Exams in a
few months and I bet there will be a few assholes who want to prove
themselves with the new boy from the west.'

Gillian laughed. And even to my still developing heart, it was a laugh filled with
music and promise.

'Oh I'm sure you'll cope. And I'm sure the girls will welcome a new good
looking addition to the area.'

Gulp. Rewind. Had the gods smiled on me within 24 hours of moving here? Did she just call me good looking? (Okay, at that age, one had a certain arrogance about one's own looks that would dissipate with age, retreating hairline and an expanding waistline)

I smiled coyly or at least what I suspected smiling coyly might look like.

'Well, if someone as cute as you thinks I'm good looking, then I'm glad we moved here.'

Bullseye!

A deep red blush had spread over Gillian's face and she now seemed to be intently concentrating on her shoes. Time to move in for the kill.

'So, where you walking the dog? I only did the edge of the estate yesterday so wanted to explore a bit further today. Fancy showing me round the village.'

Gillian finally managed to tear her eyes away from the fascinating spectacle of her shoe tops.

'Sure. I was going to take Ben a long one anyway. (Wow, a family who managed to give their dog a decent name). And we could grab something to eat and drink at the café.'

My new friend and I walked down through the estate in the cold January air. Unusually for two teenagers of the opposite sexes, conversation was easy and natural with none of the normal awkward silences that so marked similar situations. I quickly learned she was fifteen years old, had two sisters (three cute girls as neighbours? I felt like I'd won the pools) and one brother. Her dad worked at Edinburgh University library, and her mum worked in the Western General hospital. Her favourite bands were The Cure and Siouxsie (whoo!) but had never been to a gig (plan forming). We reached the end of the estate and put the dogs on leads as we came onto Bo'ness Road (to my confusion I discovered that the road behind my house, although the road to Bo'ness, was actually called Builyeon Road, and didn't become Bo'ness road till it met the road that ran through the village) and walked under the concrete and steel shadows of the road bridge. We passed the now sadly gone Vat 69 distillery at the top of Hopetoun Road (now wait, so the Bo'ness Road doesn't run through the whole village? Just from the road bridge? Which twat decided on this road system?) It was at this point (helpfully marked by aforementioned huge bridge) that the village changed character. On our side of Queensferry, most of the south was modern, with the houses mainly ranging from the 1970's onwards in age. North of the bridge and heading towards the Forth, the houses took on more character, usually built in that dark stone you see so often in this part of the world. Our chat had kept flowing smoothly all the way down the road. I had now also learned she had been single for 5 months (have I said 'whoo' already?). As mentioned a plan had been forming in my head since Gillian said she'd never been to a gig (and bearing in mind my obsession with music, I had researched upcoming concerts before even leaving Elderslie).

'So Gillian, you seem to like some great bands. How do you feel about the Teardrop Explodes?'

She almost squeaked.

'I love Julian Cope! 'Wilder' was my favourite album of last year! 'Tiny Children' makes me cry every time I hear it.'

Part of my brain was urging caution. This was the first girl I'd met since moving and here was I ready to plunge in feet first. There was also the added caveat of her being a neighbour. If things got messy, then things got awkward. The other part of my brain, ruled by teenage hormones and usually steered by little head downstairs, was urging me to 'get in there son.' In later years, with added wisdom, respect for the fairer sex and a more worldly view, the decision would have more likely swung towards the cautious decision. But I was still a teenager, and my hormones won this battle easily.

'Did you know they've got a gig at The Playhouse the start of February? I was going to get tickets next week if you fancy coming along?'

The smile that appeared on her face warmed the cold day but disappeared as quickly as a Scottish summer.

'Oh God, I'd love to, but I don't think my mum and dad would let me.'

Damn, I'd forgotten. Catholic. I should explain to you, that even in 1982, there was not the same level of enlightenment in many Catholic families that there is now. (For enlightenment, translate as 'I don't give a fuck what the Pope says.') The couple of Catholic girls I had dated so far had been ravishing beauties but with the sexual freedom of a jailed Nun (Given a video I saw some years later, this may not be the best analogy ever). The furthest I had managed to get in my (seemingly) never ending quest to lose my virginity had been some furtive feels of the breasts...through her top. Any attempt at my hands exploring beneath the material had been met with the classic 'pull away' move. Not very conducive to reaching that sexual holy grail.

'Rubbish! It's a school night so my dad will pick us up afterwards! I'm sure they'd let you go with a neighbour.'

'Well, they might, but they've not even met you yet.'

'They are bound to meet my mum and dad this week. Not as if all the houses are full yet, and our houses are only 25 yards apart.'

By now, we'd moved onto the High Street (ironically in the lowest part of the village), a quaint little road with raised terrace houses on one side and shops and the occasional pub or hotel on the other. You could see glimpses of the majestic Forth in the gaps and the odd sighting of the Forth Bridge itself rising high above the river. There didn't seem to be that much of note on this my first proper look at my new home. There were the usual suspects; butcher, baker, but no candlestick maker, newsagent, pub, craft shop, chip shop. Nothing to really titillate the excitement buds of a teenager, but then again, this was a fairly small village and there was the bustling excitement of Edinburgh to explore a mere 30 minutes by bus away. Gillian suggested we tie the dogs up and head into the café for a drink. Judging by the teenager: tourist ratio, it appeared that this was the hang out of choice for the younger inhabitants of the village as most tables were occupied by small groups of teenagers. A few of them acknowledged Gillian with waves or 'hellos' while the odd curious glance was cast in my direction. We ordered milkshakes (not my drink of choice, even at that age, but it didn't look the sort of place that would sell alcohol, let alone alcohol to a 15 year old kid). I grabbed the sole remaining table as Gillian brought the drinks over. Despite our only having met an hour or so before, there was a level of comfort between us already that would either result in us being great friends or something a little more passionate (Or a lot more passionate, as my hormones were wishing). We sat for about half an hour, discussing our favourite bands (bizarrely, like me, she had acquired a 'dual taste' in music; her older brother was a rocker so she had grown up both with the punk and new wave scenes as well as the rock bands of the mid 70's.) We didn't agree on everything. She hated the more 'Avant-garde' of my tastes like Throbbing Gristle and Psychic TV. Nor did she like the psychedelic and Kraut rock parts of my likes (Such as Gong or Can), but generally we seemed to like many of the same acts (Again bizarrely, her favourite rock band at that point was also Rush). Eventually we decided the dogs had been left alone long enough (thankfully Ben and 'The dog who shall not be named' seemed to have got along well on the walk down to the village and, as yet, had not attempted to imitate a Mongolian dog fight) (That's a dog fight in Mongolia by the way, not a fight between Mongolian dogs). We untied them and continued further along the front. As we emerged from the shelter of the houses and businesses onto the open space leading to the Forth Bridge itself, a cold and biting wind swept in from the icy Forth.

I shivered and zipped my jacket up as far is it would go. At this point I was grateful that my mum's nagging still occasionally overcame my teenage stubbornness and that I had worn a hat, scarf and gloves. The car park was fairly deserted given the sub-zero temperatures, but there were a few hardy foreign tourists strolling along, identifiable by their questionable fabric choices clothes wise, and the interminable photograph poses with the iconic bridge in the background. We stood for a while near the Hawes Pier, Gillian slightly amused at my still virginal awe of a structure she'd lived near all her life. (Before her move to Echline, her family had lived on Rosebery Avenue near my new school). Once my quickly bored sense of wonder had been sated, Gillian suggested she show me the back way along the old railway line and the area around my school. (Wasn't too sure about this; I was already dreading the 'Day of the New Boy' opening the next day at a school near me). We crossed the near deserted road and made our way up the side of the Hawes Inn. A well-worn path made its way through thick woodland where we let the dogs off their leads and they bounded away into the undergrowth barking at real or imagined creatures. After about five minutes' walk, the woods opened up onto a long unused railway track, little remaining but rotting piles of railway sleepers and the odd piece of rusting metal that had not been salvaged for scrap. There was an eerie beauty about the place, especially with the odd stray beam of sunshine breaking through the trees and lighting up frost encrusted plants and moss. The setting seemed to affect our moods, a temporary silence falling on what had been previously animated conversation. The mood was at last broken when Gillian clambered up the slight slope from the railway path and called back for the dogs to hurry up. Ben and 'The dog who shall not be named' (henceforth known simply as 'Dog') exploded from the bushes opposite us in a flurry of fur and paws. We both started laughing at the sheer silliness of the sight and that was the silence gone as talk resumed as swiftly as it had stopped. We had wandered off the subject of music now. Gillian was telling me about her last boyfriend and how her family had hated him as, not only was he Protestant, but his family were staunch members of The Orange Lodge (Gulp. Note to self: do not discuss mum's side of the family with Gill's family, only the proud Republican roots of dad's side).

The friction had caused them to break up, and she confided in me that she still wasn't really over him. (Whoa. This was putting a bit of a severe stink bomb in that day's – metaphorically speaking – summer's meadow of hopeful hormonal rushes) By this time we had emerged from the path onto Station Road proper and Gillian pointed to a monstrous 1970's building that loomed over some rather bedraggled looking playing fields.

'Well. There it is. The purgatory that is Queensferry High School awaiting its latest victim. I mean student.'

She laughed as she said this, but given the fresh revelation of her continuing feelings for her ex, the laughter did not seem quite as musical as it had earlier. Internally I shrugged. I remembered my initial thought after realising we had so much in common that we would either be great friends or something more romantic. If the romance, at least for now, was a no-go, then at the very least I had already made a great buddy in my new home town.

'Looks like an utter shithole.'

I replied, half in jest, but half horrified that yet another school I would attend was a shining example of the dearth of architectural skills in the public sector. As wonderful old stone built schools had become unfit for purpose, the councils had replaced them with buildings lacking any creative imagination (surely something that would affect their temporary inhabitants) constructed of hideous concrete and all too often packed with asbestos (yet to rear its ugly and dangerous head in the media). This would be my seat of learning for the next year or two, and, at the moment, I just felt like leaving as soon as possible.

Almost 4 years of John Neilson had produced an antipathy in me towards such buildings and I had hoped the old village may have had a school with a little more character, but the expansion of the village had seen this carbuncle built in 1970.

'All schools are shitholes in one way or another,' Gillian offered. 'They're not really places to go to enjoy yourself are they?'

I knew it made perfect logical sense, and realised that I was more nervous about tomorrow than I had thought. It was a shit time to be changing schools. My grades, which had been consistently above average for the first 2 to 3 years of high school had exponentially fallen in ratio to my cannabis use and increasing amount of gigs attended. Who wanted to spend an evening working on a German or Geography assignment when you could be stoned and listening to Howard Devoto or Julian Cope live? But I knew I had to knuckle down these next few months. My 'O' Grades were a matter of months away, and, if I wanted to go on and do decent Highers with a view to University or College then my finger had to be retracted swiftly from the proverbial anal passage. I had 8 exams to sit in May and June. Of those, I pretty much knew I'd fuck up the more science based ones like physics and chemistry. My strengths were more in the arts and languages, and that was where I'd decided to concentrate my efforts studying wise. I knew, and it saddened me, that for a few months at least I'd have to reduce the levels of partying and attending gigs. The latter would be the hardest for me. Live music had become almost an addiction for me.

The excitement would begin before even leaving the house; sticking some tunes on from the band in question while I got ready had become a ritual, and the excitement built further on the journey to the venue, the queue outside then those final breath-taking moments as you waited for the band to come on stage. Then it was (usually, barring the odd awful performance) a million miles an hour musical rollercoaster for anywhere between forty minutes and two and a half hours, with that sudden comedown at the end as the last notes of the final encore faded out and the band left the stage.

But you'd still carry that buzz for hours, or even days afterwards; from singing your favourite song on the train or bus home, to the enthusiastic and effervescent descriptions your friends had to suffer for days. But even with all the lack of common sense of a fifteen year old boy, I knew I needed a backup plan in case it took a while to get my break in the music business. And my backup plan needed a decent level of exam passes to work (not that I had any clue what I would actually do at university or college. When I was 11, there had been a brief flirtation with the idea of being a lawyer, but this had come more from my mum's dreams than my own, and my initial enthusiasm quickly waned.) So I wanted some decent passes then could make up for the lull with a summer of (hopeful) debauchery.

We started heading away from tomorrow's doom along Station Road, the dogs safely back on their leads. Gillian was asking me about girlfriends and whether I'd left anyone behind in the West. Still smarting slightly from her earlier revelation, I thought it best to play down any apparent interest I'd shown in her. So I concocted a tale of a wonderful relationship that had lasted a year but which we both had (maturely) recognised would not stand the test of even such a seemingly short distance between us (I left out that it was a few months of wild sexual exploration with a girl I stole from my best mate) The thought came that my earlier idea of us only becoming best buddies would probably be cemented by this fib, and, sure enough, my story of woe seemed to elicit an empathic sympathy in Gillian. The sensible part of me accepted that, especially given our proximity to each other house wise, this was the best course of action for both of us. The teenage boy part of me regretted that I would not get the chance to explore, or at least try to explore, the cute female body beside me.

As we talked, we'd cut up Kirkliston Road and were heading to the bridge roundabout and the final leg to our homes. Our breaths still hung in misty clouds in the frosty air, and even the dogs' exertions meant they were accompanied by their own little fogs. Traffic was busier now, people heading to visit friends and family for the day, or to do a shopping before a sedentary day in front of the zombie box. We crossed the bridge access road and made our way onto Builyeon Road. As we took the last steps towards Gillian's house, we agreed to meet up one evening after school to walk the dogs and for Gillian to hear how my first couple of days had gone. She also promised to broach the subject of The Teardrop Explodes gig with her mum and dad, and I said she could get them to phone my parents to confirm that we would get lifts home afterwards. I said goodbye, well goodbye to any romantic notions but definitely hello to a friend and gig buddy.

The house was busy and bustling, mum still emptying boxes and trying to decide to utilise all the extra space we now had (the new house was around 50% bigger than the old place). I of course offered to help by completely staying out the way. I made a couple of sandwiches and disappeared upstairs to my room to contemplate the coming horrors of the next day.

Chapter 11

I woke with mum knocking on my bedroom door. As my eyes opened reluctantly I remembered what the day held and groaned aloud. Once I showered I put on my new uniform (both my schools required the wearing of a uniform; this one was a very dark navy blue in contrast to the screaming loudness of my previous maroon one). From my window I could see it was another sub-zero day, the early morning frost glistening on the gardens in the street.

I knew the walk to school now so could avoid the embarrassment of being dropped off by mum or dad. No matter how slowly I ate breakfast or got ready, nothing was going to delay having to leave in time for school (last thing I wanted was to be even more obvious by arriving late). I retraced our steps from the previous day, taking Rosebery Avenue as the quicker route to the school that Gillian had pointed out yesterday. As I grew nearer, so did the crowds of my fellow (or soon to be fellow) pupils, all muffled up against the biting cold. I was shocked as I arrived at the gates as the smokers seemed to be more brazen here, openly puffing away right by the gate where the teachers would drive through. The odd curious glance was cast my way as I stopped beside the smoking crowd and lit my customary Regal small, but other than the odd fraternal nod, nothing was said to me. Far too soon the bell rang and I made my way to the front entrance where the office was situated. The compulsory frumpy middle aged school secretary (I'm sure there was a secret breeding farm somewhere in Scotland producing these creatures) looked at me over the counter.

'Yes?' Her query was as dry as a desert in summer and as friendly as a rabid dog.

'Hello. It's my first day here. I was told to report to the office.'

'Well your name would be helpful.'

I wondered just how many pupils were starting anew here that she was not already aware of the new boy.

'It's Graham Robertson.'

'Ah yes. Just take a seat over there. Mr Russell wants a word with you before we take you to your class.'

Great. I had sort of hoped there would be no pep talk/warning meeting with the headmaster. I sat and waited around ten minutes before an office door opened and a small rotund man in his fifties stuck his head out.

'Mr Robertson? (Mr? That was a good start). Come away in to the office.'

Okay; he seemed friendly. Perhaps he hadn't read my transcripts from my last school too closely, or perhaps (optimism on overload here) they had not even been sent. The office was the usual drab head teacher's office; grey and brown with hints of beige, the only decoration being a few sparse awards that the school had obviously bought second hand.

'Sit down then, sit down. Well, I suppose I should welcome you to the school. When did you move into the new house, eh? And how are you finding the village?'

I sat, feeling rather uncomfortable. I wasn't used to this level of joviality from a senior teacher. Usually when I was spending time in an office like this it was for a verbal bollocking or a few close meetings between hand and tawse.

'We moved in Saturday morning sir. Got a chance to walk round the village yesterday. It seems very nice.'

'Good good. Very glad to hear it. We're a nice little community. I've lived here since I was eight years old. My father used to work on the bridge you know, eh.'

I was gradually losing the will to live. This utterly boring little man was utterly boring me towards an early grave.

'Anyway, enough of the small talk.' (Thank Christ) 'Now I've noticed from your transcripts (Oh shit, here we go) that your grades have sort of slipped a little over the last year. I understand that changing schools at this stage is very difficult, but I hope we'll see some rapid improvement in time for your exams in May. I see you're taking Latin. Excellent, excellent. I myself was somewhat of a Latin scholar myself. It warms my heart to see young people enthusiastic about such a wonderful language. Non scholae sed vitae discimus as they say, eh?'

I didn't have a clue what he'd just said. I'd taken Latin as; a) It pleased mum and dad, and b) I really was interested in the history of that period. I'd originally thought it would help with that, but instead it had all been boring grammar and verb subjugation.

'I also see you've had the odd behavioural issue at John Neilson. Well, boys will be boys so we won't hold that against you. I'm sure you've matured much more now and we will not have to see you in this office too often, eh?'

My will to live had now absconded and stowed away on a freighter to Mexico.

'But let's get your school life here started, eh? I'll get Miss McIntosh to take you to see Mr Lynn your register and guidance teacher.'

Oh great, probably another dry old bastard with words of wisdom. Guidance teacher? That was a new one. Teachers at my old school just tended to shout at you. Perhaps that was West Coast guidance and the East Coast version was a bit more…twee?

Mr Russell deposited me with the frumpy conversationalist from earlier who wordlessly led me through corridors that looked like the corridors in nearly every other British school of the era. While featureless, there was a strange serenity about them when empty of noisy teenagers and I took the opportunity of this silent tour to gaze into classrooms in a futile attempt to gauge the potential talent levels (even in a state of nervousness those hormones were at work). We eventually reached a (thankfully) empty woodwork room (Hmm, a subject I'd always hated. I sensed Mr Lynn and I would not get on).

Frumpy knocked the door and entered. Behind the desk, looking through a pile of papers was a giant of a man, at least 6 foot 3, but with a jovial bearded face and eyes that spoke of arcane knowledge of mischief.

'Mr Lynn, this is the new boy, Graham Robertson. He's in your register class so Mr Russell asked me to bring him along to see you.'

'Thanks Miss McIntosh.' The voice matched the look; bassy and booming. (If I were to make a film of this period, the obvious choice to play Mr Lynn would have to be Brian Blessed)

'Right Graham, grab a seat and let's have a chat.'

I was right. Another 'chat'. It seemed to be school policy here. I wondered if it would be as vacuously interesting as the 'wisdom' imparted by Mr Russell.

'Okay then. I'm sure you've had the usual welcome to the village blah blah from Wee Bob. (Wee Bob? Only later would I learn that this was the moniker applied to Mr Russell by pupils and teachers alike). There are two things you need to know about me. Number 1; I don't like bullshit. Number 2; I don't like bullshitters. So, if you can avoid those two sins, then you and I will get along just fine. I'm your guidance teacher as well as your register teacher, which is basically just more educational psychology bullshit. But…if you do have any problems that can't be dealt with at home, then my door is always open, unless of course it's shut. (Oh great, this guy thought he was the school comedian too). Right then, I've worked out your classes and timetable for you. No real point in going into a class half way through, so your first class today will be English with Mr Sullivan. He's an American so goodness knows why he's teaching English but the pupils seem to think he's young and trendy, though personally I find him a bit of a fool. But each to their own. Next class starts in ten minutes so I'll point you in the right direction then it's up to you. Registration is at 9am sharp every morning. If you're late for me once, you get a stern look. If you're late for me twice, it's a lunchtime detention. Three times in the same week and it's an hour after school detention. Simple rules mean a simple life.'

I hadn't decided whether I liked this guy or not. My still developing senses warned me that below that outer joviality lay a dark side that you didn't want to cross. And my more than experienced hands said that, should he ever get the opportunity to use the tawse on me then my hands would remember it for weeks to come. (I didn't realise at this point that the local authority here had already banned the use of the tawse in schools)

Having pointed me in the direction of my first classroom, I was left with ten minutes to kill. Without knowing the covert smoking areas yet, and not wanting to use the far too open school gate at this time of day, I spent a wasteful few minutes looking at the wonderful (I do wish there was a 'sarcastic' font available) art work that seemed to adorn nearly every corridor wall. But all too soon I was at the dreaded destination just as a class of what looked like first years came scurrying out like little busy mice. I decided that being in first wasn't such a bad thing. Rather that than running the gauntlet of inquisitive stares. When the last mouse had left I quickly entered and nodded at the teacher. As Mr Lynn had said, he was young for a teacher. In fact, even the fuzzy facial hair that looked like someone had stuck some cotton wool on his face made him look like a 17 year old rather than someone in their late 20's.

'Well I'm sort of guessing you must be the new boy Graham.' He drawled. (I could sort of see Mr Lynn's point already. This bloke could hardly speak English, how the hell was he going to teach it?)

'Just grab a seat anywhere. The hordes will arrive soon. I'm sure Mr Lynn has told you I'm Mr Sullivan, but I prefer the older pupils call me Zach.'

(Oh great, one of those forward thinking teachers who wanted you all to be pals but were usually the worst for handing out homework and detentions)

I was only sitting for a couple of minutes when the first of my new classmates came in. As more entered, the staring intensified and was joined with the occasional questioning murmur as to my identity. By this time however, I was completely ignoring the scrutiny as all my attention was focussed on classroom entrant number 5. It wasn't that she was particularly pretty, though she wasn't ugly either. It was just that she had the most amazing pair of tits I had ever seen on a girl our age. Now you may think that these are the exaggerated ramblings of a teenage boy on heat, and to an extent you'd be correct. But these were bigger than most adult tits too (based on extensive research on various top shelf magazines by this point). I was mesmerised. I was intrigued. I was horny as hell and sporting one hell of a semi already. (And sincerely hoping that this trendy bastard of a teacher was not about to ask me to stand up and introduce myself.) There is just something about big tits that completely hypnotises a teenage boy. (Ironically, as I grew older, I sort of went off the oversized breast thing)

'Right you shower of muppets, calm down and shut up. We've got a lot to get through today and I don't want to be repeating myself two or three times. And yes, for all your gawkers, the class is one bigger today. Our new student is Graham. So stop staring. All the boys can ask what team he supports at break time and all the girls can ask if he's single at lunch time. So eyes forward and let's read some poetry!'

I could feel my face and neck redden at his flippant though welcome words. Luckily this was not noticed over the collective groan at the news of a period spent reading and comprehending (or not comprehending) the wonderful world of poetry.

The forty five minutes dragged by, but eventually the bell rang to signify the end of class and a fifteen minute respite before the next one. As we exited the classroom a gangly youth with shoulder length hair sidled up to me.

'So, Graham like then? How you doing mate. I'm Chris. So are you a smoker like ken?' (Note to readers; this was not a question as to whether I smoked cigarettes in a similar fashion to an as yet unidentified third party by the name of Ken. Ken was more an East coast colloquialism that literally meant 'know', but was also commonly used at the end of many sentences in much the same way as most Australians use that whiny and annoying upward inflection of the voice.)

'Aye mate, and I'm gasping for a fag after all that poetry pish.' (Note to American readers; in the UK, 'nipping out for a fag' means something very different as to what it means in the USA).

'Mon then. I'll show you where aw the gadgies go for a fly puff then.'

I followed my newly acquired friend out the building and round the back of one of the featureless blocks that made up the school. There were already a collection of puffers indulging in their illicit habit, and it was difficult to tell where cigarette smoke began and the frosty breath of the smokers ended. Chris approached a small group of three boys and two girls who, by their hair and blazer badges, formed part of the 'rock crowd' of the school. At least there didn't seem to be any Neanderthal types ready to challenge the new boy for his place on the evolutionary ladder of machismo. Yet.

'Arite folks. This is a new gadgie, Graham. Just started the day ken. Say hi to the gang Graham.'

Introductions were muttered. I didn't foresee any of these becoming lifelong buddies but you don't diss folk on your first day so I chatted away, talked about the bands I liked (with customised emphasis on the rock aspect of my tastes) and managed to smoke two fags before the bell rang for the re-commencement of our education and betterment. I'd scored some brownie points already though. They were impressed with the list of bands I'd seen (and met) compared to their sparse adventures in Gigland. I bade farewell to Chris of the greasy hair once I'd elicited directions to my next class; the dreaded Latin. (This query had been met with a guffaw of gargantuan proportions and had somewhat reduced my newly attained status)

The rest of the morning went by in an anti-flurry of boredom, scrutinising looks and hurried introductions. I was pleased to see that beyond the mystery lady of the huge melons, the talent ratio in my year was pleasingly high. (Though of course was yet to ascertain what percentage of the totty was single) Lunchtime came and I was at a bit of a loss as to what to do and where to go. I'd declined mum's offer of a pack lunch, and didn't fancy subjecting myself to the culinary torture of a 1980's school dinner, so the only other alternative was to seek out a local hostelry of the non-licensed but hopefully hot food type. As I made my way to the gates to begin my quest for vittles, Chris came sloping over.

'Hey gadge, what you doing for lunch like? I'm heading for the chippy down the village ken if you want to tag along. Can toke a wee spliff on the way if you're intae that?'

Result! I'd sort of guessed that Chris might be a fellow stoner but you can never take these things for granted. We made our way onto Station Road then cut down a path behind the bowling club. As soon as we were off the main road, Chris took a rather bedraggled looking spliff from his pocket and lit it.

'Man, get yer lips round this like. It's some barry gear ken.'

I took the proffered joint and inhaled deeply. Ah. Soap bar. (For those of you uninitiated in the parlance of the drugs world, soap bar is rather low grade Moroccan hashish. The stuff I usually got from John was far better quality, usually some nice black from India.)

'Aye, no bad Chris. But I'll gie you a wee smoke tomorrow that will blow you away.'

'Barry man, but I cannae see it being much better than this ken.'

I sighed. I may only be fifteen, but I felt years ahead of these amateurs on soap bar. We emerged from the leafy paths onto Newhalls Road and made our way onto the High Street and the chippy Chris had mentioned. I ordered a healthy Scotch pie supper (with that watery East coast brown sauce) and we sat and ate it at the top of the car park with the shivery silvery Forth as our backdrop.

The afternoon resembled the morning in its utter lack of anything interesting. School is school. These folk who say they're the best days of your life are talking out their arses. Sure it's a journey of discovery, blindly stumbling forward on an Everest like learning camp from Base Camp Puberty, and there are certainly moments of naïve and innocent wonder to brighten that journey.

But mostly it's about the dull grey realities of a regime driven education system sandwiched between the dull grey realities of a regime driven home system. Let's face it; a teenager is pretty much at the bottom of life's ladder. We've outgrown that cuteness of childhood and donned the cloak of surly hormonal mood swings that almost all parents dread. We're surfing a wave of resentment to a coast of adulthood that we see as impending freedom but is in fact just more of the same regime driven systems, but with the government and employers replacing school and parents. I already knew I wanted something different. I wanted to ride that wave past that gloomy looking coast and find an island beyond it where I could be me. Though to be fair, I didn't have a fucking clue what 'me' was going to be.

During the afternoon I'd clocked a few pretty girls who seemed to be paying more attention to the new boy than was normally warranted and their faces were filed away for later. And I'd chatted to a few of both sexes between classes. But my one track mind was still focussed on my buxom beauty from that morning who, sadly, had yet to reappear in my field of vision that day. Finally 3.45pm arrived and what was already my favourite bell of the day. I grabbed my bag and started for the gate, wondering if this was the time when my expected physical challenge would appear. But the journey out of school, and indeed home, was incident free. Perhaps I was being too harsh imposing the West Coast levels of physicality on my new school. I fielded the anticipated questions when I arrived home. Yes mum, the school seems very nice. Yes mum, the teachers seem very nice. Yes mum, my new classmates seem very nice. Yes mum, I'd love egg and chips for tea. (Note to the non Scots among you. We very often refer to our evening meal or dinner as our tea. Just in case you wondered why I was replacing Tetley with egg and chips). Then it was upstairs, change out of the dreaded uniform and stick on Depeche Mode's 'Speak and Spell' for some post school relaxing. All that was missing was a nice doob, but my balls hadn't quite yet grown to the size required to smoke in my parents' house, though they had seem impressed with how much more I was offering to walk 'Dog' these days.

The rest of the school week was relatively stress free. I met a few more decent classmates, found out at least two of them were fellow stoners, didn't face a single physical challenge, and, most importantly of all, I had discovered the identity of my bathykolpian beauty of the first day. Her name was Michelle and, beyond her initial buxom attraction, I'd realised she had a certain Elven cuteness that made me smile, and she was funny and clever to boot. She was in my registration, English and Geography classes and, shockingly for my self-confidence and bravado, it was Michelle who broke the deadlock of silence. It was the Thursday afternoon and we were queued up while Mr Atkinson the geography teacher was handing out a dressing down from hell to two third year pupils. (By the paleness of their faces I guessed they were mighty relieved the tawse was banned here) I was so busy watching the melodrama unfold through the window that I didn't realise my busty lust object had appeared next to me until she spoke. 'So they don't look too happy, do they?'

I jumped. Then turned around and made the greatest effort I'd ever made in keeping my eyes on her eyes rather on those true gifts of nature. I also now saw that her eyes were a beautiful and sparklingblue. This made it just a little easier not to stop my eyes wandering in a southerly direction.

'No, they look like they are in deep shit. Lucky wee bastards that he can't give them the belt because by the look on his face they would be heading home with mighty sore hands.'

'So, how are you settling in then? Seen you about the school but never had a chance to chat to you.'

'Yeah, getting there. Much the same as my old school though I'm mighty relieved the belt is banned here.'

'Oh. Were you a bit of a bad boy at your old school? I like bad boys.'

That 'gulp' that Fiona had induced so well had just returned with a vengeance. If that wasn't some form of chat up line then I didn't know what was.

'Ach, I'm not that bad (Shut up Graham!). Just got a habit of saying the wrong thing at the wrong time to the wrong teacher.'

'Well there are plenty of wrong teachers here, so I look forward to seeing you wind some of them up. Now I already know you're Graham (em…okay then) so I guess I better introduce myself. I'm Michelle. Glad to see some new blood here, especially a cute boy.'

Gulp again. I was beginning to really enjoy this new school. My natural teenage arrogance had already assumed that some of the glances coming my way from the females had been of the admiring variety, but it was nice to have that arrogance confirmed.

'I'd hardly call myself cute. Ruggedly good looking maybe.'

Michelle laughed. (Always a good sign; humour is the greatest aphrodisiac there is)

'Okay, we'll agree on that. You certainly seem to be attracting attention from the single girls in the year…and the year below.'

I was a little confused here. While loving the idea of the attention, did Michelle's comment include herself in the single girls' group? Only one way to find out.

'So, are you one of the single girls then Michelle?'

'I am indeed. And in case you're interested, yes, I have been one of the ones paying you attention to you.'

Gulp. Dance in joy. Gulp.

'Funnily enough, I noticed you on Monday too.'

'Oh come on Graham. I know exactly what you noticed on Monday, and it wasn't my eyes or my legs.'

Gulp. She had me bang to rights. But then I suppose when you had the largest chest in the school (pupil or teacher level) then you had to accept the attention you were going to get. And, if things kept going the way they had been these last 5 minutes, her breasts would be getting some very special attention from me.

Mr Atkinson had finished his bollocking and two very sheepish looking kids exited his room as quickly as they could. We began to file in and I noticed with a wry smile that Michelle chose to sit right next to me. To be honest, the following 45 minutes of glacial moraines were sort of lost in a haze of flirtatious looks and suppressed giggles. Where Gillian had quickly and appropriately been placed in the 'best friends' drawer, this looked as if it held far more promise. And her forthright manner so reminded me of Fiona that I was hoping any physical liaisons would also be in the same vein.

When the lesson finished, Michelle hung back and walked along the corridor with me. I sensed it was my turn to be forward after her earlier compliments so decided to take the plunge.

'Listen Michelle. It's only going to be my second weekend here and last weekend was pretty much all moving in and getting organised. Really don't want to be stuck in the house. Do you fancy doing something on Friday or Saturday.'

Her face lit up like a supernova. I'd obviously asked the right question at the right time.

'I can't do anything Friday as am babysitting my little cousin. But one of the fifth years is having a party on Saturday. Why don't you come to that with me? Gives you a chance to meet some of the gang outside of this shit hole.'

'Sounds a great plan. I don't want to sound like an asshole but where's the best place to get booze? I had my usual haunts back in Elderslie but unsure of the child friendly off licences here.'

'Ach don't worry about that. My brother usually gets my carry out. What do you drink? I'll get him to grab some and you can give me money on the night?'

'Brilliant. I'm easy. What do you usually drink?'

'Whatever gets me mad with it the quickest. Usually cider and vodka though.'

'I can live with that. Couple of bottles of cider and a bottle of vodka between us? My treat!'

'Why thank you kind sir. I can see I made the right choice in you.' (Gulp)

'One other thing. Will it be okay to have a smoke at this party?'

Michelle giggled.

'Well I'm sort of guessing you don't mean cigarettes. Trust me; there will be more bongs at this do than in the News at Ten titles.'

We parted ways at the bottom of the stairs, but with a promise to meet up at the end of the day and walk home together. It certainly looked like I had managed to pull my first girl after only four days at the school and the girl with the most impressive chest too!

The walk home was innocent enough. Michelle lived in Springfield, further on than I did in Echline, so we bade farewell at the top of the path to my house. We had flirted outrageously all the way home and it seemed pretty certain that Saturday would see this move up a level (Or two, please let it be two). Mum asked me why I was in such a happy mood when I got in the house but I'd never been comfortable discussing anything like girls with her. (And in fact this would remain so for many years to come). Friday was a boring day, apart from the glorious lunch hour spent with Michelle talking and laughing. My first week was drawing to a close. I'd met one or two potentially good friends, had avoided any hierarchical new boy battles, and had a date with a pretty cute elf with fantastic tits the next night. All in all a pretty damned successful beginning to my life in South Queensferry.

Saturday evening came. Michelle phoned about 6pm (thus initiating amused interrogations by my dad) to confirm a meeting point. The party was in Scotstoun so she agreed to meet at the top of the path from my house. (Though I told mum and dad we were meeting down by the bridge to avoid them taking up observation posts in the back bedroom). I chose my favourite Clash 'London Calling' t shirt, matched with black canvas trousers and a denim jacket. There was little I could do with my hair (at this point it was in a sort of unruly Julian Cope 'style' that my mum hated) but, checking the bedroom mirror, I thought I looked pretty cool for a fifteen year old. I left the house, harmless teasing from my dad echoing off the walls, and walked up to the main road. There was no sign of Michelle so I took one of my pre rolled (by John, I was yet to learn the skill of self-rolling) joints and lit it up, letting the soothing smoke calm my pre-date nerves. Finally I saw her coming along the road and as she got closer I let out a little gasp.

She was looking stunning, a red knee length pencil skirt matched with a ruffled blouse with plunging neckline (Oh cleavage, thou art my heaven) and a black bomber jacket with faux fur collar. The temperatures had risen a little that week so, though it was still chilly, neither of us was stifled by scarves or hats. She smiled broadly as she approached then shocked me by leaning in and kissing me on the mouth. I felt a warm flush move down my body and wrapped my arms around her, that first awkward kiss anything but. We eventually disentangled ourselves and we made our way along Builyeon Road hand in hand. Her brother had come up trumps and we had 2 litres of Olde English cider and a bottle of Grant's Vodka to do us for the night. In addition I had 5 nice joints from my stash so the evening was looking like a winner.

We stopped off at the Bridge petrol station for mixers for the vodka, coke for me and orange juice for Michelle, then carried on to our destination. The party was a corner house in Provost Milne Grove and as we approached there was already the sound of music escaping onto the street. The door was lying open so Michelle gave it a loud knock then led the way in. A fair crowd were already there, probably around twenty or so, and I recognised one or two faces from my first week. Chris was there, ensconced in an armchair in the corner and already looking as stoned as a Saudi adulterer. He shouted greetings above the music and gestured for us to make our way over. I took the bags with the carry out while Michelle went looking for a couple of glasses.

'Arite mate, how's it going like. Man you're one fast mover. Here a week and you're winching wee Michelle already ken. That's pretty damned barry.'

'It's only our first date bud. But aye, she's pretty damned cute. Now are you going to give us a hit of that bong beside you or are you hogging it to yourself?'

'Haha. Aye course mate. I'll just pack a wee bowl for you. It's a nice wee bit of home grown that Jason there got off his cousin ken.'

He packed a bowl, passed the bong and I sparked up, breathing in deeply then coughing like a bastard as the harsh smoke hit my lungs.

'Jesus Chris, that's a bit rough! I need a drink after that!'

Right on cue, Michelle came back with a couple of glasses. While she poured out the vodka, I grabbed the cider and took a couple of healthy mouthfuls.

'Fuck, that's better. Chris, you must have lungs made of iron to smoke that. Not got any solid on you?'

'Yeah sure, still got some of that Moroccan. Did you bring any of that good stuff.'

'Course I have. Though they are ready rolled joints.'

'Eh, how come like? Can you no roll them yersel ken?'

I suddenly realises that there was a huge chink in my hitherto cool armour. I hadn't really had a lot of 'smoking' buddies back in Elderslie. David and a couple of others, and of course John when I was up at his. But it seemed that nearly everyone at this party was either smoking a joint or taking a hit from a bong. I improvised quickly.

'Aye I can, but I'm pure shite at it. Tried and tried but always end up making a complete arse of it.'

'Ach dinnae fret man. I'm a black belt at putting a doob together. Gie me a couple o weeks and I'll have you rolling like a master.'

Phew. Had managed to not only wriggle out of a demeaning situation image wise, but also gained what professed to be an experienced teacher at the same time. I lit one of John's joints and inhaled deeply a few times before passing it over to Chris who eagerly accepted it.

'Whoa dude. That really is some nice shit ken. Barry as fuck by the way. Where you getting hold of this?'

'I get it off my cousin. He's always worked in the music business so knows a few people to get good gear off.'

'Wow. Do you think you can get us some of this from him? It's much better than whit I'm scoring these days.'

Hmmm. I had been talking to John about getting actual decent bits of hash off him now I had moved. He'd said I'd have to start actually paying for some (I'd been on freebies for some three years now). Maybe this way I could cover my costs and still get mine for next to nothing.

I'd worried about this as I no longer had any part time jobs, though mum and dad had increased my pocket money as they wanted me to concentrate on upcoming exams. I still had some earners from household chores like washing the car, but if I could offset my hash costs by selling a bit to Chris and his mates, it would leave me that money for gigs and vinyl.

'Aye, I'll have a word with him when I see him and see what I can do.'

I could tell Michelle was beginning to get annoyed that I was paying more attention to Chris and the joint than to her. She was sitting nursing her depleted vodka and looking a little petulant with a lip that could have been utilised in an Olympic diving contest.

'Hey babes, you okay?'

'Well I would be if I wasn't sitting here staring at everyone else having fun!'

'Sorry Michelle. No very nice of me. But you've got my full attention now. You want a top up of vodka?'

The smile returned and after topping up her glass I snuggled in beside her and watched the party carry on around us. The music was generally pretty naff. Though I liked a lot of rock music, this was insipid bland shit that was getting played, and not a sign of anything vaguely electronic or new wave. Michelle introduced me to a few people who I hadn't yet met and they mostly seemed sound, though one guy, Stuart, seemed to be giving me dirty looks every time I glanced up.

'What's that guy's problem? He's been staring at me like he wants to kill me for the last ten minutes or so.'

'Ah, that's my ex. He's a total arsehole and still hasn't got the message that I am not interested in him.'

Oh great. I'd managed to survive my first week with no sign of conflict on the horizon and now it looked like there may be a little confrontation coming up in the very near future. But for now I was determined to enjoy the night so in a fit of reckless abandon, and knowing full well that the wee arse was watching, I moved in closer to Michelle for our first real snog.

'Wow, where did that come from?'

'Just felt bad for ignoring you when I was talking to Chris so thought I'd give you some real attention.'

'Aye? Well give me some more. I like that sort of attention.'

The rest of the party was fairly average. I'd managed to get some Clash on and have a bit of a semi drunken jump around, and at some point Michelle had managed to blag a space on the sofa so we indulged in some prolonged snogging practice though I refrained from trying anything further while her ex was in the room. All too soon it was 11.30pm. I'd said to mum and dad I'd be home about midnight (after arguing that 11pm was far too early for a hip young cool guy on a Saturday). Michelle was in the same boat so we grabbed our jackets and said our goodbyes, though with Chris, the reply was more of a mumble as he was in a semi vegetative state in the armchair he'd occupied all evening. The night had developed a bit of a chill since earlier, and Michelle cuddled in close to me as we walked along the quiet back road. With it being so late I walked her back to hers and stood and had a lengthy goodbye on the corner of Springfield Terrace.

Once she'd headed into her house, I began to consume the necessary 6 polo mints needed to disguise my smoking activities of the evening. Dad didn't mind me having a wee drink; he'd even give me the odd lager in the house, but they were both vehemently anti-smoking. Mum was in bed when I got in, and dad was half asleep in the armchair (or 'resting his eyes' as he always retorted when mum accused him of sleeping in a chair). He woke up when I closed the front door and immediately gave me a gentle ribbing about my date, asking when he and mum would meet my new girlfriend. I embarrassedly shrugged off the queries and headed up to my room, plugged in my headphones, and drifted off to sleep to the sound of Bowie's 'Scary Monsters' with Michelle's ample bosom still in my thoughts.

Chapter 12

The showdown I'd been expecting, and dreading, didn't come till week 3 at the new school. By this point me and Michelle were pretty full on; spending most lunchtimes together and walking to and from school. I'd clocked her ex giving me the odd dirty look in the corridor but had dismissed him as unimportant and was convinced it probably wouldn't develop further. I'd kept up my friendship with Gillian (which rather annoyed Michelle) and we'd often walk the dogs together after school. Her mum had become really friendly with mine so she had even managed to get permission to do the Teardrop Explodes gig with me at the start of February (again to Michelle's annoyance). She'd loved her first taste of live music though she hadn't been impressed by the support band 'The Ravishing Beauties' (though I'd loved them as I had been well into Virginia Astley's collaboration with Richard Jobson of The Skids) but had danced like a wild thing throughout the Teardrops' set. She'd occasionally come over to sift through my still growing vinyl collection and listen to bands she hadn't really heard before (once again to Michelle's chagrin – she didn't see how a boy could just be friends with a girl). We'd met up as usual around 5pm to take the dogs round the estate and over to the big fields between us and the road bridge for a good run about. As we headed back towards our homes, I noticed Stuart and two of his pals walking on the opposite side of the road. He spotted me at the same time and started talking animatedly to his friends.

'Oh shit, here we go.'

'What? These guys from your school?'

'Aye, the wee stocky bastard is Michelle's ex, and let's just say he's none too pleased that he is the ex and I'm the current boyfriend.'

'Ach surely he won't start anything?'

'I wouldn't bet on that. The wee plamf has been givin' me the evil eye since that party we went too. I had a feeling it was only a matter of time till he took it to the next level.'

Right on cue, the aforementioned arsehole and his two sidekicks crossed the road and approached us.

'So is this you two timing Michelle already ya weegie prick?'

'One: this is my friend who Mich knows all about; two: I'm not from Glasgow so ahm no a Weegie, and three: why don't you just do one before you look any more stupid than you already do.'

'Ah, so you think yer a smartass do you? Cannae be bothered wi you West Coasters; ye aw think you're hard as nails ken.'

'Oh, and Four: my names not Ken you wee eejit.'

I knew my answers were like throwing kerosene on a bonfire but I really couldn't be bothered with this no- mark giving me dirty looks every time I passed him at school. Plus I'd always had a difficult time knowing just when to keep my mouth shut. I just sort of hoped that his two cronies had some sense of fair play and would that they would not jump me en-masse.

'Ye really think yer a clever gadgie don't ye? Well you're no going to look so clever when I gie ye a couple o slaps likesay?'

I'd never been a fighter, not because I couldn't look after myself (In most fights I'd been in I hadn't been the instigator but I had walked away the victor). I waited for him to make the first move while keeping a close eye on what his two pals were doing. Luckily it seemed as if they were both happy to let Stuart take the lead on this. He pushed me squarely in the chest. I went with it and allowed myself to fall backwards against the fence. I'd give diplomacy one more go.

'Listen Stuart. This is daft. You and Michelle split up three months ago and she's told you there's no chance of getting back with her, so why make yourself look a total arse.' (Ah, my famous diplomatic skills were at their peak here).

He swung a punch for me. I wasn't quick enough to dodge it totally and it caught the side of my head in a stinging blow. Then he tried to follow it up with a jab to the face but this time I grabbed his arm and shoved him away.

'Look mate, I don't want to fight you. You caught me a good one there; let's just call it quits at that eh?'

'No chance ya prick. You stole ma bird and now I'm going to make ye pay ken?'

My temper was starting to rise now. I moved back onto my heels and then pivoted as he rushed me, using his own forward momentum to push him into the fence. I wanted this over quickly. As he turned still trying to regain his balance I threw a right hook to his cheek that knocked him back against the fence again. Before he could recover I threw another right handed punch, but this time to the stomach (This was another thing I had to thank John for. He'd always said that if you couldn't avoid a fight, a punch to the stomach was usually enough to badly wind an opponent and end a brawl before it got too messy). It worked this time too. Stuart doubled over in pain and sank to his knees gasping for breath. I cast a quick glance at his friends who were now a few yards behind me, but they didn't seem as if they were about to intervene. In fact, one of them seemed to be quite enjoying seeing his pal cut down to size. I took 'Dog's lead back from Gillian and started walking away. Gillian was trying hard not to laugh but I was more bothered about putting some distance between us and them in case he decided that he'd not had enough yet. And thus, as quickly as it had started, my first (and only one of two to happen at Queensferry High) fight in South Queensferry was over. I needed some time to calm down as my blood was still boiling so Gillian agreed to come with me and we walked up to the viewpoint at the bridge and sat for a while. Eventually my inner calm had returned and I felt ready to go home without steam coming out of my ears. Gillian headed over to her house and I made my way up the drive and into mine. As I opened the front door, mum called out from the living room. Her voice was stern and I wondered what the hell was going on.

'Graham, get in here now.'

Oh shit.

I walked into the living room and gasped. The little arse Stuart was sitting on my sofa next to a woman I presumed was his mum.

'Graham, can you explain why you were fighting with Mrs McDonald's son today? And why he has ended up with a swollen cheek and a ripped jacket?'

This was unbelievable. Not only was this guy an arsehole, but he was a grassing arsehole too. And when the hell did his jacket get ripped?'

'Actually yes, I can explain why this arsehole has a swollen cheek, though I've no idea how his jacket got ripped...'

'Graham! Watch your language!'

'Sorry mum, but I'm so damned angry. This idiot is Michelle's ex-boyfriend. He's not happy that she is seeing me and has been giving me dirty looks and spoiling for a fight since I started going out with her. He came up and started the fight when I was out with Gillian and the dogs. So all I did was defend myself. He threw the first punch and I still tried to defuse the situation.'

My mum looked at me. Since the Sandra incident, she'd become more astute when it came to telling when I was trying to get one over on her or when I was telling the truth.

'Well Stuart? Is that what happened?'

Both mothers now turned their steely gazes on the idiot.

'He's lying! Yes, I'm not happy he's seeing Michelle, but the only reason I went up to him today was that he was kissing that girl he was with (what the hell?). I started telling him that it wasn't fair on Michelle and he just punched me then threw me against the fence. That's how my jacket got ripped. I didn't hit him once.'

I put my hand to the side of my head. There was swelling round the ear from where his punch had caught me earlier.

'Mum, if he didn't hit me once, what caused this then?'

My mum put her hand to the side of my head and felt the raised bump. Then she leaned in and looked closely.

'There is definite swelling, and the area round your ear is red. It does look like someone has hit you today.'

Mrs McDonald finally chipped in after staying silent for so long.

'Mrs Robertson, are you saying my son is a liar? Stuart may be a handful at times but one thing he doesn't do is lie.'

'Well Mrs McDonald, it looks as if he's learned a new skill then. (Go mum!). I know when Graham is trying to pull the wool over my eyes and this isn't one of those times. Someone has hit him in the last hour or two and if it wasn't your son, then who was it?'

There was a momentary silence.

'Well, whatever the truth, your son has caused my son's jacket to be ripped and I expect you to pay to replace it.'

'Now you listen to me Mrs McDonald. You came to my house making accusations against my son. It seems as if those accusations were excuses made to cover up for your son starting the trouble. I'm going to go over and talk to Gillian. There is no way they could conspire to have the same story as Graham wasn't to know your son would run crying to you (Go mum again!). If Gillian confirms Graham's story then I'm afraid you can stick your new jacket where the sun doesn't shine. (Who are you and what have you done with my mum?). Now if you leave me your phone number, I'll give you a ring once I've spoken to Gillian and let you know the outcome.'

Stuart's mum made some general grumbling noises and stood up, gave her son a look that could kill at 100 yards then made her way to the door, with the idiot following sheepishly behind her.

Once they'd left, I turned to my mum and smiled.

'Thanks for sticking up for me mum. I can't believe he came looking for a fight then went running to his mum.'

'There's no need for that smile. I'm not happy that you were fighting, no matter who started it. We've been here less than a month and I've got someone at the door complaining about you! This year is far too important school wise for any of your carry on.'

'So what was I meant to do? Stand there like a tailor's dummy and let him punch me several times? He hit me once then I pushed him out the way and tried to end it there. But he kept on coming at me. So I hit him twice to end it quickly the way John told me to.'

'Oh so John's been encouraging you to fight has he? Always thought you spent too much time at your cousin's house.'

'Ach, what's the point, you're not listening to me. He encouraged me to defend myself if these situations happened, and that's just what I did.'

I stormed out the lounge and went up to my room; with the inevitable 'Turn that racket down' following my putting on the Buzzcocks at the highest possible volume. I was a bit annoyed at mum, but equally happy she had stuck up for me as well as relieved the altercation had ended swiftly and without any real damage to me. But this situation could go one of two ways for me now. By tomorrow lunchtime half the school would know about the fight, and I'd be sure, if anyone asked about it, to throw in the fact that Stuart had gone snivelling to his mum. Now there would either be no one wanting to challenge me as they'd heard how well I'd handled myself, or there would be a queue of wannabe hard men ready to give me a square go. I sighed. Why was this growing up shit so damned hard?

I'd phoned Michelle and told her what happened once the house had calmed down. She was really pissed off with Stuart but also a little pissed off with me as Gillian had been involved in the incident, especially given Stuart had said he had seen us kissing. It took five minutes of extreme ass kissing (alas, only metaphorically) to assure her that both Gillian and I were innocents in this and a further five to persuade her not to go marching into school and kick the shit out of Stuart. When I met her in the morning she was still fuming. I tried to tell her that I didn't think there would be any more trouble as I felt I'd sorted it but she was determined to say something to him, even of those words were violence free. Once at school a couple of people already in the know came over and offered congratulations. It seemed Stuart wasn't high in any popularity charts and had a bit of a reputation for starting fights. When the part about his running home to his mum and them turning up at my house was thrown in the mix, there were laughs all round, and it seemed that this may be the final nail in the coffin of Stuart's reputation. After registration I didn't see Michelle till lunchtime and when I saw her walking towards me with a little self-satisfied smirk on her face I knew she had ignored my pleas and advice and had sought Stuart out sometime over the morning.

'Okay Missy, I already know that look on your face. What's happened to make you look so pleased with yourself?'

The grin got bigger.

'Just made sure that eejit of an ex of mine knows exactly how I feel about him...and made sure it was heard by our entire class at the time.'

Oh God. She was a feisty bitch. But that was one of the things I liked about her.

'Right then, you better tell me all about it before the school gossips come screeching around.'

'Well, we were in French class. The little dick had been avoiding looking at me because he knows he is in the wrong. But half way through Mr Jenkinson had to nip down to the office so I marched over, stood in front of Stuart's desk, slapped him on the top of the head and told him what a total twat he is. Then I had a go at him for being a grassing wee cry baby because he was scared his mum would get him into trouble for ripping his jacket. He didn't say a word back to me but everyone was pissing themselves laughing at him.'

Hmmm. This could either destroy my 'rival' for good or possibly inflame him to more confrontations. With this unpredictable fool I wasn't sure what way it would go.

But the rest of that week, and indeed the next, passed without further incident, either from Stuart's direction or other would be challengers and I settled into the heady boredom of everyday school life.

Chapter 13

In fact, the next two months went by in a tedious monotony. As we moved into March I was still seeing Michelle, though my early aspirations at imminent virginity loss had faded somewhat. She was strictly an all north, no south kind of girl, and while I was still a little in awe of those pendulous twin beauties, the novelty was wearing off in direct correlation to the number of times my hand was slapped as it attempted the perilous journey to teenage nirvana. As we reached April, mum and dad had begun imposing restrictions on how much time I spent out the house (and thus in alone time with Michelle), not over any concerns about our relationship, but purely because the dreaded exam period was hovering in the near future. What made the whole studying process more stressful was that behind the weighty stick of everlasting assessed judgement based on a two hour period, was the tantalising yet still out of reach juicy carrot of the summer holidays and freedom. My parents had also placed a temporary, and vociferously protested, moratorium on any attendance of gigs ('this is your future we're talking about.' – perhaps the most used cliché heard by 15/16 year old kids.) This was a real blow, not only to my social life, but to what I had come to see as my entire raison d'être. It was particularly hard as that spring saw a slew of bands I would have definitely been at; The Fall, The Virgin Prunes, 23 Skidoo, The Birthday Party, Orange Juice, The Cure and The Scars were just a few of the bands that fell victim to mum and dad's totalitarian ways. What made this worse was that summer tended to be a rather quiet period gig wise so there wasn't a lot to look forward to concert wise. Dad knew how much my music meant to me and in a moment of inspired, bizzare and non-prompted wonderful dadliness, had gone out and bought me tickets for The Rolling Stones at the Playhouse, Gang of Four at Coasters, and the rather perplexing mix of Queen and Teardrop Explodes at Ingliston. I hadn't been to gigs in either the Playhouse or Ingliston yet but Coasters was, for me, the Edinburgh equivalent of Tiffanys. (I would also add the Nite Club above the Playhouse to that niche later). But part of me knew I had to cram for these O Grades. I still wasn't sure exactly what it was I wanted to do after school, but university or college was certainly part of the plan. I'd heard too many stories about drunken student union debauchery and loose women with little morals not to have that firmly marked out on my limited map of my future. And to get to that little town of decadence, I needed some decent grades. I'd decided, with no consultation with the parents, to pretty much abandon physics and chemistry. I had eight exams coming up and these were my two weakest subjects, so the plan was to concentrate on the other six and get good grades there while keeping one eye on the Highers that would follow the next year (if my marks were good enough). So my bedroom went from being a place of the latest sounds and nefarious planning to a sanctum of diligent study. A timetable even appeared on one wall listing my exams and with what I was going to review and when between now and the exams. It kicked off with English on Friday April 30th, then Maths on the 6th May, Arithmetic on the 7th (in the days when they were two separate subjects), Latin on the 10th, Chemistry on the 12th (but with no place on my revision calendar), Physics on the 14th (see Chemistry), Geography on the 17th and finally, the big red circle on my schedule, German as my last exam on the 20th. Beyond that date beckoned freedom fun and frivolity for a whole ten weeks (the last couple of weeks of school would have little going on once study leave was finished). I had a good feeling about the impending summer, but to reach that valley of joy I had to first scale my revision mountain and at least come out that exam hall feeling as if I had a chance of good grades. So onto the interminable slopes of facts, numbers, formulae, verb tenses, carboniferous limestone landscapes and the intricacies of Shakespeare I plunged with reluctant enthusiasm.

The revision had not only taken a toll on my social life, but was beginning to affect my romantic life too. Michelle, though bright and clever on the outside, was not the most academic of girls, and already had a job promised to her in her cousin's hairdressing business which would include days at college, so she hardly needed to bother with the forthcoming assessments despite my argument that at least a few O Graded would be a good safety net should she hate her new career. So I was only really seeing her at school and for a couple of hours at the weekend (In their wisdom, I now had an 8pm curfew every night of the week – sensible from mum and dad's perspective, almost fascist from my own skewed viewpoint). She started little arguments with me for no particular reason and seemed fond of accusing me of being hen pecked by my parents; true perhaps, but they were doing it to ensure I got my head in my books for those final crucial weeks. Finally, a week before my English exam, the simmering resentment boiled over into an all-out shouting match as we made our way to school.

For some weird reason (I have yet, after all these years, managed to understand the intricate workings of that chaotic machine known as 'female') she was bringing up Gillian again, despite the fact that Gill herself had her nose buried in SCE Past papers, and accused me of seeing her on the side. She refused to believe my curfews were real and said they were only an excuse for me to sneak off with 'that slag'. (Again, this has always confused me. Girls/women profess to detest that word yet readily use it to denigrate those they dislike or see as rivals). I finally decided I'd had enough. With the worry of upcoming exams, the loss of any social life and the realisation that Michelle's pants were a no-go area for the foreseeable future, I took a decision that this just wasn't working any more.

'Listen Mich. This is madness. Listen to the crap coming out of your mouth. Fair enough, you've got a job at the start of the summer, but I want to go to University. And you go on and on about Gillian all the bloody time. I'm fed up saying she's just a friend. We like the same music, all the stuff you hate, so I like spending time with her, and trust me, I'm not going to risk that friendship by trying to snog her. But all this nonsense from you is doing my head right in and I really can't be arsed with it. I think it's best if we just end it now before we hate each other.'

Her face changed as quickly as the weather on a Scottish summer's day.

'You…you're dumping me? Why?'

'Why? Because you've turned from a bundle of fun to a bundle of nerves. I need to concentrate on getting good passes and I can't manage that with a paranoid girlfriend doing my head in all the time.'

The lip trembled, then trembled some more, and 4 thousand miles away a hurricane changed path.

'Oh don't cry for God's sake. It's not been going that well the last couple of weeks so surely we can stay friends?'

There was no answer; instead she turned on her heels and stomped away from me, her shoulders heaving in dramatic fashion.

I sighed. Ah well. Another experience to chalk up on the wall of life. I wasn't happy that she was hurting, but rather it happened now so I could concentrate than screwing up my exams because of all the conflict and me ending up resenting her. As I reached the school gates, I got a couple of weird looks from friends of Michelle who were used to seeing us together and I was glad that study leave started the next day. Last thing I wanted was endless questions as to what had happened from the naturally curious herd of gossips that seem to inhabit every school.

And so I lost myself in my books as the O Grade dates approached. When I did have free time I was spending it with Chris. John had given in as far as the hash was concerned and any time I was in Paisley on a family visit, I'd pick up an ounce off him. He was charging me forty quid for an ounce, and I was selling half an ounce to Chris for £35 (who was in turn selling it on at a profit too) so everyone was happy. Chris had also got me to a semi-decent level of proficiency rolling wise, though I still needed the occasional extra skin to bandage any mistakes. Despite all the negativity I was to hear later in life about smoking weed destroying any motivation, I was finding it an amazing study aid, especially with the subjects that required some critical thought like English. Mum and dad had bought me a pretty decent pair of headphones at Xmas and, after a swift walk of 'Dog' (and two quickly smoked joints), the headphones would be donned, suitable soundtracks to the day chosen and my brain would go into intensive study mode. Suddenly the hidden nuances in poems and books became more obvious; the patterns in mathematical formulae more simple, the whole process of glaciation a Technicolor movie inside my head. I began to feel that good pass marks were well within my grasp now and plunged deeper and deeper into my schedule. Chris had also given me a new addition to my radio listening. Since leaving Elderslie, I'd remained faithful (as I would till the end) to John Peel, but Chris introduced me to the local rock show on Radio Forth. The DJ (per usual for that period) was a bit of a numpty, Jay Crawford if I remember correctly, but the banter was good, and for some reason everyone who wrote into the show had adopted pseudonyms (usually names of rock albums/songs or characters from fantasy novels). I can only guess that it was a sort of spin off of the CB radio craze that was prevalent at the time but which never really captured my imagination.

Chris was already writing in on a regular basis (there seemed to be a core of 'fans', numbering around 30-50, who wrote in every week and organised meet ups) as 'The Lonely man of Pan Tang' (The Tygers of Pan Tang were a rather abysmal English metal band who, thankfully, seem to have disappeared and have not featured in the recent consciousness of nostalgia so prevalent on social media networks). He said I should write in too as requests always got played so I adopted the moniker 'The Electrik (sic) Warrior', a homage to Marc Bolan who was possibly my favourite act that John had introduced me to. I must admit, stupid though it seems in retrospect, I did get a buzz when my first letter was read out. Can't remember the exact words on the night but was something like;

'So next up we've got a new letter from a new listener; Electric Warrior down in South Queensferry. Welcome to the show Warrior. He says "Hey Jay, just moved through here from the West and my mate Lonely Man of Pan Tang introduced me to your great show. Any chance of a wee request on the show tonight. Would be great if you could play T-Rex's 'Telegram Sam' for me and dedicate it to Lonely Man and the South Queensferry crew." No problems Warrior. Hope you're enjoying your new life here in paradise and just for you and your pals, here's the amazing T-Rex with Telegram Sam.'

It may sound stupid now, but after my own experiences on hospital radio and the fun of dj'ing at the school discos, I realised just what power the world of media held. I think it was at that moment I decided what course I wanted to do at college or university; journalism. Though my mind was still focussed on being the next John Peel, I knew to get there was going to involve a long hard slog, and that having some sort of qualification would definitely open doors. I'd asked a few people at school about the dj'ing thing but apparently any school 'disco' brought in an external DJ who just happened to be one of the teacher's brother. (As well as being unbelievably shit and addicted to cheesy 80's voiceovers). So I'd put it all on hold till the exams were over, but at least now my moment of epiphany gave me a solid plan to present to mum and dad. (Who had been despairing at the repetitive shoulder shrugs that had met any career enquiries over the last year or so). I would look into courses once the exam period was over as well as investigating any other opportunities to get a DJ gig (Chris had said the Rock show mob had regular parties; not my ideal audience but I'd be happy spinning records anywhere).

With the support of my music collection, the odd spliff, my hook ups with Chris and the weekly stupidity of the rock show, the study period seemed to whizz by and before I knew it April 29th had arrived and there was less than a day to go till the English O Grade. I'd condensed all my notes down to bullet points and spent the final afternoon reading them over and over till I was sure my brain was saturated with every bit of information and critical fact that would help me walk through the exam the next day. The day itself seemed to go past in a sort of dreamy haze. I can't actually remember the half hour before the exam, or much of the actual time spent in the hall either, but there was that rush of freedom at the end then the building expectation as you met up outside and compared notes on how it went. And thus went the process for the next few weeks. I was pretty confident I'd walked the English exam, knew I'd made a couple of fuck ups in the maths one, sure I'd hit top band in arithmetic, struggled more than I thought I would with Latin, shocked myself by actually knowing some answers in Chemistry and physics and done not too badly in Geography. Then, finally came the day I'd been waiting for. Red circle day. Last exam. Gateway to freedom (for a few weeks at least) and the end of my first real period of stress (albeit one relieved by regular self-medication). German was split into two parts; written and oral. I was pretty confident about the oral side (Please, no smutty thoughts) as had been told my 'accent' and pronunciation were very good. Oral was an hour long before lunch, then it was into the final furlong; two hours hunched over a desk translating back and forth. The clock seemed to tick louder than ever before, each tiny move forward of the second and minute hands bringing me closer to liberty. I finished with twenty minutes to go, took a deep breath and scanned back over the paper, looking to see if there were any glaring or silly mistakes. Satisfied that I'd done the best I could, I put my pen down and folded my papers, glancing at the clock and seeing we were in the final four minutes.

Tick tock, tick tock, tick tock.

'Right! Time is up. Please put your pens down now and close your answer books.'

Mr Lynn's cavernous voice boomed across the hall, down the corridor and out into the open air, startling a passing flock of starlings.

'That means you too Wardell! Pen down now!' He shouted at one poor unfortunate scrabbling to write a final few words.

I grinned. A grin that was mirrored on several faces around me who shared today as the final day of exams and who knew what waited beyond those swing doors leading to the corridor.

Freedom! Music! Gigs! Alcohol! Drugs! And most of all…women! My summer holidays had unofficially started.

Chapter 14

The last couple of weeks of school term were a joke. As long as you turned up for registration the teachers didn't really give a shit if you disappeared afterwards. Now that Michelle was off the scene, I was spending more time with Chris, and the usual plan for the day, if the weather was good, was to head down to Whitehouse Bay with a few of the gang and spend the day getting stoned and drinking. Both Chris and I had continued with our letters to the rock show and were now part of the 'regular crowd'. We'd also had a bit of a giggle the last few weeks and had been writing in as two new pseudonyms; 'Dick Dastardly' and 'Penelope Pitstop'. We'd made our writing as childish as possible and had pretended we were both 11 years old but that our parents wouldn't let us listen to any rock music in the house. Jay fell for it hook line and sinker and made a huge fuss of every letter we sent, even going so far as to suggest a campaign to get our respective (fictitious) parents to drop their ludicrous (fictitious) ban. This had garnered much laughter from everyone who listened and we managed to keep it going for several months.

Chris told me there was a big meeting planned for the following Saturday and I should come along to meet some of the crowd from the show for real.

'Aye man. It'll be a hoot likesay. We're aw meeting under Albert at 1 o'clock ken.'

'Albert? What or who the fuck is Albert?'

'Ah sorry like bud. Ye dinnae ken aboot Albert. It's oor meeting place in the gardens. Albert the one oak, home of the sacred squirrel.'

'Are you ripping the piss? The one oak? Sacred squirrel? Have you been reading Tolkien on mushrooms or something?'

'Ach it's all a joke man. Lighten up ken. It's one of the biggest oaks in the gardens so for some reason someone called it Albert. And there's one wee cheeky bastard of a squirrel lives in it. Comes right up to ye and steals yer crisps like. We aw meet there and have a wee smoke then head doon to the White Hart in the Grassmarket. They've got a barry jukebox and never ask ye for ID for drinking.'

And so the scene was set for my first non-gig social foray into Edinburgh.

Saturday came, and with luck it was one of those early summer days that Scotland sporadically experiences. As Chris lived the other side of the village from me, we'd agreed to meet on the bus which passed mine at 11.30am and got to his about 5/10 minutes later. The bus journey into Edinburgh itself took about forty minutes and we soon arrived at St Andrews bus station. It was only a five minute walk to the gardens and I felt a little nervous meeting people I only knew as silly names on the radio. We headed down into the gardens and even without Chris pointing out where we were going, I knew immediately which tree Albert was. Not because of any physical attributes, but purely because there was already around a dozen people sitting on the grass drinking from cider bottles and with a haze of smoke hovering above them.

Chris made introductions as we sat and it was weird that many of the folk looked just how I imagined them from their pseudonyms. Warrior on the Edge of Time (Martin) looked the oldest of the bunch at about 30. Long stringy black hair with matching beard, denim jacket and the oh so inevitable Hawkwind t-shirt. Red Sonja (Laura) was a cute 17 year old with shoulder length red hair. Not that awful colour we call ginger, but deep red and lustrous. Though I felt more lustful than lustrous when I first saw her. But Black Betty turned out not to be black at all but a pale skinned girl from Newbridge with a bad acne problem. Someone passed me a half empty bottle of Strongbow and a joint at the same time and I immediately felt right at home. There was no sign of the sacred squirrel today though everyone was adamant that it was semi-tame and would sit in the middle of the group. I remained unconvinced and was sure that the intake of alcohol and marijuana contributed to this perspective. The group was loud and boisterous and I noted with amusement the looks of disdain that came from the blue rinse brigade on their weekly journey out of Morningside. Someone whose name escapes me had brought an acoustic guitar and was playing a torturous and clichéd cover of Stairway to Heaven. I remain convinced to this day that my psychological allergy to acoustic guitars at parties and gatherings stems from this traumatic childhood experience. We hung out in the gardens for a couple of hours then Martin, who appeared to be the de facto 'guru' of the group (and oh, that thought would turn out to be so prophetic) announced it was time to head to the White Hart. By now another four or five people had joined us so a group of around twenty left the gardens (and impressively gathered every bit of detritus from our time there and deposited it in the nearest bin – less impressive was Martin's statement that we had to do it in order to not sully the spirit of Albert) and made our way up The Mound, across The Royal Mile and down Victoria Street to the Grassmarket. The Grassmarket was a semi cobbled area with a collection of quaint looking old pubs, with the White Hart around half way along. The pub was dim and smoky, an atmosphere now lost with the draconian smoking ban. There was an assortment of customers: 3 bikers who nodded to some of our group in recognition; a couple of bewildered looking tourists who were protecting their drinks in fear of the bikers stealing them (hardly likely): and of course, the staple of any Edinburgh pub; the old men (in this case, four) sat in a corner, bemoaning the state of the world, the price of beer and how Shuggy kept cheating at dominoes. There was a large area free by the window and we immediately claimed it and began the process of sorting out the first round. As I was now well on the way to becoming a seasoned drinker, I ordered a pint of my favourite tipple (and the fashionable drink of the early 80's) snakebite and black (that's half lager, half cider and a dash of blackcurrant cordial for the uninitiated among you) Most of the gang were on the same, though Martin the elder statesman had a pint of real ale (one of the many little quirks he had). Laura went and put some songs on the jukebox and I inwardly cringed as Rainbow came on (although my tastes were eclectic, there were many MOR rock bands I just couldn't stand, and Rainbow came high on that list). The atmosphere was great. I was well stoned from the joints we had smoked at Albert and the snakebite and black was adding to the rosy internal glow I'd gained from the cider in the gardens. If this was my first social outing in the big city, then I was sure I had a good summer ahead of me. Though I was still determined to find some friends who shared my more alternative tastes in music. Martin moved over and sat beside me and Chris.

'Hey guys, you two live down in South Queensferry aye?'

'We do aye Martin, but Graham's just moved there ken. He's a weegie likesay.'

I sighed. The one thing that had annoyed me since my move (well the one of several) was the East Coasters utter ignorance of the geography of the West of their own country. To them, anyone from west of Livingstone was a weegie, whether they were from Paisley, Saltcoats. Ayr or Motherwell, and I was fed up correcting them every time they said it.

'Cool man, cool.' (I've often wondered if there was a hippy school somewhere that taught these people the clichéd and worn out phrases of Woodstock. Much the same way as some gay people, no matter their geographical or ethnic origins, seem to possess that annoying camp voice).

'Well like, I've got a bit of a plan boys. I thought it would be really cool to get all the gang together from the show and have a beach party one weekend. Weather forecast for next month is pretty good like, and the Ferry is close enough for everyone to get to. We could bring some tents and stuff and make it an all-nighter.'

'That sounds a barry idea Martin. And I've got just the place in mind. There's a wee secluded bit of shore likesay, just past Linn Mill, that would be ideal ken. No-one would bother us there like.'

I knew exactly where Chris was talking about and he was right; it was ideal. It was on Shore Road, just past Queeensferry's posh enclave of Linn Mill and there was space for tents right beside the beach. We wouldn't be bothering any locals and there wasn't a chance in hell of the police coming along. If this was how this summer was going to start then it truly was going to be an auspicious couple of months. (Little did I know just how important this party would be to my life, to my philosophy and to my very views of life itself)

'That sounds great man. I know some of you younger kids still have exams on, so I was thinking the first Saturday in June? That sound alright to you guys? My mate's got a nice loud boombox and a couple of the guys will bring guitars.' (oh whooo) (please assume use of sarcastic font in last aside).

'Brilliant Martin. Will we announce it through the show or just do it word of mouth likesay?'

'I think it best to get Jay to read something out. Can have 2 meeting points; bus station for anyone going down by bus and somewhere in South Queensferry for the local mob and anyone with a car.'

I'd mainly been silent to this point as Chris had all the local knowledge but an idea struck me.

'Why not make the meeting point in the Ferry at the train station? There's a few folk might come by train from Edinburgh or Fife. And people with cars can meet there too. One of us can lead the cars down to where it is, the other can take the rest down on the bus that goes through the village. Plus, would it no be an idea for the people with cars to do a few runs back to the bus stop under the road bridge? It's a fair walk from the bus to where the party will be.'

Chris grinned.

'Graham ma man, that's a barry idea indeed. I know a few of the gadgies have cars so they'd be well up for helping. And my big bro has an old banger and he'll want to be at this too.'

Chris's big brother, Tommy, was the proverbial high school dropout. Thicker than school dinner gravy, he was a nice enough bloke but with a notoriously short temper that I'd heard about quite quickly. He was working as a mechanic yet still seemed to drive around in cars that looked as if they were held together by sellotape.

'Great man. We have ourselves a happening planned! I'll get a good supply of weed and I'll bring the usual goodies if you know what I mean Chris.'

'Oh aye, I ken what you mean. This will be a stormer likesay.'

I was a bit lost with the last bit of the conversation and didn't want to betray my ignorance in front of everyone so determined to ask Chris on the bus home. At this point all I'd tried was weed and mushrooms (once). I knew there were lots more out there. Christ, I'd read enough of the books and dreamed of the multitude of alternate realities out there; from Cassady's amphetamine fuelled rants to Kesey and Leary's differing lysergic adventures. But, outside of John, my circle back home had been relatively inexperienced and I'd always been too nervous to ask John for anything more than a bit of weed. (To be fair, I was pretty sure he'd given everything else up when he settled down.) So I knew that the forthcoming party could be a doorway to a new part of my experiential education; I just wasn't sure which door it was I was going to be going through.

The day wore on, and the amount of snakebites consumed had begun to go to my head. I was getting (or my snakebite influenced mind said I was getting) some flirtatious looks from Laura, but with Michelle only a few short weeks behind me, I wasn't sure about going into anything else just yet, especially with the potential of a long summer ahead of me. The pub didn't do any food outside of lunchtime, so someone did a run to the chip shop down the road, a wise move as the food helped soak up some of the alcohol coursing through my system.

I already knew mum and dad would know I'd been drinking but hoped that the combination of this being my first day/night out after the exams, and how hard they'd seen me study for those exams, would lessen any thoughts of disciplinary action. Chris was on one totally though, and by half past seven was completely blootered. I thought it best if we leave soon, and though he resisted the idea at first, eventually agreed that we would head for the 8.30pm bus. The walk back to the bus station was fairly entertaining. For every 4 or 5 steps I took in a straight(ish) line, Chris was taking a couple sideways, one backwards, then a few forwards. Luckily we had plenty of time to catch the bus, and the further we went, the more he seemed to sober up with the fresh air. We got to the station with ten minutes to spare and smoked a quick couple of cigarettes before it arrived, allowing me the journey back to munch my usual dose of mints. The bus was half full, though there was no-one I recognised. By the time it had reached Charlotte Square, Chris had already nodded off; his head slumped against the window and an attractive line of drool running down his chin. When the people in the seat behind us got off at Blackhall, I jumped into the vacant seat and spent the rest of the journey staring out into the Edinburgh night, and only just remembering to shake Chris awake before his stop. He wiped his face with his jacket sleeve, mumbled something about seeing me on Monday and staggered off the bus and into the darkness.

Before the impending party I had a couple of gigs to break the parent imposed drought. First up was The Rolling Stones at The Playhouse; my first visit to what was Edinburgh's major gig venue for big bands. I'd never been a huge Stones fan but had wanted to go to this mainly because of the support band; TV21. One of the best local bands at the time, a couple of their singles had been produced by Troy Tate of the Teardrop Explodes, and Mike Scott of the Waterboys and Pete Wylie of Wah both made guest appearances on their album, so they were a band I was rapidly getting into. As I expected, they were fantastic live, full of energy, though much of that energy seemed wasted on a largely unappreciative older rock audience. It was only a couple of weeks later that I found out they split up immediately after going off stage. A sad loss to the music scene of Edinburgh. Bizarrely, The Stones themselves were introduced by Billy Connolly, something that seemed totally weird and which even Billy himself admitted a few years later was 'one of his stranger gigs'. Though previously not a huge fan, I was blown away by the band, some of the best showmanship I had witnessed or indeed have witnessed to date. The chemistry between Jagger and Richards was electrifying and they played a mixed set, with at least 3 or 4 cover versions including a raucous cover of Chantilly lace. All too soon the final bars of Jumping Jack Flash were fading out after almost two hours of high octane rock and roll and the band left the stage, only to return after five minutes of typical Scottish cheering to do a single encore of Satisfaction. I left the hall on a total high and was brought down to earth with a bang by my dad's insistence on listening to James Last on the journey home after he picked me up. I only had five days more to wait for my next fix of live music and it was another strange line up; the legendary Queen supported by MOR band Heart and my beloved Teardrop Explodes. I'd opted for my 'Julian' look even though I knew the rock contingent would be in the vast majority; ripped black canvas drainpipe trousers, my prized 'Wilder' t-shirt and carefully mussed up hair that took an hour to get looking the right version of scruffy chic. This gig was at Ingliston showground and I was a little hesitant as I'd heard folk refer to it as the cow shed and bemoan the awful acoustics of the large angular building. The queue was massive and snaked for what seemed like miles around the fence. As I'd suspected, I seemed to be the minority of one as far as Teardrops fans were concerned and managed to incur the odd hostile look from the denim and beard brigade. But my day was made when, as the queue moved forward, I noticed a small crowd on the other side of the fence having a kick about with a football. I noticed immediately that a few of them were wearing Teardrops t-shirts and then to my shock realised that one of the players was Gary Dwyer, the band's drummer and long-time friend of Julian. Like the daft fifteen year old I was, I immediately began to shout at them and, when some of them finally looked over, I gesticulated wildly at my t-shirt. With a grin, one of them came over and started chatting and realising I was primarily there to see them, told me to follow him along the fence to one of the security gates. Next thing I knew, I was inside the compound, shaking hands with Gary and the roadies and playing football with them. When the game was finished, Gary asked if I wanted to come in and meet the rest of the band. Perhaps the stupidest question I'd been asked in my fifteen years to date, but this wasn't something I was going to say and instead nodded wildly and followed him towards the main building. The support bands were housed well away from the stars of the day so unfortunately I had no chance of seeing or meeting any of Queen, but it was The Teardrops who were my priority and an awestruck teenager followed Gary into a large room populated by various band members, friends, instruments and food and drink.

I think most of my side of the conversation consisted of mumbles and shy downward glances, but as well as Gary's initial friendliness, both Julian and David (Balfe) greeted me with genuine enthusiasm, chatting to me for several minutes and autographing both my t-shirt (which was never washed again) and a tour programme (which unfortunately was dominated by Queen). Gary went and got hold of an 'access all areas' pass so I could get a decent view of the gig from the side of the stage but warned me that it was only valid while the support bands were on and that for Queen themselves I'd have to go back into the main arena. And so it was I experienced my first live gig from onstage, though of course it was from the side of the stage behind a speaker stack, but for the duration of the performance I felt like I'd died and gone to heaven. As the band trooped off stage (unfortunately to quite a chorus of boos from the Queen fans), each of them shook my hand, and Julian stopped to say a final goodbye and give me advice that would stay with me forever (to his everlasting credit and amazingly despite the amount of psychedelics he'd consumed, Julian remembered this incident many years later at a book signing for 'The Megalithic European' with the comment 'Ah yes, you were our only fan in a roomful of assholes'.) But his advice on that day was;

'Never be who they want you to be. Always follow the path you want and be the person you want to be. If you don't, they've won.'

And with those words, he disappeared after the rest of the band and left me to make my way back into the main arena. I hadn't been expecting much from Queen but boy was I wrong. While not on a par with The Stones from a musical perspective, the level of sheer flashy (and you'll understand that pun if you can remember what song they had in the charts then) showmanship was outstanding. Where The Stones had gone for a pretty bog standard lighting set up, Queen seemed to have enlisted the help of NASA in setting up their stage show, and the exuberant energy of Mercury himself had me convinced that he'd been imbibing at least half the substances I had read/dreamt about. I wasn't overly impressed with the drum or guitar solos nor their final encore song of 'God Save the Queen' but apart from that it was another two hours of non-stop vivaciousness from start to finish. After the James Last debacle of the previous journey home, I was more prepared this time and much to dad's annoyance I had a tape of one of John Peel's shows from the previous week and he managed to make disparaging 'That's just noise' type comments all the way home. But it had been a great week music wise. I'd seen two bands of legendary status who had impressed me far more than I thought they would, had seen two brilliant support bands, got to play football with some of the Teardrops and their crew, met Julian and the rest of the band, and, on a lesser note, had also seen Heart. But hey, even a perfect week can have a downside. But now there were only three days to my first party in the East, and my first ever all night party (I'd told mum and dad that me and Chris were going camping for the night outside Dalmeny. So, fourth year of school was drawing to a close but a whole new door was about to open.

Chapter 15

Saturday arrived. My plan was to head to Chris's house early afternoon with my rucksack (he was supplying the tent since we would actually be camping, just not at Dalmeny). Dad even slipped a couple of cans of lager into my rucksack when mum wasn't looking, not realising that my plans for alcohol that night extended far beyond two cans of Tennents.) True to his word, Martin had promoted the party for the previous two weeks on the radio show, and from responses the second week, it looked like we'd get a good crowd coming down. The plan was to meet at the train station from 5.30pm and give people till 6.30 to arrive. For the folk arriving by cars, either me or Chris would take them down to the location and they could set up tents, get a fire going etc. By 6pm there were already thirty or so sent on to the party site and another ten waiting – it had turned out four car loads had come down so rather than bothering with the bus through the village, we had just organised relay trips with the cars and this would work out fine unless another fifty or so arrived on the last bus or train. There were also a few folk from the show who were bikers, so we had about 10 bikes that had also headed down in the first convoy. As 6.30 approached we had around another 25 arrivals which meant there was going to be sixty of us for the party. A pretty damned good number for two weeks organising. We decided there would be no more latecomers and headed off with the final group.

I somehow got stuck with Tommy's car, a dilapidated Hillman Avenger that did nothing to inspire confidence in Tommy's mechanical skills. The one upside was that Tommy had installed a stereo that was probably worth more than the car itself, and with the volume he had AC/DC's 'Back in Black' on, I had serious concerns that parts of the car may begin to fall off on the journey. But we arrived at the venue without incident and with the car still intact, even if the local air had decreased in quality from his exhaust emissions. Things were looking well organised. People had set their tents up in small groups and some enterprising souls had already begun collecting driftwood for a central fire for later. And of course, bottles and cans had been opened and a fair few spliffs seemed to be on the go. Tommy had stopped off at the off licence to get carry outs for both himself and for me and Chris. It was the same old vodka and cider order and I hoped it would last us the night. (Though I had visions of myself collapsing paralytic into the tent by midnight). As promised Martin had arranged a boombox, a monster of a thing that looked like it had been hijacked from a Bronx street party. Someone had stuck Black Sabbath on and several heads were already nodding away in that well-choreographed 'dance' of rockers the world over. Chris and I grabbed our carry outs, took one bottle of cider each out the bags, and placed the remainder in the shallow waters by the shore to keep it cool. We went and sat in the growing circle and my backside was hardly on the ground when someone passed me a bong. It was going to be a long night. It was going to be a fun night. About one third of the crowd were female, and I took the opportunity of my post-bong head space to size up the talent available. Most of the girls looked to be a couple of years older than us, not that this was a hindrance from my perspective, but you usually found the older girls preferred the older guys. Mind you, both Chris and I could easily pass for seventeen so who knew what might happen. Laura was there, looking very cute in the tightest pair of jeans I think I'd ever seen. Black Betty (whose real name was Clare) was also there sitting chatting with couple of girls who looked like sisters. But for now, the idea of girls was on the back burner. My mission was to get totally wrecked and enjoy the company. Who knew what the rest of the evening might hold?

As the evening wore on, the behaviour got more outrageous and drunken. Several of the crowd decided to go skinny dipping in the last vestiges of daylight. I thoroughly enjoyed the sight of the three girls who participated in this activity, the sight of the five or six bikers doing so a lot less so. The sky was cloudless and as it darkened we were treated to a fantastic view of stars and an almost full moon. The fire was lit by now and the dancing flames cast eerie shadows of the revellers who were dancing/stumbling in time to the music. I was feeling quite warm and fuzzy already. The combination of cider, vodka and weed had brought me to that happy headed plateau I would come to know and love so much in the future. I'd noticed Martin wandering round the various small groups, spending some time chatting, then taking something out his pocket and exchanging it for money. My curiosity was piqued now and I decided to take the plunge and ask Chris what it was he had.

'Chris mate, I remember Martin talking about bringing goodies, and he's selling something to a few of the gang. What's he got?'

Chris's face broke out in a mischievous grin.

'Martin is our resident candy man. You name it, he can get it. But tonight he's brought down a sheet of what's meant to be amazing acid.'

My eyes boggled. This was another of my holy grails. After reading, and re-reading, the books of Kesey and Leary, I'd always known that this was something I wanted to try. And after my mushroom experiment of the previous year, albeit it with some freaky but fun visuals, I was even more determined. But just where does a 15 year old find such a thing? I'd imagined it was something I would not find till I was at university or college, but here it was, mere yards away from me and the person with it was now walking toward where Chris and I sat. Martin sat himself down (cross legged of course) and passed me the joint he was smoking.

'Having fun guys? Seems like we pulled off a good party. Nice one on finding a great location.This place is beautiful and we couldn't have asked for better weather.'

Yes, yes. Enough of the small talk. Get to the point oh bearded one.

'Anyway, I've got some really nice trips with me. Was wondering if you two planned on indulging?'

'Oh aye, barry like Martin. You ken I'm well up for it. Been a few month's like but I'm choking for a good blotter. What about you Graham likesay?'

I decided honesty was the best policy here. Though I was well read on the subject, written words and reality were two very different things.

'To be honest, I've never tried it. Took some mushrooms end of last year and loved them, but haven't tried LSD yet.'

Martin smiled at me.

'Oh don't worry man. Plenty of experienced heads here to look after you. Tell you what, just take a half just now and if you're okay later, you can drop the other half. I'll guide you through it for the night.'

I had no intention of saying no anyway, but knowing someone with experience was going to keep an eye on me removed most of the nervousness.

'Cool then. Aye, let's go for it.'

Martin took a small baggie from his pocket and carefully removed two miniscule squares of paper from it. Were they really that small? How could something that size cause the journeys in time and space I'd read so much about? He passed one to Chris and carefully tore the other in half, passing me one straight away then wrapping the other in a cigarette paper and telling me to put it away for later.

'I've been waiting to drop mine till everyone was sorted, so I'll drop the same time as you guys. Nearly everyone has taken one so it's going to be a colourful night.'

He removed another small square from the bag and placed it under his tongue, as did Chris with his. I followed suit, noting that neither of them immediately swallowed so did the same, feeling nothing more than a soggy bit of paper in my mouth.

'Does it not taste of anything then?'

Martin laughed out loud.

'No man, well not in that way. But your brain will taste the flavours soon enough. These are good ones from America; California Sunshines.'

And so began my second psychedelic journey, and my first ever with acid.

The first half hour to forty five minutes was completely non-eventful and I began to doubt the reported efficacy of what Martin had given to us. Then I began to notice a weird feeling in the pit of my stomach, almost like the nervous butterflies you feel before a first date or having to face the head teacher. I looked over towards the fire and suddenly realised that everything in my field of vision was just out of focus; like looking at something through someone else's glasses. The flames seemed to be flickering in time with the music, dancing like whirling Sufi dervishes round my mind's eye. Even what I was hearing began to appear distorted; vocals echoing and guitars developing a reverb sound where there was none before. I looked across to Martin and shrank back in terror. In the fulgurating glow of the fire his face had taken on Satanic aspects, not helped by his pointed little beard. The maniacal grin on his face only added to this sinister vision and my revulsion must have been apparent because both Chris and Martin began laughing uncontrollably. This didn't really help the apocalyptic entrance I was making to my first trip when suddenly I realised how ridiculous I was being, and within seconds I had joined in their giggling and was rolling on the ground. Martin still looked slightly sinister but the conscious part of my brain still tethered to reality was remembering what a stereotyped hippy he was and this clash of images just made me guffaw louder. I don't know how long I lay on the ground chuckling. It could have been 5 minutes or it could have been an hour. But finally I managed to bring myself back under some semblance of control or at least moved forward onto the next stage of the trip.

I realised now that it was not only the obvious visuals from the fire that were distorted in my brain. Everything around me had a surreal quality; from the trees swaying in the light breeze to the gentle lapping of the river on the shore. Then I looked up…

WHOAAAAAAAAAAAAAAAAAAAAAAAAAAAAAAAAAAAAAAAAAAAAAAAAAAAAAA AAAAAAAA.

I'd never seen the sky look like this before (remember; I had spent the mushroom trip indoors the whole time). I knew we were in an area with very little light pollution but suddenly my enhanced vision could see a million billion stars. You could visibly trace the patterns of galaxies and it made you aware of just how big the universe was and just how small we were in comparison. I found my mind detaching from my physical body and spinning off on a journey through the cosmos, defying all quantum laws and experiencing the births of planets, of stars, of entire galaxies. My immediate environment became superfluous. The people, the music, the setting had suddenly become as inconsequential to where/what/when I was as we all were to the vast superiority of the universe beyond me and the dimensions layered stack upon stack upon stack. I felt there was an answer there, tantalisingly close to the tip of my brain, yet I didn't have a clue what the question was. But every time I got close to grasping the answer, and thus by definition the question, it would dart out of reach again, hiding itself in a supernova or the depths of a black hole. I let my mind diverge; chasing the elusive 'thing' as I knew the whole world would make sense if only I could get hold of it. But it was constantly a world away from me and I could feel my cerebral energy slowly dissipate as the chase went on. I became aware of an ethereal voice coming from a small corner of the solar system I was currently traversing and turned to investigate…

'Graham man, you still with us? You a'rite like ken? Jesus gadgie, say something to me. You're messing with my buzz man.'

I blinked. And in that single instance the galaxies receded and I was once again lying on a beach in South Queensferry. Chris and Martin were staring at me with amused glances.

'Fuck's sake likesay Graham. You were out of it there for about forty minutes. Just lying on your back with a big daft grin on your face. We didnae want to do anything cos at least you were smiling but you kept saying "Oh hello there God" for the last few minutes. Ya nutter. And that's only a half!'

'Ach leave him alone Chris man. I remember your first trip last November at that party in Dalkeith. Did ye no hide in a cupboard for two hours?'

'Ah shush man likesay. I dinnae like talking about that ken?'

I laughed, and though some semblance of sanity had returned to my addled brain, the laugh sounded like someone else. Wow. That had been far more intense than the mushrooms of the previous autumn. My focus was still slightly blurred and my depth of field vision was still way off but I at least felt like I could communicate even if it was in someone else's voice. I accepted the joint proffered by Martin and took a deep drag on it, trying to soothe my battered brain. I'd loved the mushroom experience but this had taken me to another level. I was still surfing high above normality but felt that at I could at least communicate. O looked round the party site. As most of the crowd had taken some of Martin's magic blotters, it was a lot less boisterous than earlier and many of the gang were in reclining positions, either on similar journeys to my own or just smoking and drinking and chatting quietly amongst themselves. Someone had stuck Gong's 'Camembert Electrique' on the boombox and it was a welcome escape from the heavier rock of earlier in the evening. I went to take a swig of my cider and immediately spat it back out. Not only was it flat but it was distinctly warm from lying too close to the fire while I'd been on my 'adventure'.

'Martin, if I take that other half, will it get as mad as it's been the last couple of hours?'

'Nah man, it'll be cool. That was your peak, and even if you take more, it will sustain the trip rather than boosting you way back up there.'

Ah well. In for a penny, in for a pound. There was no point in hoarding that other half. I'd either lose it or mum would find it in the wash and throw it away thinking it was just a bit of paper (though she may wonder why it was wrapped up in a cigarette paper). The second half consumed, I went and retrieved a fresh bottle of cider from the river and took a long cooling drink. I could say with some certainty that this was the best party I'd ever been to (though to be fair, I didn't really have a long list of experiences to reference against at this stage). I went for a wander and mingled with some of the gang, many of whom were also basking in that post peak lysergic glow. Laura had found herself a man and was happily ensconced in his arms, but I wasn't bothered in the slightest. I was happier in the arms of my new psychedelic mistress than I could have been in the arms of any female that night. There were a few folk sitting down on the shore, mere inches away from the gently lapping waves, and I joined them with a mumble of recognition and let myself be hypnotised by the rhythmic motion of the water.

I can't remember at what time I made my way back to the tent, but Chris was already cocooned in his sleeping bag and snoring loudly. A few bodies were scattered round the fire, some still conscious (barely), some fast asleep. I took a last look round the party; it had been a good night. No, it had been a brilliant night. My body was exhausted but my mind still seemed to be working at a thousand miles per hour and I wasn't even sure if sleep would come. I crawled into my sleeping bag and lay looking as the sky lightened through the roof of the tent. My brain was whirling with thoughts and ideas. Although I'd loved the tales of Kesey, Kerouac, Thompson and Leary, an already cynical part of me had always wondered how much of it was romanticised fiction, and whether some of the experiences they had described, not only of the 'wild' variety but of the introspective philosophy that some of them described as coming with psychedelic experiences, was actually true. Now I knew. Leary had talked about the unused portions of the human brain and how he believed psychedelics could be the key to unlocking the next stage in human evolution. I now believed that. Beyond the sensory extravaganza I'd experienced there had been an underlying feeling of knowing there was something else on the other side of the world we knew. Whether this was physical, mental or metaphysical, I had no idea. I was still an inexperienced 15 year old boy. But I knew from that moment, had known from that earlier moment that the journey I had taken that night would be a journey I would be taking again and often, and determined that part of my life would be dedicated to exploring these unmapped inner spaces.

I must have eventually drifted off. I woke with the sound of voices and laughter. Laughter may be the best alarm call ever invented as even with a slightly throbbing head (which I possessed in abundance that morning) it made the waking up process a lot less stressful. Chris was already absent, and as my senses reached full wakefulness, I noticed there was a tantalising aroma of frying bacon wafting into the tent. I realised I hadn't eaten since the Steak Pie supper I'd grabbed on the final run to the campsite. Rubbing the sleep from my frazzled eyes, I emerged into a glorious June morning and had to shade said eyes from the glare of the morning sun. Someone had obviously made a run to the shops as there were several bottle of Irn Bru being passed around (though one or two of the more hardcore members of the group were still on the alcohol) and nearly everyone had a bacon roll. Chris shouted me over from a small group by the shore and I made my way down to join him.

'Graham my man. You finally woke up. You were talking some nonsense in your sleep likesay. Couldnae make most of it out like ken, but you were mumbling about wolves and planets and fuck knows what else. I think you were still tripping in your dreams gadgie!'

'I still think I am a wee bit mate. That was one mental night. But you've got a cheek slagging me for talking in my sleep. You snore like a pig in an echo chamber.'

'Bullshit man! I never snore, well at least I don't think I do.'

I laughed and left him to his thoughts and I headed over to the fire to see if there was still some vittles left to soothe my grumbling stomach. Laura had taken charge of the cooking, and I silently praised whatever clever and enterprising soul had thought to bring a frying pan to a party. She smiled at me as I approached and I inwardly cursed as even my naïve self knew that was the smile of someone who had been having the level of sexual fun I was yet to reach. Damn. But sometimes the needs of the soul outweigh the needs of the body. And sometimes the needs of the stomach outweigh everything else there is.

'Morning Laura. Please tell me there's more bacon left above and beyond what's in the pan.'

'Of course there is. Dave and Marie went into the village first thing and brought back enough bacon and square sausage to feed a small army. What do you fancy? (Right now? You). Bacon? Sausage? Or a mix of both?'

I realised I was starving.

'Can I have two rolls with a mix in it please? I feel like I haven't eaten in days.'

'Well given the nick you were in last night, not to mention your mad dancing, I'm hardly surprised you're hungry.'

Wait a minute. Dancing? When the hell did that happen? Other than the very hazy memories of my cosmic wandering, I was pretty sure I remembered most of the previous evening's shenanigans and dancing certainly did not feature in the highlights package. Damn, but there was no way I was investigating this further.

'Yeah, was a pretty wild night. You certainly seemed to have fun.' (Down thou foul green monster.)

Laura blushed.

'Ach I've fancied Pete for a while. I just needed a few drinks for Dutch courage or he'd never have made the first move.'

I grinned and left her to preparing breakfast and went in search of some Irn Bru since my throat was feeling like a litter tray after a long weekend.

Laura shouted me back over when my food was ready and it lasted all of five minutes. It may have been the best sausage and bacon roll I'd eaten in my life to that point and I slowly began to feel human again afterwards. It was now just after eleven in the morning and a few people were packing up in preparation for leaving. I'd told mum and dad that we planned on coming home late afternoon so I had a few hours to get back to an acceptable state of compos mentis before braving the journey home. I went and re-joined Chris who had just sparked a rather large spliff so my timing was perfect. We sat and shared the joint and drank in the view. I was truly settling into my new home. Where Elderslie had the wonderful Glennifer Braes on its doorstep, South Queensferry had this majestic river, miles of shoreline and the two iconic bridges. Life was good and it could only get better.

Chapter 16

The summer continued in the same heady vein it had begun. As well as Chris, I'd met up with a couple of folk who were more into the alternative scene at the Gang of Four gig in mid-June. I'd been a bit shocked to see Roddy there. I'd talked to him briefly in school but had never discussed music and I always thought he was more of a soul/funk boy by his dress and floppy hair. But it turned out that he, and Jason who was a year below us, were well into the new wave and electronic scenes so I now had musical soul mates to add to my drug soul mates.

Unfortunately, romance seemed to be a distant land that summer. Other than a couple of snogging sessions at parties, there was little happening on the girl front. Part of me regretted not persevering with Michelle, but the other part of me was glad that I had been left with the freedom to continue my experiments in altered realities over the school break.

I took acid three more times that summer; once at Martin's flat, who despite all his worn out external clichés, was actually someone I now considered my 'guru' as far as drug experiments were concerned.

He'd even shown me his 'bibles'; notebooks he'd been keeping since he was 14 and took his first trip. They were like an early version of 'Lonely Planet' but purely for LSD.

Each trip he'd taken, ever since this first one, he'd taken the time to meticulously record all the details, from how many he'd taken to what other substances he'd imbibed to a long narrative description of the effects of each one. He had even gone to the trouble of sketching the design of each blotter at the top of the entry Except for those occasions when he took liquid or a sugar cube). It was like something you'd expect to find in the journals of Leary or Thompson, a wander across seventeen years of cosmic tripping and mind exploration. I briefly considered doing something similar, and then remembered that patience was not a virtue I had in any significant amounts. I'd tried keeping a few diaries of my musical education and evolution, but inevitably I'd forget a couple of entries and by the time I remembered to go and make one, there would be gaps in the timeline. His flat was a full of clichés as he was, but the clichés added to the experience of the evening; from the Day-Glo seventies posters and lava lamps to the esoteric music collection he'd amassed from all four corners of the globe. (He'd spent a few years travelling after his parents died and had a wealth of stories from exotic locales like Nepal and China.) So that night, as well as the expected soundtrack of bands like Hawkwind and

Gong, Martin introduced me to Indian sitar and tabla players, Moroccan guembri music and bizarre Tibetan chanting. For someone who already considered themselves musically eclectic it was a complete eye opener. It made me remember that mum and dad had a pile of Turkish 78's in the loft from their time in Istanbul and I resolved to dig them out and see if there were any gems. (weirdly, when I did do this, though there was nothing of aesthetic note from my own perspective, one tune intrigued me as part of it sounded like the choral melody from Boney M's 'Rasputin.' It was only many years later with the advent of the internet that this thought returned to me and a little bit of research uncovered the fact that I hadn't been mistaken. The Boney M song had lifted a melody from an old Turkish folk song called 'Kâtibim'.) The experience at Martin's flat just convinced me all the more that the path of discovery I was choosing was the right one. In the post peak comfort we sat and discussed a hundred subjects. His book collection was as varied as his music collection and I left the next day with a number of new tomes to browse, including Hesse's 'Siddartha', Huxley's 'Brave New World' and Burroughs' 'Junky.' It was also Martin who introduced me properly to Conan Doyle, praising him as the greatest writer of the last few generations and insisting I read the books rather than base my opinions on Holmes purely on the various TV adaptations and old Basil Rathbone films. It was a fantastic, educating eye opening night and would set the scene for many of my favourite psychedelic adventures in future.

My next journey was not so private. My involvement with the rock/hippy crowd also brought my first stage of politicisation. The CND movement was pretty big in the 80's and in Edinburgh there was a SCRAM (Scottish Campaign to Resist the Atomic Menace) shop called the Smiling Sun which sold all the usual t-shirts, patches, books and posters. But it was also one of our meeting places, especially when it was too wet to meet at Albert, or too early to hit The White Hart. They'd organised a concert down at the site of the new Torness nuclear power station which the government had begun building a couple of years before.

I can't even remember the bands that were playing, though I suspect they were all local ones, as the day turned into a long hazy fluffy lysergic soaked memory of warm cider, wet kisses and funny patterns in the clouds. Martin was going to be away in London at some gig or other, but had passed on his most recent acquisition; Orange Flying Saucers, with the predictable marketing tagline of 'they're out of this world man.' There was a mini bus going down from the shop in Forth Street and Chris and Laura and a few of the usual crew were on board. The cider and lager were opened before we even reached the end of the street, the flying saucers were consumed by the time we reached Musselburgh, and by the time the bus pulled into a field near Dunbar most of the passengers were shambling giggling wrecks. It was a different vibe from the acid at the beach party. I was still learning how important setting, company, and mental readiness were to an LSD journey. If you take one when you're on a downer, the likelihood is that you'll have a downer of a trip. One of Martin's well-worn phrases was that acid was a 'synaptic amplifier' which we were convinced he'd nicked from a Michael Moorcock book, but did sum up part of the drug's appeal. And a daytime trip also affects you in a very contrasting way to one taken at night. So there I was, floating happily on a daytime Hofmann bubble and utterly fascinated by the way the clouds were dancing through my vision.

I think I spent most of the day horizontal, mesmerised by those clouds and only moving for a joint or to take another swig of cider.

There is some memory of briefly dancing to some nondescript band, and I'm convinced that's where I acquired the wet kisses from as, after a slight memory gap of some 40 minutes, I was back on my cloud observatory, still with cider and joint, but also with a rough looking punk lass called Denise who seemed as fascinated with my lips as I was with the cavorting cumulus above us. Nothing more came of it. It was a prolonged and substance influenced snogging and necking session that ended with me boarding the mini bus with her phone number scribbled on a piece of paper with a shouted promise to phone her soon. Or I suppose it really ended with aforementioned piece of paper disappearing out the mini bus window before we'd even re-joined the A1.

The third and final trip of the summer was at another beach party, this time on the outskirts of Burntisland in Fife. Mum and dad were now getting used to my regular…cough…camping trips and, if anything, dad was the more enthusiastic as he'd been a Scout and Scout leader and had also biked his way around Europe. So he saw my trips off into the wilds as the perfect antidote to the post punk teenager with a fondness for cider. How little did he know…

Chris and I used to walk over the road bridge regularly and meet up with some of the crowd from North Queensferry, Inverkeithing and Burntisland itself. They were closer geographically than Edinburgh though the walk was a pain in the arse if it was windy or wet which meant a bus fare equal to that into Edinburgh. But one day, Dave (Renegade Dave on the show for the last three people who are interested) had suggested a spot on the outskirts of Burntisland as a venue for another beach party. Everyone was (of course) enthusiastic about the plan after how good the Ferry one had turned out. Dave had phoned Martin (who really did seem to be the de-facto benevolent dictator of the group; if he said yes, the party happened) and next thing we knew; we were planning another huge event. The date was set for the 31st July which worked for me in lots of ways. We (the family) were going on holiday to Yugoslavia on the 3rd August for two weeks, and by the time I got back the new term would be right on my doorstep so this would be my last chance of a blowout before school restarted. More importantly, far far more importantly, was that it would fall two weeks after my sixteenth birthday and since we were doing family stuff the actual weekend it fell on and Chris and Martin were at a gig in Newcastle the weekend after, this would be my (un)official birthday party. I'd failed in my noble quest to lose my virginity before the date proscribed by law as it being allowed (that old rebelliousness again) but now set my heart on this party being my World Cup final and that all standards, morals and ethics would be sacrificed for the greater good. I'd run through the female members of the group in my head, but there were no suitable candidates that I did not consider friends. I wasn't looking for love, I was looking for pent up physical release at the hands of something more than my hand. So with no obvious contenders, it looked like it would have to be a random. The party was getting plugged on Radio Forth again (I often wonder if Forth realise they set the scene for the pirate radio stations advertising free raves a few years later), and there would be a huge Fife contingent this time as folk were travelling down from as far as Dundee (not strictly Fife I know) and St Andrews. Surely somewhere among the droves travelling to Burntisland would be the right woman/girl. The one to captivate my pants and lead me/allow me to lead her astray?

But before I got to that (hopefully) magical weekend, I had to traverse the horrors of a family birthday. MY plans, sown many months before, had been a marvellous maze of debauched celebration. Instead it was to be a trip to Paisley and a 'slap up' dinner with the relatives at the Watermill Hotel. It was such a predictably bland weekend that it's not even worth going into great detail. Mum and dad booked us into the adjacent hotel (with the grown up bonus of my own room – like whoop, what good was that going to do me), took me out shopping for clothes in Glasgow, got into an argument about which clothes I wanted to buy in Glasgow, gave up with an exasperated sigh and agreed to give me money to spend in Edinburgh myself (progress) and impressively and with great patience, followed me into several record shops and hovered outwith the embarrassing parent personal space zone, at least till it was time to pay for my purchases. Still remember a few of the tunes purchased that day; Yazoo's Upstairs at Erics, Roxy Music's Avalon (a bitterly bland disappointment), Simple Minds' New Gold Dream (a true classic of the era), Cocteau Twins' Garlands, and the wonderful 'Oh no, it's Devo' by…em…Devo. There were a few others that day as mum and dad, despite the fashion arguments, were in a generous mood after my pretty decent exam results.

Shockingly I'd somehow passed Chemistry and Physics (albeit with C bands), got B's in Maths and Geography, and managed A's in Latin, English, German and Arithmetic. Enough to see me sailing into fifth year and enough to keep the parents happy and relieved.

The evening 'party' was particularly unmemorable; mediocre food and mediocre chat from the cousins and aunts. I was allowed the princely total of one pint of lager shandy and two glasses of wine; hardly enough to even touch the sides on the way down. The one consolation was the presence of John. We managed to sneak away down to The Hammils for a covert spliff and he presented me with an ounce of finest Nepalese Black as a birthday present. I neglected to tell him about my further adventures with psychedelics; he'd thought me too young and immature when I'd revealed my psilocybin experiment of the previous year so I wasn't sure he was ready to know that I'd willingly plunged into the LSD pool. I got to meet up with David for a few hours while the olds went to church on Sunday morning and he was impressed and jealous of my escapades so far that summer. The news of the forthcoming beach party elicited a promise from him to come through for it though he was a bit hesitant in agreeing to do a trip with me. Then after lunch at Gran's (who had been too unwell to make the family get together) it was off back home along the M8.

Finally the weekend of my 'real' sixteenth arrived. David had come through on the Friday and we'd spent the night playing tunes and heading out with 'Dog' for the odd fly smoke. Tommy had offered to pick us up from my house but the idea of one of his clapped out cars appearing outside the house would probably have sent my mum and dad into paroxysms of fear of road accidents, so I told them we were getting the bus from the stop at the bridge while secretly arranging to meet Tommy and Chris at the same spot. The weather was not quite at the same standard as our first party; clouds blanketed the sky, but none of them looked dark or threatening enough to put a literal dampener on the night. (We did have the contingency plan of using the WWII pillboxes at the site as an inside venue). Dad had also insisted on helping by diligently monitoring the weather forecasts for that weekend and had informed me that there was little chance of rain until Sunday evening. We rendezvoused with a couple of the Fife mob who showed us the way to the site. It wasn't as accessible as our one had been; the car had to be parked some half a mile away then we skirted a housing estate on foot before coming to the Lammerlaws. There were already about 35 people at the site, though I was a little concerned at the disapproving looks cast our way by the odd dog walker. We'd had no police interference at the last one but I suspected tonight could be different. (Mistakenly so, as we didn't see a single police officer till the traffic cops stopped Tommy's hazard to health on the way home). Someone had obtained a boom box of even more epic proportions than our last one and it was already belting out Deep Purple at a hefty volume. The aromatic fog of marijuana smoke permeated the site and I remembered I still hadn't introduced Chris to my birthday present. As usual, Martin the mage was holding court by the already blazing fire and hailed us over when he saw us. I introduced him to David and sat and rolled up a joint with the Nepalese, its strength soon appreciated by those beside me. Martin advised he had another new batch of acid in (his contacts in this, and other fields of the illicit drugs industry never failed to amaze me, though I suspected a lot of it was to do with his contacts within the Hawkwind 'community'. I was finally proven right in this a year later when he revealed that his source was a chemist who was a long-time friend of the band. He even produced a commemorative blotter for their fifteenth birthday with the Hawkwind logo on it and a mighty and intimidating 250 micrograms of LSD on each blotter). David was still unsure of taking the next step and even at such a young age I tried to avoid exerting peer pressure.

He seemed happy with his whisky (he'd switched from vodka since I moved away) and his puff, so it was left to me and Chris to once again be the willing cosmonauts. This time he had 'Goofys', a design that seemed entirely appropriate given the state of mind my previous exploits had left me in, and we stuck them away safely for some post dinner madness. A few folk had brought camping stoves and were making fry ups, but the majority of us opted for a mass order from the local chippy. I would have loved to see the server's face when the order came in; 12 fish suppers, 4 Scotch Pie suppers, 5 Steak Pie Suppers, 6 battered sausage suppers, a single haggis, 4 bags of chips and a pickled egg. Personally it would have been the pickled egg that drove me over the edge from disbelief to hilarity. As everyone sat and munched in small circles I took the opportunity to switch the random radar to full power. There were quite a few girls I didn't recognise, and even one or two that wouldn't require my pre-planned sacrificing of standards. I decided there were definitely a couple that bore further investigating and some of my cheeky charm later but little was I to know that the bastard lovechild of Swiss science had other plans in mind for me that day.

The evening wore on. We'd already decided to drop our blotters around 9pm so as to enjoy a mixture of late evening light and the wonders of darkness. David was pissed as a fart by the time nine came around. He'd tanned most of a bottle of whisky and was happily ensconced by the fire with a stupid grin and a spliff.

As well as the main campfire we'd left David by, there were two or three satellite fires and we quickly identified one where there were a few fellow trippers who we knew already. Chris smiled at me across the flames.

'Well man, here we are again likesay, another party, another round of blotters. Here, I bought you an extra one. Happy birthday ken.'

I groaned. I really wasn't sure about the inherent wisdom of taking a double dunt, not at this early stage of my mental explorations.

'Fuck. Cheers Chris like. But I'm no really that sure about doing two at the same time.'

'Ach away wi you ya bufty. Martin says these ones are no quite as strong as the Sunshines ken? You'll be barry man, just barry.'

I sat with the two small squares of blotting paper in my hand. I hesitated. I thought. I considered. Then I shrugged my shoulders and swallowed them both down with a drink of cider. Now my fate lay in the hands of the chemists and the fickle Gods and Goddesses of the psychedelic universe. But as the first tickles began to reach up from stomach to brain it dawned on me that my wonderfully worked out plan of finally reaching the peak of my sexual Everest was consigned to the procrastinator's diary. Ah well, I'd been waiting long enough already I suppose. Tonight I'd be lucky to remember my own name, never mind ask a girl what hers was.

It started with the flames. (Something that seemed to be a common theme in my tripping life to date.) Like sexual partners, they entwined and danced in my field of vision, painting patterns on my retinae as the distorted music insinuated its way into my inner cerebral cortices and my consciousness began to melt. The figures around me faded into insignificant nothingness as I was raised towards platforms of all seeing knowledge. The wind caressed me like a lost lover, promising so much yet delivering so little (Something that seemed to be a common theme in my romantic life to date.) The experience was gentler this time, yet still possessed intensity beyond the ken of mortal man. I let myself float in the wind, drifting aimlessly but with esoteric purpose, my slowly evolving mind fully aware of the possibilities surrounding me in multiple dimensions. Questions morphed into answers and back into questions. Neural pathways opened up centuries before evolution intended them to and I felt my entire nervous system expand and grow at exponential rates. I walked the tightrope line between reality and dreams, seeing and understanding the patterns that had perplexed my former everyday mind. Moments of crystal clear lucidity dissolved into swirling chasms of chaos. I became aware. I awoke. I grew. The whole chain of existence, from primordial ooze to bipedal intellect lay before me like the simplest ordnance survey map. I could see the connections yet I did not fully understand them or what they quite yet meant.

And as I sensed the lofty spires recede I cast myself free and drifted gently down on gossamer paths to the mundanity of the real world.

These were the times I always treasured in my acid experiences. That peak period when the LSD was affecting you the most. I didn't yet have the wisdom or maturity to grasp all the concepts of what was happening, of what I was feeling and thinking. But I knew it was something important. I loved the other stages of the trip; the excited butterfly feeling as you were coming up, the mellow parachute feeling of lying gibbering nonsense with your fellow travellers, the haziness of the comedown as the last effects slowly dissipated. I didn't so much like the occasional refusal of your mind to switch off, even when your body had moved far beyond the normal boundaries of physical fatigue. Or the sporadic next day fogginess where functioning became an almost impossible hill to climb. But I truly felt I was part of something much bigger than me, that these practices in evolution were linking me to people I had never met and never would meet. (Maybe this was the very process that saw the internet conceived and developed?) I didn't want to start making guesses at what this enforced evolution could mean, especially given the amount of science fiction I read.

But I felt that since Hofmann's little bike ride there had been a growing movement to break down centuries of systemic brainwashing and that this had linked in with the eons old movement of worldwide use of psychedelic plants to make those intuitive leaps forward that made such a difference. Together, could we change the world? Or was I just a daft sixteen year old on drugs?

The mellow parachute stage tonight was lovely. Though the clouds had not fully cleared, they had scattered a little and a moon several days from fullness was casting eerie colours through the gaps.

Chris had somehow pulled one of the random girls from St Andrews (bastard!) and was snuggled on the other side of the fire. Of David there was no sign. This worried me at first but a quick check of the tent found him wrapped up in his sleeping bag and snoring in glorious drunkenness. I left David to his dreams and Chris to his new woman and headed over to the main fire. Someone, probably Martin, had put Hawkwind on and 'Sonic Attack', one of their brilliant collaborations with Moorcock was booming out across the party site. I sat by Dave and Laura and accepted the proffered spliff and cider and let myself drift to Moorcock's vocals on 'Coded Languages'.

The morning after the night before followed a very similar plan to the event in the Ferry. Collections were taken and brave and enterprising souls headed off in hunter gatherer mode to the local Co-Op, returning joyously within the hour bearing handfuls of slaughtered and cured pigs and flagons of Barr's most famous non-alcoholic beverage. Revitalised and refurbished, we began the process of clearing up. It had been, of course, Martin's rule that any location we held a gathering, we left it as pristine as we found it. Fires were dampened down and sand put on them, rubbish was gathered into refuse sacks that would be shared amongst those with cars and even every fag and joint end collected. And while I may have mocked his initial hippy attitude, it was a philosophy that stayed with me for life, and any outdoor party, any gathering, even any basic camping trip, came complete with major clean up at the end.

We left Burntisland just after twelve. David had the hangover from hell and despite bacon rolls and Bru, had yet to reach a stage resembling humanity. I felt surprisingly clear headed given the previous night had seen my first double dose but I knew fatigue would hit me early that evening as I'd slept for only about two hours. I'd phoned mum from Inverkeithing and told her we were on the way. So by the time Tommy had dropped us off and we'd walked across the field from the bridge, she had a huge pot of soup together with a stacked plateful of ham and cheese rolls waiting for us. Dad was out pottering around in the garage (I'm sure he did a night school course for that too) and mum was on a baking frenzy so we took our food through to the living room and vegged out in front of crap TV. Next thing I knew it was 5pm and mum was waking us both awake and sending us upstairs. The fatigue had kicked in early for me, and the hangover was still wracking David and we both crashed easily till the next morning.

Chapter 17

Last stop on the runaway train that had been my summer holidays was two weeks in Yugoslavia with mum and dad. It was my first holiday with them as an 'adult' and I knew this meant I would get away with avoiding many of the excursions they would go on. (The previous year in Austria had been a long slow fortnight of boring visits to castles and Sound of Music locations.) Our exact destination was Lake Bled in Slovenia; a picturesque looking place but not one I thought would hold too much interest for a sixteen year old. From my reading on Yugoslavia in the run up, Porec would have been my preferred destination with its beaches, watersports, pubs and clubs, but the olds were very into their mountain scenery so I had little say in the matter. We flew into Pula, a partially militarised airport and an announcement advised that taking photographs at the airport could lead to arrest. Gulp. Camera back in bag. The coach took around three and a half hours to reach Bled and even I was stunned at how amazing the scenery and Bled itself were. We were staying in a very grand hotel called the Toplice, apparently a favourite haunt of Marshall Tito, the former leader of Yugoslavia (and indeed the glue that had held all the disparate nations and ethnic groups that made up the then Yugoslavia). The big result of the day came at check in.

The Toplice was essentially split into two parts; the older and ornate main building fronting onto the lake itself, and a no less grand but more view restricted annexe behind it. When it had come to room allocation, the unknown but wonderful (in my eyes) staff member had given mum and dad a wonderful en-suite in the annexe, while I had my very own en-suite single room in the main hotel and overlooking the lake. Result indeed!

Although small, my room was far more ornate than anything I was used to; dark wood furniture and fittings and altogether far too posh for a wee Scottish boy. The parents were none too pleased about the lack of proximity between our rooms while I, of course, was ecstatic about it.

We'd arranged to meet in the lobby after an hour so I had a quick shower and change then went for a wander round the hotel environs. Everything was on a grand scale; sweeping marble staircases and ornate columns and statues that wouldn't have looked out of place in a Roman temple. I could see what the country's former leader had seen in it, but what did it have for a young ne'er do well with mischief on his mind? Outside seemed to offer the most interesting opportunities. There was an outdoor swimming pool in addition to the heated indoor one, a raised sunbathing area and a boathouse. I already knew that there weren't any real beaches so I sort of guessed the sunbathing area and pool was where all the action was going to be. I just hoped there were going to be kids of a comparable age. So far on my travels I'd only seen more geriatric holidaymakers and they were not exactly the demographic I was looking for. I checked my watch and saw rendezvous time was almost here so headed off to the sumptuous lobby. Mum and dad were already there and announced we were going to go for a walk round the town to see where everything was. Dad was in his usual foreign holiday 'uniform' of shorts, cotton polo shirt and the combination of socks and sandals dreaded by children on holiday the world over. Mum was more acceptable in a light summer dress and sandals (without socks), while I had adopted my teenager abroad outfit of black shorts, Bauhaus t-shirt and trainers with no socks. Mum, as expected, tutted disapprovingly while dad just did the time honoured rolling of eyes. The town itself was quaint; narrow winding streets and a selection of shops and cafes. We stopped off at an exquisite little konditorei and I had a slice of perhaps the best gateaux I've ever had in my life. After continuing our walk dad had to dissuade mum from raiding every souvenir shop we passed, reminding her we had two whole weeks to collect tat to take home with us. I had my girl radar on full alert and even managed to exchange flirtatious glances with a couple of local girls (Hey! A mutual fleeting look is a good place to start.)

Dinner itself was in a huge and of course grandiose dining room and it gave me a chance to scope out the hotel guests en masse for the first time. To my surprise and joy there was a good mix of age groups, and even surreptitious looks around the room identified that there were a fair few 'kids' in the fifteen to eighteen age group. And even better, quite a few of them were female and pretty. Roddy had ranted on and on about his holiday to Crete the month before and how loads of girls had thrown themselves at him, resulting in three separate sexual encounters. Now given the teenage male's propensity for exaggeration in this subject (Guilty as charged M'Lud) I'd translated his claims to perhaps three or four girls being interested and him getting to third base on maybe one occasion. But even such diluted truth gave some small iota of hope to my continuing crusade to end my sexual frustration. I had thirteen days from now in Bled, and my mission, should I choose to accept it (well duh) was to meet the girl/woman of my wet dreams. Not yet knowing anyone, I declined the olds' offer of playing cards after dinner and retired early to my room to continue my thus far uphill struggle with Hesse's 'Siddartha'. I awoke from a rather pleasant dream in the middle of the night to the sound of a major thunderstorm. I pulled back the curtains and watched the lightning play over the mountains and lake in a magnificent son et lumière that made me wish I'd smuggled a little blotter along.

The next morning saw not a trace of the biblical storm of the night before. The sky was clear and blue and even at 8am, the sun was already beating down. I made my way down to breakfast to find mum and dad already half way through. They advised me that after I'd gone to bed they had gone and looked at the excursions available (quelle surprise) and had booked several, and were leaving at 9am for a full day trip into the Julian Alps. Result #2 of the holiday. Dad gave me fifty Yugoslav Dinars (about £20) to do me for the day. And there's the hat trick on day two of the holiday given the local prices in 1982. Mum also said she'd said to the tour company representative to keep an eye on me. Not such a good result. Jesus. I was sixteen. Though that's probably the exact reason she took that course of action.

I waved them off and returned to my room to plot the day ahead. I'd pretty much decided that Plan A was the pool and sunbathing area. If the other mid to late teenagers' families were anything like mine then there should be a cluster of 'abandoned' kids whose parents were also off to spend a sizeable portion of their holiday sitting on a bus. I changed into my swimming gear, grabbed a hotel towel and my well-worn copy of Fear and Loathing in Las Vegas and made my way to the poolside.

Sure enough my Holmes like prediction had been spot on. The demographics of the mid-morning bathers fell into three distinct groupings; the families with younger kids, the older couples who'd been on enough coach excursions to reach to the sun and back, and the sporadic little oases of solo or small groups of teenagers. There seemed to be one minor gathering already with around five kids sitting at one corner of the pool.

I noticed there was a sun lounger free beside them so chose that as my site for the morning. The archetypal territorial curiosity of the teenager drew all five sets of eyes toward me as I approached and there was even a wary smile or two of acknowledgement. After getting comfy and ordering a cold drink from one of the staff I settled back to read my book, my peripheral vision constantly appraising my neighbours. There were three girls and two boys; definitely a ratio I preferred. One girl especially was ultra-cute; about the same age as me and wearing the sexiest bikini I'd seen at this range before. The other two girls were pretty too, and one had the body of a Goddess, but my eyes were drawn back again and again to the vision of cuteness in the turquoise swimsuit. Finally, after about twenty minutes of hope, one of the two boys broke the ice.

'So let me guess; Julian Alps full day excursion? Total non-interest from you. Pocketful of dinars from your mum or dad, a warning to behave yourself and the hotel or tour staff know you're on your own?'

Wow. This guy was good. He was either telepathic or was in the same boat as me.

'Bang on.' I laughed. 'Five out of five so I'm guessing your story is the same?'

His accent was American though from which part I had no clue. It was only later he'd tell me the family were from Washington DC.

'Yup, me and my sister. No way were we sitting on a bus for half a day just to see more mountains. I'm Morgan by the way.'

Okay. People were actually called Morgan. You learn something new every day.

'Hey Morgan. I'm Graham. And agree totally, am too old for those bloody excursions now.'

'Anyhow Graham, let me introduce you to the rest of the orphans. The cheeky looking one in the red top is my sister Sybil (Okay. People were actually called Sybil. You learn something new every day.). Just try and ignore her; she's been in a mood since she was fourteen.'

Sybil took this opportunity to throw me a dazzling smile while simultaneously giving her brother the middle finger.

'See what I mean? That's Else next to her, she's German. Jan is the huge guy on the other chair, he's Luxembourgian or whatever it is they call them, and lastly that's another Brit on the lounger. Roz, say hi to Graham.'

Everyone waved or mumbled a greeting. But all my eyes and ears saw and heard was Roz. I was captivated already and found myself reddening in self-awareness at my staring. This girl was 100% gorgeousness. Her accent was definitely Southern English, and well educated to boot. I offered a quick prayer to whoever the patron saint of hormonal and sexually frustrated teenage boys was that this was not the last day of her holiday and gave her my best smile.

'Hey everyone. Glad to have some company. Thought I might be stuck on my own for the day'

The stocky boy called Jan grunted. 'No way. This is the waifs and strays club. Five day running my parents go on excursions. Five day running I enjoy holiday.'

That elicited a big grin from most of the group. It seemed I'd chosen my spot well. Looking over at Roz, it seemed like I'd chosen my spot extremely well.'

'So, Roz, another Brit? Where are you from then?'

That smile again. That face again. Those beautifu…no, stop thoughts like that right there, especially in the snug shorts I was wearing. That voice again.

'Kent.' (Yup, posh). 'Tunbridge Wells to be exact.' (Oh, very posh then. Had passed through ROYAL Tunbridge Wells the year before on a visit to a distant aunt and it had seemed like a different world.) 'What about you?'

I was used to people never knowing where Elderslie was so had got used to saying Paisley, but Paisley was a bit of a shithole, so I chose my adopted home instead. First impressions were everything here and damn I wanted to impress this girl.

'We live in South Queensferry, a small town near Edinburgh.'

Her face lit up.

'Where the bridges are? Oh we were there last year. It's so pretty and the Forth Bridge is amazing to look at. We had a wonderful lunch at the Hawes Inn.'

Impressive. Hopefully impressed too. And she knew to call the old bridge the Forth Bridge and not the 'rail bridge'. Gorgeous and clever as well.

'Wow. That's so weird; I was in Tunbridge Wells last year too. My mum loved it. How long are you here for?'

The million dollar question. Open the box or take the money. Could I make the final round?

'Oh we just got here yesterday. So still got nearly all of our two weeks to go.'

Yeahhhhhhhhhhhhhhhh. Bremner scores the winner in the World Cup Final. Alan Wells takes gold again. The Associates hit number one for the third time. I did wonder if I was showing any external signs of how happy I was at this news. The only hurdles now were whether either of the other two guys had made a move yet and, of course, whether my feelings of wild lustful abandon were in any way reciprocated. (I was leaving 'in any way' open to a wide range of parameters at this point).

The other four had been here for a few more days. Jan and Else (who was perhaps the quietest girl I'd ever met, and that's a good thing) had a week left, but Morgan and Sybil (which sounded like the name either of a US sitcom or a mid-range firm of lawyers) were here for four weeks so still had most of their holiday to go. They already had a routine; sit by the pool during the morning, have lunch at the hotel (since it was full board) then hit the town to get beer and vodka. This was a routine and plan that sat well with my own holiday ideals. They'd found a couple of pubs that didn't bat an eyelid when a group of foreign teenagers walked in and ordered beer (Else was the youngest at 14, Jan the oldest at 18, Morgan and Sybil were 16 and 15 respectively and Roz was 16 the next month.) And they'd also discovered that the local supermarket shared that same unbatted eyelid when said group of teenagers bought bottles of vodka. We were less than 24 hours into the holiday and I'd already found a group of like-minded peers, discovered it was simple to obtain alcohol and had a gorgeous girl very firmly in my sights. The only things missing were some good music and a good spliff. One of those two would make an appearance in the next 48 hours though.

I tried to play it cool for the rest of the day. After lunch we followed their predetermined schedule and went and sat in a little beer garden pub at the side of the lake. The local lager was strong. Definitely stronger than the piss they served back home (the whole reason I was a cider or snakebite drinker). The combination of the beer and summer heat soon had me delightfully tipsy and I was glad to see Roz was in a similar condition. By the time Jan did a run to the shop and returned with a bottle of vodka I was pretty hammered, and by the time we'd consumed a good portion of the vodka in a local park area, I was utterly pissed. Now this is the point where your average male, be they 16 or 40, arrive at a psychological fork in the road.

Take the wrong turning and you find yourself making a wild drunken pass at the girl/woman you like, slur half your words and potentially, at some point, either vomit or fall over (which of course ruins all possible further progress down that path). Take the right direction; manage to keep your inebriated reflexes under some sort of control, don't act like a drunken arsehole and live to flirt another day, then maybe that path will lead to a meadow with the proverbial pot of gold at the end of a rainbow (or in layman's misogynistic terms, a good shag. Though to be fair, having a score count of zero, I wasn't exactly sure how to distinguish between a good and a bad shag). Somehow, from deep inside me, I managed to find the self-control to override the male arsehole gene and chose the right road.

'Listen guys. I'm a bit sozzled. Think I'm going to head back to the hotel and have a couple of hours' sleep before dinner. What do you lot get up to in the evening? I was bored as hell last night.'

Jan was clutching the vodka bottle to his chest. He'd been drinking it straight but still appeared relatively sober.

'Ja, we all tend to just meet down by the boat shed. Have a few more drinks, walk about town, see if there are any pretty local girls who want to talk to Jan.'

I liked the more drinking and strolling round town part. But I'd already found my pretty girl for this holiday.

'Cool. Will we meet down in the dining room at 7pm for food? The coach isn't due back till about 10pm.

Everyone agreed and I got up to leave. Just as I rose, Roz stood too.

'I'll get you back. I could do with a sleep before dinner as well.'

Bugger. Brilliant. Bugger. Brilliant. Was this is a good or a bad thing? Good thing = was she wanting to walk me back because the reciprocity hoped for earlier was there? Bad thing = would I rush back up to that fork in the road and choose the wrong turning this time? I had to maintain that self-control and not revert to standard steaming idiot mode. Maybe it was as simple as she wanted to go back for a sleep. Maybe she was interested. But there was no point in going rampaging in while so under the influence of alcohol. There was still dinner tonight. There was still the meet-up at the boat shed. There was still tomorrow. We left the other four inebriants behind us and walked through the town, albeit with a slightly noticeable stagger to the left. We chatted comfortably, talking about school and music. It turned out she was a damned good pianist and was considering one of the better music schools after she left her current one. But despite classical training she loved the electronic scene so we had plenty of common points of reference and taste. We soon reached The Toplice. She was also in a single room, two floors above me but unfortunately right next door to her parents' room. Once in the lift I pressed for floors three and five and an awkward silence descended for the first time. The lift stopped at three.

'Well, guess I'll see you downstairs at seven Roz.'

I went to leave the elevator and just as I stepped out she jumped forward and kissed me. Not a long kiss. Not a snog. But definitely aimed for and hitting direct on my mouth. The doors closed and I was left standing speechless in the corridor, watching as the display showed the lift taking her away from me. Wow. I guess that answered my question on reciprocal feelings then. I floated back to my room, threw off my clothes and collapsed onto my bed, that lingering memory of those soft lips the last thing I remembered before sleeping.

I awoke and checked my watch. Damn. 6.35pm. If I didn't get my arse in gear I would be last down for dinner.

I jumped in the shower then threw on a pair of canvas jeans and my favourite Depeche Mode t-shirt. I made it to the dining room only five minutes late and realised my rushing had been futile as only Morgan and Sybil were downstairs. I waved a greeting to them and made my way over to the table. Jan appeared about 5 minutes later, still looking a little worse for wear and announced that Else wouldn't be coming down as she'd been vomiting for the last two hours. Finally my English rose (I make no apologies for the clichéd wordplay here) walked into the dining room.

I think my jaw was placed somewhere on my chest as she looked absolutely stunning in a blue cropped top and very, and I mean very, tight jeans that accentuated her teenage curves perfectly.

She smiled directly at me and every part of me melted; well every part except that one part that seemed to get a little firmer. She sat beside me and immediately placed one hand on my leg. Oh God. Even firmer. This could be a long night. No-one drank alcohol at dinner as we were all worried the hotel spies could report back to our respective parents so the entire group behaved impeccably. (Though that occasional hand to my leg meant parts of me were behaving most inappropriately). After dinner we headed down to the boathouse to hang out for the evening. We weren't the only occupants; there were already four older teenagers sitting on the edge of the jetty and my well trained nostrils rapidly identified the aromatic smoke drifting my way. Yes! Dope on holiday! (Don't even think it) My happiness was complete (well almost); I had a lovely girl who was into me in what looked like a big way, a group of friends from around the world, a town where the pubs served sixteen year olds and I was about to (hopefully) have my first joint in 3 days.

The group looked up and smiled over at us. There were three guys and a girl. They all had that wonderful olive skin from that part of the world and my initial guess was that they were Italian or Yugoslav. The girl was stunning (holds Roz's hand tighter) but looked to be about nineteen. The three boys all looked about seventeen/eighteen and you could immediately tell that two of them were brothers. One of them held out the joint.

'Welcome my friends. (Yup, definitely Italian) Do you want to join our little party? Any of you like to smoke some good weed?'

I swooped quicker than an Osprey onto a fish in a loch.

'Cheers man. Don't mind if I do. (Ah. I just noticed a rather disapproving stare from Roz) You guys staying at the hotel?'

The joint giver grinned.

'Is it that obvious? Si. I'm Sergio and this is my brother Fredo. We're here with our Grandparents from Trento who have gone out to town for dinner. And our two other friends here are Aleks and Cila. They're from California but are Yugoslavs really.'

Introductions, handshakes and nods passed around the group and we all sat down beside them. Jan had been quick to dive in on my left to ensure he got the joint next, and I made sure Roz was sitting to my right. I passed the spliff to Jan and put my arm around Roz, though I could still sense a certain frosty disapproval.

'I didn't know you were into drugs Graham.' Her voice was stern but still managed to force its way inside my mind.

'It's just a bit of puff. Better than booze all the time and I hardly every touch it (liar) but thought I would since we're on holiday. I won't have any more if you don't want me to. (Cross fingers, offer up prayer, promise soul of first-born).'

'No, it's fine. Was just a bit shocked. I don't mind if it's just a holiday thing. Bit like us really I suppose.'

Why did she have to say that? Of course it was reality; Tunbridge Wells and Edinburgh weren't exactly a short bus ride apart. But I was sixteen and reality was a word for adults, not a teenager on holiday.

'No babes, we're more than that.' (Hey, let a guy have his fantasy for a couple of weeks)

She smiled and snuggled in closer. Someone had brought down some plastic glasses and the (new) bottle of vodka was passed around and we quickly reached that cosy plateau of friendship that holiday groups so easily reach. Else turned up about an hour later, still looking a little pale, and she declined any offer of vodka we had or the wine the two Italian boys had. The chat was comfortable. Other than Else, everyone's English was virtually perfect (Well, I suppose 'perfect' is not the word for the Americans in the group).

I'd been a little clever earlier and shoved a note under mum and dad's door saying I was exhausted from a day on the lake and had gone to bed with a book. I didn't think they'd be suspicious and I just hoped that they didn't plan a last stroll down by the lakeside.

But they would probably be exhausted themselves and go straight to their room and, hopefully, bed soon after. I'd added to the note that I would meet them at eight for breakfast as they were off on another full day excursion, this time to Venice. (Eh? Go to one country on holiday and have a day out to another one. The Robertsons were becoming very cosmopolitan these days). I was so lost in these thoughts that I hadn't noticed Roz was nudging me.

'Listen Graham, I'll need to head up to my room soon. Mum and dad are next door and will make sure I'm in at some point after getting back. If I'm not there before 11 they'll probably force me to go on these bloody excursions. I've maybe got another half hour or so. Do you want to go for a walk?'

Do I want to go for a walk? Do members of the family Ursidae often excrete in woodland settings? Was the Pontiff a practising exponent of Catholicism? Of course I bloody did!

We said our goodbyes and arranged to see some of the group tomorrow. One thing was for sure; I wouldn't be alone this holiday. We now had a good group of nine of us which meant that, parent dependant; there would probably always be at least 4 or 5 of us around during the day. (I think it was an internationally common contractual holiday obligation that there had to be some quality family time, though I was aiming for the minimum possible; I saw mum and dad enough the other 50 weeks of the year!)

Up till this stage of my life, I hadn't thought of myself as romantic in any way. Romance was for girls. Boys were, well, football and tits. Sure I'd sent Valentines Cards, who didn't? And yes, I'd whispered the odd sweet nothing, but usually as a platitude to enable a hand inside a bra or jeans. But tonight romance touched me properly for the first time ever. I had a warm feeling inside, yes partially helped by vodka, wine and weed. I'd even managed to get a bit of Sergio's weed off him earlier, though Roz didn't know about it. But it was more than alcohol or cannabis. The night was definitely magical; a three quarter moon in a cloudless sky reflecting on the still and placid waters of the lake. The stars seemed brighter and bigger than normal, and I had a beautiful girl holding my hand as we walked along the path. We reached a point where the path curved outwards into the lake and there was a bench situated perfectly. We sat down and cuddled in. There hadn't been a further kiss since that stolen one as I left the lift earlier, and the butterflies performing pirouettes in my gut said I was more nervous about this next kiss than perhaps any there had been before. But before I could garner courage, Roz again took the initiative, her hand pulling my head down to meet hers, my lips to meet her lips. I couldn't remember a mouth ever being this soft or lips so welcoming and welcome. There was none of the clumsiness you normally had with that first adolescent kiss. It was straight out of a Hollywood film; one take and an Oscar nomination assured. We literally had to come up for air and both let out a simultaneous sigh, which sort of led to the romance of the moment being spoiled as we both burst into giggles. Roz looked at her watch and I took the hint and suggested I walk her back to the hotel. It really had been a long day, or at least one with copious amounts of alcohol and sunshine, and all crowned with the most awe inspiring snog I'd had to date. To avoid the inquisitive eyes of staff and other guests we kissed goodbye at the hotel doors, a more restrained kiss this time but still with a fire that would haunt me for the rest of the night. She walked away from me into the lobby and I watched her go, an aching I hadn't felt before coursing through me as I turned away and stood on the terrace and looked out over the tranquillity of the lake.

The next week passed in a blur of sunny days and heavy petting. I hadn't even been disappointed when Roz had stopped me going any further than unclothed top half, though the dry clothed grinding against each other had got pretty damned ardent. I'd fulfilled the contractual obligation of family time on day six of the holiday, a surprisingly good day out to Postojna Caves and some castle whose name escapes me.

The caves were amazing; huge caverns carved out by a river and forming marvellous cathedrals of coloured rock. Not to mention the electric train ride into the cave system which had excited me more than it probably should. (And no, I've never stood at the end of a train platform, clutching a notebook and wearing a nylon anorak).

Jan and Else had left but we still had the Italian/Yugoslav mob and the Americans with the funny names. We'd also had one addition; a cocky bastard from Manchester who kept giving Roz furtive looks and who I thus found highly annoying. But nothing could spoil what was the best holiday I'd had in my life.

Not even our respective parents finding out we were a 'couple' and therefore enforcing more stringent bedtime checks than we should have had at that age. If only there was a reason for their suspicion…

Too soon the end of the fortnight approached. Roz and her parents were travelling on by train to Ljubljana and were leaving the day before us. We'd never progressed beyond the heavy petting/dry humping stage and I was strangely torn over this. Part of me would have loved to lose my virginity to a girl who had made such a mark on me and who spending time with had been my happiest days to date. Part of me had worried that going that extra step may have somehow spoiled the perfection of our romance. And then it was our last day together. Well, morning to be accurate. Roz had packed all her clothes first thing so we could have every minute till the taxi took them to Lesce-Bled station for the train to the Slovenian capital. We'd swapped addresses and phone numbers and promised to keep in touch. Though I think we both knew that those promises would fade with the memory of the holidays. As we said our final goodbyes outside the hotel, Roz was in tears and I wasn't too far off myself. Finally the taxi drove off down the narrow street and I turned back towards the hotel, my heart heavy with all the troubles of a love-struck teenager. Janez, one of the bartenders in the hotel who'd often slipped us the odd beer, was standing by the door smoking a cigarette.

'Why you not go station to say goodbye your girl?'

'No way of getting back mate. Spent the last of my holiday cash on a present for Roz.' (In a burst of romantic extravagance I'd spent all my money on a beautiful silver and crystal necklace for her).

Janez reached in his pocket, took something and threw them in my direction. I caught at first attempt and looked at the keys in my hand.

'Here, take my scooter. Romantic more to say goodbye as train leaves, no?'

I grinned and shouted thanks as I ran to the hotel car park. We'd hired scooters a couple of times during the two weeks so I was fine riding one, and the traffic round Bled, other than the tour buses, was hardly dangerous. Once my helmet was on (safety first kids) I sped off down the street towards the station. I caught the taxi about half way there but didn't acknowledge it and knew Roz wouldn't notice me speeding past as she wouldn't be looking for me. I got to the station, parked the scooter at the side and walked onto the platform I knew the Ljubljana train left from. As with train stations the world over, the platform had benches dotted along it, and most of them were vacant. I sat down on one and nonchalantly watched the world go by, waiting to see the look on Roz's face.

Around five minutes passed then I saw Roz's dad climb onto the platform with two suitcases. He saw me and smiled (luckily, despite the suspicions of potential hanky panky, Roz's mum and dad had really liked me and over the course of the holiday I had dinner with her family a couple of times and vice versa.) Roz appeared next and as she looked up and saw me her face brightened and she dropped her bag and came running over to jump in my arms.

'What are you doing here? And how did you get here before us when I waved goodbye to you at the hotel.'

'You can thank Janez. He thought it more romantic for us to say goodbye at the station than outside the hotel so he lent me his scooter.'

She laughed and held me tighter. We only had twenty minutes till the train came and I don't think we let go for a second till her dad was calling her to get on the train.

There was time for one last shared passionate kiss, the ghost of which I can still feel on my lips to this day. Then it was old black and white film cliché time. Camera pans to girl getting on train, tears streaming down face. The door closes and she leans through window, holding both hands of the lover she's saying farewell to. Guard's whistle blows and the train slowly begins to pull out station (Sadly it was not a steam train).

Boy runs along platform beside train, still holding girl's hand until platform ends. Train disappears into distance as boy stands watching the girl's final wave. Boy is left alone on platform apart from one forlorn looking pigeon. (Okay, I made the pigeon bit up). Boy turns and walks away. Screen fades to credits…

Chapter 18

It was raining at Glasgow Airport when we arrived home which seemed to punctuate the end of the summer holidays perfectly. There were two days left till school started, hardly time to recover from my fortnight of bliss never mind be ready for my most important school year ever. I'd chosen to go for five Highers in one year; didn't want the add on of a sixth year and wanted to get my rapidly evolving ass out into the big bad (but exciting) world to see what it held. On the back of my O Grades, I'd chosen to go for Maths, German, English, Latin and Geography. Maths was going to be the most daunting. Though I felt I was very proficient in the arithmetic side of things, I tended to get a bit lost when it came to algebra and quadratic equations and all that weird stuff that no-one will ever need in their day to day life…ever. I was pretty confident on the other four subjects and also knew that I'd have to maintain a fairly decent study-life balance, well at least from Xmas onwards.

The only good thing about this time of year and the ending of the summer was it meant that gig season was back with us again. I already had a good few tickets for the coming months, partly subsidised by birthday money and partly by the old parental blackmail method of 'Look, I want to go to gigs so I will have to get a part time job and won't be able to study as much.' This had resulted in the Chancellor of the Exchequer (Mum) renegotiating the child funding budget for the remainder of 1982 with definite advantage to the receiver. Already bought and paid at the Playhouse were Elvis Costello on the 17th, John Martyn (a definite taste I'd acquired from John) on the 27th of the month, Roxy Music on the 1st October, AC/DC on the 11th (with Chris and some of the radio show gang), a hectic week at the end of October with Depeche Mode (with Roddy and Jason), Hawkwind (with Martin), Japan and SLF all within a nine day period, another busy week in November with Siouxsie and the Banshees, Ultravox and Yazoo (last two again with Roddy and Jason) on consecutive nights and a rare (in fact the first) trip to a gig with my dad for Billy Connolly on the 25th of November. I also had to fit in gigs at Coasters (Oh what a task). I had Simple Minds there on the 9th September (supported by the fantastic Hey Elastica!), Culture Club the night before the mad week at The Playhouse started, Bow Wow Wow as an appetiser for the 3 consecutive Playhouse nights in November and The Birthday Party and Orange Juice a week apart at the end of November(Both of which David was coming through from Paisley for) So all in all a fantastically filled diary of musical eclecticism. And in between all that I had to attend school, do some studying, have other nights out and continue the saga of the Long Distance Virginity Loss Seeker. Graham was going to be a busy boy.

School started with a wet blustery day typical of a Scottish August. I still had a (much depleted) register class with Queensferry's answer to Brian Blessed and he imparted his pearls of wisdom to us as to how this was a year that would decide the rest of our lives, blah blah blah, and how we had to apply ourselves to get positive results, blah blah blah, and that we had to avoid the temptations of any distraction that would keep our heads away from our boo…

When I awoke after a verbal valium assault, it was time for first class. One advantage of fifth year was that our timetable was far reduced from the previous school term which meant that we had more free time. The disadvantage was that even if our first proper class wasn't till 11am, we still had to be there at 9am sharp for registration (and any daily blah Mr Lynn saw fit to impart). Luckily another advantage was that we had our own common room, so there was somewhere to hang out between classes, play a game of pool, listen to some tunes and generally just laze about for an hour or two. Chris was gone.

He'd applied for Stevenston College to do an Automotive Vehicle Maintenance & Repair course so he could go into business with Tommy. So Roddy was my daytime companion (though he wasn't a toker) with Jason making the odd appearance.

First gig of the 'season' was Simple Minds at Coasters. These were their last dates in small venues as their popularity (and egos) was growing. After this UK leg came some international dates then it would be gradually expanding venues capacity wise. It was an energetic and brilliant performance, and by the end of 'I Travel' towards the end of the set, I was drenched in sweat. The Costello gig on the 17th was just as impressive, Elvis running through a massive set list that covered all his albums to date.

Then September was wrapped up musically with the folking superb John Martyn (and yes, there were several joints smoked pre-gig).

If only my romantic life was as event filled as my gigging one. Since the holidays there hadn't even been a sniff of possible romance other than an anonymous stalker on the radio show who kept declaring her undying love for me. (Unfortunately I suspected, though he never admitted, that Chris was behind this). I'd been writing to Roz every few days and in the immediate aftermath of those glorious two weeks in Yugoslavia we had been phoning each other every second days. But alas, as with most holiday romance, no matter how wonderful they are, the ardour soon fades in the harsh reality of everyday life. We were now down to weekly phone calls and it had been over a week since I'd received a letter from her. I'd never really expected anything more to come of it but it had been such a fantastic time together that I was still clinging to the paling memory of our passion. I'd sort of given up on the active pursuance of getting laid and resigned myself to the fact that it would happen when it happened. September turned to October. Schoolwork got a little harder and given the amount of gigs I was attending, I had to keep my side of the agreement and do a fair bit of studying in the gaps between concerts. I hadn't had a trip since the Burntisland party and didn't know when I'd get a chance to have one. There was no way on earth I was taking one at a venue as I had no idea how I'd react in such a large crowd. The musical highlights of October had to be Roxy Music and Depeche Mode. Roxy were superb (a pleasant surprise after how bland the album had seemed earlier that year) and it was also my first introduction to Robert Fripp's wonderful King Crimson who supported them on the tour. But Depeche Mode were just a class apart from anything I'd seen (or would see) in 1982. They had already taken a deserved place as one of my favourite bands and the Broken Frame tour just cemented that position. They were another band in transition; though in their case they were one step ahead of Simple Minds and on the brink of making the change from large venues to stadiums. Gahan has always been the consummate showman, often relegating the other band members to nothing more than supporting roles. From the opening bars of 'My Secret Garden' to the encore of 'Dreaming of Me', he held the audience in the palm of his hand. It was Roddy and Jason's first time seeing them live, and indeed it was Jason's first concert of any type. Both of them left awestruck and I left smiling from ear to ear.

Before I knew it, we were into November, another busy month band wise and only two months from the dreaded but meaningless mock exams. One of the highpoints of the month (but not THE highpoint) was my first Marillion gig on November 12th. Long a favourite of the rock show, they were playing a homecoming gig at the Nite Club above The Playhouse. Martin (of course) had some guest passes and invited me and Chris to join them. They were marvellously theatric, combining Fish's story telling with almost operatic stage antics. Martin knew them well so we ended up drinking with the band afterwards and a long friendship with Derek (Fish) that saw many drunken escapades. But it also brought with it a new episode in my life and one that I'd been chasing and waiting for since I hit puberty and it all began when I was sitting killing time in the common room when Roddy sauntered in.

'Hey man, what's happening?'

'Bugger all Roddy. No got a class for another hour so trying to get my head round this German essay.'

'Cool. You got any gigs on this weekend like?'

'Nope, no plans at all. Thought I might nip into town for some vinyl and a pint. What's your plans?'

'That's why I'm asking. Bongo fae sixth year is having a party Saturday. Fancy checking it out?'

Ah, sixth year. Separated by a mere 12 months or less in age terms, but an often impassable gulf in many other ways. It was rare for any of the sixth years to socialise with us lowly fifth years, but I knew Bongo quite well and he was definitely one of the good guys. I'd not been to a decent party since the Fife one in summer so this sounded like an ideal plan.

'Aye deffo mate. Let's go for it.'

And so, unbeknownst to me, the seeds were sown for life changing events.

Saturday came and I headed over to meet up with Roddy and Jason. I'd used the trade-off system and spent the whole of Saturday daytime studying so mum and dad would cut me some slack for the party (and more importantly the likely recovery time on the Sunday).

Once Jason had arrived (late as usual) we collected carry outs from our favourite local Asian shopkeeper and made our way to Bongo's house which was only a couple of streets from the school. When we arrived there was already a good few people sprawled about as well as at least half a dozen in the back garden drinking and smoking joints. Good sign. I still had some of my birthday Nepalese left and had brought a few grams as well as a bit of 'bog standard' black. We exchanged hellos with people we knew then headed into the kitchen to get glasses for the vodka and to stash some of the cider in the already full fridge. Bongo himself had commandeered a sun lounger and was stretched out happily, a can of lager in one hand and a huge hash cone in the other. His girlfriend Marion, who I'd met once or twice, was by his side and I gave her a smile. Though she lived just up the road in Kirkliston, Marion went to a 'nice' school in Corstorphine; Edinburgh's famous Royal High School. I grabbed a seat on the grass beside Roddy, took a long swig of vodka and coke and lit up one of my pre-rolled spliffs. (Though I was now more proficient at rolling, I always liked to go to parties or gigs with a few numbers prepared.) Now comfy in mind and body, I looked around at the rest of the 'outdoor' crowd.

Then I saw her.

I knew instantly that she was Marion's sister. She had lighter colouring, almost fair hair where Marion was dark, but the similarities were there in droves. And she was totally and utterly gorgeous. It didn't look as if she was with anyone, but that didn't mean she didn't have someone. There was also a chance she was telepathic as it seemed like she sensed me looking at her and returned my stare immediately. Eyes locked. Chemical reactions initiated. Hormones accelerated. Instant attraction. She smiled. The smile of a Goddess. (Sorry Roz, it's relegation time). I smiled back. In that moment, it seemed like an unspoken understanding was reached. At some point that night we would be together. It didn't have to be now, or even in an hour, but the time would come when we would find ourselves side by side and then those primary sparks would become an emotional conflagration. I guessed (and hoped) that she was Marion's older sister as I knew Marion was in fourth year. She didn't look younger and even with that initial telepathic chemistry I wasn't sure I wanted to get off with a third year (though after a few ciders…fuck it).

The party trundled on. It seemed every time I tried to get close to her, she had either Bongo or Marion by her side and I wanted our proper introductions to be while we were on our own. The crowd had moved inside as the November air got chillier and there were now about 40 people scattered throughout the house. Roddy had pulled one of the girls from our year; a pretty nondescript lass called Susan, but they seemed happy curled up on a seat in the corner and trying to swallow each other's mouths. I headed through to the kitchen and topped up my vodka, deciding that I fancied some of that cold night air while I enjoyed my last pre-rolled spliff. I stood with my back against the house and lit the doob, inhaling the fragrant smoke and trying to blow smoke rings into the wintry night. I heard the door open and glanced to my right. At last! She'd obviously seen me leave and had taken the opportunity we had both been seeking all night.

'Hey.'

'Hey back. I'm guessing you're Marion's sister. You're the spitting image.'

She giggled. A light airy sound like the gurgling of a mountain stream that brought a smile to my heart.

'Is it that obvious? She's the one that got the good looks.'

'Hell no. Are you mad. You're gorgeous.' (Yeah that's right, play it cool you idiot)

She did that thing girls do when you say something nice; the bit where they look down and find something fascinating on the tips of their shoes. Just where did they learn this stuff? Were there some secret classes they took where all these little feminine habits were taught?

'So…(quick change of subject) are you at Royal High too? I'd even wondered if you and Marion were twins. What's your name by the way? (That's even better; turn it into an interrogation)'

'Wow, so many questions at once. Yes, I'm at Royal High, No we're not twins, I'm a year older than Marion (Quick inebriated calculation followed by relief) and my name's Sharon. And I know you're Graham.'

'Eh? How do you know my name then?'

She giggled again. Back to that smiley mountain.

'Well that's a bloody easy question; I asked Marion who the handsome boy staring at me was.'

Handsome? Those sparks were beginning to get near the flame stage. I offered her the joint and was pleasantly surprised when she took it as I hadn't even seen her smoke a cigarette all night.

'So I suppose I should ask another question. No girlfriend Graham?'

'Nope, and there hasn't been since before the summer holidays (I couldn't really count Roz, could I?). What about you?'

This time her laugh was louder.

'Oh I definitely don't have a girlfriend.'

'You know what I meant!'

'I know, I know. Sorry. And no, there's no boyfriend. Not yet anyway.'

Hmmm. Was that a major hint? Flames were growing.

She proffered the end of the spliff back to me, then and as I went to take it, pulled it back towards her. I didn't need any more signs and moved in closer, relieved that I'd read the situation all night correctly as she lifted her face towards mine. That first kiss had none of the natural smoothness that there had been with Roz. It was clumsy and sloppy and tasted of a mix of cider and smoke. But it was totally and utterly wonderful. We kissed again, harder and deeper than before and Sharon pressed herself against me. Ooops. I felt myself harden, something I thought I had more control over these days, and I pulled myself away from her.

'What's wrong? Do you not like kissing me?'

'God yes, but it's bloody freezing out here and I'm dying for the loo. Let's see if we can find a space then I'll jump upstairs. Hey, Marion or Bongo won't mind, will they? That we're together I mean?'

'It was Marion who sent me outside after you. She's been telling me to talk to you ever since I said I fancied you.'

Sharon wasn't shy in admitting her feelings, and I had to admit I had that warm fuzzy glow thing going on and it definitely wasn't down to cider and cheap vodka.

We returned to the party, knowing smiles being exchanged between the sisters and Bongo giving me a nod as if to say it was cool I was snogging his girlfriend's sister. Not that I'd have been much perturbed had he not given his imperial approval, but you don't want to rock the boat and I'd managed to keep my head down since the incident with Michelle's ex. I jumped upstairs and joined the inevitable loo queue. By the time I got back down to the living room, Sharon had appropriated an armchair and was sitting giggling away with her sister. Marion moved to make room for me and gave me a look that said 'I'm glad you've got it together with my sister, but if you mess her about, I'll remove your testicles with a rusty tin-opener.' Or at least that's what I thought the look said. I leaned in and kissed Sharon on the mouth and Marion made a vomiting noise in the background. I laughed and sat back; getting all the things out my pocket I'd need to roll a joint.

The party began to wind down about 1am. I'd said to the olds I would be home by two so this suited me perfectly. Sharon's mum had arranged to come and pick them up whenever she phoned so the last twenty minutes or so was spent in intensive snogging and that first furtive creeping of the hand towards the mammary region. I met no immediate resistance but settled for the subtle 'stroking of the side of breast with thumb' move so favoured by Sun Tzu. No point in going in all guns blazing for now. We'd already swapped phone numbers and I'd said we would arrange a meet up in between all my forthcoming concerts. Finally, we heard the beep of a horn outside and the girls kissed us last goodbyes and headed out the door. We were down to the detritus now; Roddy had left with Susan earlier, Jason had disappeared, so there was only myself, Bongo and a couple of others who looked much the worse for wear. Now don't get me wrong; Bongo was a nice enough guy. But he was perhaps the most boring person I met throughout my school years. Dull. Greyer than a Scottish summer morning. As interesting as the patterns on a golf ball. About as intellectually stimulating as dandelions. So I didn't really fancy sitting about chatting with him. I even suspected he was the sort of guy who would want to compare notes on 'progress' with respective girlfriends. And despite all the other failings I had as a hormonal teenager, or even as a still hormonal twenty-something, grope and tell was not one of them. Excuses were made, thanks were offered and, all etiquettal niceties observed, I exited stage left. Or front door forward. Or something. As I walked back towards Echline, my jacket collar raised against the biting wind, I reflected on the year so far. It was coming up to the end of my first year in the East and those first weeks here already seemed like a memory lost in time. There had only been one major thing missing in recent months, and that vacancy looked as if it had been filled tonight. I'd managed to make a good, and diverse, and occasionally mentally disturbed, group of friends. I was again attending my beloved gigs on a regular basis. I was doing okay at school (though knew had to actually make some half-way concrete decisions soon as to the next step). And of course, I was getting a regular smoke and had expanded my consciousness, literally and metaphorically, several times that year already. The only other thing I was sort of still missing was any form of DJ'ing. The local hospital radio wasn't that local, and the school disco was a no-no. It was something I still wanted to do, and something that had informed some of my 'maybe' choices life wise in the shape of journalism courses, but there just didn't seem to be any chances to get involved anywhere. I decided that this would be the next priority on my 'to do' list.

Chapter 19

As we went into December I was riding the crest of a happy wave. November had been a brilliant month both musically and romantically. Sharon and I had slipped into a comfortable and easy going relationship. Her music taste was second to none. Well it was second to mine I suppose. Her favourite band was Depeche Mode and she was the first, but not the last, person to point out that I looked a little like Dave Gahan. I'd never seen it before, but I'd radically changed my hair at the end of the month from my previous floppy Cope hairdo to a slightly bouffant flat top which was, without meaning it to be, very like Gahan. Do we sometimes subconsciously imitate our heroes? Who knows? But it was very flattering and I took to spending money on hair products other than shampoo for the first time ever. Okay, I added products to mum's weekly shop; something dad found highly amusing. We were speaking on the phone nearly every night, had met up a good few times and had even had the unadulterated joy of a double date with Bongo and Marion. The only problem was the distance between us.

Although Kirkliston and the Ferry were not far apart geographically, there were no buses that traversed that short distance. So it was either beg a lift from mum or dad (Only a success when the winter weather was at full scale) or face a half hour walk up to her Gran's house. Her parents were semi-strict and didn't like the idea of Sharon having a boyfriend till after her Highers. (Yet Marion was okay as O Grades were just a stepping stone. Sigh. Adults were weird) So we used her Gran's for meetings instead. Luckily her Gran adored Sharon, thought I was wonderful, and was more than happy to be part of an unwritten plot in our relationship. Her older cousin stayed with her gran but he spent most nights at his fiancée's house, so we had a bedroom to sit in, listen to music (not his; it was mostly shit) and practice our snogging and heavy petting. And boy did we practice.

That initial clumsy nose-bumping kiss had swiftly developed into Lancaster/Kerr level snogging (just without the beach) and we'd refined out technique along the way. She was, for a 16 year old, a very tactile person. We hadn't moved much beyond basic fumbling, petting and groping at this stage but I had a feeling in my boner that there was indeed a hint of Eastern promise at the end of the petting rainbow. Xmas was fast approaching and I had already formulated a plan for New Year's fireworks of a different kind to normal.

The olds had already said they expected a certain level of studying for my mocks over the holidays but I wasn't placing a huge amount of importance in them. They were meant as a guide to how well you would do in the real exams, but I saw them more as getting a rough idea of what the real exams' content would be. For me, the holidays were going to be just that; a time of relaxation and enjoyment before the run up to the end of fifth year and the real stress.

I'd started quite seriously looking at university and college prospectuses. There were now a few candidates on the list and I had to start applying soon as the deadline was mid-January. My shortlist included Journalism at Napier in Edinburgh, Journalism Studies at Sheffield, a combined studies degree in Swansea and a degree in media studies in London. There was also one wild card in the pack; a degree in German at Edinburgh University. The wild card had come about after reading a recruitment pack for the Navy at school careers day. Now I'd never in any way considered any of the armed forces. Remember; I was a bit of a Bolshie sort and supported CND etc. But the guy from the Navy at careers day tempted me into considering it. Mainly because they would sponsor me at University with money above and beyond my grant (And thus no budgeting) but also with the fact that my degree would allow me officer entry level as a communications officer, world travel, and, when and if I chose to leave, the chance of a very lucrative job working on an oil rig or similar. The figures he was talking were, to a young kid, mad money, and the temptation was enough that I had filled in the Navy forms and was due for an interview the first week of January. So, I had to consider at least applying for the degree in German in case I defied the odds and plumped for the wild card. But my main focus was still on becoming the next John Peel. I didn't even have a clue how much someone like Peel earned, but it had to be good. And never mind the money; think of all that free vinyl he must get sent!

I'd resolved to fill in all the UCAS (Universities and Colleges Admissions Service for all you non-Brits) in the last week of the Xmas break so had around three weeks to make my final decisions. Another factor that was, only now, influencing my decision, was Sharon. We seemed to have got serious pretty quickly and I could see us being together for a while. But I'd always imagined University as a decadent playground filled with all manner of exciting adventures. And by adventures I meant copious amounts of sexually liberated women, ludicrous levels of alcoholic inebriation and inspiring levels of substance experimentation. Now suddenly a girlfriend was thrown in the mix and I was torn between the promise of numerous peccadilloes and the potential guarantees that a regular girlfriend brought with her. It sort of brings me back to an earlier point; people think 'childhood' is the easiest time of your life when in fact it offers up more stress than you ever experience in adulthood. Not necessarily because the actual events and decisions are more stressful per se, but because you lack the experience and psychological maturity to make those decisions in a balanced way. So here I sat, ready to decide life directions based almost purely on likelihood of regular sexual congress.

Sharon planned on doing a degree in teaching and we'd co-ordinated our searches and she'd identified degrees in Edinburgh and Sheffield that suited her, so we had some crossover that would allow us to be close and maybe even live together. (A thought that frankly, despite the joy of that first blooming of romance and semi-sexual liaisons, had me totally petrified.) I thought I might be in love, but this was based purely on a notion that had no frame of reference to validate it.

And my cynical side worried that we could make all these plans then fall out just as university approached. After all, at that age, love can be a fleeting and transitory companion, and what one week can be a wonderful and joyous union of two people can the next week turn to hellish indifference. With all this in mind, undecided, confused and unsure were three words that immediately sprang to mind when considering my options. This brought me back to my New Year plan. I'd resolved that I had to have sex with Sharon to see if my post-coitus feelings were still strong enough to justify a long term relationship. Was this really love? Or still the hormonal imbalances of unfulfilled desire? There was only one way to find out and I was determined that I'd know one way or another by the time my UCAS forms had to be sent off.

And here was Xmas; a time of family, fun and festivities. Or alternatively, a time of gluttony, greed and grumbling depending on your perspective. I'd already sourced and bought mum and dad's presents; for him a box set of the Fiddlers Rally on fancy new CD and for mum a couple of model house ornaments from the new Lilliput Lane collection. I still hadn't decided on Sharon's present though a moonstone necklace I'd seen in Cockburn Street was current favourite. Dad had asked me the month before what I wanted and, mindful of the possible fleeing of the nest in the coming year had gone slightly over the top and optimistic in my request and asked for a new hi-fi. I had contemplated being really cheeky and asking for a Linn Sondek but realised that there was no chance of that and anything to go with it, so with some careful research had listed my ideal set up; (warning; geek alert! If unimpressed by boy toys, please skip three sentences) a Thorens TD160BC turntable, a NAD 3020 amplifier, a pair of Kef Coda IIs and a pair of Sennheiser HD40 headphones. All fairly entry level gear but quality nonetheless. I'd bought a few hi-fi review mags and compared all the different combinations. It was still serious money (for 1982); a total of about £320 but I hoped my good results in the last lot of exams, my doing well to date this year, and the frequent deliveries of prospectuses would all combine to cause an overwhelming outbreak of parental generosity. I didn't have a clue if they'd even looked at my list with any seriousness, or whether I'd receive a shitty gift voucher for WH Smith come Xmas Day, but I had my fingers (and toes, and legs and various other anatomical appendages) crossed in hope.

So school ended for the Xmas break. Last minute shopping was done; I'd plumped for the moonstone necklace for Sharon as well as a few other bits and bobs for family members. We were hosting Gran, Moira, Duncan and Elizabeth for the first time that year; an event I looked forward to with unbridled joy and enthusiasm (please insert sarcastic tone here). Sharon was spending the day at her Grandparents in Dunbar so we had made plans to spend most of Boxing Day together. I spent a large part of Xmas Eve either wrapping presents or helping dad with preparations in the kitchen. I'd sneaked a look under the tree and much to my disappointment there did not seem to be anything resembling hi-fi separates, merely two small indeterminate boxes with my name on them (I didn't include those parcels that were obviously jumpers, underwear and socks). Xmas morning arrived and the three of us gathered for the traditional exchanging of gifts and bacon rolls in the living room. My disappointment was almost palpable as I opened the two unknown boxes to find a book and a video. Ah well. It had always been a longshot.

'There is one other present for you.' Said Dad. 'But we didn't put it under the tree. It's in the dining room cupboard.'

Well at least it had to be more exciting than a book and a video, even if it wasn't the longed for and dreamed of hi-fi. I went through to the dining room and opened the cupboard. There sat four boxes neatly wrapped and stacked. Could it be? Surely not. I ripped the paper off with all the subtlety of a drunken six year old. Yes! Everything that had been on my list was sitting there in all their glory. I ran back through to the lounge and gave mum and dad a very uncharacteristic (for a 16 year old) hug.

'Thank you! I can't believe you got them! Is it okay if I go and set them up in my room?'

Dad laughed.

'Aye of course. Just no playing that noise you call music at full volume!'

'Aw dad, I need to test the speakers out at least. I promise no more than ten minutes though.'

I went back to my pile of loot and carefully carried them upstairs. I reverently unboxed each item and stared in awe at the sleek black sexiness of the system. My old stereo was rejected; tossed aside like a forgotten lover and removed from its previous place of prominence. With great care I wired each component together and placed them on the stereo unit. I realised with dismay (and a slight selfish greed) that I really should have asked for speaker stands too. But then I remembered an article from one of the hi-fi mags that had shown how to use a small pile of bricks to the same effect and resolved to try this out as soon as possible. Once the separates were all combined I faced my next dilemma; which vinyl should be the first to grace this awesomeness? Hawkwind? Depeche Mode? Rush? Gary Numan? Finally I plumped for The Associates' 'Sulk' and retrieved it from my collection.

Ensuring the amplifier was turned down I switched all the power buttons on and was greeted by a satisfying, almost sexual hum, as the machines kicked into life. I gently placed the vinyl on the turntable, put the needle on the record then turned the amplifier up, initially to '3'. The difference to the old system was incredible. As the first chords of "Arrogance Gave Him Up" filled the room, I was awestruck by the crystal clarity, the way each note stood out and the way McKenzie's voice soared like an earthbound angel. As the next track "No' came on, I decided it was time to test out the capabilities of both amplifier and speakers. '4'; still that audio perfection, '5'; not an iota of difference, '6', '7', '8'; still the components performed together in total perfection, an experience only marred by the sudden intrusion of dad's voice shouting 'turn that bloody racket down now'. Time to test out the headphones. I plugged them in, placed them on my head, and thus was born a lifelong love affair with Sennheiser headphones, an affair perhaps truer than any human one I've had. I was in audiophile heaven, and I'd have been happy to have stayed in my little bubble of nirvana all day if it wasn't for the impending arrival of the dreaded and beloved relatives.

The rest of the day followed the usual yearly pattern of boredom, crap jokes and the odd argument. The latter mainly coming against me with everyone else united. In those days most of my family were slightly to the right of Goebbels. And my increasingly left/anarchist leaning politicisation made an easy target for people who believed Thatcher was a second coming. I argued my points vehemently and with passion, throwing in statistics willy-nilly along with the odd de rigeur phrase like 'mutually assured destruction.' Thankfully the day also followed the other usual pattern of all the adults being virtually fast asleep by around 7pm so Elizabeth and me escaped upstairs where I wowed her (okay slight exaggeration; she wouldn't know the difference between a Binatone and a Thorens in a hundred years and her music taste was, to be kind, utterly shit.) with both equipment and vinyl. Finally it grew late, final coffees were drunk and mince pies eaten and we waved off the relatives with sincere hopes of not having to do it again for 12 months. I helped mum clear up the last of the cups and glasses then took 'Dog' out for a final walk and a chance for a good night spliff. By the time I got back to the house mum and dad were in bed so I gave

'Dog' some scraps and retired to bed to listen to the wonders of Gong's 'Camembert Electrique' through my new headphones.

Boxing Day; traditional day of leftovers and hangovers. Lunch, unsurprisingly, was comprised of various cold turkey and ham cuts, 'spiced' up with mayonnaise and cold boiled potatoes. Once the joys of such fare were finished, it was time to get ready to go and see Sharon. Her Gran was off visiting friends in Newbridge and wouldn't be back till late, and Paul was at his girlfriend's so we would have the house all to ourselves. I still had my Hogmanay plan in mind and today we would decide where we would be celebrating the bells. There were two choices sitting on the table; number one was to see the bells in on the Royal Mile after drinks at the White Hart and with a party in Leith to follow. But Sharon wasn't too enamoured of the rock crowd or indeed of the music, so that was a bit of an outside contender. Choice two was in Kirkliston itself. One of my fellow fifth years, Stuart Wardell, lived in a mill conversion on the edge of the village and, with his parents away in Spain for a week, had decided to throw a major New Year's party. This choice had a couple of advantages; it wasn't far from home so thus did not entail a major journey back the next day, and it was close to Sharon's gran's house so if my plan went according to plan (and there were no suitable rooms at the party) it was just a short walk for the final instalment of my long running quest. I pretty much knew it was going to be choice number two but it was a nice psychological advantage to let Sharon think she'd won a discussion/argument. In the post Xmas chaos, I'd filched a bottle of white wine and added it to my bag containing records and three quarters of a bottle of vodka.

It had been Paul who'd really got me into the idea of hi-fi separates (though John had lit the initial flame) and it had only been in the last few weeks that he'd let me use his beloved system.

Despite being well wrapped up, the biting cold of the weather struck me like a fist as I left the house. Although it hadn't been a white Xmas, it had been a damned cold one. Although sub-zero, the day was beautiful; clear blue skies juxtaposed against rows of frost sparkling fields. But the wind was vicious and seemed to infiltrate every nook and cranny of my body despite the layers of protection. By the time I reached the outskirts of Kirkliston I was frozen through and looking forward to the roaring fire I knew awaited me not far away.

Sharon's gran lived just off Main Street on Liston Drive, so it was only another ten minutes walking and I was knocking at the door. Sharon opened it soon after. Wow. Just wow. She looked totally and utterly stunning; purple flared knee length skirt with matching blouse (with just enough buttons undone to let me glimpse that cleavage I loved and to start a small wave of warmth in my loins) with a pair of cute pixie boots that I hadn't seen before (and thus guessed that they were a Xmas present). She threw herself into my arms and gave me the biggest and warmest kiss I'd received to date.

'Happy Xmas babes. So missed you.'

'Aw Happy Xmas to you too Sharon, but is there any chance of getting inside before I freeze to death?'

She laughed and led the way through to the lounge where, sure enough, a huge fire was roaring in the grate. I peeled off my jacket, scarf and gloves and crouched in front of the flames, feeling some semblance of life begin to return to my extremities.

'Do you want some mulled wine Graham? Gran made enough to keep Scotland going for a year and it's bloody good.'

'Damn right. Beginning to thaw on the outside but my insides still feel like frozen peas.'

She went off to the kitchen and returned with two generous mugs of spicy aromatic mulled wine. I took a deep drink and could feel the warmth spread through my veins.

'Damn that's good. So, do you want your present honey?'

'Of course I do. I'll just get yours too.'

I had a feeling she'd bought me some records as the last couple of times she'd been at mine (Rule number one; bedroom door to remain open throughout any visits by female friend) she had spent ages going through my collection and I was sure she was making sure I didn't have the tunes she'd decided on. Yup, right again. The parcel she handed me was approximately 12 inches by 12 inches so she had either bought me a load of calendars or some vinyl. I handed over her present and took mine in exchange.

'Oh Graham, this is absolutely gorgeous. Thank you!'

Good result. I had thought she would like it and I had been bang on the money.

I opened mine and flicked through her choices. Brilliant! Not only did she have fantastic taste in men (cough cough) but her taste in music was nearly as good. She had obviously thought about it and not just rushed into the shop and grabbed a handful of albums. There was; XTC 'English Settlement', Thomas Dolby 'The Golden Age of Wireless', Front 242 'Geography', The Birthday

Party 'Junkyard', Laurie Anderson 'Big Science' and Wall of Voodoo's 'Call of the West'. Nearly everything she'd bought was already on my 'to buy' list with the exception of the Front 242 album as I hadn't really heard much by them yet (though they had been gaining some good write ups.)

'Stick one of them on the stereo if you want babes.'

'No offence Sharon, but I wouldn't let any of my vinyl near your Gran's stereo. I think she last replaced the needle in 1967. I'll wait till we've finished this wine then I'll give some of them a listen on Paul's system.'

She laughed.

'Fair point. I don't think Gran is very up to date on hi-fi's let alone the stuff you and Paul are into.'

We finished off the mulled wine and headed upstairs, Sharon carrying the vodka and me carrying the mixers and my records. I let her go first, a gesture that was not only gentlemanly, but also one that allowed me a wonderful up-skirt view as she moved; a view that had all the right anatomical parts responding. While Sharon poured two vodkas, I switched on Paul's system and let the amplifier warm up. Pride of place went to his Linn Sondek, certainly the best turntable on the market at the time (and Scottish too).
Once I'd allowed for the amp to warm up it was time to choose the first of the new albums to play. I decided on Birthday Party's 'Junkyard' and was in love with it from the moment Cave's vocals growled out on "She's Hit". I accepted my vodka from Sharon and leaned back against the bed as I built a spliff. Once 'Junkyard' was finished, I moved onto the Front 242 album and had to agree with the rave write ups the band had been receiving. We'd moved onto the second spliff and third vodka by the time Laurie Anderson had started playing but Sharon was getting a little bored with my concentration on music and not her.

'Hello there. Boyfriend. Remember me? I'm really glad you're enjoying your new records but your girlfriend would like a little attention too.'

I laughed.

'Sorry Sharon. It's your own fault for buying such good albums. Give me two minutes and I'll put on a couple of Paul's CDs on shuffle then I'm all yours.'

I chose a couple of more chilled albums and set Paul's CD player to shuffle. Relighting the joint I'd left forgotten in the ashtray I joined Sharon on the bed and kissed her on the forehead.

'There we go. Music sorted and 100% attention on my gorgeous girlfriend.'

'Well if it's 100% attention then I expect a kiss somewhere better than my bloody forehead!'

I moved in closer and kissed her gently on the lips.

'Is that better?'

'Well it's a start.'

She pulled me towards her and kissed me greedily on the mouth, our tongues entwining like two love-struck snakes. Despite the room only having a radiator to ward off the winter chill I could feel a heat rising from deep inside me. We fell back against the pillows, still kissing, and I could feel that passion was increasing from both of us. I reached down and pulled her blouse out her skirt, Sharon twisting slightly to make it easier. My fingers found the buttons on her blouse and began to clumsily undo them; a task that seems to defeat many men no matter their age or experience.

'Here, let me.'

She expertly unbuttoned her blouse and discarded it to one side. I stared in wonder at the soft material of her bra and the heaving breasts pushing against the cloth. I began to kiss her neck languidly, hearing soft moans escape her throat as my mouth found the places where she was most sensitive. Then my lips moved downward, nuzzling at that cleavage I found so alluring and hypnotic. My fingers fumbled at the clasp at the back and, wonder of wonders, I somehow managed to unhook her bra at the first attempt. She shrugged her bra off and for the first time I had her semi-naked before me. As the thumb and forefinger of one hand took one nipple in their grasp, my mouth found the other and her gasps took on a greater urgency that matched the rising ardour.

'Oh God yes, that's so nice.'

I switched nipples, my tongue now focussing on her left breast while my hand massaged the right. She'd turned towards me and was pressing against my now obvious hardness with all her might. Moving my attention away from her breasts I held her with my right arm while my left hand began to caress the back of her knee before moving slowly and carefully upwards to her inner thigh. My fingers traced circles on her skin and I could feel her body respond. As I realised I was meeting no resistance but only passive encouragement, I moved onwards and upwards till my fingers met the soft silky material of her panties. I could feel she was already wetter than a Scottish summer and her gasping was now loud enough to wake the neighbours. This was further than we had ever gone before. I'd seen tonight as a sort of dry run for Hogmanay but it was rapidly turning into something far less dry. Finding the waistband of her panties, I began to gradually pull them down her legs, stopping only briefly to ask an important question.

'Do you want me to stop?'

'No, no, God no.'

I slipped her pants down and off her legs and returned my attention to her waiting wetness. Her clitoris was already engorged; something Fiona had taught me meant that the woman was very aroused. I lightly began to massage her clitoris and with the increasing volume I was relieved her Gran was several miles away (though there was still a chance she might hear). Leaving my thumb placing light pressure on her clit, I let one finger slip inside her. She let out a long happy gasp and arched her back in the air.

'Yes, yes, God yes.'

Fiona had taught me well. It was as important to give pleasure as to receive and right now, Sharon knew what pleasure was. I began to move my finger in and out of her pussy faster and faster while at the same time increasing the pressure on her clitoris. Suddenly she let out a long cry and her back arched to an almost impossible angle.

'Oh my God. Graham, Graham, that's amazing. I want us to have sex now. I thought I wanted to wait a while but I need you to be my first.'

This hadn't been in the plan at all, but I wasn't going to turn back when finally the repository of the Holy Grail lay before me waiting for me to enter.

'Have you got any condoms?'

'Yes baby, just hold on.'

I fumbled in my pocket looking for the condom I knew was there. But...where was it? No, I knew it was there. It was always there just in case of an event like this. I began to panic and sat up, desperately searching each pocket in turn.

'What's wrong Graham?'

'This bloody condom. I know I had it, I'm sure I had it but...'

'Never mind. Paul is sure to have one. Check the bedside drawers.'

There then followed perhaps the most frenetic search in the history of searching. With no regard for Paul's private space, we rifled drawers and cupboards, finding things we definitely weren't meant to (Polaroids still being de rigeur in those days. Wait…is that Paul in that pic?) But not a bloody condom to be found. I was almost in tears when I realised Sharon had collapsed on the bed in fits of laughter.

'What the hell are you laughing at?'

'Oh Graham, look at the state of the room, look at the state of us! It doesn't have to be tonight; that's just the way things were going. We've got Hogmanay a few days away. What more special way to start a new year than by losing our virginity to each other? Now stop being a silly bugger and come back to the bed.'

I laughed with her. She was right. And Hogmanay had been the original plan anyway. I joined her on the bed and held her tight and we laughed our problems away.

Chapter 20

Those next five days may have been the longest five days of my life. Knowing that my quest of years was about to end, and that it was going to have a meaningful end with a girl I loved/lusted after/was very fond of, meant that every day seemed 48 hours long. Chris had phoned me the day after Boxing Day and said he would come to the Kirkliston party as he'd had a fall out with Martin (Given Martin's hippyness, falling out with him must have taken a monumental effort). I just hoped he wouldn't cramp my style on the night, though I had a feeling that Sharon and me would rather sneak off to her Gran's at some point after the bells rather than risk being interrupted from a drunken reveller. But what had me almost as excited (okay, okay; that's a blatant lie) as my impending virginity loss was the fact that Stuart had phoned me and said he had borrowed a set of decks (for set of decks read one of those dodgy Citronic systems I mentioned earlier) and asked if I wanted to DJ for some of the party. There was a partial dilemma in answering this request; this was going to be a very special night, a coming of age ceremony that was long overdue. I wanted to give Sharon as much attention as possible and make the night as magical as it could be. But I had really been missing playing tunes to a crowd and this would be a great chance to play a good set. I eventually compromised with Stuart and agreed that I'd play for a couple of hours before the bells but wanted to be off the decks at 11.30pm (and those of you in the know will realise how hard a decision it was to give up a set through the bells at Hogmanay). I told Sharon about it when I called her and she was happy that I was getting to spin some vinyl but happier that I'd given up the midnight set so I could be with her. I now had to plan two hours' worth of music that would suit the crowd. There was no way I could go too weird so most of my leftfield stuff and older Krautrock was a no-go. But most of my electronic tunes would go down fine and I'd even (aaargh) throw in a bit of 'acceptable' pop. It just felt good knowing I'd get to DJ again after a year's absence and I hoped a few more gigs would come out of it somehow (even if it was just invites to play at parties)

Finally the big day came. Friday 31st December, 1982. D-Day. Pivotal moment. The dawning of a new epoch. All my preparations were complete and I was as ready as I'd ever be. My records were chosen and packed away with a note of the set list (I'd decided to go out on a disco note with Donna Summer's 'I feel love' which I'd found on twelve inch in a second hand shop on Leith Walk). My alcohol was bought and in a bag (much to my shock, dad had sneaked a bottle of vodka to me under mum's nose). I had two different types of hash in my box and half a dozen ready rolled joints for when I was on the decks. And, most importantly, I had six condoms in my wallet (and a further two in my pocket just in case I lost my wallet – Be prepared!). Now I don't know if I'm weird in this, though I certainly wouldn't think so, but I'd already used around five condoms by practising putting them on. There was no way I wanted the spiritual awakening of my sexual activeness to be ruined by fumbling in the dark. So, when I knew the olds were safely out the way I'd sat and went through some test runs; firstly with light and then in the dark, till I was confident that I could put one of these buggers on one handed. The olds had agreed to let me stay out all night (though they didn't know the extent of the party or the plans for virginity loss). I was planning on heading to Stuart's early on to have a mess about on the system and check sound levels. Sharon would arrive at about the same time as the rest of the crowd who had been told the party was starting at 9pm. After a hearty dinner of steak pie and mash, dad ran me up to Stuart's house (Carrying 100 records, a carry out and a change of clothes would just have been too much for that walk) and with some sort of weird telepathic thing left me with the words 'If you get up to anything, make sure you wear a condom.' This was bizarre on several levels; firstly that he should offer such advice on the very night I actually needed it.

And secondly from the perspective that we had never ever discussed sex. Ever. At all. It was one of those almost taboo subjects that I certainly wasn't going to bring up and they never seemed to want to either.

Stuart had done a good job with the house. He'd also borrowed a couple of UV tubes and a few basic lights so, together with the decent sound system that accompanied the woeful Citronic Hawaii, – hello old friend – there was an almost club like ambience to the house.

Another great factor was that the mill house was pretty isolated; thus reducing any chance of interruption by police, neighbours or the dreaded zombie gatecrashers. There was a small crowd already gathered and Chris had arrived early too, claiming the huge armchair in the corner and already swigging cider and rolling joints.

I said my various hellos then had a good look over the DJ set up. Someone had brought a microphone as well as one of those cheesy 80's 'phone headphones' but I'd be using my prized Sennheisers and there was no way I was going near the mic. (I just hoped and prayed that its only purpose was to count down to the bells at midnight.) I had a mess about with my first two tunes (The 12" mixes of Heaven 17 – 'Play to Win' and Depeche Mode – 'Meaning of Love'). Happy that the system was sounding good, I went and joined Chris for a joint and a few drinks before Sharon arrived.

'How ye doing Graham, I've no seen you in weeks likesay. You seem pretty loved up wi this Sharon lass. Ye doin the dirty wi her like?'

'Fuck off Chris. That's bugger all to do with you. Anyway, what's happened with you and Martin? How the hell do you manage to fall out with the biggest hippy in Scotland?'

'Ach he was being a right prick ken? He had some real dodgy acid; nowhere near as strong as normal and I'm sure they were cut wi something dodgy likesay. I had a pure louping belly for two days. But he widnae listen tae me. Said ah wis full of shit ken. So I telt him he was a long haired wanker and walked oot. Sure we'll kiss and make up next week though.'

I laughed aloud. Whereas I was taking my first steps into the psychedelic universe with great caution, Chris had gone plunging in like a complete lunatic. From what I'd heard, he was tripping nearly every weekend, and I was sure that this couldn't be good for your mind or your body. We settled down with a spliff and had a good catch up. What with Chris having college and work with Tommy, and me having loads of schoolwork and a girlfriend, we hadn't seen as much of each other over the last couple of months. In fact, our last night out had been the Marillion gig in November; an occasion where Chris had (again) managed to get so drunk he sent half the concert puking in the toilets. I was in the middle of telling Chris an anecdote about the 'party' afterwards with the band (which he had spent sleeping in a chair) when my mouth fell open. Sharon and Marion had just walked in and in retrospect, I'm sure my lower jaw was sitting somewhere mid-chest. I already thought, no, I already knew she was beautiful, but tonight she had taken the art of looking stunning to a whole new level. Before tonight she had quite long hair down to just past her shoulders. But now she'd had it cut short and sleek into an utterly gorgeous bob a la Louise Brooks (though at this stage of my evolution I didn't know who Louise Brooks was, never mind what a bob was). But whatever it was called, it was damned sexy. She was wearing a black knee length pencil skirt with the minutest of splits at one side showing just a hint of that leg I'd caressed so lovingly only days before. It had been matched with a blouse of the deepest purple with that Sharon trademark of enough buttons undone to show just a hint of cleavage shadow. Chris was forgotten and I shot off the chair to embrace Sharon, much to Marion's comedic disgust. Bongo came shuffling in last, consigned to carrying the girls' bags for them and looking as interesting as ever. I bribed a partially disgruntled Chris with a bit of black if he'd give up the armchair for Sharon and me. The next half hour or so was spent in exchanging both knowing glances and long wet kisses. You could tell we were both nervous and excited but Sharon did her best to keep our concentration on the now rather than the later.

'You excited about your DJ set then?'

'Course I am. But I'm more excited about our New Year plans for later. (Yeah, that's right; spoil your girlfriend's distraction techniques and make her blush at the same time.) I've got my set pretty much sorted; left a bit of room for manoeuvre in case tunes aren't going down well but I think I'll be okay.'

'You'll be brilliant. Let's be honest, you've got the best taste in tunes and the best record collection of anyone I know. (That's it baby, massage that ego.) I'll probably be dancing like a mad thing the whole two hours.'

'Well as long as you bring me a drink every now and then, that'll be great. I'm on in about twenty minutes so I'll go over in about ten to get the tunes sorted.'

By now, the party was beginning to fill. Over the open plan living and dining room where the main focus was, there was already about 45 people, and there were several others wandering in and out who were obviously scattered throughout the house. The guy who was on before me, a rather weedy looking guy called Mickey, had been playing some pretty dire soft and middle of the road rock for the last hour and, as yet, not one person had been drunk or brave enough to dance. Stuart had dimmed the lights just before 9pm and now the large room was a UV heaven with some coloured lights in the corner. What was making Mickey's set worse was that he was a microphone DJ; every gap between track was being filled by inane vocal dribblings. (Hey, that was the mighty Rainbow with 'Since you've been gone.', now here's a classic from Fleetwood Mac') I was on the verge of inflicting violence on him, and I'm sure several others were too, going by the regular looks of unadulterated disgust being thrown his way. Whether that intended violence was because of the awful music or the awful talking between tracks only the people involved knew. I did wonder how on earth he'd managed to persuade Stuart to let him play, and it was only later I discovered that all the equipment had been borrowed or hired from Mickey's brother with the proviso that Mickey got a set at the start of the night.

At last his set drew to a close. I was already behind the decks waiting; tunes sorted, bottle of cider in one hand and the old trusty doob dangling from my lips as I waited for him to play his last record. Then I heard the opening bars. Oh sweet fucking Jesus.

'Thanks everyone, this is my last tune. The fantastic Toto with 'Africa'. Next up spinning some great records is DJ Graham with some wicked electronic sounds.'

This guy was not only an asshole. He was King Asshole, Emperor Asshole of Assholia, The Grand Galactic Overlord Asshole of the Seven Galaxies of Assholus. He was playing music most dads wouldn't even listen to, and his patter was so shite it left skid marks on the microphone. He turned and smiled at me, receiving only a mocking grimace in return, and the microphone he passed to me was immediately unplugged and discarded to the side. I swapped the stupid phone headphone for my beloved Sennheisers and cued up the remix of 'Play to Win' by Heaven 17. It was time to put some funk into the evening; an antidote to the ninety minutes of dreary dad rock we'd all endured. As the first beats kicked in, the mood in the room seemed to palpably change. Heads began to nod, and in a show of support Sharon dragged Marion up onto the floor and began to dance. This was all the catalyst that was needed and by the time the second record was on, there were about twenty people up and dancing their little drunken asses off. Now by now you'll have realised that music plays a very central part in my growing up (and, later on, in my not growing up). Although I had by this time had a few shots as a DJ, it had mostly been for short periods of half an hour or so (I'm not counting my shows on hospital radio here). So in many ways this was my first 'real' gig (yeah, I know; it was just a party in a house). It was the first time I'd played for any length of time and it was the first time I was 'up close and personal' with the crowd (the sets at school discos had been played from the lofty isolation of the stage). I therefore make no apologies for including my set list in this story; the night of 31st December 1982 was a major milestone in my life in two ways and the music was a big part of it.

From start to finish, these were the tunes that kept the 'dancefloor' virtually full until 11.30pm;

Heaven 17 – Play to Win (12" mix)

Depeche Mode – Meaning of Love (extended version)

Culture Club - White boy (Extended Version)

Human League - Mirror Man (12")

Soft Cell - What (Full Length Version

Depeche Mode - See you (Extended Version)

A Flock of Seagulls - Space Age Love Song (12" Mix)

Thompson Twins - In the name of love (12" railroad mix)

Visage - We Move 12" [Dance Mix]

Siouxsie & the Banshees - Israel (pre-mix version)

Talking Heads - Once In a Lifetime (original 12 inch)

Soft Cell - Tainted Love/Where did our love go (12" remix)

Depeche Mode – New Life (12" remix)

The Cure – Let's go to Bed (extended)

Visage – Fade to Grey (Dance mix)

Japan - Life in Tokyo (remix)

Simple Minds – I travel (12" mix)

Donna Summer – I Feel Love (12" remix)

By the time I put on Simple Minds' 'I Travel' the room was full of drunken sweaty people. The proximity of the crowd made me realise for the first time just how much power a DJ could have. It was akin to conducting an orchestra; depending on the direction I took the music, the crowd would change from frenzied movement to slower funky flowing. I was in the grip of ecstasy, especially when I knew the reward that awaited with me when Sharon and I found some privacy later. The little darling had spent almost my entire set dancing in front of the decks and I swelled with pride at the fact that the best looking girl in the party was all mine. She had also kept my glass full throughout the set and it was only as 'I Feel Love' drew to a close and Stuart got ready to go on after me that I realised I hadn't had a toilet break the full two hours despite ingesting copious amounts of alcohol. I left Stuart to start his set, mumbled an explanation to Sharon and then raced to the nearest toilet.

When I returned the party was still in full swing as Stuart built up towards the bells. Sharon had taken a breather and had reclaimed our armchair from earlier. I sat beside her and gave her a long passionate kiss.

'Graham, that was fantastic. Why don't you play more often?'

'Where? Can't get a go at the school, am too young to play in clubs, so there aren't exactly many opportunities for me.'

'Well I know the teacher that organised the events at Royal High so I'll have a word with her when term starts. See if I can show you off to all my friends.'

'Wow, cheers babes. That would be great. Looks like it could be a great 1983 ahead.'

'Definitely. And what a start we're going to have once we head back to my gran's.'

I gulped. Although (of course) the impending frolics had been on my mind all night, all day, in fact every waking second since Boxing Day (not to mention a few rather naughty dreams) I suddenly realised that zero hour was fast approaching. And now it was so close, I was absolutely terrified. Yes, we'd come close on Boxing Day, but that had been spontaneous. This was all planned out and that foreknowledge had me frightened half to death. Thank god for the saviour that was alcohol. I was already pretty tipsy, but had held back from an all-out assault on the carry out until my set was finished. Now that it was just Sharon and me it was time to get pissed quickly and there was only 20 minutes or so till the bells. Onwards the clock ticked. Someone switched on the television set as it got close to midnight and as the coverage went over to Big Ben live, Stuart turned the music down and someone upped the volume on the TV.

10, 9, 8, 7, 6, 5, 4, 3, 2, 1...

As the fireworks soared over London, the television was turned off again and Stuart blasted into Dexys Midnight Runners' 'Come On Eileen'; one of the biggest tunes of the year. Everyone was hugging and kissing. I only managed to grab a brief embrace with Sharon before being manhandled by half the crowd, but in those stolen seconds, I took the plunge and uttered words that had never before escaped my lips.

'I love you.' I whispered in her ear before Chris grabbed me in a crushing bear hug and poured a swig of whisky down my throat. It was five minutes, though seemed like an hour, before I was able to return to her arms and hold her close.

'Graham...what did you just say?'

Oh hell, it was done now.

'I said I love you Sharon Patterson. I totally and utterly love you.'

She squeezed me tight and kissed me.

'I love you too Graham. Have wanted to say it for weeks but just didn't know how you felt.'

'I was too scared (liar). I've never said it to anyone before (true) but I know no-one has ever made me feel like this before (true) and that I'm so happy we're losing our virginity to each other (very very true)'

I'd crossed another threshold of growing up. How true the love was I had no idea. Looking back from a viewpoint of gathered wisdom I think I really did love her. Maybe not the deep lasting love you experience as an adult. But from the perspective of an arrogant 16 year old with a lack of any real life experience it was the most marvellous feeling in the world. Right there, right then, that moment truly encapsulated love for me. And I think it would have been the same even if we hadn't planned to sleep together later that night. The whole night had me buzzing with the sheer perfection of it. I'd played my first ever party set, I was comfortably stoned and drunk, and I had a beautiful girl with a loving heart in my arms.

'Graham. Can we leave quite soon? I really want to be with you.'

For one of the few times ever in my life, the idea of leaving a party early that was still in full swing was not a hard decision. The night had already moved far beyond the boundaries of 'special', and now it was about to go so much further again. I looked around the room; people were dancing, drinking, sleeping, snogging, or just generally having fun. But all I wanted at that moment was to be alone with Sharon and with an inward smile I realised that this would have been true even if there was no sex on the menu; even if all we did was cuddle in for the rest of the night, I no longer wanted to have to share this magic with anyone but her.

'I was just thinking the same thing. Wasn't sure if you wanted to leave Marion quite yet though.'

'Ach she's big enough to look after herself. And Mr Interesting is here as her bodyguard so no harm will come to her. What will you do about your records?'

Hmmm. Good point and one I hadn't thought about. I had brought a lot of tunes above and beyond my planned set just in case things went awry with my chosen records, or indeed in case I ended up playing a second set at some point. But they would fit in the two bags I had easily and it was only a fifteen minute walk to Sharon's gran's house. There was no chance of phoning a taxi at this time. Most of the local ones would be on runs into the city and we'd probably have to wait at least an hour or more. If Sharon could carry the remnants of the carry out, I'd manage to carry my vinyl no problem (how little did I realise that the walk that night would be a portent of many, many nights of humping boxes and bags of vinyl ludicrous distances). There was also no chance I was leaving my prized tunes here. Some bastard could either use them and scratch them or nick them.

'Well if you can manage the rucksack with the carry out, I'll carry my records and headphones in the other two bags.'

'Problem solved then! I only have that shoulder bag with me. What booze will we take back with us? No point in taking it all. Can leave some with Marion or your mad mate Chris.'

'Take the half bottle of vodka and the bottle of cider. Give the rest to Marion; that's more than enough for us.'

'Definitely. Plus I've got a bottle of fizzy wine in gran's fridge. Put it in there just for us.'

We spent the next twenty minutes saying goodbyes (knowing smile from Marion, offensive remark from Chris) and gathering together our stuff. I said thanks to Stuart and we agreed that we'd made a good team and should do another party, albeit one with absolutely no 'DJ Mickey' on the decks. As we left the mill house, the magic of the evening continued to elevate as it had just started snowing. Nothing heavy, and thankfully with no wind it wasn't blowing in our faces, but just for a moment it seemed like it was another perfect part of the perfect plan for a perfect evening. We started making our way along the dark country lanes when, unbelievably, whatever Goddess or God was watching over me ramped that amplifier of magic right up to '11'. From out of nowhere a local taxi appeared, obviously on its way into Kirkliston from a Newbridge or airport run. Sharon waved her arms frantically and the driver saw us at the last minute and pulled over twenty yards up the road. Even after only a few minutes in the initial snowfall, the taxi was warm and inviting.

'Alright kids? Happy New Year to you both. Now what are you doing half way down a back road at this time of night?'

Sharon answered him.

'Party at the old Mill House but it's pretty boring so we're going back to my gran's to see the family (clever girl). Can you drop us at 48 Liston Drive please.'

'Course I can love and tell you what; there's no charge. I've got a pick up at Allan Park going to Livingston and that's worth a few quid. The missus thought

I was mad working tonight instead of boozing it up but by the end of my shift I'll have made as much in one night as I normally do in a fortnight.'

Now this is not something I've researched, but over the years I've sort of formulated this theory that within the majority of taxis there exists an unseen flaw in the fabric of space and time; a sort of border between dimensions. This flaw makes nearly all journeys seem interminably long no matter how brief the actual geographical distance. Now stay with me here; this is where my theory gets a little weird. I further believe that both the causes and purposes of these rips in the fabric of reality are the taxi drivers themselves. Now while I scoff at UFO sightings and abductions, it is only because I believe them to be distraction techniques to turn our attention away from the true aliens among us; the taxi drivers. Now whether they are extra-terrestrial or extra-dimensional I have no idea. But rather than dismissing my theory with offers of free tinfoil to make myself a pretty little hat, just think about it for a moment. When you travel alone in a taxi, how much of the journey can you actually recall later? See! You're more intrigued now. If you take a solo taxi trip there will be huge holes left in your memory afterwards. The drivers' vocal chords have some sort of metaphysical or technological quality that, while seeming to your subconscious memory to be droning on about weather/football/that bloody government/cost of living/what was on TV last night (delete as appropriate), are actually sending you into a temporary trance like state so that they can carry out nefarious experiments or study you or peek at your underwear…or something. Okay, I haven't quite got the last part of the theory regarding motive quite right yet but you can see some credibility to my idea, can't you? Can't you?

The short journey seemed to take forever, not so much for the wacky reasons outlined above, but because I think we were both impatient with desire. But eventually the cab pulled up outside number 48, we thanked the driver/alien and made our way into the warmth of the house. Sharon stoked the fire in the lounge while I poured drinks and rolled a joint. Though that simmering impatience was just below the surface, we were both equally aware that we wanted to maintain the magic that had seemed to permeate the entire night. The fire was soon back to roaring flames level and what little chill we'd collected was soon banished. For the next half hour or so I don't think we said a word; merely lay cuddled up and sipping vodka and watching the curling wraiths of spliff smoke perform aerobatics against a background of dancing flames. You could almost taste the perfection of the evening in the air, and I think we were both nervous and a little shell-shocked from our earlier declarations of love. When the vodkas were finished, Sharon said she'd get more drinks after she nipped to the loo. I sat, hypnotised by the flickering light and by the experience of the evening so far.

'Graham, can you come upstairs a minute?'

I headed up and saw that there was dull light coming from Paul's room. Pushing open the door I stepped inside then stopped in abject shock. Some of what Sharon had done could only been prepared in advance; she'd only been gone from the lounge for about five minutes or so. The bedroom was bedecked in candles; around twelve of them at various points around the room. She'd also used some of her 'hippy scarves' (as I called them) to soften the expected masculinity of Paul's space. One was carefully draped over the bedside lamp; bringing its usually 40 watt light down to a soft diffused glow. Others had been placed over his posters of semi-clad girls and performance cars to create an overall atmosphere of romantic idyll. Sharon herself was sitting on the edge of the bed holding two glasses of what I presumed was the 'fizzy wine' she'd mentioned earlier. But it was what she was wearing that grabbed my full attention. She'd changed into some sort of nightie; though this was nothing like the flannel burqa type monstrosities my mum wore. No, this was small and black with less material than there was flesh on show. It was almost sheer and even in the muted light I could see her beautiful nipples straining against the silk or lace or whatever it was this wonderful item of nightwear was made of.

'Do you like what I've done with the place?'

'God yes, it's gorgeous, you're gorgeous. What is that you're wearing?'

Sharon giggled coquettishly. (Another of these strange female traits that they seem to learn from some arcane path of knowledge)

'Don't you like it? I went shopping with Marion yesterday and thought you might like it. I can't let mum or dad ever see it though; they'd go totally mental.'

I was utterly lost for words; a rare occurrence in my life. But the layers of magic in this evening seemed never ending and by the movement I felt stirring in my loins, the magic was going to continue for a while longer.

'Why don't you grab a shower? I just had a quick one and you must be sticky as hell from the party.'

'Okay babes. I'll be back in a few minutes; don't go anywhere will you?'

'I'll be right here. Will even roll a joint for you coming out.' (Sharon had very quickly developed a high level of proficiency in rolling a doob and, to be honest, her spliffs were better than mine now.)

I gave her all the equipment and supplies she'd need then jumped out to the bathroom on the landing. I showered quickly; I had indeed needed it after those two hours behind the decks. When I returned, Sharon had put on the dreamy sounds of the Cocteau Twins; the perfect choice of soundtrack to the end of the evening (or to the beginning of a new stage of my life). In my short time away she'd managed to roll a joint, put on some tunes and was now reclining against the pillows, shrouded in aromatic smoke and looking as sexy as anything I had ever seen before. No, scrub that; looking sexier than anything I had ever seen before.

I joined her on the bed, fumbling with the towel round my waist in an effort to preserve some modesty. Which was sort of ironic given that full nudity was an essential part of our forthcoming activity.

'Have I told you I love you?'

'Yes Graham. Several times. But don't stop saying it. I like hearing the words. And I love you too; completely and with all my heart.

She passed me the joint and I lay back, happy and content. A glass of interesting bubbly in one hand, a spliff in the other and a stunningly good looking girl with her head on my chest. We stayed like that for what seemed like a lifetime; exchanging the joint, drinking the wine and occasionally indulging in long sigh inducing kisses. Finally I extinguished the roach and placed my glass on the bedside cabinet.

'You know Sharon; I think this may have been the best night of my life so far.'

'Me too. And it's not finished yet.'

Her head was still on my chest, but her hand began to trace light circles on my stomach, raising the temperature by several degrees and the towel by several inches. Fingers played with the towel where it was knotted together and before I could utter a cry of protest (Unlikely I know) the towel had fallen away and I lay exposed and very aroused. She reached down and gently took me in her hand. A sigh escaped me that, had there been an audio dictionary, would have been the leading contender for the definition of 'sigh'. Fingers ran up and down my shaft, eliciting further gasps from me then she shifted position slightly and took me inside her mouth. I moaned loudly enough to wake the dead in Kirkliston Cemetery, and for a moment I worried that it might all be over too soon as I could feel a tsunami of pleasure rise from deep inside me. Trying to control my breathing and my excitement, I concentrated on a random spot on the wall to try and quell the orgasm I could feel building inside of me. Just when I thought all control would be abandoned, she pulled away, as if some feminine sixth sense had told her I might peak too soon. Moving back up my body she planted small butterfly kisses everywhere, tingles running through places that had never experienced tingles before. We kissed again; a kiss deeper and with more meaning than any I think either of us had experienced before. I gently pushed her onto her back, my fingers tracing the hardness of her nipples through the flimsy cloth. It was Sharon's turn to gasp and sigh now, and she did both in abundance. The feel of the material was almost as arousing as the responses from her body and my hand gradually moved lower, repeating the circles she'd made on my own stomach shortly before then going further downwards till I reached her pubic mound and the dampness beyond. Sharon was writhing in pleasure and expectation now as my fingers toyed lightly with her clit and my lips teased at her nipple through her nightie. She pulled the garment up and over her head, allowing me unrestricted access to her now naked body. My tongue treated each nipple equally, lightly licking at them before lightly nibbling at them with my teeth, elucidating further gasps of pleasure. Then in one movement, my tongue traced a line from the valley between her breasts straight down to her clitoris. Her body rose from the bed by several inches as a first orgasm wracked her body, then continued to push against my mouth as I lapped at her clitoris and then at her inviting wetness.

'No more Graham, no more please. Make love to me now.'

I reached back to the bedside cabinet and grabbed one of the condoms I had placed there. My practice paid off as it slid smoothly over my erect penis and I turned back to her.

'Are you sure about this baby? We don't have to go any further.'

'Yes I'm sure; more sure than anything I've ever wanted.'

I positioned myself between her legs and gently pressed against her swollen lips. Slowly I pushed forwards; a slight resistance bringing a small cry of pain from her that almost panicked me, but she immediately reassured me.

'It's okay. I knew it would hurt a little at first, but don't stop. It's beautiful.'

Now at this point I would love to say that there followed a bout of lovemaking equal to anything in a pornographic film. But the truth of the matter is that it was the first time for both of us, and I was already so close to the ultimate heights of pleasure that in all fact that first sexual act lasted only three minutes or so. All too soon I could feel my blood pumping faster, my heart beating at twice it's normal rate, and a deep unknown ecstasy rising from the very depths of my soul. I let out a cry as a huge orgasm tore through my very being; unlike any I had experienced from self-pleasure or even oral fun. I collapsed on top of her, and was shocked to find that there were genuine tears in my eyes. Those three short minutes (and the build up to that final sprint) had affected me on physical and emotional levels I couldn't have believed existed.

'My God. My God. That was simply amazing. Are you okay Sharon?'

'Okay? I'm feeling wonderful. I thought the first time might hurt a bit more but it wasn't bad at all. I just hope that...oh bugger.'

'What is it? What's wrong?'

'We've made a right mess of Paul's quilt cover. My blood is all over it.'

And so, for a little while, the magic bubble was burst as Sharon stripped off the cover, put it in the washing machine then put a new one on. But within half an hour the spell had resumed and we lay cooried up in bed whispering to each other and kissing in that warm rosy afterglow. Eventually we drifted off to sleep in each other's arms with a feeling of utter contentment watching over us.

We woke in the morning to the sound of birds outside the window and the feel of a naked body lying next to each other; a new experience for us both. Neither of us had slept (in the sleeping sense) with anyone else before, just as neither of us had slept (in the sexual sense) with anyone else before, so it was strange to wake up to someone next to you (and a struggle to avoid that half-awake male thing of raising a leg in the air and letting out a mighty sleep-fermented fart). We kissed, oblivious to that stale post-party taste, then made love again, this time far slower and less frantic, yet as exhilarating and wondrous as it had been the night before. We dozed for a while again afterwards then Sharon cooked up a humungous fry up while I took a shower. Now satiated with food and love, we cuddled for a while on the sofa with crap television on. Then it was time for the magic night/morning to finally end. I phoned dad and said I was getting a lift up to Kirkliston Cross and could he meet me there in half an hour. I gathered my records together and said a long emotional goodbye to Sharon. We both knew this was a milestone in both our lives, a turning point in growing up that neither of us would ever forget. The events of that night are forever etched in my heart. Does anyone ever forget their first true love?

Chapter 21

January turned into a smorgasbord of pleasure. Every opportunity we could take, Sharon and I were at it like cocaine-fuelled bunnies. We were thankful her Gran was a little hard of hearing as it meant she always had the TV turned up loud, thus drowning out the creaky bed and cries of lust emanating from Paul's bedroom. Weekends were best as it was the only time I could escape revision for more than a couple of hours. We'd even entered the exciting world of alfresco sex (sheer madness in Scotland in January but when you're young and lustful, you don't really notice the frostbite on your ass cheeks) a couple of times; once in the woods near Sharon's school and once down by the shale beds on the river front when walking the dog (poor 'Dog' was tied to a tree for half an hour while we indulged in further anatomical exploration).

I wasn't putting a lot of effort into mocks revision; I saw them as a pointless exercise and would rather reserve my study energy for the real thing coming in a few short frightening months. And anyway, life was getting too exciting to concentrate on meaningless pretend exams. As well as my sexual awakening finding new paths to tread, my DJ set at Stuart's party had somehow turned into something of a legend. Stuart had phoned me a few days after and said his cousin was organising a club night at the Hoochie Coochie Club above Coasters in Edinburgh and would we (Stuart and I) like to be the warm up DJ's. It would only mean us playing from 9pm till 11pm but we'd get paid five pounds each and his cousin (Tom) would give us a lift home afterwards. A paying gig! £5 may not seem like a lot now, but to be paid for playing records that I loved just seemed like both the greatest and the stupidest thing at the same time. That was due to start on the 4th February; other than Stuart and me, there would be Tom and his mate Rabbit (don't ask) playing tunes. They were calling the night 'Vortex' and the music policy was electronic, post-punk, new wave and, as Tom described it, 'anything Avant garde'. His last bit of ambiguity had me excitedly wondering if I could get away with a bit of weirder stuff like Can or Throbbing Gristle. The club was bimonthly (as in the every 2 weeks version) and Stuart and I had agreed to swap round time wise for our sets. Then as if 1983 hadn't already begun in a truly exceptional way, a chance meeting with Martin the second weekend of January brought an offer that would be another foundation stone in my life ahead.

I'd headed into town to buy some vinyl (quelle surprise) and had bumped into Martin at the bottom of Cockburn Street. After exchanging New Year's greetings and regrets that we hadn't met up, he invited me for a pint in the Malt

Shovel and once we'd got our drinks and found a quiet smoky corner, he put his idea to me.

'Wee Chris was telling me you're a bit of a star DJ Graham.'

'Well I wouldnae go that far. That's my first gig in a year but it seemed to go okay.'

'Do you ever get to play your weirder stuff? Or do you just play all that electric pap?' (It's 'electronic Martin, not 'electric', but never mind)

'Not yet, but I'd love to. Have made up a few tapes at home but don't have decks so I stick wee mad bits of talking I've recorded from TV or radio between the tunes.'

'That's what I like to hear, and that's exactly what I'm looking for.'

'Are you going to tell me what you're talking about Martin or are we playing three guesses?'

'Aye, aye, I'll tell you. You've read Tom Wolfe's book about Kesey, haven't you?'

'Of course I have; about three times. Probably my favourite book of the last couple of years. Why?'

'My Uncle's got this wee farmhouse out past Bilston, right at the foot of the Pentlands. No land anymore; he sold it off when he retired. But it's a good sized house plus a couple of outbuildings.'

I still wasn't sure where Martin was going with this.

'Anyway, he's off to Spain for three weeks with my auntie and he wants me to watch the place while he's gone. That's when I had the idea.'

'Nae offence Martin pal, but what fucking idea?'

'Graham; we're going to have an acid test.'

He sat grinning like the proverbial cat while he watched the idea sink into my subconscious.

'Okay Martin; you have my full attention now. What are you planning?'

'Well, first of all, I just took delivery of some primo LSD crystal. Half a gram of White Fluff crystal to be exact. That's just about the best crystal you can get and is enough for about 5,000 doses or so. (At this point, despite being unable to whistle, I believe I let out a long astonished whistle). Obviously I need to sell some of it, but it's been a good winter and I can easily afford to give a chunk of this away. So I'm throwing a party. In fact, I'm throwing the best fucking party Edinburgh has ever seen. I've got the guys from Silly Wizard (Long standing Scottish folk band), Chasar (Rush sound-alikes from Alloa) and a couple of the boys from Chou Parrot (legendary Scottish Beefheartesque band of the 70's) all playing live. Wee Boab (lighting manager at the Playhouse and the Nite Club) is getting me a load of top notch lights and projectors, Davy (guy who ran a PA business in Leith) is giving me two sound systems. And I'm organising pick-ups from Loanhead and Penicuik. Man, I've got this all planned. But I want two music spaces; one for the live bands and for folk to have a jam, and one with DJs and the maddest most mental music for people to trip out to. Cushions and bean bags everywhere, brilliant lights and a few mad psychedelic backdrops. I know you've got a great record collection so I want you to be my main DJ for the night and play two nice long sets. Are you up for it?'

Was I up for it? Was I up for reliving a scene from my favourite book? Was I up for emulating Kesey and Owsley and Garcia and the Pranksters? Fuck yes I was up for it.

'Damn right mate. I'm totally up for it. When is it happening and, more importantly, how are you actually going to do the acid test bit?

'It's happening on the 11th February; a Friday so we can go all through Saturday too. And we're taking it the same way Kesey and his Pranksters took it.'

'Eh? Kool-aid? But you cannae get that here.'

'You're right Graham. But we can get Irn-Bru. We're going to have bottles of Irn-Bru marked 'with' and 'without'. Just in case anyone doesn't want to go the full trip path.'

'That sounds a brilliant idea. Utterly mad but totally brilliant at the same time.'

'Isn't it just? We, my friend, are going to hold The Electric Irn-Bru Acid Test.'

I sat in stunned silence as I sipped my pint. Since I'd read Wolfe's book, there had been a melancholy yearning inside me to have been able to be part of that scene; a feeling that had only increased with my recent psychedelic experiences. But I'd thought it merely fantasy; nothing (outside of perhaps a Hawkwind gig) came close to recreating those heady days of San Francisco.

But with one earth-shattering idea, Martin had transported me back in time to Haight Ashbury and given me an opportunity to be part of something uniquely different in this day and age. It was going to be a big challenge on two fronts; firstly putting together two very long sets (Martin had said around three hours plus for each). It had taken me a while to put together the Hogmanay set and that had only been two hours of tunes; this was going to be a lot harder if I was going to include spoken word stuff and samples. Secondly, I'd never attempted to play records before while 'under the influence' and boy, was I planning on being under the influence at this party. Sharon would be a no-no. Though she smoked as much as me when we were together, I wasn't sure what her views would be on acid. Plus, if, no, since she'd never taken anything like that before, I didn't really fancy having to babysit her with everything else going on. It wouldn't be hard though; she hated that whole scene so would hardly want to spend a weekend in a draughty farmhouse in the Pentlands.

One thing was for sure; this party, if it went to plan, would go down in the folklore annals of Edinburgh. Finishing my pint, I bade farewell to Martin and headed off to do my record shopping, though now my initial ideas for purchases were side-tracked and I found myself browsing the weirder and more psychedelic sections instead of electronica. I ended up with some pretty mad stuff; 'Trans' by Neil Young, not my usual cup of tea but he'd gone all experimental with a vocoder on this one and I thought it would fit right in for the acid test. Choice two was something I'd been meaning to buy for a while; Zappa's fantastic 'Joe's Garage'. Number three; Tom Waits' 'Frank's Wild Years', an artist I'd only recently discovered. I also took the chance to pick up a couple more Gong albums for the collection; 'Angel's Egg' and Allen's offshoot 'New York Gong' album. Finishing off that day's buying spree was 'Church of Hawkwind', which brought my Hawkwind album count at home up to seven. More than happy with the day had turned out, I headed off to the bus station and the journey home. I had a date with Sharon that night which meant that there was some sweet dessert to end the day.

January plodded on, alternating between beautiful clear winter days and miserable wet ones. As said, Sharon and I took every opportunity to shed our clothes and continue practicing our new skills. The mocks came and went and, as I knew I would given the level effort I put in, I did pretty much somewhere between abysmal and average. Of course the parents were furious but providence sent a placating message in the form of provisional offers from UCAS and accompanying promises to really knuckle down and study to get the grades I needed. My wild card had been discarded in the third week of January after an interview with a Navy officer to determine my 'psychological suitability'. I'd passed the interview with flying colours but had fallen foul of regulations with my medical declaration. From about age 9 onwards, I had suffered from terrible hay fever several weeks a year. It had seemed to disappear a year or so ago but it was still a medical condition that the Navy didn't like at all. My arguments fell on deaf ears; like seriously, how the fuck does hay fever affect you if you're on a ship hundreds of miles from the nearest pollen? But I'd received provisional offers from Sheffield, Swansea and London. London wanted minimum three 'B's' and two 'C's' while the other two wanted a minimum of two 'B's' and two 'C's' so it was easily doable. Sharon had also received a provisional for Sheffield so it looked like that would be the choice of both of us if everything went smoothly.

Chapter 22

Before I had time to catch my breath January had become February and we were only three days away from my first ever club gig (and ten away from the insanity). I'd spent every free (non-Sharon) moment working on both sets. For the acid test I now had around 15 cassettes with various mad samples and things culled from radio and TV.

I'd also thought ahead and spent some time at Stuart's (whose rather wealthy family had splashed out on his own set of citronics) both practicing for the club night and also making some 'emergency tapes' for the farm weekend. The idea of an 'emergency tape' was in case I ended up in too ludicrous a state to press buttons or lift records (a very possible scenario). Then I could simply throw on a tape that would give me forty-five or sixty minutes grace to get back to some level or normality or for a substitute DJ to be found. But for now the focus was on 'Vortex'. We'd even managed to drum up our own 'fan club' and a few of our mates from school had promised to attend. Sharon and Marion would both be there of course, which unfortunately meant I'd have to suffer Mr Boring's company for part of the evening. To decide which of us would take the first (empty room) set, Stuart and I had simply flipped a coin. Luck was with him and I was consigned to the 9pm to 10pm slot. But to be honest I wasn't too bothered. I'd get the better set in two weeks and it also meant I could come off the decks at 10pm and have a few drinks with Sharon. We arrived at the club early and wandered into the DJ booth. Not only was this my first club gig; it was going to be the first time I'd played on real equipment. Till now I'd thought of DJ decks as the Citronic monstrosities, but tonight another love affair with hardware would begin for me. The DJ box was raised above the dancefloor, bringing back my idea of the DJ conducting the orchestra of dancers.

But it was the technology that was grabbing my attention at this point. (Warning; further geek alert. Please skip six sentences if unimpressed by tech talk). The decks were Technics SL 1200 mark 2's. Not only was I amazed that someone had translated the purism of home hi-fi to the club space, but I was gobsmacked when Rabbit told me that there had been various versions about since 1972. That night gave birth to a new relationship; a happy one that still sees three more recent models sitting in my 'workroom/study/studio'. The rest of the equipment was all made by Akwil; a 4 channel Digitheque mixer linked to a Video4K lighting controller then a Disco V 5 channel DJ mixer. This was heaven. If I'd known this sort of shit existed I might not have been so quick to ask for the hi-fi separates for Xmas and would have gone down this route. There was about an hour till the doors opened so Tom and Robert gave us a crash course in how to work all the gear we were confronted with. Luckily the lighting controller was pretty much automatic and you didn't have to touch it unless you wanted to. I loved the crossfader on the mixer; meant you could flip from one tune to the other so much easier. Once we both had a rough idea, we had a couple of shots each at spinning some tunes until it was time for the doors to open and my first record to play. Amazingly, around thirty people were in the club by five minutes after the doors opening, and we only knew three of them (Yes; Sharon, Marion and the Interesting Man). I'd opened with Fad Gadget's 'King of the Flies' (a flexi-single give away from some magazine I forget) and then moved onto a promo one of my friendly record shop guys had given me; Cabaret Voltaire's dark 'Crackdown' that had a throbbing bassline that had me mesmerised. Of course, Sharon was on the dance floor by the time my second track had finished. I won't bore you with another tracklisting but I felt I was already growing in confidence, especially with the fantastic equipment I was getting to use. By 9.30pm, there were a good sixty or so people in and by the time my last tune (Throbbing Gristle – 'Hot on the heels of Love') played there were well over a hundred. Around seventy were dancing which I thought was a great result for my first club set, especially given the early time slot. I left Stuart to build the crowd up even further and went to join Sharon by the bar. We'd discussed leaving early to head to her gran's house in order to make the most of our extended curfews, but had decided it wouldn't be fair on Tom or Rabbit after giving us such a big chance. So we had to be contented with extended snogging sessions at our seat in the corner, interspersed with the odd dance. Stuart managed to put in a good show too, alternating between new romantic classics and some wicked electro funk. I'd never heard Tom or Rabbit play before, but their performances showed why so many had turned up for a first night (by the time Rabbit took over at 11pm, there were well in excess of 200 people in the club and the dance floor was hot and sweaty. They took the crowd on a musical journey; from obscure 70's disco to weird Italian electronica to more well-known tunes. I hadn't heard half the stuff they were playing and I resolved to get a list of recommendations from the both of them. This record buying was becoming semi-obsessive; every spare bit of pocket money was going towards tunes, as well as the now regular income I had from passing on hash to Chris. Now I was over 16, John was being a bit more relaxed about the whole thing. He was giving me two to four ounces at a time, and at cost, and I was passing them onto Chris who was adding extortionate mark ups. But it meant I was getting my own smoke for free and, on average, earning about £100 per month from my side-line. I'd invested in a set of scales; pretty little bronze ones from one of the shops on Cockburn Street. Each ounce was then cut up into exact quarters of seven grams each. Chris was shaving a gram off each of them and selling them on. A six gram quarter was about average in those days so he wasn't ripping anyone off. (Though I did hear one guy have a right good moan at him about the size one weekend). Sharon wasn't overly happy about my business venture, but she realised I wasn't really involved beyond the weighing and passing on to Chris to sell so she (mostly) kept pretty quiet about it.

As the night began to wind down, some people began to leave early but the faithful party heads kept their spots on the dancefloor right to the very end. Tom ended up bunging us both a tenner as they had done better on the door than they had expected. He declared himself very happy with both our sets and even went as far to say that in a couple of months we could swap with them and have the later sets. My John Peel dream was still in the sights of reality.

Saturday was spent recovering from the night before. As usual we ended up at Sharon's grans but it was a very down tempo evening. Not a drop of alcohol; just some juice and snacks and a couple of good videos. She was in a bit of a bad mood with me to be fair. Her happiness levels regarding the forthcoming acid test were non-existent. I'd tried telling her how much she'd hate it, but the green monster had raised its ugly head for the first time ever; she was convinced that the convergence of me, party, alcohol and drugs meant that I would automatically be off chasing other women.

Finally she realised that my enthusiasm for the next weekend was purely based on my love of music and my burgeoning affair with psychedelics and agreed that it was probably best that she didn't attend. With the mood finally lifting, it was back to a couple of practices of our naked wrestling before walking back down the long, lonely road to Queensferry.

The rest of the week was spent putting the final touches to my sets for the coming weekend. Unlike my last two gigs, I hadn't planned it out record by record. Instead I had separated it into sections and had certain records/bands in each one. My genre list was the most eclectic I had attempted; there was everything from Krautrock to classical, experimental to accapella, and the samples and word bits I had culled from TV, radio or tunes I owned were all written down in a little pad so I knew which tape they were on and where on that tape to find them. Martin had phoned on the Wednesday night; everything was prepared, the weather forecast was clear but cold, he had a man with a van doing the pick-ups, and he'd even organised a bar to cover some of his costs. He'd made up little photo copied flyers; a spoof on some of the posters from the 60's, with a picture of an Irn-Bru can on a psychedelic background. By the sounds of it, he was expecting around 150 people to turn up. This was a little nerve-wracking; I'd never done acid with so many other people at the same time and I just hoped that I managed to keep a firm grip of the plot throughout the night.

Friday arrived at last and I headed off into Edinburgh to get the bus up to Loanend. I had my records, my tapes, some spare clothes, and half an ounce of nice black. Chris was getting our joint carry out and of course Martin would be providing the other necessary ingredient for the weekend.

It was time for the Irn-Bru acid test; it was time for the next stage in my evolution.

Chapter 23

A psychedelic experience is a journey to new realms of consciousness. The scope and content of the experience is limitless, but its characteristic features are the transcendence of verbal concepts, of spacetime dimensions, and of the ego or identity. Such experiences of enlarged consciousness can occur in a variety of ways: sensory deprivation, yoga exercises, disciplined meditation, religious or aesthetic ecstasies, or spontaneously. Most recently they have become available to anyone through the ingestion of psychedelic drugs such as LSD, psilocybin, mescaline, DMT, etc. Of course, the drug does not produce the transcendent experience. It merely acts as a chemical key — it opens the mind, frees the nervous system of its ordinary patterns and structures.

(Leary, Alpert & Metzner – 'The Psychedelic Experience')

The weather looked foreboding; from Edinburgh city centre you could see dark heavy clouds sitting over the Pentlands like some iron-fisted judge about to pass a death sentence. I met Chris at St Andrew's bus station and we got on the first Loanhead bus that was leaving. Despite the oppressive skies, we both had a sense of eager expectancy about us. This was far beyond the chaotic but fun beach parties of the year before and somehow we both knew that the next 48 hours would be forever engraved on our memories. We got off the bus at the junction of High Street and Clerk Street and Chris jumped into the nearest phone box to call Martin and let him know we were awaiting pick up. As we waited, lit cigarettes in hand, the skies chose that moment to open and send down chilling winter rain that sent us scurrying for shelter in the closest shop doorway. I just hoped that this would not be the pattern for the weekend or it would put a real dampener (sorry) on the party.

After about twenty minutes and old battered Ford Transit pulled up beside us; its colour hidden by years of rust and grime. Martin was in the passenger seat and a grizzled biker type dude was smiling at us from behind the wheel.

We jumped in the back and I grimaced at the detritus we had to shift to sit down; bits of wood and bike parts were everywhere and I knew my jeans would be maukit by the time we reached the farm. Not that it mattered; a weekend partying on a farm was hardly going to leave you looking like you'd walked out of a Persil advert. The rain began to slow a little as we drove the last couple of hundred yards up a narrow winding track. As we pulled into the farm, you could see Martin had been busy. The courtyard between the main farmhouse and the outbuildings had been swept almost pristine, and everywhere you looked there were lights and lanterns hanging. There were a couple of big bikes parked at the side of the barn, and another dilapidated transit in front of the main house. There were a few bikers within our rock crowd and, contrary to public perception; they were not all Neanderthal maniacs intent on spreading disorder. Other than one arsehole from Dundee who seemingly revelled in initiating confrontation at every event, they were some of the friendliest buggers I had met, and would always go out of their way to help you.

Also off to the side of the barn was the 'outdoor area'; a non-musical space for people to gather round a fire and chat or chill. There looked to be enough wood to burn down Edinburgh gathered under a tarpaulin, and another tarp was stretched from the barn roof and secured at an angle to two large poles driven firmly into the ground. This would provide some shelter should the weather remain inclement across the weekend though if it remained as cold and wet as it had been that late afternoon, I sort of guessed people would much rather be inside. Martin took us on a tour of the site; the barn was the live music area and was already set up with a p.a. system and several spotlights. A small stage had been constructed from skillets and wood at one end of the barn and the floor was covered in easily brushable straw to soak up any wetness from boots and shoes. A couple of backdrops on the side walls completed the decoration and you could almost believe this was a permanent venue. Once he'd shown us where the bands would be, he took us over to the main house. For some reason I'd been expecting a cramped and miserable wee farmhouse, but instead what we got was a large and surprisingly modern space. Martin's Uncle had obviously invested the proceeds from selling off the land in bringing the old house (Martin had already told us it dated from the early 19th century) up to scratch. Downstairs mainly comprised of a huge open-plan living/dining space that had been transformed by Martin and his decoration pixies into something right out of a Grateful Dead tour. A lot of the furniture had been removed for safe keeping, leaving only a large sofa and a couple of cavernous armchairs. These had all been covered with throws and blankets to protect the upholstery underneath from the carelessness of the party-goers. Fairy lights were strung along the ceiling in every direction and a couple of UV tubes had also been hung from nails; I was guessing where paintings or pictures used to be. Almost every inch of wall space was otherwise covered in marvellous psychedelic backdrops; their themes everything from the Alice in Wonderland caterpillar to Tolkienesque landscapes. I could only imagine what they would look like once the black lights were switched on. One corner had been transformed into a DJ booth; a large table was stacked with the equipment that I, and others, had requested. Through his myriad of contacts, Martin had managed to get hold of three Technics decks; they were only Mark I's but still streets ahead of the Citronics. He'd got hold of something called a GLI PMX9000 as a mixer; I'd not heard of it before but it really looked the business. Completing the hardware line up were two tape decks and two CD players as well as a reel to reel player that someone else must have asked for (later I was to realise just how amazing this latter bit of equipment was for cutting and pasting music and samples). The system for the house was a 1K system which would be more than enough for the space and there were four speakers in the corners of the room as well as a couple of bass bins and a monitor for the DJ. Completing the décor for the room were a couple of groovy oil projectors and various bean bags and cushions which gave the room a very overall Bohemian feel. It made me think of Leary's former base at Millbrook and I was sure the Professor would have given us his approval had he seen how the setting had been set for that weekend's explorations of the consciousness. I dumped my bags of records, CDs and tapes by the equipment and followed Chris into the kitchen while he found space for some of our cider and hiding places for the spirits we had bought. Even if I wasn't planning on imbibing silly quantities of LSD that weekend, there was enough alcohol to keep us going for a week. As well as running a bar to raise some cash, Martin had also organised food, and the room-sized fridge was full of sausage rolls, burgers and pasties. I had wondered what we would do for meals (though I'd also wondered if we'd want to eat at any point) but it looked as if any attacks of the munchies would be well taken care of. And, of course, there were numerous bottles of Irn-Bru on the worktop, already labelled with the aforementioned 'with' and 'without' stickers, though Martin advised he was yet to add the magic ingredient.

More than impressed with the preparations the old hippy had put into the party, I grabbed a can of cider from Chris and headed off to roll a spliff and chill for a little while before the insanity commenced.

Martin had intimated a 10pm kick off for the party, but by 9pm there were already around a hundred people milling about the farm. Some had arrived in their own transport, and there were now several bikes, cars and vans parked along the side of the track and the buildings themselves, but many more had utilised the 'ferry' service from the nearest towns. I'd checked that all the equipment was in working order once someone more technically minded than myself had wired them together. The sound quality was sublime and I knew this was going to be one hell of a fun weekend. Some of the live acts had arrived earlier too and the early part of the evening had been punctuated by snippets of distorted guitar and manic drumming as they also sound checked in the barn. I'd chatted to a couple of the other guys who would be DJ'ing; Baz, an old friend of Martin's from London who'd made the trip up especially for the party and who'd spent time with Kesey in the states in the 70's (And yes; this sixteen year old was in utter awe of his stories). There was also a guy called

Pete, who turned out to be the owner of the reel to reel tape deck and whom I would learn much from in the coming months. He cut and pasted snippets of movies and news broadcasts into songs as well as cutting up various parts of tunes to create whole new musical soundscapes. I felt like I was both in exalted company and a bit of an upstart for presuming to be on the same 'bill' as these two psychedelic and musical veterans. But they treated me not only as an equal but as a long lost friend and I only hoped my sets could justify the trust and openness they showed.

In preparation for the coming madness I stoked the engine with food from the barbecue outside and the stream of hot pastries coming from inside. I was being careful with the booze intake; had interspersed my cans of cider with Irn-bru (without) and had so far avoided any vodka at all. The rain had petered out around 8pm and although the sky was still dark and overcast, it seemed to be staying dry for the foreseeable future. In the live arena, a couple of bikers were (surprisingly skilfully) jamming and Pete had started off proceedings in the DJ room; melding long progressive and psychedelic rock tracks with his own brand of remixes on the reel to reel. What he'd done with sounds was breath-taking; tracks would jump from one to the next but in a creative seamless way and I realised this guy was years ahead of his time (something that time itself would prove me right in) and even to my still straight mind you could hear and feel the layers he had created for the senses. Martin had set midnight as the kick-off for the psychedelic side of things and, knowing him, I was sure he would introduce some element of ritual into the proceedings. I'd had discussion with Baz and Pete and we'd sort of agreed to keep the set times informal and to be aware of what mental state the other DJ's were in. Looking back, I think there were elements of kindly Uncles to them both; they realised I was still, in comparison to them, very young (Baz was in his early 40's and Pete was about the same age as Martin). Their life and LSD experiences were leagues ahead of my own, and given that Martin had obtained high strength crystal, I think they knew there may be points in the weekend where I was incapable of playing records (Or indeed walking or basic speech). We'd loosely agreed that Pete would do a sort of warm up till just before midnight, then I'd take over for a couple of hours after the 'ritual' or until my capabilities vanished into the cosmos. Baz would do 2-3 hours after that, followed by Pete again etc etc. As the party was planned to last through to the Sunday, no-one would lose out and this informality allowed us time to both space out and grab the odd snooze here and there.

As midnight approached, an air of excited expectancy seemed to grip the party and conversations and music both became slightly more subdued. Chris had appeared in the house to tell us that Martin wanted everyone to gather by the fire in the courtyard and I immediately knew my suspicions re a ritual were about to come true. Sure enough, Martin had, in my humble opinion, taken things just a teensy weensy bit too far. The skies had mostly cleared and, although there was no moon, the courtyard was bathed in the light of several flaming torches held by his chosen 'acolytes' to form a pathway to where he waited by the main fire. Martin himself had found some type of druidic robe from somewhere and was standing behind a small table set up by the flames on which the sacred Irn-bru bottles had been placed along with dozens of small paper cups. I worried slightly that this was taking on aspects of the Jonestown ceremonies rather than the La Honda ones but at least I knew that in this case there was no cyanide involved. Martin had to have that dramatic flourish; and I don't mean that in a bad way at all. But for me it seemed a little over the top even after reading the stories of Kesey and Leary. Then again; tonight was his baby and I realised that when I looked back on this, even those flourishes would become part of the magic of the evening.

As people stepped up to the table, Martin simply asked them; 'with or without?'. There was no avoiding the question, nor was there any judgement if your answer was 'without'. Acid wasn't everyone's cup of tea (I'm sure there's a mushroom joke in there somewhere) and I estimated that of the 180 or so that were there, around sixty or so chose to pass on the laced Irn-bru. That still meant that in excess of one hundred nutters would shortly be running, falling, walking, stumbling skipping, flying and levitating around the venue, not to mention the hordes of mythical creatures that each of us would be experiencing. To give Martin the due respect he deserves, he knew just how strong the crystal he had was, and by controlling each person's intake this way he was ensuring that no-one overdid it too much at first. Finally it was my turn to pass between the fiery torches and approach the High Priest of Silliness.

'Welcome Graham. With or without?'

'Em...with please.' (I resisted the temptation to coax an astonished look from Martin by saying 'without')

He proffered me a cup of the magic elixir and smiled benevolently.

'Enjoy my brother.'

I wandered off and stood by Chris who had been one ahead of me in the queue.

'Well, here goes the weekend.' He said with a mischievous smile on his face.

We both drained the cups and smiled. There was no difference to the taste and I worried for a minute that maybe Martin had got the bottles mixed up. Still being a relative newcomer to this whole game, I'd expected the crystal to add some sort of aftertaste to the fizzy juice but there was nothing at all. Making my way back to the DJ room there were already a few people gathered and not a bit of music playing so I swiftly grabbed my tune bag and threw on a bit of Zappa to start. I had planned on a more dramatic start to the set; I had some recordings from the Apollo missions which included a countdown and that had been the intended introduction. But first rule of being a DJ is that the crowd are your boss (well, apart from not allowing them to make requests of course) so I didn't want to keep anyone waiting any longer. The room was looking fantastic now; the backdrops had totally come to life with the addition of the UV lights, and the two oil projectors were casting swirly mind-blowing patterns on the ceiling that I knew would be a black hole for my mind later on. But for now I lost myself in the music; jumping from Zappa to Tangerine Dream to Can and Kraftwerk, and dropping some of my collected samples either over the top of instrumentals or in between songs with vocals. It seemed to be going perfectly; heads were nodding and I even got a thumbs up from Baz, which boosted my confidence no end.

After about 35/40 minutes I began to feel the first tell-tale tickles in my stomach. My head started to fill with helium thoughts carrying me slowly away from the grounded reality I was trying to maintain. From my previous trips I estimated I maybe had another 45minutes or so till the peak kicked in. I had one of my pre-mixed tapes close to hand and put it in the player and cued it up, ready to be the inevitable 'press in case of emergency' back up that I would so obviously need. You could sense an almost palpable change in the atmosphere of the room as the acid began to take hold of minds and bodies. It looked like we only had trippers in here; the non-indulgers/pissheads had mainly congregated in the barn or outside by the fire. Dropping into a bit of Amon Duul, I tried to guide the cerebral cortices of those around me to a higher plane, conscious that even though I too was coming up, I had a responsibility to the people around me. As the clock hit 1.45am, I knew I wouldn't make it through those last fifteen minutes and signalled to Baz to see if he was ready to take over. If he wasn't, the pre-mixed set would suffice for another 45 minutes or so until he, or even Pete, was in a state where they could deal with the equipment. Baz looked spaced out too but acknowledged he was compos enough to play for a while. I finished off with Can's 'Soup' from their 'Ege Bamyasi' album; over nine minutes of psychedelic German madness that gave Baz time to sort out his first few records.

'Those were some damned good tunes Graham. I was expecting more modern stuff given your age but you certainly know your classics. Well done for hanging on this long; I could see the trip coming up on you even from the other side of the room.'

'I've had some good teachers over the years music wise mate. But aye; it was getting a little hard towards the end there. Could hardly read any of the labels on the records and was having to go by the pictures on the cover then trying to remember where each track was. Enjoy your set. I'm off to melt in a corner somewhere.'

Freed from the servitude of the decks I took over the voluminous bean bag Baz had just abandoned. Chris was in the armchair to my left, (he seemed to have an uncanny knack for getting the comfy seats at parties) and immediately passed me a rather large joint.

'That was barry like Graham. Really trippy tunes ken. Cannae wait to hear more later on.'

I found myself unable to answer. It was if leaving the decks behind had released the trip from its starting position and I found myself falling and soaring into clouds of smoke and swirling light. Whether it was the purity or the way we'd imbibed it, I'm not sure, but it somehow felt different to my previous trips. It was almost as if I was watching myself experience this from outside the room, outside my body even, and I observed as I gradually let go of the cosmic strings holding my mind anchored to the mundane realities of everyday life and slowly slipped into a dimensional whirlpool of awareness. The lights from the projectors were like watching universes being born; clouds of interstellar gas merging and exploding to form a million galaxies and infinitesimal worlds. My whole life was flashing before my third eye and I could see every crucial moment in my sixteen years with absolute clarity. I watched with fascination as I was born and, just for a minute, it seemed like that new-born I was aware of the cosmic me observing from another dimension and looked me straight in the eye. Although I was aware that on the physical plane there were other entities surrounding me, they were inconsequential as I strode across space like a God of Gods. This was where divinity lay; not in some badly translated book that sought to maintain hierarchical structures, but in the mind of every one of us. Leary and his peers had been absolutely correct. These substances were the key to our future evolution; to unlocking the secrets of mind and matter or indeed mind over matter. My trance like state brought me visions of beauty and horror simultaneously. The myriad of possibilities that time and space held lay unfolded before me like a simple AA road map. I could see how each decision on which path to take caused ripples to spread outwards to those around you as your choices altered destinies with every small adjustment. My fascination with the processes of evolution grew as I touched an alien world and brought life to it. Abiogenesis led to diversity led to complexity led to awareness led to an awakening of consciousness and the beings I had created went from blind worship of the divine me to the realisation I had already had; the divinity was within each of us. All you had to do was find the key and unlock it and everything was possible. I drew back from my evolved aliens and strode back across time and space, gradually approaching my home world, my home, my me.

Brain parachute, floating back down to some semblance of almost normality. Conscious of all that had gone before; the things I had seen and the worlds I had visited, but now only seeing that which was around me. Distortion of lights and sound still present but almost feeling like I could communicate in more than non-verbal ways. Those who were in the same physical space as me were split between their own personal journeys and sharing that airy parachute back to the world of beanbags and strange music. I looked to my left. Chris was in an almost foetal position, a cushion gripped in both arms as he continued his own personal journey. I reached for the joint I had left abandoned in the ashtray and lit it once more, feeling the tendrils of smoke reach within my body and my soul. For I now believed in a soul, but not in any religious way. We were our own Gods; that was the gospel in my head. Forever and ever, amen.

Chapter 24

The night progressed on in a hazy, dreamlike state. Although now back on Earth, my mind was still awash with distorted fluctuations in reality. I wandered from place to place; pausing to chat to people I know, to share a joint, or merely to soak up the atmosphere around me. Despite the temperatures being around the freezing mark, the outside area was surprisingly warm and cosy; perhaps because of the roaring fire that seemed to send elongated flares up into the night sky. I'd managed to catch a chunk of Silly Wizard's set in the barn and had been impressed by their melding of traditional folk music with more modern rock styles. Frenzied dancing occupied the majority of the barn floor space while they were on; all accompanied by ecstatic whoops and whistles from a crowd either inebriated or tripping their boxes off. The two guys from Chou Parrot had been on before them; jamming with a couple of other folk and producing some off the cuff madness that sounded like outtakes from a Captain Beefheart recording session. Unfortunately I'd missed most of their 'set' but the last half hour I had caught was wonderfully psychedelic and suited the mood of the weekend completely.

Martin, in an ongoing bout of weirdness, was still wearing his druidic robes from earlier, and was wandering the site with his trusty bottles of Bru and offering top-ups to those who wanted one. I didn't feel anywhere near ready to boost my own experience, though I sort of planned on doing so at some point during the second part of the party. He saw me sitting in a corner of the barn and beckoned me outside.

'So Graham, how's your night been so far then?'

'Wicked mate, totally wicked. That's some damned good shit you've got in that bottle. Definitely the most vivid trip I've had to date. One thing's for sure; people will be talking about this party for months if not years to come.'

'Cheers bro. Are you wanting another cup yet?'

'Nah, not just now. Thinking maybe later on Saturday but am happily fuzzy for now. Plus I'm due back on the decks in an hour or so. I had to come off a little early at the end of the first one as the peak was hitting me.'

'Yeah, I caught some of your first set. Damned good sounds. Chris was bang on in saying I should give you a go. How are you getting on with Baz and Pete?'

'They're cool guys. Loved listening to Baz's stories about his journey across the States. I can't believe he hung out with Kesey in Oregon for a fortnight. Lucky bastard.'

'I've said he should write a book about that trip. Sounds like it was a modern version of 'On the Road'. There's not much I get jealous of in this world, but Baz's American adventure is definitely one of them. Anyway, enjoy the rest of the night. I'm off to spread peace, love and LSD to the masses.'

Martin headed off into the night, his robes trailing behind him, and I wondered if he would ever leave this lifestyle behind. I loved these experiences, and was coming to love them more and more. But I could never see me doing it full time like Martin. I wanted to travel like Baz and to travel these days you needed a bit of cash. And with university coming up (hopefully) after the summer, I knew things would be tight for the next few years unless I could earn some money from this DJ'ing lark. I knew I'd only made a tenner from the Vortex gig but we'd been promised more wages if the numbers kept up and I felt that I would grow both in confidence and skill as the opportunities to play increased. One thing I was sure of, even if it did sound a little arrogant; I had an uncanny knack of picking the finest tunes to suit where I was playing, and I knew my record collection was more eclectic and bigger than any peers in my age group. Now it was just a case of getting out there and playing more clubs and parties and letting people know who I was. Pete had mentioned the possibility of starting a rock club but, to be honest, I wasn't sure it was the direction I wanted to go. One off events like this were all fine and well, but I felt in my bones that DJ'ing at rock nights would be a very niche market. The future lay in the electronic scene, and I was pretty sure it was a scene that was going to grow and grow.

There would come a time when I would have to make real choices regarding my record buying habits; playing more gigs would mean buying more vinyl, and with a fairly limited budget some of my more eclectic tastes may have to be sacrificed for those tunes that were going to be popular on dancefloors.

I left the barn and made my way back into the main house. Pete was playing and I grabbed myself a drink from the kitchen and sat by the DJ booth. Chris was nowhere to be seen and I realised I hadn't seen him for a couple of hours. There was no way he'd pulled tonight; the state he was in earlier meant he could hardly talk, let alone chat some girl up, so I decided he was monged out somewhere clutching a joint and a bottle. Pete was in a world of his own; he had some mad spoken word stuff on the reel to reel that sounded like lysergic inspired poetry and was playing it over the top of a Tangerine Dream instrumental track that I couldn't remember the name of. All the bean bags and chairs were occupied so I had to make do with a combination of carpet and discarded jackets to find some semblance of comfort. Once settled, I started to attempt to build a joint; a process that took around thirty minutes due to my still addled brain. Finally I managed to produce something that was smokeable and didn't look like it would fall apart with the gentlest breeze. This room definitely seemed to be the magnet for the party goers who were still in the grips of their journey or simply wanted to crash in a more ambient atmosphere for a while. The ratio of glazed eyes was certainly a lot higher than the other areas of the party and I started planning how I would start my next set. The evil part of me wanted to come in with something loud and raucous that would wake the dead, but the kinder side of me knew that to do so would be inherently cruel. Although I'd so far declined a second dose, there were a good few people on their second or even third doses, so there were a fair number still in the grip of dimensional adventures. I abandoned the evil idea altogether and decided to do a Gong homage for the first half hour or so of the set; that would certainly suit the trippers. I passed the joint to Pete before I bogarted it right to the end and he advised he fancied a break in thirty minutes or so. This suited me perfectly; I'd have a quick trip to the loo, see if I could find Chris and replenish my drink(s) before going on. At this time of the morning (It was just after 6am) it could be a long set and I wasn't sure if or when Baz would want to go back on. I knew I would want to sleep, even if only for a couple of hours, before part two of the party kicked in on the Saturday. Reassuring Pete that I'd be back shortly, I left my things by the decks and went to the downstairs bathroom. This had not been a bathroom earlier in the evening; it had been a portal to other worlds. What was meant to be a swift visit for a pee had turned into around forty minutes of staring at my metamorphosing face in a mirror lit by flickering candlelight. It was something I had never experienced before; not only observing oneself while under the influence of acid, but watching your face melt and distort into demonic entities right before your eyes. But this time my senses were far more grounded and I was happy to see my own, albeit slightly bedraggled, face in the mirror above the sink.

I found Chris by the fire, enveloped in a blanket and proving my earlier prediction right; one hand held a smouldering joint, the other a bottle of cider. He mumbled something to me, but it sounded like he was talking in an obscure dialect of Aramaic and I suspected that he'd had at least one more of the 'with' cups during the course of the night. Knowing I'd get no more sense out of him but relieved that he was safe and close by, I went back to grab more drinks and sort the start of my set out.

My choice for first song was 'Tally and Orlando Meet the Cockpot Pixie', an almost lullaby-like song from one of Daevid Allen's solo albums, and I planned on dropping into 'Angel's Egg' from that. Pete was on his last leg (and his last legs by the looks of him). I didn't have a clue what the hell he was playing; it was another of his weird remixes on the reel to reel and seemed to be a chaotic and almost cacophonic mash-up of snippets of song, music and samples. It shouldn't really have worked at all, but it did, especially given the mental states of the listeners. I'd already asked Pete earlier if he would teach me how to do the mad shit he did with the reel to reel and he'd invited me up to his flat/studio in Liberton next time we both had some free time. Peter left the decks with 'Lookin' Out My Back Door' by Creedence Clearwater Revival playing; not a tune I'd heard before, but the lyrics seemed to encapsulate the spirit of the weekend perfectly. At least this time I had a chance to use my Apollo mission samples and as the countdown finished I brought in the Allen track and was happy to see that it produced a sea of smiles across the room.

My set was much smoother this time; probably due to the increased control I had over my faculties compared to the previous levels of madness. Despite the late/early hour there were still plenty of people carrying the weekend forward, and I was glad that I had an attentive, if occasionally bewildered audience.

I pulled out all the stops, deviating by a long way from my prearranged set and wandering through several genres and using every mad sample I could think of. Joints were passed back and forth, drinks were proffered (though I again passed on the 'with' cup) and I lost myself in my music. Somehow over three hours passed and I only realised the time when Baz reappeared and asked if I wanted a break. When I replied that I'd only been on the decks for an hour, he pointed out that it was 9.30 in the morning and I was in my fourth hour of playing. How the hell did that happen? There was no way it felt like that long but then I looked at the disorganised pile of played and discarded records behind me and knew that my lost in music thought had been truly accurate. Happy to hand over the reins to Baz, I happily grabbed a just vacated armchair, made myself comfy and settled back to chill out to the lush tunes being dropped by Baz.

A hand shook me awoke, and through sleepy eyes I looked up to see a grinning Chris.

'Hey man, you wanting some food likesay? I'm just going to throw some burgers on the barbecue outside ken.'

'What time is it? I feel like I've been run over by a JCB.'

'It's nearly 4 o'clock; you've been crashed out for hours. Mind you, so have most folk. I slept in the barn for a few hours ken. But what a barry night it's been.'

I groaned as my body became aware of the awkward angles it had been subjected to in my slumbers.

'I'm aching all over. Do you think Martin would mind if I grabbed a shower?'

'Och aye man, go ahead likesay. He said anyone could help themselves to showers or food. He's awa a mad walk up the hills with a few of the others. Some of the part-timers have buggered off home but including the ramblers, there's just over a hundred of us left. And Martin reckons there will be some new blood here tonight to do it all over again. Now go and jump in the shower likesay man, and I'll have grub waiting for you when you come out.'

I found fresh towels in the linen cupboard in the hall and got in the shower eagerly. It felt like I'd accumulated a year's worth of grime in one short night and the hot water felt more refreshing than any shower I could remember. My clothes still stank of smoke and I was glad I'd packed a change of underwear and t-shirts; the days of going entire festivals in the same set of clothes still lay well in my future. There was a still packaged toothbrush in the bathroom cabinet and I cheekily borrowed it to invigorate a mouth that felt like it had been used as a party venue all on its own. Feeling like a new man, I headed back out to the courtyard where a surprisingly lively bunch were gathered round the now subdued fire and the aromas coming from the Chris-operated barbecue. I hadn't realised just how hungry I was until I smelt the burgers and sausages sizzling away and accepted a plate of munchies enthusiastically and gratefully from my culinary inclined friend. Once fed and watered I went for a wander round the farm and took in some fresh air. I'd sort of finally decided what had been on my mind since waking up; I wasn't going to indulge in nay more acid that evening. There was a fraying round the edges of my brain from the previous night's adventures and misadventures and I wasn't sure taking more LSD was going to be any help whatsoever. Both my mind and body were totally fatigued and I knew I'd be much happier with a few drinks and spliffs and enjoying playing more music. In some ways I felt like I was letting Martin and myself down, but right from the off I had resolved that I would only ever take any substances because I wanted to and not because someone else was telling me that I should. With mind made up I went off to find a quiet corner to nap for another couple of hours.

When I awoke again it was nearly 8pm. I felt a lot better than I had but was still staying away from Martin's concoction for the night. Some new faces had arrived and some of the old ones had come back to life so there was already a good vibe when I took a walk round the three main areas.

Martin and the rambling crew had long returned from their adventure into the wilds and Martin had donned his slightly grubby robes again and was offering communion to all and sundry.

'Graham! You're awake again. Now young sir; would you like 'with' or 'without'? As if I didn't know...'

'Actually Martin; it's going to be 'without' tonight. (I ignored his startled expression). Feeling a bit rough round the edges so am just going to stick to the booze this evening.'

'That's cool Graham. First time on the crystal can take anyone a little by surprise. Are you still going to play a couple more sets?'

'Oh fuck yes, that's an absolute definite. And at least I'll be able to concentrate a bit easier on what I'm doing.'

He laughed out loud.

'You coped better on the decks than the two veterans. I think Baz put the same record on three times in half an hour! Do you fancy a little dab of speed to keep you going?'

I hesitated. To date, this was an avenue I had never gone down. My experimentations (outside of cannabis) had been reserved purely to the psychedelics and though plenty people around me had been doing speed at the parties the summer before, and indeed last night, it had never felt like something I wanted to try. But I was still feeling knackered and a bit out of sorts, so maybe it would be the pick me up I needed.

'Well...okay, but just a little bit. I've never tried speed before so am a bit unsure of it.'

'Och don't worry man. The shit I've got is really good and quite pure. I'll stick a tiny amount in a cigarette paper for you; just enough to perk you up without getting you off your tits.'

He fiddled beneath his robes (don't!) and came out with a clear baggie filled with glittering white powder. He carefully measured a tiny amount out onto his hand then placed it in a skin which he folded and handed to me.

'Just swallow it down with a drink. Here, have some Irn-Bru, and don't worry; it's from the 'without' bottle.'

I accepted the wrapped up speed for him and nervously swallowed it, forcing the awkward parcel down with a hefty gulp of lukewarm Irn-Bru. Ugh. How did people manage to do this on a regular basis? It was almost as if your throat knew this was something that shouldn't be swallowed and resisted attempts to make it go down.

But there was no going back now and I'd now added another substance to my repertoire of recreational drugs. Whether it was something I liked very much remained to be seen. Thanking Martin and leaving him to his dispensing duties, I joined Chris by the fire.

'Alright gadgey? I just took another dose of that mad shit. What about you? You indulging likesay?'

'Nah mate; I'm giving it a miss tonight and going to concentrate on the tunes. But Martin just gave me a bit of speed to wake me up so we'll see how that goes.'

'Ach I dinnae like that shit ken? Makes me loopy as hell. I'll stick with my acid and my booze thanks. Just be careful mate.

'I only took a tiny bit. No sure of it myself either but am still half asleep here, and Martin says his shit is good.'

'Aye well there is that likesay; his gear is always good, well apart fae thae dodgy trips he selt me a few months back ken, but thon speed is something I wouldnae be touching like.'

'Fuck's sake Chris; don't let Martin hear you slagging that batch of blotters again. He's one sensitive big hippy, remember.'

'Aye, aye; it's cool. The big man's no about ken. He's wandering about the barn gieing his unholy communion to aw thae disciples likesay.'

I had to laugh. Martin was one of our closest friends, and he had done so much for me over this last year, but sometimes his hippy ways did verge on the ridiculous. He was forever stuck in an era he hadn't even taken part in, other than as a child, and though there was much to admire of that era, it seemed s little out of place in 1980's Scotland. Still laughing, I left Chris smiling by the flames and went to see how Baz and Pete were getting on.

I would love to be able to say here that my first experience with amphetamine was an unpleasant one, and that I never went near it again, but the truth is that it really gave me an alertness that night that was a new feeling. Although I had only partaken of a minuscule amount, the combination of fatigue from the night before and the LSD already in my system combined with the speed to leave me talking at 100 miles per hour and aware of everything around me. It was a completely different awareness from that experienced on acid; with LSD you become aware of the hidden realities around you and the layers upon layers that exist in life. With speed you became hypersensitive to the people and conversations around you. The paranoia would be a much later experience and, for now, I was enjoying the buzz without completely falling in love with it.

The rest of the night went fairly smoothly. The three DJ's all produced wonderfully meandering sets that took the crowd on a journey through the leftfield of music over several generations. The bands who had remained from the previous night were again superlative and this time I managed to catch the Chou Parrot jamming session in its entirety. Although there were still scores of people tripping their little mad heads off, the whole evening was slightly more subdued than the insanity of the first night and it seemed to begin to wind down around 3am with people finding corners or chairs to curl up on and fall asleep.

Martin had locked all the bedrooms, but there was a twin guestroom on the first floor which he offered to Chris and me to crash out in. My only thought was; why didn't he say this last night when I was developing back problems in that awkward armchair? Chris was still on Planet Outthere and was happily listening to Baz play more madness down in the DJ room. But for me it was the end of the weekend. Every bone was aching, every fibre of my being was exhausted and all I wanted to do was get a solid sleep before facing the olds the next day. Bleary eyes and a dishevelled face would only invite unwanted interrogation though to date there appeared to have not been an iota of suspicion re any drug use. I made my way up to the guest bedroom, pulled back the covers, undressed and collapsed. As my head hit the pillow, all systems powered down and I fell into a long, deep sleep.

I was woken by the charming sound of a long and loud flatulent Chris. I'd been so dead to the world I hadn't even heard him at whatever time he'd staggered into the room. Glancing at my watch I realised it was already past 11am and I wondered how many casualties remained from the night before. Dressing quickly I left Chris to his dreams and farts and made my way downstairs.

The music was off in the DJ room and it resembled the aftermath of a particularly nasty car crash. Bodies were strewn everywhere and at angles that somehow defied human anatomy. The smell of stale sweat and biker feet was overpowering and I hurried to get outside and breathe in the fresh air of the Pentlands. Outside some life existed at least; some enterprising and helpful guests had made a start at clearing up after the party and were collecting empty cans and bottles while another had found a brush and was sweeping up the inevitable fag and spliff ends. Someone else had decided to man the barbecue and cook up the last of the food and I found my stomach grumbling in appreciation of the smells wafting over towards me. I exchanged hellos with the few sorry looking souls huddled round the last of the fire and asked if there was any spare grub. Thankfully there were a few burgers left though all the rolls had long gone. But a plateful of burgers and a pint of milk purloined from the fridge later and I felt myself once again nearing a state of humanity. I found Martin in the barn, dead to the world and still wrapped up in his now filthy robes. It didn't take a genius to guess that he'd had a corker of a weekend. He'd been in his element playing the 'high priest' role and he'd certainly gained some new disciples this weekend which would bode well for his ongoing 'business concerns'. I really doubted if he would have lost any money over the weekend.

Most of the equipment had been loaned rather than hired, though I was sure he'd have slipped the people concerned a few acid or similar. And even though he'd given out a heft amount of the crystal, he'd made a fair bit of cash back on the bar and also on donations for food. But where he'd really win was on the long term business side. There had been a lot of new faces at the weekend, and now that they knew he provided the best acid available in the Lothians, he'd have a string of new customers. Plus there were his side-lines of speed and herbal weed so I doubted he'd be worrying about expenditure over the weekend. Once I'd had a spliff I joined in with the clear up, grabbing a bin bag and starting to lift empty cans from the barn. The musos had all packed up their gear and were long gone and all that remained equipment wise was the pa system in the barn and the equipment in the DJ room. Within an hour we had the barn pretty much returned to pre-party state and the pa equipment disconnected and stacked up by the doors. I went to help with the same process in the DJ room but it was already done. What had resembled a morgue/accident scene an hour or so before was now back to its pristine glory, windows wide open to let the cold but refreshing air blow away the smell of spliffs and socks. Chris had even managed ro resurface and was sitting by the window looking slightly confused and unsure of his surroundings. The only thing left to do in the lounge was to pack up my tunes. Someone, probably Baz or Pete, had carefully moved all my carelessly abandoned records and cd's to a neat pile by the side of the table and all I had to do was pack them away in bags. That done, it meant that we could leave anytime, or at least at whatever time Chris managed to remember his name and where he lived.

'Earth to Chris, Earth to Chris; come in Chris. Is there anyone in there?'

'Aye man, ahm fine ken. Just a wee bit rough roon the edges likesay. I didnae come to bed till aboot 6 o'clock. Ye were snoring like a pig gadgie.'

'Whatever mate; I know I don't snore. Sharon would have told me and have fallen asleep beside her often enough.'

'Ach yer a bufty man. Imagine fallin asleep next to that wee doll. I often do imagine it.'

His ducking to avoid the cushion I threw at him impressed me with it's speed, a speed, and indeed reflex action I wouldn't have expected from him from current appearances.

'Anyway ya numpty, what time do you want to head back to the Ferry? I'm all packed up and can go any time. Don't want to leave it too late. Plus it looks like it might piss down later and really don't want caught in the rain with these record bags.'

'Give me half an hour to get ma heid together eh? Then we'll cadge a luift doon to Loanhead ken.'

Leaving arrangements in hand, I left Chris to sort himself out and went to see if Martin had risen from the dead as well. But unfortunately he was still wandering the land of nod and was immune to the light attempts at waking him up I made. Which led to the next problem; how were we getting back to Loanhead? The van we had come in seemed to have disappeared that morning and I didn't know who of the crowd left was in possession of a vehicle or indeed in the right state to be able to drive. The next ten minutes were spent asking the remaining weirdos if anyone could give the two of us a lift down to the town. It was finally Baz who came to our rescue, appearing from the back door rubbing his eyes and stretching.

'Sure Graham; I can give you a lift down. I'm staying with Martin for a few more days but I fancy hitting the supermarket and getting some decent food in. All that fatty food hasn't agreed with me this morning.'

'Cool. Cheers Baz. When you thinking of heading down?'

'Let me splash some water on my face and I'll be right with you. Cheers for coming up by the way; thoroughly enjoyed all your sets over the weekend. If you're ever down London way give me a shout and I'll set a party or gig up for you to play at.'

Wow. This new career was taking off like a runaway freight train. Getting offered gigs in the capital after so few appearances was a huge boost to my ego.

Unfortunately I didn't see me getting there any time soon unless the London college was the one I chose (or that let me in). But for now I wasn't bothered about colleges or DJ gigs; all I was bothered about was coping with the two buses home to the Ferry, having some good home-cooked food and snuggling up in my own bed in recovery for the school week ahead. I left a thank you note for Martin with a promise to call during the week and went to grab my bags and to round up Chris.

Chapter 25

I'd made a decision after Martin's party that I wouldn't be touching any more psychedelics till after my exams. It had taken several days to completely recover from the mind exertions of that weekend and I just had too much at stake with my Highers to let partying ruin it altogether. One thing I didn't want was to do a sixth year at school because my grades were too low. Freedom was beckoning, and with that I mean no disrespect to my mum and dad; they had always been semi-strict but fair and, as I got older, had gradually allowed me more latitude in staying out at weekends. But the whole idea of having my own place, even if it was a pokey little room in halls of residence, was exhilarating, and the possibility that I might share this new life with Sharon was equally thrilling. And so, from mid-February, my life became an almost precise schedule of studying for the exams in May. Of course, there was still recreation time; but that consisted of time with Sharon, playing Vortex every two weeks, the odd concert and the occasional trip to Edinburgh to buy vinyl and meet up with the rock crowd for a few pints in the Grassmarket. The olds were well impressed; I don't think they had ever witnessed me commit to anything quite as much as I seemed to be those three months. There were even a couple of subjects that Sharon and I crossed over on which meant we could combine study sessions with more glorious sex.

Vortex was definitely on the up too; crowds were averaging around 250 people every two weeks and Stuart and I were now earning a huge £30 per gig. From the mid-march gig, Tom and Rabbit began mixing up the DJ rota so that both Stuart and I got later sets. My first 'headline' set was at the end of March and I don't think I've ever been more nervous as when waiting to come on after Rabbit. We had one of our bigger crowds that night too; 320 people and I was convinced I would fuck up in a big way. But everything went just right; my choice of tunes worked on the dancefloor junkies as well as eliciting praise from my more experienced mentors and I even got away with finishing with a new track out of the States; the seminal White Lines by Melle Mel, which few had heard until that March evening but which would rocket up the charts within four short months.

The huge mix of genres from the four DJ's was a big hit with the often fussy Edinburgh crowds and we even managed to get mentions and reviews in a couple of the local fanzines though mass media exposure still escaped us. The olds were amazed that a 'hobby' could actually earn money, though of course it was still mere pocket money level (well, damned good pocket money level). I knew the club gigs would be one of the things I'd miss most about Edinburgh but remained convinced that this 'hobby' was a huge part of my future pathways. And given the time and money invested in my record collection (I was now up to 176 12" singles, 206 albums, and around 300 7" singles and flexi discs) I sort of hoped that it would always be a parallel if not primary career. For now I was happy to be doing something I loved and even happier that other people enjoyed it. To me, that was the principal reason for doing it; there was no sense of egotism, just an overwhelming desire to share the music I loved with people who either loved it too or hadn't heard it yet. And the fact that they were dancing their sweaty little socks off AND I was getting paid to do it were just added bonuses. The clubbing scene was gradually changing and moving away from the meat market pulling parlours that had been the norm for so long, and more towards cathedrals of music where who you took home was of secondary consideration.

Concert wise, I was maybe a little quieter than I had been the year before over this period. But I still managed to fit some great gigs into that first half of 1983. From Echo and the Bunnymen in January, The Stranglers and my last ever U2 gig (they were getting boring by this point) in February, Thin Lizzy, Fun Boy Three and The Undertones (at the latter of which I made the huge mistake of grabbing Feargal Sharkey's microphone stand and got a swift kick to the chest that pained me for weeks) in March, to Marillion, Orchestral Manoeuvres/Cocteau Twins and the marvellous and ever improving New Order in April, even a reduced gig calendar was filled with quality.

And then came the coup de grace; an uncharacteristically brilliant idea from Chris that provided a real incentive to work through the impending exams and start my new life/summer with a true bang. His idea came as we sat quaffing two fine pints of cold cider in The White Hart one day. He'd been browsing through NME when he turned to me with a smile.

'Hey Graham; I've had a brilliant idea ken. I have a couple of weeks off work in June cos Tommy is off to Spain likesay. How do ye fancy doing the Glastonbury Festival?'

Now I have to admit; I'd thought of Glastonbury to this point as a bit of a hippy thing and the idea of going never even crossed my mind. But as Chris read out some of the line up my excitement levels rose and the idea began to seem a bloody good one.

'Look who's playing like; The Beat, Marillion, UB40, Curtis Mayfield (wow), Dennis Brown and Aswad, A Certain Ratio, Fun Boy Three (had just seen them but hey), Julian Cope (wow again), The Chieftains, and hunners more ken. Don't tell me that disnae appeal to ye gadgie?'

Chris was bang on; I couldn't tell him that didn't appeal to me, and what a way to celebrate the end of exams and school life. The only stumbling block would be mum and dad, but given it was after exams and also considering I'd be leaving home two or three months later, I was sure I could talk them round.

'You're on Chris; let's do this man. Our very own road trip down to Somerset which means loads of bloody good cider as well.'

'Aye and dinnae forget the birds man. Tommy telt me these festivals are hoaching with lassies dying for a shag.'

This last selling point I was less sure of. Bands and cider? Oh yes. The inevitable good weed and acid there would be? One hundred percent. But I'd been totally faithful to Sharon and have to admit I was pretty hooked on her. So I'd let Chris sow his wild oats and I'd dance in sunny fields to rhythms from around the world while gulping vast quantities of locally brewed scrumpy. I was a little worried about sharing a tent though; there was no way I was lying in a sleeping bag while Chris did the beast with two backs beside me. But the road trip rules could come later. For now it was getting the idea past the parents (and indeed Sharon who hated the idea of me being anywhere without her that had other females present) and keeping on with the studying.

Amazingly, the idea of Glastonbury was easier than I thought to sell to the olds. Dad, who had spent months travelling round Europe on a motorbike before he met mum, saw it as a true coming of age experience (when did he turn all hippy-like on me?) and once he was on board mum soon followed, though I had to make a whole list of promises about being careful, phoning when I could, staying away from strange people (this last one would be difficult given the very nature of the event we were attending), not drinking too much, etc. etc. etc. Promises were made, and planning the trip became an integral part of my hook-ups with Chris.

And so April began to fade away and examination dates loomed ever closer. I was now studying around three hours per night when on my own, and maybe half of that in my study sessions with Sharon (Even a studious teenager needs a bit of recreation time with his girlfriend.) But I was feeling confident and on top of things as the first date approached. Then the date was here. And gradually I ticked off some of the most crucial days of my young life to date. Maths; done and dusted, struggled a bit, but it had always been the weakest of my Higher subjects. Geography; completed, no real issues, fairly happy with how I answered questions. English; finished, my best subject and walked out of the exam hall certain there was a good mark waiting. German; over and done with, very happy with the oral exam, bit less happy with a couple of parts of the written exam. And then that final morning was here; last exam. Latin; gone forever, so-so in places but overall pretty sure I had a decent pass.

The last week or two of school was inconsequential and attendance was more about some strange reluctance to leave a part of your life behind that had governed it since you were five years old. It becomes almost ritualistic; something you hate but don't want to let go of as a weird nervousness about truly entering adult life sets in. You begin to question your own abilities and maturity and there was even a fleeting moment when the fear had me considering staying on for a further year. But like many fears, I worked my way through it and accepted that it was time to walk away. I wasn't planning on staying to the very last day, nor indeed were any of the other fifth years who were leaving for good. So we had one last June day of madness; rules we'd followed (and broken) for so many years discarded in a chaotic teenage embrace of anarchy. Alcohol was smuggled in, trousers were stolen and hoisted on the school flagpole, teachers were terrorised by pranking guerrilla warfare and general mayhem was the order of the day. All too soon that final day was over and we gathered with mock sombreness by the school gates to burn our hated school ties and walk away from the monstrosity of a building one final time.

The first major defining episode of my life was over. I was officially a school leaver and adult life beckoned. But first there was a summer of partying and fun to indulge in before the mantle of responsibility was once more donned.

It was June 10th, 1983; I was free, I was young, and there were seven days to Glastonbury.

3620B445R00113

Made in the USA
Charleston, SC
27 November 2014